BEATIFIC
VISION

JORDAN SPIECE

authorHOUSE®

AuthorHouse™
1663 Liberty Drive
Bloomington, IN 47403
www.authorhouse.com
Phone: 1 (800) 839-8640

Published by AuthorHouse 07/30/2018

ISBN: 978-1-5462-4880-4 (sc)
ISBN: 978-1-5462-4879-8 (hc)
ISBN: 978-1-5462-4878-1 (e)

Library of Congress Control Number: 2018907647

Print information available on the last page.

CHAPTER 1

CHASING DREAMS

September 15, 2035

He was engulfed in a white sea of nothingness. An endless void stretched far and wide about him as the sounds of countless words and songs rushed to him like twinkling light from distant stars. What he was feeling was a dreadful cold, one that cut him to the bone and burned his soul; strangely enough, it was not uncomfortable, and he did not shiver.

Suddenly, a low, vibrating, humanlike voice laced with frantic whispers echoed through his entire being, plucking the hairs within his ears.

"No fears, do not fear, we will protect you," reassured the voice. "You are here with friends. We meet you here in the void between life, death, and the eternal. In the abyss—paradise, purgatory, or Sheol—know that our Father protects all his children, no matter their place of being. He is here with you and with us." Giuseppe felt strangely serene listening to the droning, bodiless speech.

"Child of God, do not fear us."

After these words, Giuseppe was greeted by an image of two beings standing before him. It was an image that could have frightened any man into insanity, but Giuseppe was not an ordinary man. Instead, it left him smiling, feeling triumphant and hopeful. He knew what these creatures were—messengers, sons of God, angels. It was not the sight of these beings that brought him feelings of hopefulness, but rather the realization that they were there to deliver a message from something divine in nature.

1

The two beings were immersed in a light blinding to any mortal who looked upon it. It radiated from behind them, creating a halo effect not unlike the corona of a solar eclipse. White fire leaked through their eyes, mouths, and nostrils like water dripping from holes in a dam. Loose black robes were wrapped around them, floating and waving within the windless void. Each one had familiar symbols adorning his forehead, red symbols pulsating to the beat of Giuseppe's heart. The being on the left stood still, red flames dancing from the top of his skull, his right arm cradling a sword. In his left he held a small, ghostlike infant by one leg. The being on the right appeared to be floating underwater, with moonlit ripples swimming over his body. In his left arm, he cradled an identical sword as the being next to him, and in his right hand he held the same infant by its arm.

A thick fog began to rise from below the three before him. It also throbbed to the beat of Giuseppe's heart. More red symbols moved within its misty tendrils. Soon the fog consumed everything around it, and only the silhouettes of the two men and the infant remained in view. The fog touched everything, heard everything, and was everything.

"Giuseppe. We are coming. Your worries are over. Giuseppe. Giuseppe …"

Giuseppe.

Giuseppe Morreti opened his eyes effortlessly to the realization he was lying in his bed in the barracks, surrounded by bookshelves and a large wooden desk situated under a curtained window to his right. *Was I dreaming?* The cold that he'd felt was still with him. The all-consuming fog he'd envisioned seemed still to be dissipating. The images he'd experienced remained vivid in his mind. Could they simply have been fabricated by his sleep-deprived mind? It seemed a likely explanation.

Even after his release from the otherworldly dreamscape, the whispers and musical incantations still echoed through his thoughts. Dreamless nights were a rarity for him, but his usual dreams were nothing compared to the realism and lucidity of this latest experience. As quickly as he was cast back into reality, Giuseppe hazily scribbled down the elements of his dream experience, being sure to include the symbols adorning the beings' foreheads. He felt certain the symbols were from the Hebrew language, but their translation was unknown to him. Intrigued to learn their meanings, he tucked away his notes to have the mysterious messages translated later on.

Giuseppe Morreti commanded an elite branch of the Vatican City military known as the Milvian Guard, a unit shrouded in mystery even from its violent and heroic beginnings as the force that expelled Aurean occupiers from the Vatican at the forefront of Domus Aurea's rise to power. Giuseppe was a seasoned leader at the age of fifty-four, with a history of loss and triumph behind him that would have broken a lesser man or given him a false sense of valor and godliness. Whatever befell him, Giuseppe Morreti kept his calm composure and humble personality.

The man was a hero in his own right, but traditionally heroes were vibrant, tireless, and full of life. He, in contrast, seemed old, broken, and weary, or at least it was how he felt about himself. Three years ago he'd been a different man. Three years ago he could have led an army and skillfully destroyed wicked men, casting them into oblivion. Today, specters of his past haunted him, relentless in their whispers of defeat. They robbed him of sleep and energy, but not his spirit. Although Giuseppe was noticeably weaker and older, his mind was still sharp and his disposition still optimistic.

He was not a frail man by any means, but the wrinkles on his face, along with the gray and white hairs that peppered his head, spoke plainly of his past and the horrors he had faced in the last three years. During the Aurean occupation of Vatican City in 2032, Giuseppe had led a successful revolt against the city-state's captors. Later, with the help of the Swiss Guard, he and his subordinates had barricaded themselves into the Vatican, keeping chaos, disaster, and the entire world locked out.

Still lying in his bed, Giuseppe peered out his window at the gray sky outside. It seemed to him that the world had finally accepted its fate and saw fit for nature to reflect the hell unfolding in Rome. Drops of rain landed lightly on the windowpanes, making it difficult for him to avoid falling back to sleep. Just as the luxury was beginning to envelop him once again, it was ripped away by a quiet but steady knock from the other side of the two large mahogany doors enclosing him within his sanctuary. At first he wondered if he had imagined the knock, but after a few seconds, he heard two voices whispering to each other.

"You call that a knock? If he's even awake, there's no way he heard it," said one of the voices.

"Fine. You do it if you're such an expert at knocking on doors," replied the other.

The second knock was much more forceful.

"Crown Morreti, Inspector General Gabrieli sent us to retrieve and escort you to the gardens," said the first voice.

Giuseppe rolled over and peered, once again, outside into the overcast sky. He hoped and prayed it wasn't an omen for the day to come. After rubbing his eyes and sitting up in bed, he gave a raspy response.

"I'll be out in a moment. Wait in my office."

"Yes, sir," responded four or five voices in unison. This chorus of voices gave Giuseppe a sudden jolt of energy. Why had the inspector general sent so many men to escort him?

After a few minutes, Giuseppe emerged from his room. Standing in his office were five officers of the Vatican gendarmerie.

"We're ready when you are, sir," said one as he opened the door for them to depart.

Giuseppe had questions, but he knew to save them for when he reached his destination. If he knew the inspector general as well as he thought, it was safe to assume the man wouldn't divulge information to those who didn't need to know it.

As the group left the Milvian Guard barracks, Giuseppe gazed into the sky. A steady breeze blew the rain, and as the cold drops hit his face, he was awakened to the reality around him. The city-state was no small place by any means, but the walls that surrounded it had closed in over the past three years. Claustrophobia didn't seem like something one could suffer from by living in such a large place, but many besides him had felt its effects. Ever since the city walls were closed to the outside world, there had been a wave of suicides inside. Perhaps it was why the inspector general, Adriano, had called Giuseppe. *Maybe there's been another suicide. Maybe I'm needed to help identify the body.* But the seasoned man knew better. Something strange was in the air, and Giuseppe was aware of it.

From his current location, Giuseppe could see the dome of Saint Peter's Basilica rising over the buildings of the Vatican. The beautiful architectural accomplishment used to stand for something bright and hopeful, but it had become a dead husk, empty and void of the voices that had once echoed within its massive and grand interior. Saint Peter's Square was just as vacant: silent and abandoned. The only signs of life were the ranks of Uriel's Sword, soldiers in the Milvian Guard who patrolled and stood watch at its entrance. Sharpshooters were intertwined among the statues of Christ and his apostles at the basilica's facade, which was a sad contradiction in Giuseppe's eyes.

As the group neared the gardens, Giuseppe noticed a large number of gendarmes scouring the area, each glancing at the approaching men as they closed in. The Crown of the Milvian Guard, as the rest of the guard knew him, began to run every possible scenario through his head. The worst would be the assassination of the pope, but Giuseppe knew that whatever it was, it was serious enough to warrant his attention. The looks on the men's faces around him expressed that clearly.

All of it was especially distressful to Giuseppe today. He had long roamed the grounds of the Vatican gardens as an escape from the strange new world inside. The trees hid the sight of the massive stone walls surrounding him, and the sounds of the birds that dwelt there took him someplace else, somewhere far and away. Now it seemed that Giuseppe's paradise had become the very same hell that burned and festered outside his walled in home.

Giuseppe and the men arrived where Adriano, the inspector general, had told them to go. He could see yellow crime scene tape surrounding a small area around Saint Peter's statue, with several gendarmes standing within it. Directly to the right of the scene stood several cardinal priests, which served as some relief to Giuseppe; if the pope had been assassinated, every cardinal within the Vatican would have immediately rushed to the Sistine Chapel.

"Giuseppe!" yelled Adriano from within the crime scene. "Over here!"

Giuseppe held out his hand to let his escorts know that he would continue the rest of the way on his own. As he lifted the crime scene tape, Giuseppe looked around to see if he could gather what he could about the situation encompassing him. Nothing out of the ordinary seemed to stand out, but the air around him had an eerie and electrified feel about it.

Again Giuseppe looked to the sky. The clouds were moving faster than when he left the barracks. A storm was coming, and he knew that it wasn't just one within the realms of nature that he should worry about.

"What's going on, Adriano?" asked Giuseppe once he reached the inspector general. "It can't be something simple, can it? That would make my life easier."

"I only wish it was," said Adriano as he motioned for Giuseppe to follow him. "A priest found him this morning next to Saint Peter's statue."

As the inspector general and Crown of the Milvian Guard neared the statue, Giuseppe noticed a white cloth covering a man just below the statue's pedestal. It wasn't anything he hadn't seen before. Compared to the hundreds of mangled bodies of those who served under him during the Vatican Revolt, this was nothing. But Giuseppe still felt strange and sickened by what he saw. Something wasn't right, and he could feel it in his soul.

A small gust of wind blew past the two men from the direction of the body. With it Giuseppe could hear the voices of the men around him talking among themselves, but there was something else layered beneath all the scattered conversation—something that stood out and made the hair on the back of his neck stand on end.

Adriano stood facing the corpse while scratching the back of his head. "I've dealt with death and the likes of it before, but this ... this is something entirely different. Take a look."

Giuseppe took a closer look at the covered body, but noticed some movement underneath the white blanket. Upon removing the covering, Giuseppe searched for any signs of what may have caused this young man's untimely demise, but there was nothing that could be seen. In fact, the color in his skin had not faded, and his eyes seemed uncannily alive. Giuseppe had stared many times into the face of the dead and dying. Enough times to recognize it when he saw it. This man was dead. The young man was staring into the face of God or the black abyss of nothingness, depending on how he had lived his life. But it wasn't the lively look to the dead man or the mysterious circumstances of his death that perplexed, frightened, and chilled Giuseppe to the bone. By all accounts, death had taken this man, but dead men do not speak, and this man was speaking.

A horrid and breathless voice rose from the mouth of the man. At first, the words were meaningless clicks and vibrations to his ears, but slowly Morreti could distinguish a message.

"The sons of God will be punished, and the owl will emerge from her place of rest to dwell on the shores of the sea. Her children will again know dominance and cleanse their world of filth. The three will vanish, and God will turn his head. Your soul will be forgotten, and your world turned to dust."

It was something Giuseppe should have expected, but not what he desired. He stood and placed his hands in his pockets. To him the message was clear, but telling Adriano the meaning would land him in a worse predicament than he was already in, if that was possible. He would either have to avoid the emerging questions or fabricate answers.

"I have to say, Giuseppe, this is not something I'm used to. Normally when I'm investigating a mysterious death, I'm attempting to give a voice to the departed. Not trying to decipher what the dead are saying to me. What do you make of it all?" asked Adriano, breaking the silence.

Giuseppe opened his mouth attempting to assemble a believable lie when a voice from across the gardens yelled his name, saving him from having to mislead his longtime friend.

"Giuseppe Morreti! I demand that you speak with me at once!" screamed a stout and pug-looking cardinal behind the crime scene tape.

"Oh no. It's Alban," said Adriano, laughing with pity as he spotted the short, red-robed cardinal priest.

Giuseppe placed his face in his hands and rubbed his forehead. He had been brewing a headache ever since he woke up from his dream, but he knew it was about to get worse.

Alban Sommer was a cardinal priest who loved to spend his time torturing Giuseppe. Or at least that's what Giuseppe thought. Alban had a false sense of superiority when it came to his position and a small understanding on what he was able to get away with. This earned him the title as the bane of Giuseppe's existence.

"Maybe if you ignore him he'll go away," said Adriano in an attempt to cheer his friend up.

"Not this time," replied Giuseppe as he walked toward the group of cardinals.

Morreti prepped himself for the argument that was about to ensue.

He knew that rationality and reason were mostly absent in any type of conversation with Alban. Today would not be any different, he feared.

"What is it, Alban?" asked Giuseppe dryly after reaching the crime scene tape.

"Morreti, what is the purpose of your position? Is it not to command the soldiers in your guard?" questioned Alban facetiously. "The same group that is supposed to guard and protect our home and our people? Then how is it that this has happened?" asked Alban angrily.

"Alban, this has nothing to do with you. The matter is being taken care of by the gendarmerie, and I would appreciate it very much if you would just leave," responded Giuseppe, ignoring Alban's inquiry. "How did you get past the barricade?"

"I'm asking the questions here! I knew it was ill-advised to appoint you as a leader. You are obviously not worthy of this responsibility." screamed Alban, pointing in the direction of the body.

"You had nothing to do with appointing me. For that, I am eternally grateful, Alban," said Giuseppe, again dryly and sarcastically.

At this point, Alban's face resembled a cherry about to pop. Never had anyone been so impolite to him—and in front of his peers nonetheless.

"That's 'Your Eminence' to you!" yelled Alban as Giuseppe turned around and walked away. "You will not speak to me in such a disrespectful manner! As far as I'm concerned, you are inadequate and unable to hold your position! This will be brought to His Holiness immediately!"

Giuseppe simply waved his hand in the air without turning around. "It's a good thing your opinion doesn't hold much weight then."

Alban attempted to respond, but he was at a loss for words. He simply stormed off in the direction of the Apostolic Palace, hoping to find someone who would listen to his grievance.

Although Giuseppe didn't necessarily agree with Alban's way of expressing the issue, he did agree on one point. If what he was witnessing was as he feared, the repercussions could cause those in a position of authority to reevaluate Giuseppe's worth. It was his duty to protect the occupants of the Vatican, from both visible and veiled threats.

"Should I call a priest for you? You know, to perform last rites?" laughed Adriano.

Giuseppe just shook his head and sighed heavily. Even though Alban held absolutely no authority in matters such as these, Giuseppe knew that he would be lectured for his confrontational and disrespectful demeanor toward a member of the Holy See. At the present moment, though, he was drawn to more pressing matters.

"All right, Giuseppe," said Adriano, scratching the back of his head, "what do I do with this thing? A storm's blowing in."

"I don't believe there's much more we can do right now," said Giuseppe. "Have your men get whatever they need from around the body and then have it moved to the morgue. Maybe an autopsy will reveal something."

Adriano agreed and called over a few of his men to move the body. They hesitantly crouched down to lift it onto a stretcher and then began to wheel it away just as rain started pouring. Both Giuseppe and Adriano stared in silence, listening to the mysterious voice as it dissipated.

"I'll get everything cleaned up here and then report any findings back to you once the autopsy is complete," said Adriano as he flagged a gendarme down to relay orders. "I'll have the coroner record the message before he does any cutting and have it sent to your office."

Giuseppe nodded his head and began walking away. "Good. I'll head that way now, but I'm not sure how long I'll be there. I imagine I'll be called to the palace any moment now."

Adriano laughed, and the two waved to each other as Giuseppe walked toward his escorts. By this time, Giuseppe's headache had escalated to a new level. With Alban breathing down his neck, the oncoming storm, and lack of sleep, it was a typical day in the life of the Milvian Guard's leader, but one thing stuck with Giuseppe. Alban's comments about his failure to act seemed to ring true. After the Vatican Revolt and the Aurean Army's expulsion, not a soul had left the city-state's grounds for any reason. Giuseppe felt too constricted and completely useless with the restrictions placed upon him. It was counterproductive; if he was allowed to leave the city for any amount of time, so much good could come of it.

As the group approached the Milvian Guard's barracks, Giuseppe noticed a man standing outside waiting for them. Raul Vezzi was his name; he was a lieutenant colonel under the rank of Uriel's Mouth and leader of a third of the Milvian Guard's troops.

"Care to share why you're being escorted by five heavily armed men, sir?" asked Raul as Giuseppe entered the barracks.

Giuseppe avoided the question and motioned for Raul to follow him to his office. The two walked through the halls of the newly built structure. It was constructed after a suicide bomber failed to destroy the Apostolic Palace by missing his mark. Several members of the Swiss Guard successfully diverted the man into a market by their barracks, destroying it and clearing a large area. Standing at four stories tall, with a basement, it was large enough to house the entire guard. The basement housed locker rooms, an armory, an indoor gun range, and a gym. On the first floor were several meeting rooms, cafeteria, and small hospital while the second, third, and fourth floors housed members of the guard and Giuseppe's office.

After reaching the third floor, Giuseppe and Raul were met by two soldiers standing atop the stairs clad in ceremonial uniform. The top floor was more heavily guarded than any other, as it housed Giuseppe's living quarters. His office was a large room at the end of the hall, separated into three sections. The first was a waiting room and secretary's office, while the second and third were Giuseppe's office and bedroom. As the two entered the quarters, Giuseppe walked over to a fireplace and stared into the leaping flames. Raul walked to Giuseppe's desk and hung up a phone that was off its hook.

"Her children are becoming bold," said Giuseppe to Raul, breaking the silence. "I don't know how they did it, but they got into the gardens last night; left us a little something too."

Raul shook his head in disbelief. "That can't be. I was in charge of the night shift last night, and I can vouch for my men. No one got through these walls. And what do you mean they left something?'

Giuseppe turned to face Raul and sighed. "Someone got in last night and left a body lying in the gardens. I don't know how they did it, but it happened. I'm not blaming you or your men for this at all. Whoever did this used … unorthodox tactics to gain entry."

Raul looked at Giuseppe with a confused look. "What kind of unorthodox tactics?"

"I don't know for sure," said Giuseppe as he rested his arm on the fireplace mantel, "but the body … the body had some supernatural elements working through it. With that in mind, it's obvious who is behind this. Trying to understand how they did it isn't what we need to be focusing on right now. We need to figure out why."

Raul rubbed the stubble on his chin as his mind flooded with thoughts. "So what do we do?"

"As far as anyone else knows, this is just an act of terrorism by the Aureans. The best we can do is allow them to continue thinking that," said Giuseppe.

"A cover-up? Everyone who saw that body knows something strange is going on," said Raul with slight sarcasm.

Giuseppe sensed the derision in Raul's voice but decided to overlook it. "I'll let Adriano take care of that," he said. "The only people who were there were gendarmes and a group of cardinals."

Raul smirked, knowing that Alban must have been one of the cardinals there, and chimed back, "So what did Sommer have to say this time around?"

"I wasn't really listening, much like always," said Giuseppe, smiling, "but he did reaffirm something. We're not able to perform our job correctly. It's completely counterproductive to be restricted to the city and be expected to prevent things like this from happening. We need to get permission to leave the city."

"How do we manage something like that? The probability of us getting out of here is slim to none," said Raul distressfully.

"We're just going to have to go straight to the top. His Holiness has a good head on his shoulders. I'll talk to him about it, and maybe we can come to an agreement," said Giuseppe. "Do me a favor and gather up all the other colonels. We need to discuss the matter of what to do if we gain some freedom. I'll call Elia myself."

Raul nodded his head and left to find the remaining lieutenant colonels. Giuseppe walked around his office thinking about the events of the day. If he could convince the pope to allow them to leave the Vatican and Adriano's autopsy revealed anything helpful, they could be well on their way. The message left for them by the mysterious intruder called for immediate action and could not be overlooked. Perhaps this would be the deciding factor to gaining their freedom.

With everything that had unfolded so far that day, Giuseppe still had something else burning in the back of his mind. He reached into his pocket and pulled out the small piece of paper he wrote the Hebrew letters on that morning to glance over them. His close friend Elia Serra, another lieutenant colonel and personal advisor to Giuseppe, had extensive knowledge on the Hebrew language and would be able to decipher the meaning easily. Giuseppe picked up the phone on his desk and dialed Elia's room number, hoping that he would be there. The distraught man needed some answers today, and he knew Elia could give him some.

CHAPTER 2

HOPELESS

September 15–16, 2035

The streets of Aurean-occupied Rome were devoid of the fascination and grandeur that once captivated the imaginations of tourists and locals alike. The once historically colorful ancient city had become a dark and lifeless tomb, a stark contrast to life as it once was. There were no smiling faces or wide-eyed onlookers wandering the city to behold the feats achieved here. There were no loud conversations nor whispers speaking of past achievements held by the people of this city. With Aurean patrols constantly roaming the streets actively looking for punishable occurrences, individuals took roundabout ways and back alleys to their destinations, hoping to avoid any and all confrontations.

Daven Jones and Adam Gilmour had several reasons why they needed to avoid the ever-watchful eye of the Aurean military. The two men in their early twenties were visiting Rome as part of a university trip to study the city's architecture when the Reclamation of Domus Aurea broke out. However, their stay was elongated when Italy's inhabitants were trapped in the cage of Aurean power held by Lucius Nero.

No one could have been prepared for the complete obliteration of Italian society, and anyone caught in the restructured country not of Italian descent was arrested and shipped off to work camps. Everyone within was forced to prove their citizenship and Italian heritage. This made life rather difficult for the two pale-skinned individuals, but both men succeeded in evading their hunters, unlike their classmates, who were not so fortunate. Being in Rome, the heart of Domus Aurea, made it especially dangerous for the two, but to them, the hand of God himself closed the eyes of their pursuers and guided them both to a safe haven.

That safe haven would be in the care of Abele and Eula Fortuna. The two had been living in Rome after moving there in 1990 during the second year of their marriage and had bought a small house just minutes away from Vatican City. The couple had been married for forty-four years when the events of 2032 unfolded.

Abele had been expecting the worst the night after the invasion when a knock was heard on their front door. Because of their location, it was either an Aurean patrol or thieves looking for an easy target. The aging man had acquired a small pistol earlier in life and decided to make then a good time to test its effectiveness, but as he opened his door, two longhaired, bearded men crouched on his front step, looking up at him with fearful eyes. It was obvious to him at that moment what these two were doing, and without hesitation, Abele brought them in and tended to them.

For three months, Daven and Adam hid away from the eyes of Nero in a small, cold wine cellar, all the while being cared for by Eula and guarded by Abele. A strong relationship was built by the four, and not even the forces of hell or the Aurean military could tear them apart.

A year into their seclusion, Adam and Daven decided it was necessary to aid Abele and Eula monetarily, but in order to do so, they would need to venture outside of the Fortunas' residence, a risky endeavor. Fortunately for the family, a friend of Abele's volunteered to allow the men to work as apprentices in his bakery, and despite the danger involved, both agreed to the offer and began work.

Three years had passed, and the two men were becoming used to a life of hiding in the shadows. Working at the bakery gave both men a much needed escape from their cooped-up existence inside Eula and Abele's house, and it also created a tight bond with the owner, Lorenzo, who considered the two as close as brothers.

"I don't suppose you two could speed this process up at all, could you?" inquired Lorenzo to his two flour-covered workers.

Adam picked up a wad of dough and tossed it into the face of his employer. "There. Put that out for your consumer base," he said dryly.

Adam was a redheaded man at average height with green eyes. He was relatively well-built and kept a full beard and shoulder-length hair— something to shave off to easily alter their appearance in case they needed to avoid being apprehended by Aurean officials. He was born in Birmingham, Alabama, in the United States and was a married man with a newborn daughter. He was overly distressed knowing that his young daughter was growing up without her father, and he felt unbearable guilt remembering that it was his decision to leave his family in the first place.

Daven was a taller and thinner man, with brown hair and hazel eyes. He also wore the same long hair and beard but kept his hair tied at the back of his neck. He was born on the eastern coast of Canada in a small town named Nain, Newfoundland and Labrador. As a child, he loved to walk the docks and beaches, fishing or collecting rocks and listening to the waves. In his early teens, however, he was almost drowned when the riptide carried him out to sea, and because of this, he had a crippling fear of the ocean.

Lorenzo proceeded to wipe the remaining residue off his face as the two others laughed at him. The young baker humored the two, knowing the hell they had been through. Once communication was cut off to Domus Aurea, the men had no means to contact their families or anyone for that matter. To their loved ones, both Daven and Adam were presumed dead. At that point in time, they had only each other, and they would protect one another at all costs.

Lorenzo's bakery was located in a busy marketplace to the south of Vatican City, but the busyness made it surprisingly safe for the two to hide. Aurean patrols only watched businesses that were at high risk for theft, and a bakery was not one of those. This made it simple to keep the men's existence a secret, and with secrecy came a more comfortable atmosphere to work in.

Daven's and Adam's presence was not known within the group of business owners, but questions did arise as to how Lorenzo managed to run a bakery when no other workers were outwardly present. Of course Lorenzo never denied or confirmed any theories as to how he ran his business. Aside from the frequent questions, there was little risk to Daven and Adam involved when working with Lorenzo. It was he who was taking the risk. If any word was to leak out about his involvement with Daven and

Adam, he would be charged with harboring and aiding fugitives, which was punishable by death.

As closing time drew near, the two began cleaning while Lorenzo watched from a small wooden chair. A massive storm pummeled the streets with high winds and piercing rain, but as others would see the raging weather as intimidating, Daven and Adam were comforted, knowing there would be few patrols roaming the streets that night.

"Do you really have to sit right in the middle of the floor?" asked Adam as he swept the flour-covered room.

"And is it necessary to make a bigger mess?" added Daven as he swept up Lorenzo's purposefully created pile of orange peels.

"Well, I can respond to both those questions with a simple answer." Lorenzo smiled as he chewed vigorously on an orange slice. "And that answer is—", but before he could respond with the predictable yes, a knock was heard at the back door of the bakery.

Lorenzo rose from his chair and kindly kicked it back into a corner to clear space for the hardworking men. Adam stuck out his broom handle, tripping Lorenzo on his way to the door as payback for making their jobs much more difficult.

"Can I help you?" asked Lorenzo, directing his question to the individual outside.

"It's Abele, Lorenzo," responded the man from the other side of the door. "Open up. It's storming something dreadful out here."

Lorenzo opened an eye-level slot to get a closer look at the man. It was indeed Abele, but the joking baker decided to have some fun with the soaking-wet old man.

"Can you come a little closer … Abele, is it? My vision isn't what it used to be," said Lorenzo as he popped another orange slice into his mouth. "Can't be too careful these days, wouldn't you agree?"

Abele wasn't in the mood for games and opened the door, forcefully striking the baker in the nose.

Lorenzo rubbed his face. "I guess I should be thanking you," he said, looking up at Abele, who walked in laughing. "That door should have been locked."

As Abele shut the four men in, the strong winds howled and whistled through the shrinking opening. The interior became peaceful as the storm was closed out, and the warmth of the quiet space cloaked its inhabitants.

"Are there any patrols out tonight?" asked Daven. It was a question he was sure to ask every night.

"Not a one. I guess even the might of the Aurean military can't withstand a little rain," said Abele with a grin.

"We're in luck then," said Adam.

"Let's still be cautious," answered Abele. "We never know who could be watching. We'll be the only ones on the roads tonight. Which means we'll be the only ones to be watched if anyone passes us by."

Both Daven and Adam nodded in agreement. They knew how much Abele was risking by doing what he was doing. It wasn't something they overlooked, and it burdened their thoughts knowing that if anything were to happen to Abele and his wife, Eula, it would be their fault.

The men gathered their belongings for the trip home. Abele and Lorenzo always left the store first to scout out their surroundings. It was a short distance from the back door of the bakery to Abele's small car, but any distance was a treacherous one when a small mistake could mean so much. There had been reports of stowaways being captured by Aurean officials in the past. All of which ended in terrible and public acts of violence. Most of those who aided the refugees were imprisoned and hanged for their treason. The convicted fugitives were tortured and later crucified.

Adam and Daven walked out into the damp night after Lorenzo and Abele gave the all clear. The misty atmosphere clung to their faces, washing away the day and revitalizing their tired bodies. Before walking farther, the two men looked down the alleyway toward the street. Even around this time of night, voices could be heard speaking to one another about the day's events and evening plans, but tonight was different. Tonight was silent on all accounts, except for raindrops dripping in puddles on the streets and sidewalks farther out. A cold chill ran up Daven's spine, along with a sinking feeling in the core of his body. Thoughts and wishes ran through his head like a tornado of anxiety. He longed for his life to once again become normal as it had been, sitting on the rocky shores of his hometown. The idea of seeing his loved ones both excited him and crushed him, all in the same breath. It was a pipe dream, but at the same time, it moved him through the day.

Adam was less optimistic about his current state of being. Anger consumed him much of the time, while questioning thoughts flooded his already disturbed feelings. It wasn't just his longing to be with his family once again that caused this despair, but the knowledge of that family's dependence on him that darkened his days and made the minutes seem like hours. On a nightly basis, he would lie in his bed and visualize his young family's faces, smiling back at him in the silent distance.

The three said their goodbyes to Lorenzo and walked to Abele's vehicle. They began their nightly routine of situating themselves on the floorboards of the car's back seat, peering out the windows to view what little of the world they were allowed to see. It wasn't a long drive to the Fortunas' residence, but when so much was at stake, the mile-long trek seemed like a daylong journey.

Streetlights and building tops were the most Daven and Adam could see on the way home. Occasionally, a sight of the moon would shine through the spaces between structures. Its light would reflect off windows, staring like eyes at the night sky on the face of hypnotized stone giants. The two men would normally take the time to rest during the short drive, but each night, they were able to catch a glimpse of the dome of Saint Peter's Basilica. It was uplifting. Although there was no escape, no sanctuary, no peace or strength left within the walls of the Vatican, it still stood for something that no man could conquer: faith. To Daven and Adam, their faith was pivotal to survival. Anger toward their God was still faith. Distrust and impatience still rang true to faith, still directed toward the Divine, the unseen omnipotence that guided them, forgave their faults, and loved them when their hearts sank and eyes grew dim.

As Abele pulled up to the front door of the Fortuna residence, all three men opened their ears, listening for footsteps, conversation, or anything that could become an immediate threat. The old man exited the vehicle and unlocked the front door to his house. It was the custom for Daven and Adam to await the signaling of the porch light being turned off to show safe passage. In the past, there had been nights spent confined to Abele's car. Patrols of Aurean officers were constant in the early days of Daven's and Adam's covert existence, but as of late, there was some relief. A careful eye and listening ear would keep them safe as long as the two never became too comfortable with their surroundings.

"Are we good to go?" asked Daven to Adam.

Adam lifted his head to peer out the window above Daven's head. "Light's off. Let's go."

The street was deathly quiet and the rain had long since ceased, but no patrols could be seen. It was both comforting and ominous, but the two decided to be thankful for an eventless night. There had been numerous close calls in the three years that the two men had been hiding out within the Fortunas' care, but it had been mostly encounters with neighbors and family friends. Cautious behavior kept danger at bay, but all involved in this secret life were sure to not let comfort and lowered guard seep in and cloud their awareness of threats.

The two entered the security of their home. It was essentially their home at this point in time, and the Fortunas made sure they felt at ease and included in their household. Abele and Eula Fortuna worked as a sort of foster family to Daven and Adam. They loved the two men, and that love was reciprocated toward them as well. Any one of the four individuals would lay down their lives for one another without hesitation, but it was as simple as making a meal for the three men in her life that Eula showed her dedication toward her family.

"Everyone come to the kitchen! Supper's ready," called Eula when she heard the front door close for the second time.

As Abele, Daven, and Adam entered the quaint little kitchen toward the back of the Fortunas' house, Eula greeted each of them with a kiss on the cheek. She was a naturally happy person and wouldn't show any kind of dark mood or anger around her two adopted sons. She knew she was looked at as a pillar of strength by them, and any sign of weakness or unhappiness would leave Daven and Adam without a light in their otherwise bleak existence.

"I hear you had quite the uneventful evening," said Eula as she took off her apron and sat down.

"Very uneventful," replied Abele. "Not a soul on the streets tonight."

"I just wish we could take advantage of it," said Adam. "You know ... take a walk. Enjoy the night. Just to be outside."

"Aside from the occasional smoke break out back at work, right?" said Daven sarcastically.

"I wish you wouldn't smoke, Adam," said Eula. "I don't even know how you're able to keep getting cigarettes."

"He steals them from Lorenzo," said Daven, smirking. Adam scowled at the man but chose to keep silent.

Abele and Eula stole a glance and smiled secretively at each other. Adam noticed and decided to make it a part of the conversation. "I saw that, you two. Let's keep it PG in here. Especially at dinner."

Daven laughed. He knew the two older individuals wouldn't understand the reference or the joke, but any chance to find humor in their lives was taken.

"Although I do love my wife very much, that wasn't quite what you thought it was," said Abele.

"We have a surprise for you two," said Eula as she reached for her husband's hand.

Daven and Adam looked at each other and then back at their guardians. It was impossible for thoughts not to flood their minds, but the Fortunas didn't leave them wondering.

Abele looked at the two men with a smile while Eula put her arm around her husband. "We may have a way to get you two boys home," said the woman with a grin.

Immediately Daven and Adam felt a sense of light-headedness. These had been the words they had longed to hear for three years. Both Daven and Adam had the mind-set to never get their hopes up, but at the sound of this, it was impossible not to feel hopeful, even if it was a false sense of the feeling.

Several seconds passed by without a word being spoken, but finally Daven opened up. "How?" was the only word he could get out.

"I have an acquaintance living in Fiumicino," began Abele as he sat back and put his arm around Eula. "He has had contact with an individual in Corsica for about four months now. I had mentioned to him about your situation, and he spoke to his friend in your regard."

Adam, who had been lost in his thoughts, finally came to and joined the conversation. "What did he say? Is there any way for this to work?"

"He told me that the man is willing and able to help you," said Abele.

At this moment Daven couldn't control the emotions that had been building up inside him. Tears streamed down his face at the thought of escaping and seeing his father and mother once again.

"How will he be able to help us, though?" asked Adam with slight disbelief.

"That's the best part," said Abele. "The Corsican is a fisherman. He knows the Tyrrhenian Sea and the Aurean sea patrols. If we plan well enough, there's nothing that can stop you two from returning home."

"When can we see this man?" said Adam. He too was ready and eager to return home to his family. A vision of his little girl's smiling face flashed within his mind and nearly caused him to weep.

"After your shift tomorrow at the bakery, we will drive to Fiumicino to meet him. We have been planning your escape for some time now, and we both feel you will be out of here within the week," said Abele with confidence.

Daven and Adam looked at each other with amazement. As wonderful as this news was, it was still extremely overwhelming and stressful. So many questions were racing through the heads of the two men. How could they sneak past the Aurean patrols on land and out at sea? How trustworthy was this acquaintance of Abele's? What would happen if they were caught?

"I know you two must have a thousand questions screaming through your head right now," said Abele. "But I believe right now it would be best for you two to get some sleep. We will save your questions for Jean tomorrow."

Adam nodded his head in agreement and rose from his seat along with Daven. The two shared their good nights and prepared for the long sleepless night ahead of them.

The wine cellar the two had been living in for the last three years had become quite cozy, in stark contrast to what it was before. Both men remembered in detail their first night within the cold basement. Abele and Eula didn't drink wine, or any alcohol for that matter, which left their crypt-like underground room unattended to and abandoned. Even with the cobwebs, dirt-covered floor, and musty atmosphere, the men slept soundly, knowing they were hidden from the eyes of their pursuers. It was now more like a hotel room rather than a prison cell. Two beds adorned two corners, with stairs leading up to the Fortunas' apartment fixed in between. Two curtains surrounded each bed, concealing them from any would-be invaders, with a single lamp sitting on an ornate nightstand situated under the stairs. A large cabinet sat at the bottom of the wooden steps, keeping the men's meager wardrobe organized and clean. It was warm, peaceful, and a world away from the Aurean streets above.

Daven sat wide-awake as he stared at the wooden support beams of the house's floor.

"Your mind is keeping me awake," said Adam sleepily and jokingly.

Daven laughed and collapsed back onto his pillow. "I can't help but wonder what'll happen to Abele and Eula. I'd feel guilty if we left and never looked back."

Adam rolled over on his back and crossed his arms behind his head. He had been thinking the same thing but hadn't mentioned anything to Daven. "Do you think they would want us to worry about them?"

"I know they wouldn't, but we both know that's going to be impossible. I want to do something … anything that could help them. They saved our lives, Adam. We owe them theirs," said Daven as he tried to come up with ways to assist their saviors.

"Well, the first step is to get out of here," said Adam as he tried to keep focus on their present dilemma. "Once we arrive in Corsica, we'll send word to Jean, and hopefully from there we can think of something. We will rescue them … I promise."

The following morning arrived quicker than expected. Adam woke first, but the man didn't feel the same sensation of dread and despair he was used to. Instead, hope and optimism welcomed him with the new day. Daven spent most of his night lying awake with thoughts of Abele and Eula flooding his mind, which had taken its toll as he hadn't yet woken from his sleep. As Adam rolled out of his bed, the sound of the heavy cellar door could be heard opening.

"You boys awake down there?" asked Abele from the top of the stairs.

"We are," answered Adam as he threw a pillow at Daven to wake him up.

"All right. I'll meet you at the bakery once your shift is over," said Abele. "We can head to Jean's right after. I'll be waiting up here to take you to work once you're ready to go."

"What time is it?" were the first words out of Daven's mouth every morning, but the answer never changed.

"Five in the AM, Daven," said Adam as he walked toward the stairs. "I'm going to take a shower."

The stairs creaked under Adam's feet as he climbed to the top. It was a familiar sound to him now, and so was the early rise to begin his day. The house was quiet, as it always was that early in the morning. Eula still slept, and Abele had gone outside to enjoy the morning air. It was at this time of the day that Adam's thoughts were their loudest, and the morning shower served to amplify the noise pummeling his brain.

Adam sat crouched down in the claw-foot tub as the water dripped off his nose. It was therapeutic and reminded him of rainy days in his home in the southeastern United States. The warm water relaxed his tense body and prepared him for the day to come, but he couldn't help but think of what Daven had mentioned the night before about the Fortunas. What would become of their rescuers once the two men left? They had already seen the ruthlessness of Nero. The man had effectively killed thousands of non-Italian citizens during the construction of the Wall of Dominance, but what would happen when his supply of workhorses was depleted? Would he then claim the lives of those he professed to rule over? These questions weighed down Adam's mind and outweighed the luxury of enjoying the thought of returning to his home.

After making the short car ride to the bakery, their workday began like any other. Daven tossed Adam an apron after the two washed their hands and drew back their hair. Lorenzo waved to them from the front of the store while signing for a morning delivery. It was quiet and peaceful. Nothing out of the ordinary occurred, and it seemed like that would continue.

Daven knew that Lorenzo would need to know about Abele's plan to smuggle the stowaways out of Domus Aurea, but he was reluctant to speak up. He didn't want to come across as ungrateful to the man who risked life and limb to employ the two boys.

"You two are quieter than usual today," said Lorenzo, breaking the silence.

"A lot on our minds, I guess," said Adam, avoiding eye contact, trying to think of a way to break the news.

"You care to share?" asked Lorenzo. The man was uncomfortable with awkward silences.

Daven looked at Adam with questioning eyes, waiting to see if his friend was going to tell Lorenzo the latest, but he chose to speak first when Adam remained silent. "We may be going home," he said with a barely contained smile.

Lorenzo looked at the two with a stern expression. His reaction was what Daven and Adam had feared, but to their relief, Lorenzo then clapped his hands together and laughed.

"That's wonderful! When? How?" asked Lorenzo with excitement.

"We're not sure yet," responded Daven. "Abele knows someone living in Fiumicino who may be able to get us out."

Lorenzo scratched the back of his head, attempting to come up with words to express his excitement for the boys.

"I'm really happy to hear that," began Lorenzo before being cut short by the front doorbell. "Hold that thought, guys."

Lorenzo left the back room and walked up front to welcome his patron. The man had never lost his caring attitude toward his consumers. Most of his peers in the market district had lost their compassionate frame of mind once the Aurean regime choked the joy of life out of the Italian people, but this only fueled Lorenzo's ability to make people smile. It was the least he could do to shine light on the gloom around them.

Once Lorenzo left the room, Daven turned to Adam and began to inquire as to what was ailing his longtime friend.

"What in the world happened back there, man?" asked Daven. "You of all people should be the happiest about getting out of here!"

Adam looked down at the flour-covered table he was standing behind and attempted to pull himself out of whatever hole his mind was in.

"All I can think about is my family, Daven," replied Adam with a quiver in his voice. "To them I may as well be dead. It's been three years! How do I know my wife hasn't found someone else? How do I know that my daughter isn't calling someone else Daddy? It's killing me just thinking about it. One part of me wants to run home and leave all this behind, but there is this pain that I feel that keeps me attached to this godforsaken place. I don't know what I could handle more easily—staying here and fighting to survive, or going home and finding out that everything I knew is gone."

This sudden outpour of emotion and vocalization rendered Daven speechless. He always knew that Adam's imprisonment in Domus Aurea was more difficult to handle, but he never knew of the torture that Adam endured on a daily basis. The man had a brand-new family—a wife and child. Adam was only eighteen when his college sweetheart, Brooke, became pregnant, but he wanted nothing more than to take care of her and start a family. Adam was ready to quit school and start working in order to support his wife, but she convinced him to pursue his dream. It was a decision he would come to regret and still regretted. The reason he was in Italy at the time of Nero's rise to power was because of his dream chasing, and it ate at him every day.

Daven sat for a moment trying to think of words to console his troubled companion, but he stopped short after sensing something was different and out of place at the front of the store. He peered through the small circular window placed inside the double swinging door that led to the counter. For a moment, all he could see was the back of Lorenzo's head, but as their supervisor moved out of sight, Daven saw something that made his heart stop and his blood run cold. His head began to swim, and the room around him spun like the second hand on a clock.

Three men stood in plain sight on the other side of the counter, and five others stood behind them: the Primus Palus of the first cohort in the Lazio Legion; its legate; five members of the Praetorian Guard, Nero's personal bodyguards; and Domus Aurea's supreme ruler and founder, Lucius Nero himself. Nero was a relatively young man, who had an extremely charismatic personality. He wore a dark-blue frock coat underneath an intricately designed breastplate. Adorning his shoulders was the emblem of the emperor himself, a symbol of fascism in earlier days. It was a bundle of equal-length sticks tied together at the bottom and top, with an ax-head situated on the right and left sides. On top was a clenched fist, symbolizing Nero's authority, and a green laurel contained the symbol. Lucius was tall and imposing, wielding a gladius on his side and a pistol on the other. He had jet-black hair and dark walnut-colored eyes that hypnotized all who looked into them. Nero smiled and spoke to Lorenzo calmly and politely, but the legate, Adamo Gozi, and Primus Palus Benito Gozi, Adamo's younger brother, stood by with a look of disdain and boredom.

"Adam," said Daven in a daze, "we need to go. We need to go now."

Adam looked in Daven's direction trying to figure out what had happened that required them to run, but before he had the chance to get the words out, Daven had already bolted out the back door.

"So how long have you owned your business here ... Lorenzo?" questioned Nero.

Lorenzo fumbled about trying to act busy, attempting to buy Daven and Adam enough time to notice who had entered the bakery. "Um ... I'd have to say close to fifteen years, Your Highness," he said, not really knowing the correct title to use. "I normally work alone, as you can see. I don't get as many customers as I used to."

Nero hadn't caught Lorenzo's underhanded stab at the emperor's inability to keep his people happy, but his subordinates did, and they weren't pleased about the comment.

"Why the sudden drop in business?" asked Adamo sarcastically. "Is there something you think may be hindering your ability to function?"

Lorenzo stopped what he was doing and tried quickly to pull his foot out of his mouth, but Nero carried the conversation forward, ignoring the comment.

"Would you care to give us a tour of your establishment here?" asked Nero quickly, sensing the tension between Adamo and Lorenzo, but in reality, he had just unknowingly signed Lorenzo's death sentence. Typically, if any Aurean patrol had found Daven and Adam in the care of Lorenzo, he would have been arrested on the spot, but with the supreme ruler of Domus Aurea in his presence, Lorenzo would probably be executed without hesitation.

In a matter of seconds, Lorenzo experienced an overwhelming flooding of emotion regarding his own death. Anger, sadness, despair, and even the acceptance of the inevitable rushed through his mind in what seemed like an eternity. He felt the cold bite in his stomach and the blood rush out of his feet. But there was nothing he could do. The only hope he had was that Daven and Adam had disappeared.

"Absolutely," said Lorenzo in a daze. "Where would you like to begin?"

"Why not show us where your livelihood is made?" said Nero, trying to act like the caring man he was not.

This wasn't what Lorenzo wanted to hear, but he had no choice, so he motioned for the group to follow him. He was so sure that these final few seconds would be his last as a living man, and so he made peace with his God and prepared himself to be arrested or shot on the spot, but as he made his way into the kitchen, it was not Daven and Adam who awaited him.

Two Italian men covered in flour up to their elbows were kneading dough in front of Lorenzo.

"Your Excellency," said the two men in unison as they bowed their heads to Nero. *Excellency* thought Lorenzo in a small moment of epiphany.

"Didn't you say you normally worked alone?" asked Nero, smiling.

Lorenzo hesitated for a moment as he tried to comprehend what was happening. These were obviously not the two men he had just spoken to not ten minutes ago. He felt as if, for the moment at least, he was the brunt of a very bad joke. In fact, he laughed nervously and almost maniacally when he saw that his life had been spared by some freak miracle.

"Uh … normally yes. These are volunteers f-from the baker's guild," said Lorenzo, still in a daze, knowing full well there was no baker's guild.

Adamo leaned in and whispered something to Nero, which left Lorenzo wondering if the officer had noticed the nervous store owner's pale and sickly complexion. The constant thought of having his cover blown left him feeling drained and exhausted. He just wanted the day to be over.

"Well, I believe we have overstayed our welcome … as I am being told," said Nero as he glared at Adamo.

Lorenzo attempted not to act excited toward the idea of them leaving, but holding back the feelings proved to be quite difficult.

"No! Don't feel rushed on my account. Business has been slow today, and I enjoy the company," lied Lorenzo through his teeth without hesitation.

As Lorenzo shut the door after the group had vacated, he sat for a moment to breathe a sigh of relief. He had never run into trouble before with Aurean officials, and so he was convinced that this was an omen of some sort. The last few minutes were cutting too close, and he knew that things needed to change before lives were lost.

It was difficult for him to even think about what he was about to do. Daven and Adam were more than just friends; they were family. Knowing that the decision he was about to make might cut ties between the men forever made it all the more heart-wrenching. He didn't want to walk through the door. He didn't want to see the smiles and laughter he knew he would hear as the two spoke about the close call they all had averted. But it was unavoidable.

Lorenzo walked into the kitchen as Daven and Adam were shaking hands with the two men he had seen earlier with Nero.

"Lorenzo!" said Adam, laughing, his eyes wide open. "This is Gabriel and Michael. We found them walking past the alleyway when Emperor Psychopath showed up. They actually agreed to help us ... I can't believe they actually agreed to help us."

"They didn't even hesitate," added Daven as he pushed his hair back with his hands.

Lorenzo laughed, trying to forget what needed to be done. It ate at him like fire in his stomach. He needed to release it before it consumed him, but the thought of speaking those words pained him more.

"I thank you two from the bottom of my heart, but I must ask," said Lorenzo as he shook the hands of the strangers, "why were you in the alleyway?"

"Divine intervention," said Michael with a smirk. "I guess the universe had a plan in mind."

Lorenzo wasn't entirely sure what Michael meant, but it didn't matter. He had just dodged a bullet thanks to these men, and he wasn't about to question any further.

As the sun set and Michael and Gabriel departed, Lorenzo was left without any more distractions. He promised himself once Abele arrived to retrieve the boys, he would speak to them about his decision. It was the furthest that he could delay the foreseeable. This had to end; as much as he wanted to look the other way and continue on with his charitable actions, he feared for his life and that of his two friends.

CHAPTER 3

A HEAD START

September 15, 2035

Elia Serra sat lost in a book. It was the third time he had skimmed the pages of this particular novel, but it served as an escape from reality and, therefore, it was a good story.

The man had bookshelves strewn across each of the four walls in his quarters. Above his bed, lining the doorframe. From corner to corner. He had read each and every book at least once.

On his nightstand lay a small lamp and phone. He never spent much time in his room, but when he did, it was to not be disturbed. Regularly the phone was left off the hook, but after many a lecture, he was obligated to leave the avenue of communication open. Giuseppe made it a point never to call Elia unless it was important, which is why Serra's phone began ringing.

At first, the ringing went unnoticed. He had reached a favorite part of his book, and because of this, he was far too engrossed to notice anything around him. It wasn't until he heard Giuseppe's voice on the answering machine that his thoughts were interrupted, and he picked up his phone.

"Giuseppe, what seems to be the problem?" asked Elia.

"No problem, Elia, just a question. Can you come to my office? I have something to show you," replied Giuseppe through the shrill earpiece.

Elia hung up the phone and scanned the room, looking for his shoes. His gaze caught sight of the mirror, and he was quickly reminded of a moment in his past. During the Vatican Revolt, Elia fought side by side with Giuseppe on the front line in Saint Peter's Square. It wasn't until after the skirmish that Elia was made aware of an injury. A bullet had damaged a portion of the left side of his face. His eye was destroyed, and so to this day, he wore a cloth to cover the injury.

As Elia made his way to the top floor of the Milvian Guard barracks, two Swords, foot soldiers of the guard, stopped and attempted to start a conversation with him. Serra was known for being extremely approachable and lax when it came to visual forms of respect. As unorthodox as his methods were, Elia's company of Swords were the happiest, most respected, and most fit for battle of all their peers.

After shaking the two soldiers' hands and continuing on his way, Elia noticed Giuseppe's door hanging open. He could hear Giuseppe talking to someone as he drew near but couldn't make out the words that were being spoken. As Elia entered the office, Giuseppe set down his phone and turned around with a look of petulance on his face.

"Is it a sin to wish harm upon your peers?" asked Giuseppe after seeing Elia.

"I'm sure you know the answer to that question, Giuseppe," answered Elia, smiling.

"Ah. So it is," said Giuseppe sheepishly, looking down at his feet. "Elia, I hate to have called you up here only to leave so abruptly, but I've been … summoned to the palace. Probably to be reprimanded for my unsavory actions this morning."

"I can only imagine," said Elia.

"In the meantime," said Giuseppe, reaching into his pocket, "can you translate this for me?" He handed Elia a small folded piece of paper. "I saw it in a dream last night."

Elia reached out as Giuseppe handed the slip to him, walking away.

"Oh, and hang around here. Raul left to gather the other lieutenant colonels. I have something to discuss with you. I won't be long!" yelled Giuseppe as he disappeared down the stairwell. And with that, Elia was alone.

Adriano had just received a call from the chief medical examiner about the dead man from that morning. He never liked meeting with Doriano. Perhaps it was the nature of the man's profession, or maybe the coroner's odd personality, that made Adriano feel awkward and uneasy. Either way, he wasn't fond of morgues.

As he passed the Church of Saint Anne on his way to the coroner, Adriano could see Giuseppe leaving the barracks, heading toward the Apostolic Palace. He was reminded of the night Giuseppe and he met in secret inside the church to discuss an eviction of Aurean power from the Vatican. It was a time of great fear. Aurean soldiers patrolled night and day inside the former city-state's interior, never granting the inhabitants a moment's peace.

It didn't take long to learn the patrol routes, making slipping past unwanted attention rather easy. Still, the risk was great, and being caught, much less while staging a coup, meant certain punishment or death. Even so, Giuseppe and Adriano had been determined to take back their home, and their combined prowess had eventually proved formidable in ousting great powers.

He entered the gendarmes' offices and made his way to the stairwell. The lighting was different in the basement of the building, emitting an electric-blue fluorescent hue. It bothered his eyes, and the almost inaudible buzz of the bulbs irritated his ears.

The hallway leading to the double doors of the morgue was long, slabbed with stainless steel panels. That, along with the cold tile floor, reverberated the cold, but it was nothing compared to the frigid interior of Doriano's haunt.

His footsteps echoed through the passageway, the hard soles of his boots clapping with every step. It wasn't uncommon to hear Doriano speaking to himself loudly from the opposite end of the hall. The coroner claimed he did it due to a self-diagnosed psychosis, but most believed it was because he felt uneasy with the natural silence associated with the dead. Today was different, though, and Adriano was well aware of it. At first, he thought that Doriano had simply stepped out for a moment. It was quiet on the other side of the doors, but after entering the morgue, he saw the examiner standing over the body with his back turned toward the entrance.

"Doriano," said Adriano, announcing his presence.

The silent man jerked slightly as he turned around. "Oh, Adriano. I didn't hear you come in."

"Is everything okay?" asked the inspector, noticing his peer's clearly shaken state.

"I'm fine. Just a tad mentally displaced is all."

"I see." Adriano walked and stood over the dead man. His skin was noticeably pale, and the life that was once eerily present in his face was gone. It was normal and yet still unnerving.

"I made sure to record and transcribe the speech before cutting," said Doriano as he walked to a stainless steel table to the left of the body. "I also did some feeling around in his throat before damaging the larynx. I found this." Doriano handed Adriano a small glass container with a tiny flower petal inside. "As soon as I removed it, he stopped talking. It's unique and could point you directly to your next location. If you're even able to get there."

"Where?" asked Adriano, still inspecting the small petal.

"I'm no botanist, but what I do know is that this particular flower only grows in Orto Botanico, Rome's botanical gardens."

Adriano went from optimism to aggravation in seconds. His crime scene had shrunk immensely, making it that much easier to narrow down their list of suspects; but unfortunately, those inhabiting the Vatican were restricted to its grounds. There were no exceptions: resident, officer, even pope.

"You don't seem very impressed, Adriano," said Doriano as he rubbed his chin.

"Oh no, it's not that in the least," said Adriano. "I'm just stuck. At a point where I'm equipped with all this information, but I can't utilize it."

Doriano nodded in agreement. "Understandable, but I do believe we're approaching a time of liberation. His Holiness is an admirable man. His hands have been tied with all the advisement he's been receiving from his cardinals. While it's all in the best interest of the Vatican, I know it has constrained your movements significantly."

"Liberation, you say? I guess I'm cautiously optimistic," replied Adriano. "It is a dangerous world we live in, but this," he continued, holding up the glass container, "this is a step forward. I'll be sure to show this to Giuseppe. I wish I had caught him earlier. It looked like he was heading to the palace."

"Do you think it has something to do with all … this?" asked Doriano, looking at the body.

"I don't know, but I have a feeling that whatever it is, it's about to change everything."

Giuseppe stood in front of the Portone di Bronzo, delaying his entry. The air still had an electrified feeling about it that had never dissipated since that morning. The storm was moving in swiftly and menacingly, and Giuseppe felt he was its sole destination. He stood, staring at a Swiss guard who stood at the entrance of the pope's residence. Another paced back and forth within the hallway inside the large bronze door. These men dedicated their lives without question to the leader of one of the world's greatest institutions. They were admirable men, who never voiced aloud any complaints or grievances. This made Giuseppe feel like a chastised child. The argument with Alban that morning was avoidable and immature. He was certain that whatever could befall him at this point was of his own doing, and he was prepared to take full responsibility for his actions.

A single raindrop landed on the tip of his nose. He looked up as the clouds began moving quicker with the increased speed of the wind. He decided to make his way indoors.

"Crown Morreti," said the stationary guard at the door as he saluted.

Giuseppe wordlessly nodded back and hastily moved inward. The Papal Apartments lay on the third floor of the square building. The ceilings and walls of the interior were adorned beautifully with sweeping art and precise stonework. The images he beheld were associated with pleasant memories and aided in suppressing his anxiety, but that peace was soon shattered.

As he climbed the staircase to his destination, an unintelligible and angered voice echoed down to his ears from above him. The voice was immediately recognizable as Alban's, but as to the recipient of the incensed words, Giuseppe was unaware. He knew there was no avoiding a confrontation, but he vowed to himself and God to make it as painless as possible. He didn't know what conversation or lecture by his superiors lay ahead of him, but this small encounter with Alban was one he could control.

As Giuseppe rounded the first bend of the stairwell, his eyes met immediately with Alban's, but to his surprise, the cardinal quickly averted his gaze. Following behind him was the Dean of the College of Cardinals, Camillo Lombardi. The kind-faced man stopped as Alban continued, and smiled at Giuseppe.

"Hello, my good sir," said Camillo as he watched Alban continue on.

"Your Eminence," greeted Giuseppe warmly.

"I understand your morning has been quite ... problematic," said the Cardinal Bishop. "I can only pray it begins to alleviate quickly."

"Thank you. I can only pray with you in that regard."

"I understand how hotheaded Alban can be at times," said Camillo, "but I can assure you he only means well ... in his own fashion."

Giuseppe was not convinced. He was positive the man was put on the earth only to torment and annoy him, but nonetheless, he smiled and silently agreed.

"I also want you to know that I am staunchly supporting your work," said Camillo, "and I will do whatever it takes to relieve whatever pressure I am able to when it comes to freeing your movements."

Giuseppe was grateful for this. He needed every supporting hand he could muster up if he was to continue his work unhindered. Camillo was a powerful ally to have, and he could only hope that he found the same willingness in the man he was about to speak with.

Camillo smiled and extended his hand. Giuseppe grasped it firmly and smiled genuinely. The two parted ways with no more words spoken, but an understanding of the work that each was attempting to accomplish.

Giuseppe reached the third floor and stopped short just before reaching the pope's office door. He had nothing to fear from the man, but still his nerves got the better of him. Pope Innocent XIV was a kind and gentle man. It was not a stretch to say that he was loved by every human soul within the Vatican, but even so, he was still the most powerful individual within the city walls. As Giuseppe walked through the office door, he breathed deeply and accepted fate as it would be.

"Giuseppe! Come in, come in!" said the hunched man with glee in his voice, walking from behind his desk. He had a short, shuffled stride that scraped the floor as he walked, always keeping his hands outstretched, prepared to give a two-handed handshake whenever he was obliged. "Please have a seat!" he said after grasping Giuseppe's hand. "You know, this city is far too small that we should go so long without exchanging words," said Innocent as he moved back behind his desk.

"You are not wrong, Your Holiness," said Giuseppe as he took his seat.

"Giuseppe ... formalities. Why keep such traditions when the world is not watching?" said Innocent in regard to being referred to as holy.

"Shall I call you Inigo then?" said Giuseppe, playfully sarcastic.

Innocent smirked. Inigo had been his name before his papal inauguration. "I don't suppose I would even answer to such a name anymore. So unfamiliar ... Why I chose to be called Innocent, I will never know. I'm far from being so. But I didn't call you here to discuss names or lapses in friendship. Nor did I call you here to discuss the incident with Alban this morning."

Giuseppe breathed a sigh of relief. It was now obvious as to why the cardinal priest left Giuseppe unacknowledged in the stairwell. The cherry-faced man did not obtain what he desired as Giuseppe's punishment.

"I was in the wrong," said Giuseppe abruptly. "I should have kept my mouth shut."

"We are not faultless beings," said Innocent. "Besides, it has been addressed and concluded. We have more pressing matters to discuss, don't we?"

The sudden coolness in the pope's voice caught Giuseppe off guard.

"Obviously the incident that occurred last night was unavoidable. It is not the fault of any direct party, but I cannot help but feel responsible for the constricted environment we insist you work in. This is not the work of the Aureans. You and I both know this. It is the work of our hidden enemy, but not one we are familiar with. It is an impatient darkness. One that will go to any length to achieve its goal. They share the same desires as the ancient ones, but not their strategic grace."

Giuseppe listened intently but impatiently. Innocent's mention of the Milvian Guard's restrictions in a negative light gave the man hope. Perhaps the shackles would be loosed, and he would be able to work freely to protect those under his watchful and caring eye. "If that is so, we cannot take a reactive approach to these threats anymore. It's time to take the offense."

"You have my unwavering support when it comes to making your job easier, my friend," said Innocent, "but I still have some restrictions I must be unmoving on."

"What would these restrictions entail?"

"If your guard is able to move freely away from the city, and I am sure that is what you desire, I cannot allow you to move with them. You are too great an asset. However, you will be allowed to send whomever you wish out into our enemy's territory. Within a responsible number of course."

"There is nothing more I can ask for, then. If the guard is able to move freely, within caution, I will be satisfied."

"Good," said Innocent with a pleased grin. "Now … with that being said, I must insist on being included in every decision made by you and Adriano. I may act as a stressless and carefree individual, but I am capable of handling much in the ways of responsibility and knowledge."

"You would not be our leader if you were not," said Giuseppe. "You have my word that nothing will proceed unless you are notified in full."

"Then there is nothing more even I could ask for," said Innocent, still smiling. "You are a great man, Giuseppe. You bear the weight of the world on your capable shoulders. Something no one, including myself, could possibly accomplish."

"It shows in the wrinkles on my face and the gray in my hair." Giuseppe smiled.

Innocent laughed and patted the table as he stood up once again. Giuseppe stood as well and nodded his head as if to bow. He could not help but show at least some form of respect toward Innocent, even in the vaguest ways imaginable. He loved this man dearly and envied his ability to show no signs of worry or anxiety, no matter what the situation. There was nothing he wouldn't do for the Holy Father, and he knew the feeling was reciprocated.

As Giuseppe stepped outside into the brisk air once again, he was immediately called upon.

"Giuseppe!"

He whirled around to see Adriano walking quickly toward him. He waved his hand to acknowledge that his attention was received and began moving toward the inspector general.

"Giuseppe," said Adriano as the two met, "I've an update from Doriano."

"Couldn't come at a better time," said Giuseppe. The chains had finally been lifted. He was prepared and eager to receive any news, knowing he could respond without hindrance.

"You'll have to fill me in, but in the meantime, maybe you can make some sense out of our new findings where I cannot."

Adriano began to relay everything he had learned from the coroner. Giuseppe immediately formulated a plan of action. It was liberating to let his imagination run freely with plans and solutions. It was almost overwhelming.

"So where do you go from here?" asked Adriano.

"I believe I'll have some Eyes tour Rome. Perhaps the botanical gardens. I hear it's beautiful this time of year."

"Indeed it is," smiled Adriano. He tucked his hands into his jacket pockets and looked up. "There's a wind of change in the air. I do believe things are looking up."

"I'm optimistic," said Giuseppe, "but one can't help but feel the pang of defeat even in the most promising times. Especially here."

"You know the cliché. God has a plan and works in mysterious ways."

"True, but so does our enemy. You are correct, though. Maybe my pessimism is encumbering me more than I'd like to admit. I'll adopt your frame of mind. Positivity may beget positive results."

"There's the idea," said Adriano, smiling. "Oh, I do want to put this offer on the table. Feel free to utilize the gendarmerie's CSI when need be. Might as well be thorough with whatever you undertake from this point."

"Thank you," said Giuseppe. He could see the pieces falling into place with every step. The floodgates of fortune had opened, and it was plentiful.

The two exchanged goodbyes and went their separate ways. Giuseppe was excited to return to his office and share the good news of his exploits that day with his lieutenant colonels. He found himself jogging back to the barracks and skipping steps on his way up to the third floor. There was a fire within him that hadn't burned for years. His heart raced, and his senses heightened. Adrenaline pulsed through him like cold water and revitalized his tired mind.

He could see Raul standing outside his office doors as he reached the top of the stairs at the opposite end of the hall.

"We're all here, Giuseppe," said Raul.

"Why are you standing out here then?" questioned Giuseppe.

Raul rolled his eyes while gesturing over his shoulder. "Margo is going on and on about how incompetent I am. He thinks it's my fault that someone got in last night."

"You don't believe that, do you?"

"Not anymore. It's obvious we're dealing with something out of the norm. But I still don't like being falsely accused."

Giuseppe patted Raul on the shoulder as he walked past into his office. Elia and Margo turned to look at the two men as they entered.

"So how do we handle this, Giuseppe?" Margo asked as he cut his eyes toward Raul.

Raul had been passive up until this moment, but he knew Margo would continue crucifying his reputation if he didn't speak up. "Don't be coy. Margo. I'm not fooled by your falsely concerned inquisition. You're asking about me, and you know it."

Giuseppe silently agreed with Raul but spoke up in an attempt to defuse the situation. "Raul …" he said, trying to rein in any brewing anger.

Margo stuck his hand out to stop Giuseppe from interrupting. "No! Let him finish. Only the guilty need to defend themselves so belligerently."

"And only the ignorant falsely accuse," snapped Raul.

Margo finally had enough. In his mind, Raul had failed in his responsibilities and put the city in extreme danger. He felt compelled to make Raul admit to his wrongdoing. "They were *your* soldiers who were guarding the wall! You chose who to place where! You should have known who was capable to stand watch! As far as I'm concerned, it was *your* responsibility and *your* failure to choose wisely that got us in this situation in the first place!"

"Enough!" yelled Giuseppe, having let the argument go on for too long. "While I cannot condone Raul's incensed response to your angry accusations, he is right in defending himself. Not even I know for certain what occurred last night, but I do know that Raul isn't to blame—or anyone else for that matter."

"Fine," said Margo, bowing to his wrongful allegations, "but I know we can all agree that this blatant and bold attack means we need to act. We should have acted long ago, but it is imperative that we do now."

"Which is precisely why I've called you here. The familiar, patient persistence we've become accustomed to in our adversary is no more. Their passive nature has turned aggressive," said Giuseppe, moving the conversation along.

Raul sat down and placed his face in his hands. "That goes without saying. But what can we do? Our hands are tied. We've never been able to leave the city, even from the onset of our battle."

Elia broke his silence. "I know I've always been perceived as foolishly positive," he said with his arms crossed as he leaned against the fireplace. "But I can't help but think that the tides will be turning in our favor very soon."

"And I may be frustratingly pessimistic at times, but I can't help but agree with you. Change is in the air," said Margo.

Raul remained uncertain. "Well, I'm happy to hear that our future may be less bleak in a matter of time, but forgive me if I'm not convinced quite yet."

"Then allow me to ease your worried mind," said Giuseppe with a smile. "Apparently the events of this morning have lit a fire under the feet of our superiors. His Holiness has lifted the hand of suppression and freed our movements. As of today, we are free to leave Vatican grounds to move about Rome when need be."

Elia stood straight up and dropped his arms. "No restrictions?"

"Only that I myself must remain here within the city at all times. Otherwise, we can send whomever we want into the heart of Domus Aurea within a reasonable number," said Giuseppe.

"Then I'm no longer a doubting Thomas!" exclaimed Raul. "I'm willing and able to take on any task you see fit, Crown Morreti."

"Perhaps we should meet with Azael?" said Margo, with ideas flooding his mind. "I believe his team would be best suited for this particular task."

"I agree," said Raul.

"As do I," said Giuseppe as he walked behind his desk. "In the meantime, meet with your lieutenants and update them on our newfound freedoms, but keep tight restrictions on when they should be allowed to set foot into enemy territory. We may have been liberated, but we have also stepped into a much more dangerous dominion."

"Yes, sir," said the three men in unison.

While Raul and Margo made their way out of Giuseppe's office, Elia stayed behind to speak to the man about the writing he wanted translated. He waited for the other two men to step out of earshot range and turned to Giuseppe.

"I have a few things to ask you about that dream you had …"

"What were you looking to know?" asked Giuseppe.

Elia stood for a moment in silence, trying to piece together the proper way to present his question. "Was there … anything overtly strange about the dream itself?"

Giuseppe smirked and looked at Elia with silent inquiry. "Elia, the whole experience was out of the ordinary. It felt so real. The cold, the sounds, the images. Everything. Even now I feel as if I truly experienced it. When I wake from any other dream, I immediately realize how illusory they were. But this … I feel like I could revisit every aspect as if it were contained in our realm."

Elia tilted his head and smiled with a look of affirmation. "That's what I thought."

"What are you thinking?"

"This writing is clearly Hebrew, as I'm sure you guessed," said Elia as he unfolded the paper. "That's obvious. But I didn't have to do much thinking when it came to a translation." Elia walked to Giuseppe's desk and said, "I recognized these from several books I've read. More specifically from the Alphabet of Ben Sira."

"Sounds enticing," said Giuseppe as he took the paper.

"More informative than entertaining, but its usefulness has shown itself. These are not just mere words or phrases. They're names. Names that I recognize from the Alphabet's story of Lilith," said Elia as he pointed at the names: "Senoy, Sansenoy, and Semangelof. The three angels sent to punish Lilith for her disobedience against Adam."

"Lilith. Why would I dream something related to Lilith?" asked Giuseppe, clearly confused.

Elia returned the look of confusion but in a different manner. "Why wouldn't you? She is the source of our problems. But even so, I don't think it can be chalked up to stress or anxiety. I don't even believe it was a dream at all."

"Not even a dream? What? You think I had a vision?" Giuseppe asked with a questioning tone.

"Is that so unbelievable?" asked Elia with slight defense. "God spoke to the prophets through dreams. Our Milvian Guard was created specifically to fight the unreal and insane. Why should we dismiss the same when it shows itself?"

"No, I suppose it isn't so unbelievable," said Giuseppe, sensing Elia's frustration. "If it was a vision, I can only draw positive interpretations from it."

"You're already witnessing the positive outcomes. Our liberation is one, I believe, Giuseppe, and that is a significant victory."

"So perhaps that is the interpretation. Us being graced with freedom."

Elia made his way toward the office doors to take his leave but turned around once more. "I believe that is part of it. But I also believe there is much more to follow. I'll keep you informed with any other news that may come about."

Giuseppe smiled as Elia walked out of the office. He was then alone and finally able to reflect on the events of that day. So much had occurred, and he was attempting to absorb it all before he was called upon once more, which occurred sooner than he expected.

Giuseppe walked outside into the cool night. It was calming and serene, without a cloud in the sky—starry and limitless. Giuseppe never felt unsafe when walking the grounds, even at late hours. The nighttime air felt cozy and comforting, like a blanket around his shoulders.

He was meeting Azael at the radio station, directly west of the barracks next to the western wall. He decided to take his time and enjoy the peaceful serenity of the crickets chirping all about him, their tempo quick and all encompassing. Azael Vargas was the commanding officer of the reconnaissance branch of the Milvian Guard. They were trained for less conspicuous activities regarding the safety of the Vatican and were able to carry out dangerous missions in the name of the guard. They were officially known as the Eyes of Uriel, and the name was befitting regarding their responsibilities.

Giuseppe stopped at the memorial to Saint Peter just shy of the station and directly in the center of the city. It was where just thirteen hours before, he was staring at a talking corpse. It had been busy and crowded, with people of all sorts witnessing the havoc surrounding such a supernatural occurrence. Now it was deathly silent, without a soul to be seen. A chalk outline lay at the base of the statue, but otherwise, there was nothing to mark the catastrophe that had occurred.

Giuseppe placed his right foot forward after he had finished reflecting on that morning, but before he could move any farther, the chirping crickets fell silent. Even the wind ceased to blow past his ears. Only the sound of his breathing and the beating of his steadily quickening heart were heard. Suddenly he felt as if he was being surrounded by a multitude of unseen eyes. The hair on the back of his neck stood on end, and the feeling spread down his back and arms. His vision began to fade, the blood rushed from his head, and the sound of his breathing and heartbeat slowed down like a dying record player. He felt himself falling backward, and after what seemed like hours, he could see the blurry twinkling of the stars above him as his head and body met the grass and concrete below.

He lay there, with the hazy statue of Peter peeking up from his vision's horizon. Then, like an eclipse, a dark figure moved in slowly from his left, replacing the white statue with shadow.

"Does it make you feel … hopeless, Giuseppe, to know how insignificantly small you really are?" said the low rumbling voice, coming in from all sides, whispering and echoing. "Twice I have walked past your impenetrable line of defense to the very center of your home." The voice grew louder and more terrifying. "You cannot stop us. You will try, but you will fail."

Giuseppe could not move. His senses failed him, but his mind was still fearfully intact. He was completely aware of who this strange visitor was, and it scared him to death.

The shadow crouched closer to the man's face. Giuseppe could feel the black silhouette's cold breath filling his nostrils, freezing his unfocused eyes. "My name is Charles. Charles Monroe. You and I both know that is not my true name, but that is how you will refer to me."

"Ch-charles," Giuseppe stuttered out. He couldn't tell if his voice shook because of fear or because of cold.

"That's right, Giuseppe. Charles," said the blackness. Giuseppe could see the edges of the silhouette's face tighten up. The creature was smiling, and his confidence was terrifying.

The shadow reached out and touched Giuseppe's face. Its hands were surprisingly warm. It comforted Giuseppe, while continuing to frighten him. "You thought you were fighting the world, didn't you? Domus Aurea chokes you … walling you in like a prisoner, keeping your defenses on edge. They are a visible threat, but they are not what truly frightens you, are they? No … that would be … *us*."

The being's hand grabbed Giuseppe's jaw and clenched it. "But not even *they* are worthy of your fear. You're a formidable opponent, one that I truly respect." The shadow rolled Giuseppe's head from left to right, inspecting him in judgment. "And I am worthy of your fear."

The man dropped Giuseppe's head and stood up. "My brothers and sisters, the *true* enemy, are slow. You hold a secret that both they and I desire, one that we will eventually attain, but they are pensive … inactive. They are like children testing hot water, never committing to the plunge. I do not share their patience."

Suddenly, as if an echo sprang from large canyon walls, Giuseppe could hear his name being called out. The shadow lifted his head, looking into the distance that seemed so far away to Giuseppe. "We will meet again." And with those words, the man was gone.

"Giuseppe! Giuseppe! Come on, boy, answer me," said the echoing voice, closer now and real.

"I'm fine," groaned Giuseppe, almost inaudibly. "I'm fine …"

He attempted to rise from his cold, concrete bed, but dizziness and a head full of rushing blood bore down upon him.

"What happened? Are you all right?" asked Azael Vargas as he reached his fallen comrade.

"I'm fine, my friend. I just tripped is all," responded Giuseppe as Azael helped him to his feet.

"Tripped? You were completely laid out on your back," said Azael, unbelieving.

"Best bit of rest I've had all week," jested Giuseppe.

"Look, we can talk later if you'd like," said Azael. "I know today hasn't been very enjoyable for you."

"No, this is important, but if you don't mind, I'd like to have that talk right here," said Giuseppe, smiling, but still visibly shaken from his encounter. "I'm sure you've probably heard by now, but the Milvian Guard has been given free rein over Rome. After our encounter this morning, I feel we need to be quick and hasty with our response. I'd like you to assign me three of your best men to accompany some members of the gendarmerie to the Orto Botanico tomorrow morning. Keep them safe, but also keep their identity a top priority. Have them assist the investigators in any way possible. I'll be speaking to Adriano when I arrive back at my quarters. You can reach me there when you have decided whom you would choose."

"I can do you one better," said Azael. "Scott Farrell, Deirdre Burke, and Marco Riccardi. Those are your operatives. I'll gather them to the gendarmerie's barracks in twenty minutes. After you've spoken with Adriano, we'll proceed from there." Azael paused and looked at Giuseppe inquisitively. "Are you sure you're fine?"

Giuseppe smiled and placed his hand on Azael's shoulder. "Never better."

The two parted ways and headed to their destinations. Giuseppe was nervous and cautious. He focused heavily on his peripheral vision and checked behind himself frequently. The electrified feeling of the stranger's eyes inspecting him was pleasantly absent, but he still felt afraid of the darkness around him. He was ready for the day to be over. Tomorrow was a considerable leap forward in the battle to protect his home and the secret that he was entrusted with, one that was sought after by men not of his understanding.

CHAPTER 4

A SLIM CHANCE

September 16, 2035

"I'm so sorry, boys," said Eula as she cut vegetables. "I know how much you needed Lorenzo in your life. I do hope you're not angry at him for his decision."

"Of course not," said Daven. "Today was a close call."

"That's putting it lightly," said Adam. "It's one thing to cross paths with a patrol, but Nero himself?"

"The odds were not in our favor. At all," said Daven, with raised eyebrows and wide eyes.

"I don't even want to think about it," said Eula, hands outstretched in the air. "If anything had happened to you, I don't know what I'd do."

"Not a soul in Domus Aurea could withstand the torrential anger of Eula Fortuna," said Daven with a grin.

"Even so, I don't want any hard feelings to be had between you two and Lorenzo," said Eula, ignoring Daven's quip.

"It really doesn't bother us. Besides, if this plan works, we'll be leaving soon anyway. It was going to happen eventually," said Adam, indirectly reminding Eula of her impending loss.

Eula stopped her cutting for a split second and started up again without speaking. Adam knew he had hurt Eula by reminding her of their departure. He remembered how his own mother felt when he left for a school four states away. This was worse. These four had shared a bond through horrific times. Eula had been their mother for three years, holding them through a storm of fear and depravity. She fed them, clothed them, healed them, and reminded them of the good in the world even when there was none.

"Eula …" said Adam as he wrapped his arm around the woman, "this isn't the end. Don't think for one second that we're going to leave you here and never look back."

Daven joined the two at the counter. "We owe so much to you and Abele. The least we can do is get you out of here."

Eula smiled, with tears streaming down her face. She turned around and hugged the necks of her adopted sons. She never had children of her own, but the need to care for the boys came naturally. There was nothing she wouldn't do for them, and Daven and Adam appreciated it more than she knew. "I know, I know," she said, wiping away the tears. "I just worry. You're my boys! How can I not?"

"We're resilient," said Adam. "You have nothing to worry about. We've gone this long and have stayed safe. We won't let anything happen."

"Let's just be sure that we don't get ahead of ourselves," said Abele as he walked into the kitchen. "This is still Domus Aurea, and we are still under close watch. We will handle everything as we always have. Nothing changes until you are safely in Corsica."

"Yes, sir," said Daven. "We won't do anything to jeopardize you or your friend."

"I know you won't," smiled Abele. "But careful words still need to be spoken."

The conversation then shifted as a commotion could be heard from the street. Muffled angry voices breached the curtained windows, and all within the Fortuna household bolted into a practiced routine. Daven and Adam immediately moved the table resting on top of their cellar home. Eula yanked the large Persian rug away as Abele locked the front door and sat by the window. As he peeked outside, he could see a lone man with his hands in the air standing on the sidewalk outside. Across the street, eight uniformed men, an Aurean tent group, stood with guns fixated on the individual.

"I saw it, sir!" yelled one of the patrolmen to his superior. "I saw it under his jacket!"

"Do not move! You hear me? Do not move an inch!" shouted the officer to the visibly shaken man. "You two," he said, pointing to two of his subordinates, "search him. If you find a weapon, take care of it."

The two men quickly skated across the wet street to the man. Abele could see the barrel of an assault rifle peeking out from underneath the man's thick jacket. He knew instantly who this random stranger was, and he knew the man was in grave danger.

Directly after the onset of Domus Aurea's march across Italy, San Marino, a small enclave microstate located in northeast Italy, instantly took an offensive stance against the invaders. They immediately sent out militias capable of wreaking havoc around Domus Aurea wherever they were stationed. This man was a militiaman, and Abele knew he wouldn't be alone.

Instantly two sharp pops rang out, and the two patrolmen immediately dropped like rag dolls to the ground. Four more men ran from the left and right of the remaining Aureans and demanded they drop to their knees.

"Why did you shoot them?" yelled the man outside of Abele's window. "Oh, God, this isn't good!"

The six Aureans got on their knees and placed their hands behind their heads. The other Sammarinese began taking guns, walkie-talkies, ammunition, and whatever else they deemed worthy of acquisition.

"Shut up!" yelled one of the men to his peer. "What were you doing on the street anyway? We stay *off* the streets! Off! How hard is that to understand?"

The two men met in the middle of the street next to the bodies of their enemies. Abele turned to look at Eula, Daven, and Adam.

"Get down!" He forcefully whispered to family, "This street is going to be crawling with Aurean patrolmen within the hour. These idiots just killed two of them."

Eula shut the wooden hatch and covered it again with the rug. Abele was helping her move the table back when more gunfire rang out. He ran to the window and saw the two men in the middle of the street bolt away from another oncoming patrol. The rest of the Sammarinese ran as well, firing in the enemy's direction. The remaining six Aureans joined with their fellow soldiers.

"What do we do, Abele?" asked Eula, obviously shaken. "They'll question everyone on the street for a mile!"

"Then I'll have to meet them in the middle," said Abele, walking toward the door. "Perhaps I can give them what they want enough to leave the house unsearched."

Eula peeked out the window as Abele walked to the remaining officers of the second patrol. The rest had gone ahead in pursuit of the Sammarinese militia. A steady fog was rolling in, blanketing the street in a gray haze. The streetlights shone like floating white orbs, supernatural in their appearance. Eula could only see her husband, the two dead men, and the Aureans, pointing in directions to explain what had just transpired. The woman feared for her husband's safety, as Aurean patrols were known for being dangerous and impulsive. After what seemed like hours, Abele bowed his head and bid the patrolmen farewell.

As Abele walked through the front door, Eula ran to him and embraced his neck. "Please, next time you're feeling especially suicidal, try not to do it in front of your especially nervous and anxious wife."

Abele smiled and kissed his bride. "I promise to give you fair warning next time."

The man once again walked to the front window to assess the situation before calling on Daven and Adam. The two Aurean men had removed their jackets and placed them over their fallen comrades. Abele watched as one of the men placed his hand over his eyes and began weeping. It confused and depressed him, seeing whom he had labeled as evil men showing such compassion for another human being. For years, Abele believed he lived in a black-and-white world, those who suffered under the regime of Nero and those who worked to further the tyranny.

"Abele, maybe you should wait to take the boys. It's too dangerous right now," said Eula quietly, hoping Daven and Adam wouldn't hear her.

"I know it seems like a safer option, but getting them away from here is probably the best idea," said Abele. "These men are tenacious and will not stop searching until their friend's killers are found. We need to get them away from here."

Abele walked to the wooden hatch covering the two refugees and lifted it just enough for his voice to carry to the men. "Okay, boys. Grab something to cover your heads and follow me to the car. Be quick. We don't have much time before more patrols show up."

The three said their farewells to Eula and made their way outside behind the home. Once in the car, Daven and Adam situated themselves in the trunk under a false bottom that Abele had constructed two years ago. Vehicles at one point in time had been searched by a more prevalent Aurean force. To drive a car was to be pulled over on a regular basis. Most individuals began to ride bikes or walked to their particular destinations. The men had even seen a rise in equestrian transportation. Luckily, after the first year of occupation, the searches became fewer and less frequent.

After Abele spoke to the two patrolmen he conversed with earlier, answering any questions they might have had, the three men were on their way to liberation and a better life. Deep down, Abele was truly happy for the two men he had cared for for so long, but at the same time, he *had* cared for them for so long. Three years was enough to create a bond so strong that it hurt to think of saying goodbye. Especially when that goodbye could mean forever, but in the end, it wasn't about Abele. It was about seeing those two men happy again, truly happy; and if Abele could lend a hand to aid in that transition, he was obliged to do so.

September 16, 2035

Joseph slowly picked himself up from the ground, holding his jaw and tasting blood. "Okay ... I deserved that," he said, squinting his eyes while groaning in pain.

"You're lucky, you know that?" said Salvador, rubbing his knuckles. "We'd all be dead right now if that fog hadn't rolled in. So tell us, what the hell were you doing in the middle of the street?"

"Salvador," said the fire squad's commanding officer, Michael Dina. He was also the lieutenant colonel of the First Battalion in the Guard of the Phoenix. The guard was three hundred men strong and was tasked with aiding those unfortunate enough to be trapped in Domus Aurea. Dina's battalion kept watch in Rome, while the other half of the guard was spread out in the northern half of the peninsula. There were two more guards that made up the San Marino Militia, the Guard of the Rock and the Guard of the Council; both kept watch in San Marino. "If you keep yelling like that, you'll be just as guilty of getting us killed as Joseph," said Michael. He then tilted his head and cut his eyes quickly toward Joseph. "But I would like to know as well, Joe … What were you doing in the middle of the bloody street?"

Joseph fell backward and sat on the ground, still dizzy from Salvador's hit. "I don't know … I'm sorry. The fog came in so thick and so fast. I don't even remember moving, but when I finally could see where I was, it was in the middle of the street."

"So you mean to tell me that you just magically appeared there?" said Salvador condescendingly.

"I know it sounds ridiculous, but that's what happened. All I can remember before they saw me was looking down the street and seeing this silhouette just materialize out of nowhere. I swear, its eyes were glowing this yellow-orange color … It took all I had to break away. If the Aureans hadn't yelled at me, I'd probably have walked straight into the darkness that thing came out of."

"Unbelievable," said Salvador. "So not only did some ghostly fog move you from one point to another; an *actual* ghost tried to steal your soul?"

Joseph looked down and rested his forehead on his knees. He knew whatever had happened to him sounded like complete rubbish, but it was the truth. Odd occurrences had been more frequent of late, and it seemed that the silence that came with the rain and fog that day brought with it a strange presence. It went unspoken, but those within the militia felt it, every one of them.

Michael peered off the edge of the building they were hiding on. The fog was still thick, like mist floating over a lake early in the morning. He had sent two of his men to follow their pursuers in order to gauge when the five could regroup with the rest of the militia. The three shook with a jolt when the fire escape ladder began to shake. It came as a natural response to take a defensive stance, hiding behind whatever could be used as protection, aiming their firearms at the oncoming unknown.

"The streets are clear," said one of the scouts Michael had sent out.

"Good. Can you place our pursuers?" asked Michael, coming out from behind his hiding spot.

"We followed them back to the origin of the firefight. There were at least two more patrol groups that I saw. If we're going to go, we need to move now," said the second scout.

Salvador and Joseph stepped out into the open. The two scouts stared at Joseph's injuries but said nothing to bring any attention to them. Michael commanded the rest of the group to gather their belongings. "We'll make our way to Fiumicino. Rome will be dangerous tonight, so we'll take our leave and contact our superiors in the morning."

The four subordinates saluted their commander and made their way into the alley below. Even with the happenings of that night, the city was quiet. The men knew all too well that silence was just a precursor to a storm, and they hoped that they were moving quickly enough to avoid the thundering ferocity that was moving their way.

Michael readied his weapon as he neared the street. He moved his head past the corner of the building he and his men were lined up against and looked back and forth. It was still and void of life, which still unnerved him, but he signaled to his men, and they made their way to the street, disappearing into the fog-filled night. It was a half day's walk to Fiumicino and eight hours until daylight. Michael silently prayed for a quick pace and an uneventful trek, but most of all, he hoped for peace and quiet— something he hadn't felt for a long while.

September 16–17, 2035

"What's worse …" began Adam as Daven and he crouched behind the front seats of Abele's car, waiting for the signal to go inside and speak to their contact in Corsica.

"Not this again …" said a clearly annoyed Adam. Daven loved to play games like this. It passed the time but wore on Adam's nerves heavily.

"It's better than *what does this smell like*? Don't you think?" smirked Daven.

"Okay, fine. What's worse than what?"

"What's worse … being thrown off the Wall of Dominance or playing this game?"

"I heard free falling is a rush …" said Adam, but before he could answer further, the front porch light flicked off, signaling safety and freedom from Daven's mentally taxing games.

As Daven and Adam entered the street-corner property, they were immediately grabbed by Abele and his friend and taken to the center room of the house.

"We'll try to stay away from any windows. Safest bet, I'd say," said the homeowner, "but where are my manners? Hello, boys, my name is Jean. Pleasure to finally meet you." The man extended his hand to the two men but was instead embraced and overly thanked for his part in their story.

"I don't know how we're ever going to repay you," said Daven, "any of you. We will find a way to end this hell. In whatever way we can."

Abele and Jean simply smiled. No words needed to be spoken. Even if the likelihood of deliverance was microscopic, the two old men were thankful that they would not be forgotten.

"How about we take a seat?" said Jean, motioning toward a table in the middle of the room.

The four sat down. Spread out in front of them was an unfolded map of the Aurean coastline. There were lines drawn in patterns all over the water, with times written out, and a single line drawn from Corsica to a point about one mile from the shore.

"I've studied Aurean ship routes, patrolling relatively close to the beach. They try to keep a small window of distance between individual ships," said Jean, pointing to the lines on the map. "It's very precarious, but I think there is an avenue of escape early in the morning around five o'clock."

"What's that line coming from Corsica?" asked Adam.

"That, my boy, is your saving grace," said Jean with a toothy grin. "A man whom I've been speaking to has been able to evade attention on several occasions and has offered to aid in your escape."

"Does our liberator have a name?" asked Daven.

"Not one that he has been willing to give," said Jean. "But I'm sure once you are introduced, he'll be happy to relinquish it to you."

"So how does this plan work?" asked Abele.

"Have either of you had any scuba diving experience?" asked Jean.

After a moment, he was met with a predictable no."

"Well," Jean began, "you won't be doing much diving, so it won't be very difficult to achieve."

"Figures we would take the most terrifying avenue of escape possible," muttered Daven.

Adam laughed at his friend's phobia of open water and patted him on his shoulder.

"Well, this could be considered the lesser of two evils," said Jean while shrugging.

"Still not comforting," said Daven, "but I won't complain."

"So what do we do?" asked Adam impatiently.

Jean stood up and walked over to an armoire situated behind his chair. "You'll swim," he said as he opened the ornate wooden doors, "and you'll swim far."

Jean grabbed two snorkels and two flippers and threw them on the table. Daven and Adam looked at the equipment in disbelief.

"You can't be serious," said Abele, vocalizing the thoughts of the dumbstruck boys.

"Unfortunately, I am very serious," said Jean as he sat back down. "Given the amount of security spread out on the beach and in the water, using a boat to get to your meeting point is not possible. You'll have to stay underwater and swim about one mile into the blue."

"I'm gonna faint," said Daven, resting his head on the table.

"You won't be swimming blind, though," said Jean, standing up again. "You'd never make it to the rendezvous point without help." Jean opened a drawer on the same armoire and pulled out two devices. "These will get you to where you need to go. Tomorrow I'll speak to the Corsican and program a set of coordinates into these GPS's. Then all you'll have to do is follow the dotted line to your meeting point and jump onto his boat. From there, you'll be home free."

Adam picked up a GPS and looked it over. He thought of how surreal it felt to know that the key to his freedom was so small and so simple.

"So we're leaving tomorrow?" asked Daven as he placed his hand on the GPS.

"I don't see why you shouldn't," said Jean. "In fact, I would suggest staying here tonight, but I'm sure you'll want to say goodbye to Eula. However, you should be prepared to leave tomorrow at exactly five in the morning. It's still dark, and the coast guard will be far enough away to allow the Corsican an open opportunity to get you."

"That doesn't give us much time," said Abele, "so we should probably get planning. Eula isn't going to make this farewell a quick one."

Daven and Adam agreed with Abele, and after a few hours of going over last-minute details, the four men made their way to the front door.

It was early in the morning of the next day when they made their way outside, but it was still dark. The day was tranquil, and the smell of the sea was ever present. The men were tired but excited, and their minds were fogged with thoughts of escape. Daven shook whenever he thought of submerging himself in the darkness of the night sea, and at the same time, he shook with the thought of rising from that darkness to the light of a new life. Like rising up from a baptism.

After shaking Jean's hand and waving goodbye, Abele turned toward the street and stopped cold. Adrenaline rushed from his heart, causing his hands and feet to turn ice-cold. His heart began pumping fast and hard, and his eyes shot open with fear.

"Boys," he said without breaking his gaze, "I want you to run. Run hard and fast and do not look behind you until you are well hidden."

As expected, Daven and Adam stood still in confusion, but Jean had already seen what Abele was seeing. "Run! Now!" he yelled, pushing the boys off the stairs at the front of his house.

The two began running toward a set of buildings across the street. Adam turned to look at what could be chasing after them but only saw the back of Jean's head explode in a mist of red and gray as a sharp snap rang out.

"Hold your fire, dammit!" yelled an unfamiliar voice. Adam looked in the direction of the command and saw the danger that had caused Abele to leap into action. A tent group of Aurean soldiers, jumping like lions after them.

"Why, why, why, why?" screamed Daven as he rounded the corner, heading into an alley.

"Don't stop; they're right behind us!" yelled Adam, still watching behind him. Five soldiers were quickly approaching, firearms pointed directly at them.

As the two ran farther into the alleyway, they were met with a tall brick wall, cutting off their escape early in the chase. Adam stopped to look behind at the oncoming soldiers and froze with fear. There was nothing to be done. There was no reasoning with these men, these violent men indoctrinated with the lies and fear of Lucius Nero. All they could do was accept fate as it was given to them. Adam slowly fell to his knees and looked to the night sky above him, waiting for the end. But it was not the starry black that was spread out above him. Daven flew headfirst over Adam into three of the men from a fire ladder. He had quickly climbed the metal rungs the instant the wall before them rose to stop their steps.

"Get up!" Daven yelled as the remaining two soldiers ran to the aid of their friends.

Adam quickly rose, grabbing a piece of cracked concrete, and flung himself toward the Aureans. As the two men lifted their rifles in an effort to stop the fugitives, Adam hurled the slab of stone into the face of the man closest to him. He fell backward, his weapon firing straight into the chest of his counterpart. Daven reached out to grab the now crumbling bit of rock and brought it down into each of the three men's faces who lay below him. As their blood poured from the wounds inflicted upon them, Daven fell backward, dropping the bloodstained stone.

"Come on," said Adam as he reached down to help his friend up. "We can hide here until everyone goes away."

"I killed them," said Daven with a quiver in his voice. "I just … smashed their faces in. I can see their brains." Daven lifted his hands up, shocked at the blood that ran through the creases of his palms.

"Yes," said Adam, grabbing Daven's face, "but they were going to do much worse to us. Now climb the ladder to the roof, quickly. They'll have heard that gunshot and will come looking for their friends."

Daven nodded, showing that he understood what his friend was telling him to do. He raced up the fire escape and cleared the edge of the roof, disappearing from sight. Adam raced to two of the men, grabbing two pistols along with what ammunition he could find. It wasn't for self-defense that he felt the need to take the weapons. He knew that if the two of them were to be apprehended, they would face a fate worse than death. These tools of sleek metal would allow for a fast end, which would be far from what the Aureans would deliver. Hearing frantic footsteps quickly approaching, Adam scurried up the ladder and joined Daven on the roof.

"This way," said Daven as soon as he laid eyes on Adam. "I think the building's abandoned. We can hide in here until things quiet down."

The two entered a door leading to the top floor of the building. After clearing the stairs, they made their way to the ceiling and crawled until an opening into the walls presented itself. It was a tight fit, but they felt secure, even with all the spiderwebs, rat carcasses, and old insulation that littered the area around them. As their minds slowed and bodies settled to the turmoil of the night's incidents, the thoughts in their heads raced uncontrollably, asking every question that could be inquired and arriving at every possible conclusion.

"I heard a gunshot," whispered Daven. "Did you see who got hit?"

"It was Jean," responded Adam. "He didn't make it."

Daven sat quietly for a moment before whispering, "They're going to kill Abele …"

Adam had become angered at Daven's pessimism and decided to act on his aggression. "You need to pull yourself together," he whispered forcefully. "I know that everything that just happened is going to be hard to process, but right now we don't have time to do that."

"You're right," said Daven. "We should wait for this area to cool off and only move at night."

"We're on the run, I guess," whispered Adam sadly. "We can't go home. They'll be expecting that."

"Then we make our way to the Vatican," said Daven. "Abele always said they would take us in. They have to …"

Before Adam could respond, a multitude of voices could be heard from the alleyway below. The men couldn't decipher exactly what was being said, but they could hear anger and sorrow in the muffled voices that rose to their ears up above. They knew that the buildings and streets around the scene would be heavily searched, so they ceased any conversation, made themselves as comfortable as they could, and waited.

September 16, 2035

Deirdre Burke looked up into the sky above her. It was the same as it ever was, but it was a sky from a different perspective, one that she hadn't seen for years. She was a soldier in the Milvian Guard's Uriel's Eyes branch, a group of men and women dedicated to reconnaissance and special operations. Today they found themselves in the Orto Botanico, following a lead taken from the body found within the Vatican. She, along with Scott Farrell, Marco Riccardi, and three gendarme investigators, was sent by Giuseppe to gather information regarding the ambiguous message received from the previous day.

Deirdre was a twenty-four-year-old redheaded Irish woman from Jordanstown, Northern Ireland. From an early age, she wanted to travel the world, and at the age of eighteen, she found herself working in the Vatican. She was chosen by Giuseppe after he witnessed her ability to lead during the revolt and asked her personally to join the Eyes. Today was the first day she had seen the world from outside of Vatican City in a while, and it was everything she hoped it would be.

She had visited the botanical gardens before the Second Great Fire and had not found it particularly impressive, but now was different, and the beauty she saw before her was new and rich. Deirdre made it a point to take in everything she had the opportunity to witness with the utmost gratefulness since the initial cataclysm. Even after being trapped within the Vatican for three years, she consciously made the effort to appreciate the artistry of all the ancient structures inside the city and marvel at every detail she could see. She was now in the midst of a sensory overload—the smell of the plants and flowers, the sight of the trees and fountains, the sound of the birds and wind blowing through branches and bushes. It was beautiful, and it would always be beautiful to her until the day of her last breath.

"Deirdre," said Scott, trying to garner the attention of his friend's wandering mind, "you there?"

"Sorry." She laughed. "I'm just … taking it all in."

Scott smiled, understanding her fascination. He was an even-tempered man, with a head of bright golden hair. Scott hailed from Seattle, Washington, in the United States and had been branded as the "grunge man" for his love of nineties rock, which he would blast from his room late at night. He was one of the Eyes' best marksmen and would sometimes bet members of the Swiss Guard and Milvian Guard cigarettes to see if he could shoot specific points on a target. Because of this, he had enough cigarettes to kill himself at a very early age.

"Believe me, I am too," Scott said, turning to face a man who was following behind him. "This is Johan; he's the lead security officer here in the gardens. He says he's going to let us take a look at some footage from the night of the incident."

Deirdre grasped the officer's hand. "It's a pleasure, sir," she said. "Thank you for your cooperation."

"Pleasure is mine, my friend," said the officer, a short, chubby man with salt-and-pepper hair. "Anything I can do to stick it to Emperor Nero."

Those of the Aurean population who were vehemently against Lucius Nero's regime nicknamed the man Emperor Nero, drawing similarities between him and Nero from Roman antiquity. The ancient Roman emperor was especially unbalanced and cruel, and the populace of Domus Aurea drew the comparison as a slight against Lucius.

"Well," began Deirdre, "we're not really sure if the Aureans were even involved, but I'm hoping we'll be finding out very soon."

"Well, if you'll just follow me this way," said Johan, motioning toward a building at the end of the walkway, "we can find out right now."

The three investigators stayed behind, searching the grounds for any sign of the type of plant that drew them to the gardens in the first place. As Scott and Deirdre followed Johan down the white walkway, Deirdre stopped and looked around in confusion. "Where's Marco?" she asked. Scott looked behind her and pointed with his forehead to a fountain in the middle of a grove. Marco had situated himself on the bench circling the pool, lying face up, hands cradling the back of his head.

"Let him sit," said Scott, shaking his head and smiling. "He looks so peaceful. It's adorable."

The three quietly laughed and made their way to the security outpost. Once inside, Johan led the two Eyes to a large monitor farther in and explained how to operate the database.

"You can choose the date here," he said, pointing to a calendar on the screen. "Once you choose the date, you can select what camera angle you want and then use these knobs to tweak the speed."

"Seems fairly straightforward," said Scott as he began searching for the correct date.

"I know," said Johan. "Can you believe they pay me to do this?"

Deirdre laughed. "I'm sure you've dealt with some interesting occurrences in your time here."

"The occasional streaker, your frequent vagabond slumber party ..." said Johan, rubbing his forehead. "But people don't visit the gardens that much anymore. I miss those days."

Deirdre rested her hand on the old man's shoulder. "If history is any consolation, men like Nero meet bitter ends."

"I pray you're right," said Johan as he turned to look at Scott. "Have you found anything?"

Scott turned around and motioned for Deirdre. "Look at this, because I don't know what I'm looking at."

Deirdre walked to Scott's side and focused on the screen. Scott turned the knob left to rewind to the beginning of a clip he had found. "Take a look," he said as he pressed the play button. Immediately Deirdre recognized the man from the previous day, whose body turned up inside the Vatican. He was visibly shaken and erratic and ran to the middle of the frame. He then held his hands up as if he was begging an unknown individual offscreen and then dropped like the life was drained instantly from his body.

"What happened?" asked Deirdre.

"Just keep watching," said Scott.

Deirdre looked closely, searching for someone else to appear on-screen, but instead, the monitor began to glitch.

"No," she said with heavy disappointment. "Tell me it clears up."

"Just keep watching," said Scott again impatiently. "It's like watching a movie with my wife. If I had a wife."

Deirdre then noticed what she thought had been a digital anomaly moving closer to the fallen man, stopping right above him, and then moving downward, as if someone was crouching to inspect him.

"Now that is strange," said Johan, squinting his eyes.

"Give it a second," said Scott with an unbroken glance.

Suddenly, as the anomaly crept closer and further downward, a brilliant flash of light shone with a hot white burn and then disappeared without a trace. The man on the ground had vanished, and the grounds within the frame remained still and lifeless.

Johan and Deirdre stared at the screen trying to process what had just transpired.

"I'm not sure I really know what happened there," said Johan, speaking up after a moment of silence.

"Neither do I," said Scott. "But can you take us to the area in the tape?"

"Yeah … yeah, it's not far from here."

The three individuals walked outside and immediately noticed Marco wasn't lying down by the fountain anymore.

"I wonder where he went," said Deirdre.

"He probably just wandered off looking for us," said Scott. "This place isn't too big. We'll find him."

"Come. Follow me this way," said Johan. "It's right over here."

The three began their walk to the next location after signaling the three gendarme investigators. Deirdre panned the landscape, taking in everything that she could see.

As the six drew closer to their destination, Scott noticed Marco, a short man with curly black hair, standing in the middle of the walkway. "Marco!" he yelled, trying to get his friend's attention, but Marco just stood eerily still, staring at the ground.

"Marco?" Deirdre asked as she slowly made her way forward. "Are you okay?"

"He's standing right where that man fell down," whispered Johan to Scott. "Either he's a very talented investigator, or he is just extremely lucky."

Deirdre came up from behind Marco and placed her arm around the young man. "Marco," she said softly, "what are you looking at?"

Slowly Marco crouched down and picked up a small business card that was lying in between his feet. Everyone knew Marco to be extremely laid-back and lax in his duties, but he was well-liked and went out of his way to be the positive light in a dim situation. As he stood up, Deirdre noticed that Marco jerked his head slightly, and his eyes darted back and forth. It seemed to her that Marco had just been woken up, like waking a sleepwalker, and was confused by how he ended up where he was.

"W-what?" stuttered Marco. "I was just lying by that fountain … How did I end up here?"

"That's what we were wondering," said Scott as he joined the two Eyes.

"I don't remember falling asleep or anything," said Marco as he scratched his head. "I just woke up standing right here."

"What did you find?" asked Deirdre, reaching for the card.

Marco handed it to the woman and then crouched down, as he was feeling fairly dizzy. Deirdre ran her fingers over the raised lettering, reading the contents. *Hotel San Pietro* was written in bold, black lettering.

"It's a business card for a hotel north of the Vatican," said Deirdre, handing the card to Scott.

"Can't get any easier than this," Scott said, waving the card in the air.

"I guess it wouldn't hurt to look around just a little bit more," said Deirdre, scanning the landscape. "We'll meet back here in about an hour."

The six agreed to Deirdre's plan of action and then left to search the rest of the park. The clouds rolled back, revealing the hot early-morning sun. It brought new life into the plants and trees around them, amplifying the colors and adding a deep contrast to different hues. They were all bound and determined to procure any knowledge they could on who or what had been causing so much trouble for the people of the Vatican, and none of them dreamt of letting Giuseppe down. Deirdre, Scott, and Marco all silently feared the identity of the otherworldly character involved with this mystery, but they knew that this was their responsibility, and they were ready to put their talents to good use.

CHAPTER 5

THE ROAD LESS TRAVELED

September 17

"**A**dam," whispered Daven with slight annoyance, "Adam, wake up." Adam opened his eyes to darkness, waking to a moment of confusion, wondering where he was and how he got there. The smell of mildew and rot was pungent and served to further the nausea he had been experiencing since last night. He had surprisingly fallen asleep, albeit very uncomfortably, and woke drained. His neck pained him, and he let out a groan as he looked from left to right.

"It's so hot in here …" Adam said, trying to move his shoulders. "I'm itching all over."

"That's because we're sitting in sixty-year-old insulation," said Daven. "My skin is burning."

Adam attempted to stretch but was hampered by the limited amount of space around him. The blood in his extremities began flowing once again, feeling like millions of tiny ants crawling through his veins, paining his hands and feet. He was completely miserable, with his shirt sticking to his chest and back, tiny bits of insulation and dirt irritating every square inch of his body. He was completely ready to get moving and was restless with anticipation.

"So, did they ever leave the alleyway?" asked Adam, worried about the long distance they needed to travel to get to the Vatican.

"Yeah, I think so," said Daven as he shifted his weight. "They looked around in here for a little but didn't stay too long."

"I must have been asleep for that," said Adam. "I can't believe I was actually able to sleep."

"Neither can I," said Daven with a hint of spite in his voice. He was completely unable to rest, much less close his eyes. His mind raced out of control, and his thoughts forced themselves into being. He felt sick and knew today would be difficult considering the distance they would be undertaking, but he shook with anxious excitement nonetheless.

"So how do we want to do this?" asked Adam. "Should we wait until nightfall, or should we try to blend in with whatever crowd we can find?"

Daven sat for a moment and thought to himself. It was hard to keep concentration when all he could think about was Abele. Adam reassured Daven more than once about Abele's well-being, but he still feared for his friend's life. Daven didn't try to convince himself of something that he didn't believe to be possible, but he knew that even a small amount of false hope was allowable, even healthy.

"I know what you're thinking," said Adam, sensing Daven's stress. "And I told you, Abele is fine."

"As fine as he can be considering the situation, I guess," said Daven. "But you're right. We need to come up with a plan."

The two sat for a moment running ideas through their heads. They knew they couldn't just jump into the fray without a set path to follow, and it was at least a half day's journey from their current location to Saint Peter's Square. It would require a strategic mind-set, sharp senses, and no small amount of luck, but their lives up until then had helped hone their skills and gave them enough confidence in their abilities to take on such an intense task.

Before either of the men could come to a decision, Adam heard footsteps quietly making their way to their floor. Daven also heard the footsteps and instinctively held his breath, hoping to avoid giving away their position. Their hearts began beating in their throats, producing a powerful pressure in their skulls. They were unbearably frightened and were completely unable to move. All either man could hear was the sound of his own beating heart pounding in his ears and the footsteps growing louder and closer.

"You saw them come in here, right?" asked one of the muffled voices in the stairwell.

"Yeah," answered another. "They climbed onto the roof, ran through the door, and never left."

"Are you sure they didn't leave through the door in the alleyway?" asked a third.

"Not unless they wanted to walk straight onto a crime scene filled with Aureans."

The two stowaways listened as the three men reached their floor. Daven continued holding his breath, while Adam slowly shifted his head to a small hole in the wall to see who was standing on the other side. He saw three men in the center of the room, scanning the ceiling, checking behind old furniture, and looking for prints on the dirt-covered floor.

"Look at this," said a man in a long brown jacket, pointing below him. "They ran through here and then stopped right where the hole in the ceiling is."

The taller man, who wore an old green jacket, walked over to the hole and looked up. It brought him within feet of the two men hiding in the wall and elevated their level of panic. Adam could see the man squinting his eyes, trying to see into the large opening. The man then walked to the wall and began tapping it with the knuckle on his middle finger.

"These walls are at least a foot thick," he said as he placed his ear to the partition, listening for anything out of the norm.

"You think they might be hiding in there?" asked the man with the long jacket. "I can't even imagine what might be creeping around in there."

"I would jump into a used toilet if it meant avoiding a patrol," cracked the third man, still unseen by Adam.

After hearing the mystery man's dry witticism, Daven couldn't help but let out a small, whispered laugh—and the tall man heard.

"Is anyone here?" he asked. "We're not here to hurt you. We're here to help you."

Adam continued peeking through the hole in the wall, trying to figure out who these men were and what their motives might be.

"I know you're scared," he continued. "I know you feel like you have nowhere to go, but you're not alone."

"I saw what happened last night," said the man in the long jacket. "I saw them shoot that man in cold blood. They took the other one. They didn't harm him, but I can't say he'll stay unharmed."

Adam shifted his sight to the third individual. It looked like he had been injured; he had bruises on his face and a split lip. He tried to remember if he recognized the man or remembered hitting one of the soldiers in the face, but none of them sustained that type of injury.

"I don't know what we can do to make you trust us," said the tall man. "But I can promise you that if you let us, we can help you, and we can get you somewhere safe."

"As long as one of us doesn't wander into the street again and get us all killed," muttered the man in the long jacket.

"For the hundredth time," said the man with the split lip, "I'm sorry! I didn't consciously wander into the street on purpose. You need to let it go!"

At that, Adam recalled the unrest outside of Abele and Eula's house. Abele had mentioned that a man with a gun under his jacket had wandered into a patrol's line of sight. He looked at the injured man and saw an assault rifle barrel peeking out from underneath his jacket, just like the one outside the Fortunas', and realized that this man was the same individual. Adam finally decided to act and knew that Daven would probably pass out if he kept holding his breath any longer.

Adam looked at Daven and nodded, but Daven, with wide eyes, vigorously shook his head in protest. Adam placed his hands on the wall and pushed with all his strength. The wall came tumbling down, and Adam fell onto the floor in front of the tall man. He waited to see what would happen, whether the man would kill him right there, arrest him, or help him up.

"Hello," said the man as he offered his hand to help Adam. "My name is Michael. I'm a lieutenant colonel in the San Marino Militia, and I'm here to help you."

Adam grabbed Michael's hand and immediately embraced him. He was unable to fight back the tears that had been welling up since the start of their misfortune, and he began to weep.

"We're going to get you somewhere safe," said Michael, embracing Adam. "We're going to make sure you're safe."

Finally after a moment, Daven pushed his way out of the wall and brushed the drywall and insulation off himself. "We need to get to the Vatican," he said, regaining his balance.

"Agreed," said the man in the long jacket. "My name is Salvador."

"And I'm Joseph," said the man with the split lip. "I'm glad we finally got to you. We would have come sooner, but this place was crawling with Aureans up until only a few hours ago."

"Did you see what they did with the other man?" asked Daven hastily. "The one they took away."

"They escorted him away fairly quickly," said Michael as he looked out a window facing the street. "But I was concentrating more on you two. After they shot the other man, I was sure you would be next. Especially after hearing that gunshot, but then Salvador here saw you on the roof."

Daven dropped to his knees and then sat back. "I killed three of them," he said with a distant look in his eyes. "I killed three of them like a mindless animal."

Salvador walked over to Daven and held out his hand. "Before this is over," he said, "I would expect that you will have to do it again."

"We've all killed our fair share of men," said Joseph. "But it's only when it becomes routine and you feel numb to it that you should really be worried."

"But that's neither here nor there," said Michael, walking away from the window. "We need to start moving now. There will be heavy patrolling in this area around nightfall, and we want to be far, far away before that happens."

"Lead the way," said Adam.

"Just follow and do everything we say without fault, and you'll be in Vatican City before you know it," said Salvador. "I'll check the streets from the rooftop, and then we'll be on our way."

Michael motioned for Daven and Adam to join him in the center of the room. "I want to tell you this before we do anything else," he said quietly, gripping their shoulders. "I know once we get you to the Vatican that you'll want to seek out whoever has been hiding you. Please, for their sake and yours, do not give in to this temptation."

"How do you know we even have anyone to go to?" asked Daven.

"You wouldn't have lasted this long without help," said Michael. "And you were especially worried about that man who was arrested."

"So why shouldn't we go home?" asked Adam, needing an especially good reason to follow through with Michael's advice.

"By now," began Michael, "Aurean officials have an address. They've probably incarcerated your friend and anyone else associated with him. Wife, children, relatives. They'll take everyone. Once they have a location, the Aureans will wait there until you come back looking for your loved ones. But I would stay far away. They've risked their lives for you … Don't negate that by getting yourselves killed."

Neither Daven nor Adam could argue with what Michael said. They wanted so badly to be reunited with the Fortunas, but they knew if they did, it would mean the end for all of them.

After a short time, Salvador came back downstairs from the roof. "It's all clear right now," he said, closing the door behind him. "We'll stick to alleyways and rooftops. Shouldn't take us long."

"All right," said Michael. "Let's get going."

The five men quickly made their way down to the ground floor and then into the back alley. Daven noticed four chalk outlines lying in a straight line to his right. Each contained a large pool of blood that had dried and stained the concrete.

"The fifth man must have lived," said Adam. "Which means they have our description."

"No time to sit here," said Salvador. "Move out."

Daven peeled his eyes away from the aftermath of his brutality and followed close behind his saviors disappearing into the shadows of Fiumicino.

September 17, 2035

"I've never actually seen you sit in here," said Felice Savoca as he walked into the Golden Palace's Throne Room, formally the Pantheon. The palace itself was constructed after the outlying land had been leveled in order to complete the massive construction. It spanned several blocks and housed everything from Nero's living quarters to political offices. It was a sight to behold, with golden corners and marble walls, and was lined with statues in the likeness of Rome's historical rulers. But even with all its glory, there were none to gaze at its beauty, and none who desired to walk its ornate halls. Nero had made Domus Aurea a silent tomb, though a beautiful one at the very least.

The throne room itself was mostly the original layout as it once had been, the largest difference being the absence of religious icons from its former stint as a church and the addition of Nero's throne in the far niche opposite the entrance. The original coffered ceilings were still intact and lined with gold. The oculus was the only source of light and air circulation. The niches situated along the circular walls were empty and void of all the paintings and statues that once populated them, with members of Nero's Praetorian Guard replacing them. Surprisingly enough, Nero felt a need to keep the tombs within intact and untouched. He felt he needed to bask in the company of those great men, in his words, being that there were no other great men around him. His throne replaced the high altar of the former church and sat atop a red dais. It was a dark walnut-colored wooden throne, with carvings of lions' paws as the legs and unfurled eagles' wings as the chair's arms. Two muses leaned against the back of the throne, carved out of white marble, arms draped over the top, their faces gazing at the throne's occupant.

Felice's boots clicked loudly and echoed around the large circular room as he made his way across the multicolored marble floor. He was a short man with brown hair and was known to wear his ceremonial military uniform even though he was more of a messenger than a soldier.

"What do you want, Felice?" asked Nero, irritated, as he slouched in his throne. "I'm feeling especially cantankerous today, and I don't need your trying personality making it worse."

Felice stopped just short of the steps leading to the impressively large throne. "I have a message from our friends in Rome," he said, slowly bowing.

"Which ... friends?" asked Nero sharply.

"Our ... supporters hiding in the city," said Felice nervously. He knew better than to annoy one of the most dangerous men the Italian peninsula had seen since Mussolini.

Nero sat up in his chair and rested his head on his fist. "So what is your message, Savoca?" he asked, picking at the woodgrain on his throne.

"The leader of this particular order of rogue extremists said he was willing to offer his power to further your empire," began Felice as he stood with his arms intertwined behind his back. This piqued Nero's interest, but the remainder of Felice's message would dim his excitement. "If only you would aid him with a certain undertaking."

Nero sat forward and rested his face in the palms of his hands in an attempt to sooth an oncoming headache. "This potential ally must know that I cannot grant that particular request; we've already discussed this," he said, trying to hold back the anger within him. "A power much greater than himself, a power that he was once loyal to, has stayed my hand from removing that superstitious blight from Rome."

"I believe this man said he could take care of that issue as well," said Felice calmly and soothingly.

"Promises, promises," said Nero, flicking splinters off the throne's armrest.

"Your apprehension is well placed," said Felice, dipping his head, "but our new friend seems to be refreshingly competent, and I believe he can be of some benefit to you and your ultimate goal."

"And what goal is that, Felice?" asked Nero, looking up to make eye contact with the man for the first time. "World domination? It sounds so trivial when it's expressed in those words. No … I want a united earth. One that mirrors the great empires of the old world. A world under one culture, one economy, one language … one man."

"A worthy endeavor," smirked Felice, trying to keep Nero's temperament under control. "One I'm happy to be a part of."

"Such a worthy endeavor …" mimicked Nero, his voice trailing off as if he was falling into a trance. "A worthy endeavor …" He began digging into his armrest again, and his eyes began drifting out of focus.

"My liege …" Felice's voice crawled like a spider into Nero's ears, pulling him back into his body and shortening his fuse.

"What is it, Felice?" he asked with extreme rage.

"I only ask for an answer to return with to our friends," Felice said with a quiver in his voice. "They promise—"

Nero jumped from his throne and launched a candelabra clear across the circular room. "I don't need empty promises!" he yelled, his voice bouncing all around the circular walls and domed ceiling. "Three years I've waited patiently, to no avail! These … allies that they call themselves have sat back and done nothing but observe as I cage myself in this stain of a city!"

Nero stomped down the steps and across the marble floor straight to Felice, stopping inches from his face. "They tell me to keep away from the priests and nuns," he hissed sternly yet quietly to Felice. "They say watch them, keep them imprisoned, build a wall to keep the world out, and in return, they'll give me an empire worthy of the Caesars." He then gripped Felice's jaw and stared into his eyes, seeing only fear and weakness. "Oh, Felice," he said, smiling, changing from raw anger to loving pity. "Don't be so nervous. You're just the messenger … correct? Don't kill the messenger is what they say. I can follow rules." Nero walked over to the candelabra he had catapulted across the room. "Tell this … supporter that he will need to prove his ability to keep his former allegiance from interfering with my plans, and then I will consider his offer." Nero picked up the tall brass candleholder and carried it across the room. "Now leave. I can't hear the Pantheon speak to me when you're muttering in the corner."

Felice bowed, hands still behind his back, and twirled around to walk quickly and rhythmically out of the throne room, but before he reached the door, Nero spoke once more. "Oh, and Felice," he said with unnerving playfulness in his voice, "if you wear those boots one more time, I'll cut your feet off myself." Felice turned, bowed once more, and left the room.

September 17, 2035

Claudio's breath shook tremendously with every tremor his body was experiencing. He couldn't see, but he could smell wet concrete and damp, rust-covered metal. It was humid and cold where he was, and whatever sounds he could hear traveled far and echoed back to him from a considerable distance. He was in a large building, he thought, and it felt old and dirty, but other than that, he was unfamiliar with where he was. His hearing was elevated with the absence of his sight, and every unnatural sound he heard caused him great distress. He wasn't sure, but he thought he could hear footsteps, but he was too frightened to call out. His arms were cramping, and his core was burning. Claudio had tried to free his arms from the chains binding him to a pipe above, but the blood had drained from them, and his wrists ached.

"Who's there?" he asked finally, sensing someone standing in front of him.

He didn't receive an answer, but he could feel a presence inches from his face.

"I don't know what you want," he began with all the courage he could muster. "But whatever it is, I'm sure it's very important to you. I can do whatever you need me to do if you'll just keep me alive."

Claudio waited for what seemed like an eternity before he was answered. "I do want something," responded his unknown captor. The man's voice was interlaced with a demonic whisper. "But I know you can't get it for me."

Claudio began to hyperventilate, and his mind went wild with fright. "H-how can you say that? You don't know what I know!"

"You're right," answered the disembodied voice, "but I already have a purpose for you, and I won't deviate from it."

"No ... please, just let me go," begged Claudio hopelessly. He knew that nothing could be said or done to see his life spared, but he was still adamant regardless.

"I should stop you right there," said the man without any emotion. "Before you embarrass yourself further. You are going to die tonight, but why should a man like you fear death?"

"What do you mean? Why shouldn't I fear death?" asked the prisoner, attempting to prolong his life, even if it was a pointless endeavor.

"Do you fear God? Have you not lived your life in accordance to his will?" asked the darkness. "You are a man of Christ, are you not?" Claudio did not answer. "I see ... So you fear the eternal nothingness that awaits you. But you should be overjoyed!"

Claudio hung his head in crippling desperation. "Joy? No joy. Not for me."

The man lifted the hostage's head by his chin and inspected him. "Did not Yeshua himself say 'Greater love has no one than this, that someone lay down his life for his friends'? Well … you will be giving your life to save hundreds. Do not fret the hereafter."

"That's surprisingly ineffective coming from you," said Claudio sarcastically.

"Ah, so you jest at your own demise? You must be coming to terms with your fate. So … shall we begin?"

Claudio's body went limp with despair, and he began to weep, his frame convulsing with every labored breath. An unsettling but comforting warm feeling draped itself over his tired body, giving him some sense of relief, but even with it, he continued sobbing.

"You children of Eve," said the man, his voice shaped by an obvious grin, "your emotion is so colorful. It's what separates you and me, you know? I have desire, make no mistake of it, but I will only move forward and prevail, while you sit in the dust and pout."

"What is my purpose then?" asked Claudio numbly and without energy. Before he was answered, his vision was restored, though with it he came to the realization that he wasn't wearing a blindfold. "W-what did you do to me?" he asked, bewildered, seeing that he was in a small room, carpeted and dry. There were no pipes, no rust, no age—nothing he had sensed before.

"Where … where am I?" asked a clearly shaken and confused Claudio.

"I have power that you can't even imagine," said the man, still invisible to Claudio. "I can control every pathway of your consciousness, make you hear, see, and smell what I want you to." Finally, Claudio's eyes were open to an unnaturally tall man with thin, translucent skin. His hair was slick and black, and his eyes were deep pools of emptiness that stared through Claudio's skin, muscle, and bone. He was draped in a long Victorian-style overcoat, complete with an outfit to match. He walked with such care that he seemed to almost float. "What do I have in store for you?" he asked, only inches from Claudio's face. "I want you to fly."

At this command, Claudio's body tightened into a rigid straight line, his spine losing all mobility. His rib cage clenched his lungs like fingers squeezing a rotten piece of fruit, preventing him from breathing. The blood drained from his head, causing him to go completely blind, bringing with it an overwhelming sense of panic. His skull shook with such ferocity that he lost all sense and passed into death.

"Fly for me, my friend," said the tall man as he caressed Claudio's cheek with the back of his gloved hand. "In the coming days when my kind has taken this garden for ourselves, you will be remembered as a stepping-stone that brought us to our rightful place."

He then walked behind Claudio's limp body, blood pouring from the dead man's eyes, ears, and nose, to a small white flower sitting on a metal chair. He picked one petal from it and cupped it in his hands. As he walked back to face the dead man, he lifted his hands to his mouth, the flower petal almost touching his lips as he whispered some inaudible words into his palms. After finishing, he held the flower petal between his index finger and thumb and pried the dead man's mouth open. "Another message for you, Giuseppe," he said, slipping the petal into the man's throat. "May you heed this one with care."

As he loosened the chains around Claudio's wrists, he whispered again. "For you, Mother," and the same voice that cackled out of the dead man found in Vatican City days before came out of Claudio's mouth. His body crumpled to the floor, lifeless and cold.

"Let's take you somewhere for you to spread your wings," he said, grabbing the ankles of the corpse. "I think I have just the place."

CHAPTER 6

A New Purpose

September 17, 2035

Four men sat waiting in a meeting room just inside the Papal Apartments. No conversation was had, and no eye contact was made. It was the first time these particular men had met in this fashion for quite some time. Giuseppe sat next to a small podium to his left, resting his elbows on the heavy wooden table. In front of him sat Pope Innocent, who had a perpetually smiling face, even through sheer boredom. To Giuseppe's right sat Rudolf Anrig, the commander of the Swiss Guard, dressed in his regular duty uniform, his arms and legs crossed in silent annoyance. Anrig was a tall and well-built Swiss citizen, with overabundant Scandinavian features. His hair was almost bleached blond, and his eyes were deep pools of crystal-blue. He was a kind and fair man, who would do anything to keep his friends and loved ones safe, and he took his duties with the utmost seriousness. To Pope Innocent's left sat Camillo, the Dean of the College of Cardinals, who was asked personally by Giuseppe to sit in attendance. The four men sat, waiting for the fifth member of the group, Adriano, who was running late.

After about ten minutes or so, Adriano made his appearance, muttering under his breath. "For a city filled with Catholics, we're not lacking for thieves and liars." No one spoke as the inspector general sank in his chair and sighed with exhaustion. "I apologize, my friends. The duties of my particular rank have me going at all hours and for all lengths of time."

"I can empathize," said Rudolf, leaning forward in his chair. "Dangerous times call for tighter security and longer hours."

"At half the pay," scoffed Adriano with a smile.

"You get paid?" joked Rudolf, allowing for some of the tension in the room to dissipate slightly.

Pope Innocent grinned giddily. "How about a nice holiday for everyone in the room?" he said, running with Anrig's invitation for humorous banter. "A week of paid rest on the beaches of the Italian coastline. I hear it's quite empty this time of year."

Everyone laughed at Innocent's uninhibited accentuation of the unsavory state of affairs they all were privy to. His joy and bright outlook on life were indeed infectious, and anyone who was privileged to spend any amount of time with him was better for it.

"There, now that everyone has cheered up a bit, we can begin," said the pope as he looked to Giuseppe to begin the meeting.

"First, I want to apologize to those of you who received an impersonal request to attend this meeting," said Giuseppe as he stood up and made his way to the entrance of the apartment. "I have been quite busy since the events of the fifteenth and have been delegating much of my office work to my secretary." Giuseppe then shut and locked the two large wooden doors adorned with four intricate wood carvings and turned to face those in attendance. "The four of you are here because you command and lead the main branches of Vatican City military, police, and religion … and you are responsible for her survival. All of you are aware of the events that took place just a few days ago, and I'm sure you have many burning questions you've been waiting to ask, but right now, I won't be clearing anything up unless it involves our future." He then pulled the recorder Doriano had used to record the ghostly message out of his pocket and pressed play. Each man listened intently, their skin crawling with every word that clicked and crackled into their ears, knowing full well that the words uttered came from the mouth of a dead man.

"You could say that this message didn't come from anything human, and you would be correct," said Giuseppe as he slipped the device back into his pocket. "Although the inhumanity isn't found within the vessel of the deceased, but from those who sent it."

"You are quite cryptic, Giuseppe," said Rudolf, "but I feel that our time would be better spent getting to the point."

Giuseppe nodded in agreement and then took his seat. "I sent three of my best men and women, along with three gendarme investigators, into Rome yesterday, specifically the botanical gardens, chasing a lead found by Doriano during his autopsy … and they found something."

"Well, that's great news!" said Camillo excitedly. "What did they find?"

Giuseppe sat back slowly and crossed his arms. "They found something that they were meant to find …" he said, slanting his lips and rubbing his chin. "Which is why I wanted to meet with all of you before I made any … critical decisions."

"What do you mean they were meant to find it?" asked Adriano, scrunching his brow.

"They acquired some security footage that led them to an area in the gardens where the man was murdered," explained Giuseppe. "And they found a small business card sitting out in plain view exactly where the man fell, pointing us in the direction of a hotel in the city."

"Are you sure it didn't just fall out of the man's pocket?" asked Rudolf, not entirely convinced.

"Positive. There was absolutely nothing left behind. No footprints, no blood, not even hair," explained Giuseppe. "The victim ran straight onto the scene stumbling and eventually falling. Not even his footprints were visible. Even the scene itself looked to be overly clean, almost as if it was purposefully left that way. But before we go any further, I'll show you everything we gathered." Giuseppe then pulled several photos from a manila folder bearing images from the scene of the murder. Included among these were pictures showing the strategically placed business card.

After the photographs were passed around, each man sat in silence once more, mulling over the considerably weak evidence in their own minds, picking it apart to see how well it could hold up under scrutiny.

"Did our operatives search the entire garden?" asked Adriano. "I'm just not entirely convinced we're dealing with a murdering businessman."

Giuseppe sneered, diverting his gaze, feeling the pang of Adriano's jab, but he had more to show, and he knew that it would change the course of the meeting. "I guess I can't expect to convince all of you with only this unimpressive bit of information," he said as he reached down beside him, pulling up a laptop and setting it on the table. "I am sure that this, however, will change your minds."

Innocent, Camillo, Adriano, and Rudolf all leaned in closely to witness what Giuseppe was about to show them. Each man watched as the all-too-familiar talking corpse they were acquainted with moved into the frame as a living man. After a few seconds, the now-confirmed blurred and static-laden image of the ghostly suspect made its way across the screen, causing the man to collapse and die.

Giuseppe watched as the expression on each man's face changed from a look of inquisition to one of perplexity. Their bafflement would only deepen as the remaining footage played out and ended. "I want you to look closer at the remaining moments of the video. Just observe where this individual has fallen and what he is replaced with once the light diminishes."

Giuseppe clicked through the footage slowly, making sure to allow for time to absorb what was being seen. "Now be sure to focus on the area about a foot away from the body; right here," he said, pointing to the particular spot. "Watch what appears." After Giuseppe let the clip move forward at regular speed, all in the room watched as the light dissipated and the small pixelated image of the business card appeared, lying in a spot that was once empty.

"Why didn't you show us this first?" asked Rudolf, slightly irritated.

"It's easier to explain something from a simple beginning," said Giuseppe. "A mysterious circumstance explained through unbelievable avenues would confuse. The card served as an anchor to reality."

"Could it be said that this evidence is meant to lead those involved into a trap?" asked Adriano, noticing the suspicious nature of the carefully placed evidence.

"It's most definitely meant for that purpose," said Giuseppe. "But we can't allow men like this to believe they are untouchable."

"What do you think should be done, Giuseppe?" asked Camillo.

Giuseppe sat for a moment, trying to piece the words to his plan together. "We watch and wait," he said simply. "I would like for two of my soldiers in the Eyes to sit and gather information from a safe vantage point for a few weeks and then report back to us with their findings."

Each man in the room nodded with approval and waited for Giuseppe to continue with the remainder of his thoughts.

"I believe we are approaching a time when our enemies are going to take any course of action to achieve their ultimate goal. We must be proactive, and I believe jumping to meet them on the field of this battle we will ultimately fight will be effective. They've watched us for too long as we've sat and cowered in our prison, and they expect us to flinch at anything they throw our way," he said just before a frantic knock pounded on the locked door.

Adriano jumped up from his seat and opened it, seeing one of his officers standing outside.

"What's going on, Leo?" he asked the panting man.

"Shots fired, sir," he said through labored breath. "Lieutenant Colonel Dina's fire squad and two men ran into the square just moments ago. They were being chased by an entire century, and the centurion leading them is threatening to move on us."

Rudolf and Giuseppe fired out of their seats, sending them skating across the room. Anrig bolted to Innocent's side, laying a careful hand on the Holy Father's shoulder and pulling a walkie-talkie off his belt. "I need *everyone* to the Apostolic Palace immediately. Man your posts," radioed Rudolf to all Swiss Guard members. "Quickly! This is not a drill!"

Adriano and Giuseppe sped out of the room, leaping down stairs and sprinting through hallways. A standoff such as this had not taken place since Domus Aurea's occupation of Vatican City, and Giuseppe remembered how devastating it had been. He was terrified of what he was about to see, and in his mind, all he could remember were all the hundreds of brothers lying in pools of their own blood, slowly dying, eyes staring into the sky.

Adriano ordered all the gendarmes in the city to set up roadblocks at all the entrances to the Vatican and to hold down the city.

Giuseppe readied his own weapon as he flew onto the scene, running toward the front of Saint Peter's Square. He looked to the basilica as he passed Caligula's Obelisk, hoping the sharpshooters he had posted there were ready, and to his relief, they were, aiming their scopes at the mass of enemies below them. He couldn't completely see the century Leo had mentioned, but he knew once he broke the line, he would be presented with a terrifying reality. Once he reached the opening to the square and pushed past the few men who were positioned there, he finally saw what Leo had described, and it caused his heart to sink and his palms to sweat. Eighty fully armed men were standing with weapons fixated on only about twenty of his own and ten gendarmes. There were a little over four hundred and fifty Milvian Guard Swords in the entirety of the city, but they were all spread out stationed at various checkpoints and standing atop the city walls, making sure the Vatican was safe.

Slowly Giuseppe lowered his weapon and stepped forward out into Rome. Every Aurean soldier he could see snapped their weapons toward him, waiting for the command to end his life. The perfectly positioned century blocked Giuseppe's view of the Via della Conciliazione, creating a sense of entrapment and constriction to those staring down the barrels of their enemies.

"Let's just … stop and talk for a moment," he said, holstering his weapon. "My name is Giuseppe Morreti, and I'm the commanding officer of the men before you."

"I know who you are, Crown Morreti," said the centurion with complete disgust standing in front of his century. "So how about you just tell your men to step aside so I can take my prisoners?"

Giuseppe turned and looked behind him. He hadn't seen the prisoners the centurion was talking about, but the three San Marino Militiamen who had run into the Vatican walked around the corner with their weapons drawn. "What prisoners?" he asked with his arms extended away from his body.

"Don't be coy, Morreti!" yelled the centurion. "Those … men behind you killed ten of my own on their rampage through the city!" he said, referring to Michael, Salvador, and Joseph. "I want the men they were transporting given to me now as compensation for my dead brothers, or I will give the order to fire!"

Giuseppe felt the air being sucked from his body. The fear he was feeling created a viselike grip around his heart, causing shortness of breath and dizziness. Though he wanted to cower in the presence of such power, he instead calmly turned his head and looked at the angered leader through his peripheral vision. "You and I both know you won't do that …" he said with forced confidence.

The centurion lifted his weapon, gripping it with white knuckles, his chin jutting forward, breathing heavily through his nose. "I won't?" he yelled. "What makes you think I won't kill you where you stand?"

"The same reason why we've stayed in our city untouched for two years," Giuseppe said softly and carefully. "Nero will kill you himself if you harm any of us."

The centurion knew what Giuseppe was saying was true, but he was stubborn, and he wouldn't let his enemies win so easily. It was an abhorrent quality of a leading officer in the Aurean army to be seen as weak or short tempered. If this centurion walked away with his tail between his legs or flew into a fit of rage, he could be demoted quickly without question or publicly punished in front of his former century.

Instead, he lowered his weapon, stood straight, and smiled a smile that curdled Giuseppe's blood. "There are more ways to cause you pain rather than through a bullet," he said calmly and coolly. "We'll part ways today, but I will see you suffer very soon."

The centurion turned to face his men and belted out a command that caused even Giuseppe to marvel. Each soldier spun in perfect unison 180 degrees and rested their rifles on their shoulders. As soon as their commanding officer gave the order, each man marched away from the square and down the Via della Conciliazione, their boots rumbling through the street into Giuseppe's soles, sending tremors through his bones.

The Crown of the Milvian Guard stood waiting as the remainder of the century marched out of view. He had avoided a catastrophe, but he also knew that it wasn't the end of the matter. Aurean military leaders were a tenacious lot and would go to great lengths to punish and torture those they deemed worthy of such unbridled castigation. Giuseppe turned around to gauge the current state of his men and saw that the twenty Swords who had positioned themselves in between the century and Saint Peter's Square still had their weapons drawn but had long since lost concentration and were staring into the distance as the last Aurean soldier rounded the corner. Adriano stood to the right of the Swords with his gendarmes and the militia, gazing in Giuseppe's direction, waiting for the man to speak. Giuseppe took a deep revitalizing breath and exhaled as he began walking in the direction of the inspector general and Lieutenant Colonel Dina. As he walked from one end of the long line of Swords to the other, he made sure to tell them know how brave he thought they were for staring down their enemy without flinching.

"Lieutenant Colonel Dina," said Giuseppe, arriving where the militia and Adriano stood. "It's good to see you again."

Michael extended his hand to Giuseppe and squeezed the man's hand with vigor. "I apologize for this fiasco," he said with genuine regret. "This should not have escalated the way it did."

Giuseppe embraced Michael, seeing just how torn apart the man clearly was. "I'm not entirely sure what happened," he said, standing back and gripping his friend's shoulders, "but everyone seems to be in one piece."

Michael, Salvador, and Joseph diverted their eyes and scanned the ground with sorrow on their faces. "We lost one of our own on the road here," said Michael, with sadness and anger in his voice.

Giuseppe rubbed the stubble on his chin and looked at the three men with empathy. "What happened?" he finally asked.

Michael began describing everything that had transpired from meeting Daven and Adam to arriving in Rome. The man explained how the initial journey to Rome went with speed and without hindrance and how they met with the remaining members of their fire squad at the city's southern end. "We're always careful," he said. "We take caution very seriously. Which should go without saying, but we can be overly safety conscious when it boils down to it." He then explained how he'd noticed Aurean tent groups marching about in greater numbers than he was used to seeing. The militia had stuck to alleyways and were sure to keep eyes on every pathway, fearing a confrontation. "Then … the worst that could happen happened."

Michael had been carefully scanning a street they were about to cross, making sure to take into account the routes previously witnessed tent groups had been following. "But they must have been expecting us. There's no other way to explain it, because the farther we got into the city, the more we noticed men on rooftops scanning the streets below them. I've never seen patrolmen on rooftops," said Michael, continuing on. "That's when everything went wrong. If the soldier above us hadn't yelled out, it might have been worse."

"Who are these men that all of Rome would band together to stop them?" asked Giuseppe, marveling at the lengths Domus Aurea had gone to catch Daven and Adam.

Michael shrugged, unable to answer Giuseppe's question. "I don't have a clue. I don't think the boys know either," he said. "But I lost a good soldier getting them here, so please, Giuseppe, keep them safe."

"You don't blame these men, do you?" asked Giuseppe, interpreting Michael's comment as disdain toward Daven and Adam.

"Of course not," said Michael. "Not even a little. We were the ones who pulled them from their hiding place and dragged them into enemy territory, but I know they probably blame themselves," he said, turning to Salvador and Joseph behind him. "So we should probably go see how they're doing."

Giuseppe motioned to the three militiamen to lead the way. The San Marino Militia was welcome in Vatican City, and the men were very knowledgeable of the layout of the city. They led Giuseppe to the Milvian Guard barracks and descended to the sublevel, where there was a gym, firing range, locker room, and armory. As they made their way down a central hallway leading to the range, Giuseppe turned into the locker room where Daven and Adam were hiding.

The room was a long, thin chamber filled with blue lockers covering every wall. In the middle were several long benches placed end to end from wall to wall. The walls were stacked cinder blocks painted white, and the floor was covered with a thin navy blue carpet,

Giuseppe could see two men at the very back of the room, sitting on one of the benches, hunched over with their fingers interlocked behind their heads. He could feel the fear these two men were experiencing, and their body language reflected their sorrow and horrible regret.

"Daven … Adam," said Michael softly, announcing their presence, "how are you two feeling?"

As the men's faces came into focus, Giuseppe was broadsided by shock. *It's them*, he thought to himself, *it's them*. Instead of viewing the men as exhausted and disparaged human beings, Giuseppe saw them as the two angels from his dream. He couldn't speak. His words hung on the edge of his tongue, and the more he stood with a dumbfounded expression draped across his face, the more everyone in the room took notice.

"Giuseppe …" he heard Michael say as if he was far away, "Giuseppe, are you okay?"

Giuseppe blinked quickly a few times, trying to rid himself of the floating feeling he was experiencing. "Yes … I'm sorry. I just thought I recognized them," he said in a far-fetched attempt to see if he actually did recognize the two outside of the dreamscape and their likenesses appeared in his dream because of the subconscious recognition.

"No … I'm sorry, but I don't think we've met," said Daven with a distant sound in his voice and a bemused look in his eye.

"Well, my name is Giuseppe Morreti. It's a pleasure to meet you," he said, keeping his distance. Both men glanced quickly up at him and nodded with a silent response. Giuseppe knew these men were brought to him for a reason, but he decided to tuck any thoughts of what that might be away until the time was right.

"Michael …" said Adam, clenching his teeth, balling his hand into a fist, "I'm so sorry … I'm so, so sorry …" The man had tears running down his face and an anger in him that was directed only at himself.

"Stop, Adam," said Salvador. "You are not going to blame yourself." Salvador made his way to Adam and knelt down in front of him. "Ric did not die because of something you did. He died because he gave his life to keep all of us safe."

Joseph buried his face in his hand and fell against a wall of lockers. Ric was one of his closest friends, having been in his fire squad since the beginning of Nero's so-called reclamation across Italy. It was a heavy blow to him, and he wept bitterly. knowing that his friend's body would never see peace or a proper burial.

"The best thing you can do now is live," said Michael. walking to sit beside his newfound friends/ "Live and rise to your new life and fight with everything you have."

"You're right," said Daven, "you're right … I can't thank you enough …. I'll never be able to thank you enough."

"No, you can't," said Salvador, smiling, slapping the two men on the shoulder. "But you'll never have to."

Giuseppe was taken aback by the amount of compassion these men had for each other. They had only just met earlier that morning, but the bond of friendship was strong within each of them. After witnessing such intense horror, which had also caused the death of one of their own, time was an irrelevant factor in the growth of their union.

"I know you all must be tired after everything that has happened," said Giuseppe. noticing the lethargic look on all their faces. "Rest here knowing you'll be safe."

Michael wanted to say no, but his exhaustion was exceedingly prevalent, and he knew he would be useless unless he got some rest. Many factors were working against him, both physically and mentally. The long journey from the coast, the elevated sense of impending doom, depression and anxiety. His body was stretched and wrung out like an old rag, frayed at the edges and falling apart. "I'm too tired to argue with your offer," he said while rubbing the back of his neck. "But only for a few hours, and then we'll need to make our way back to San Marino to let Ric's family know what happened."

Giuseppe led the party of tired warriors and prisoners to the third floor of the barracks and to their individual rooms. Michael was given the guest room in Giuseppe's suite, while Salvador and Joseph were given an empty room at the opposite end of the top floor, and the remaining militiaman stayed with a Sword. Giuseppe then turned to Daven and Adam and led them to their quarters. "Since you two are fugitives of Domus Aurea, we'll be keeping you away from any prying eyes until everything settles down," he said, not knowing how to approach the situation. "Look, I know you've been through more than anyone should ever have to go through, but you're in a safe place now. You can rest at ease in that fact. I'll have one of my people come and help you get settled. Soon, when you're able to leave the barracks, I'll show you around the city, introduce you to the people you'll be living with for the time being."

Daven looked up at Giuseppe and forcefully, yet genuinely, smiled at him. "Thank you, Mr. Morreti," he said tiredly. "We really are grateful for what you're doing. I know our faces aren't reflecting that, but we are."

Giuseppe smiled and turned to unlock the door they were standing outside of when he heard his name called from down the hall. The three men looked up to see Deirdre walking hurriedly toward them. "Oh, I'm sorry," she said, noticing the two unfamiliar men staring at her. "Are these them?" she asked Giuseppe rather vaguely.

"Well, they are our newest addition if that's what you mean," said Giuseppe with repressed sarcasm.

Deirdre tilted her head to look behind Giuseppe at Daven and Adam.

"Hello," she said with a sympathetic smile. "My name is Deirdre Burke. I hear you've been running all around Rome today."

"You could say that," said Adam after noticing how taken Daven was with Deirdre. His friend was wide eyed and mindlessly gazing at the attractive woman standing in front of them. Of course Adam only had eyes for his own wife, but he understood Daven's overly creepy expression. The men hadn't seen a woman, aside from Eula, in years, so this was a special occurrence.

"And your name is?" she asked, looking at Daven, noticing his mindless stare.

"Uh … Daven. Daven Jones," he said, trying to wipe the ridiculous grin off his face. "It's good to meet you."

Deirdre smiled at him, silently laughing at the obviously enticed man. "Well, it's good to meet you too," she said with an equally awkward grin.

"Um, Deirdre," said Giuseppe, stopping the painfully uncomfortable exchange before it got worse, "how about you wait for me in my office, and I'll get with you about what happened. I'll need to run some new ideas by the Eyes anyway."

Deirdre's countenance immediately changed to one of solemnity, and she made her way to Giuseppe's office. Daven tried to inconspicuously steal one more glance at the woman, but his efforts were in vain as Adam elbowed him in the ribs, causing him to hunch over in pain.

"You two get some rest," said Giuseppe, smiling, knowing the incident with Deirdre had brightened their day, if only a little. "I'll send someone in a few hours to check on you."

After Giuseppe had closed the two boys in their room, Daven and Adam stood for a moment, taking in their new living space. Two beds sat in either corner of the tiny box on opposite sides. On the back wall, a small window opened to a view of several buildings and a chapel. Farther out, the Vatican walls could be seen rising above the other structures. Two dressers sat against the wall on opposing sides of the door. The room was small and comfortable, but the two missed their even smaller space below the Fortunas' house. As cozy as this new situation may have been, it was still unfamiliar, making it difficult to rest easy, no matter how safe they were.

"You do realize we have to go back to check on Abele and Eula," said Daven.

Adam had been tossing the idea around in his head ever since they arrived in Vatican City, but he was unsure on how to make it happen or if it should even be done. "I don't know …" he said, hanging his head.

Daven spun around with a look of complete astonishment on his face. "I can't believe you would even hesitate!" he barked at Adam. "We have an obligation to make sure they are safe!"

Adam was shocked at the sudden outburst from Daven, but he understood the release of anger. He wished to see his protectors once again just as much as Daven did, but he was more even keeled and careful than his friend. "Daven …" he said softly. He wanted to explain his reservations and his caution, but all he could say was, "Okay … we'll go see them. But we need to wait until Rome quiets down. I don't want to get caught, and I don't want to put Eula and Abele in any more danger than they already are."

Daven nodded and sat down on his bed. "Well, then … I guess we don't have much we can do except for sleep."

"I need a shower is what I need," said Adam, still feeling the itch from their stint in the walls down in Fiumicino.

"I'm sure Giuseppe will send someone soon to show us around. Until then, let's just crash."

Adam walked to the foot of his bed and fell face forward into his pillow. Within minutes, he had fallen asleep, and his mind dreamlessly allowed him peace for the first time in days.

CHAPTER 7

Not My Will

September 18, 2035

Ronaldo had been a sharpshooter in Uriel's Swords since its inception. He was a soldier in Elia Serra's company and was handpicked by the lieutenant colonel to be a sniper. Every day, he made his way to the facade of Saint Peter's Basilica, then situated himself behind the statue of Christ the Redeemer. He had never really acclimated himself to the overwhelming irony of sticking his barrel out from below Christ's cross, but he knew he was protecting his friends by doing what he was doing or what he might have to do.

He gazed out onto Saint Peter's Square and the colonnade surrounding it. Giuseppe had positioned two companies of Swords to watch the main entrance to the city after yesterday's events, but even with three hundred men spread throughout the entire plaza, it wasn't enough to stop whatever Domus Aurea could throw at them. He could see quite far: the Castel Sant'Angelo was to his left; the ruins of the Passetto, which had been destroyed to keep Aurean soldiers from using it to infiltrate the Vatican, ran below it; and the Ponte Sant'Angelo extended from the castle and over the Tiber. It was a view that he never tired of, and from where he stood, it was peaceful. The people populating Rome seemed too small to cause any harm from his vantage point, but he knew better.

Ronaldo couldn't figure out why, but he felt extremely dazed and tired that morning. He had slept well the previous night, and nothing had happened to him that would have caused the exhaustion and heavy eyes. The elevated wind speeds he felt from his nest were ideal for keeping him awake on long watches. He looked around at the other soldiers along the facade, and it seemed that they too were feeling the same effects as he was. Some were hanging their heads, eyes closed, using their rifles as canes to keep from falling over. As he scanned the square below him, Ronaldo noticed several men leaning against pillars or simply sitting on the ground. "What's … going on?" he asked himself, trying to keep awake. His eyelids grew increasingly heavy with every breath, his heart rate slowing, and the blood pressure in his veins lowering to a languid flow made it difficult to even stand. He knew he was about to lose consciousness, and in order to keep from falling to his death, he knelt down to the stone railing, looked up at the obelisk in the middle of the plaza, and blacked out.

When he opened his eyes after what only seemed like a few seconds, he noticed a crowd of Swords standing around the obelisk he was staring at before he fell asleep. They were all staring up at the tip, pointing and scratching their heads. As he shifted his sight to the top of the obelisk, he could see what looked like two arms sticking out from either side. He aimed his scope to get a better view and was presented with the image of a man, arms extended outward like a bird spreading its wings, facing the basilica. Ronaldo looked at his watch to see how much time he had lost but saw that it had only been a few minutes, which caused him to scratch his head even more.

Suddenly the radio on his hip hissed, and the voice of Giuseppe came on with a short and straightforward message of, "Don't touch him. I'll be there in a moment."

Ronaldo could see Elia and Raul running onto the scene, screaming at their men to get back to their posts. The Swords in the square immediately dispersed, hustling to their assigned positions, never looking back. Not long after Elia and Raul arrived, Margo, Giuseppe, and Adriano appeared, walking with haste toward their comrades.

"I'll call for the fire brigade," said Adriano, looking up at the twenty-five-meter obelisk.

"We're dealing with something powerful for it to cause three hundred men to black out at once," said Margo, also staring into the sky.

Giuseppe rubbed his eyes with his right hand. "I don't think we're dealing with just one of them," he said, knowing his enemy all too well. "But that doesn't matter right now."

"How could that not matter?" asked Margo, confused by Giuseppe's nonchalance.

"Because first we need to know where they're coming from and how they're doing what they're doing," said Giuseppe, looking especially distraught. "I don't believe this is the same enemy we've been dealing with for the past few years. This has to be a rogue faction."

"What about the why?" asked Margo.

"I know the why," said Giuseppe with confidence. "To cause panic. The thing that's executing these disruptions has the ability to get to me whenever it wants," he said, referring to the night of the fifteenth. "But it wants to show everyone in the city what it is capable of, and it wants to put fear in all of us."

"Why do you think this is being done by rogues?" inquired Margo much to Giuseppe's growing impatience.

"Because in the last three years, these are the first overly public displays of raw power shown by their kind. Those that we've been accustomed to dealing with are extremely patient. These … not so much," said Giuseppe, pointing upward to the newest corpse to garnish the Vatican.

"Maybe those we've been accustomed to dealing with are finally losing their patience," said Margo, unaware of Giuseppe's growing desire to slap silence into him.

"Maybe I am."

It took Margo a moment to catch Giuseppe's slight, but by the time it came to him that he had been indirectly annoying his superior, the fire brigade Adriano had called for arrived with a truck.

Giuseppe watched as the long white ladder was extended vertically along the monolith to the mystery man's resting place. The two pulling the man down used the sign of the cross before reaching for the target above, hooking him to the ladder. Giuseppe listened intently, waiting for that moment when another otherworldly message he knew would be delivered to him would come within earshot. Just before the ladder came to rest on ground level, some gendarmes arrived to whisk the body away, hoping to avoid a bigger spectacle than had already been witnessed.

Once the body had returned to earth, Giuseppe quickly made his way to the stretcher the officers had brought with them. Strangely enough, he couldn't hear anything odd worming its way from the lips of the deceased. He looked down into the face of the departed and instantly recognized who he was: Claudio Renzi. A member of Uriel's Swords under Margo.

"No …" said Margo after pushing his way to the core of the huddle. "Not Claudio … he went missing on the sixteenth. I never imagined …" he said, drifting off, unable to finish his thought.

"Why wasn't I aware of this?" asked Giuseppe, becoming more and more annoyed with Margo.

"You've had so much on your plate lately," he said, shading his eyes. "We didn't want to burden you with more.

Giuseppe was surprisingly reassured by this but still uneasy about how close this particular tragedy hit personally. He could tell that this man had been dead for at least a day given the marbled appearance of his skin and stiff limbs. He remembered that the other victim had seemed so lifelike, even though he had also been dead for the same amount of time. He wondered if Claudio had been a casualty of the same monster, but his questioning mind was immediately laid to rest.

As he was following the dark blue veins lining Claudio's face, the dead man's eyes shot open to reveal foggy orbs, piercing straight into Giuseppe's soul, causing him to recoil and scowl in disgust. Everyone surrounding the body jumped back, shocked with the presentation of undead movement. Claudio's mouth gaped open with a ghoul's maw, and his head rolled slowly until his ghostly eyes met Giuseppe's.

"It will only get worse, Giuseppe," began the familiar clicking and clacking of the mystical message prerecorded on Claudio's mind. "Give me what I want, and your troubles will be over."

Giuseppe waited for more, but as the last words left Claudio's lips, he silenced and drifted back into death. The weary Giuseppe commanded the gendarmes to remove the body and take it to Doriano in the Gendarmerie barracks.

Raul and Elia made their way over to Giuseppe and Margo after commanding their respective companies to keep quiet about what they saw. After they arrived, Giuseppe ran through what Margo and he discussed earlier on, with the addition of this new message and the dead man's identity. Little was discussed among the three lieutenant colonels and their commander, and each was told to keep the situation under cover as much as they could. After all was said and done, Giuseppe glanced at Elia and motioned for him to stay once the others had moved away.

"Please tell me you have some good news," said Elia after his colleagues had moved out of sight.

Giuseppe looked up at the facade of the basilica, noticing a lens flare just under Christ the Redeemer. "I might …" he began, hesitating with slight nervousness. "Do you remember what you said when we spoke about my dream? You said that we were put here to 'fight the insane.'"

"I believe these last few days have proven that point," said Elia, curious to see where Giuseppe was going with his question.

"Yes … yes, that is correct," he said finally. Turning to face Elia, he continued, "You and I questioned whether or not we had seen the full message of my dream played out. While I do believe that our recent liberation is part of that translation, I think I've seen another fulfillment of that vision. Yesterday actually."

Elia crossed his arms and tilted his head, silently waiting for Giuseppe to continue. As his commander looked into the sky and smiled, Elia could only imagine why Giuseppe was so hesitant to impart his recently acquired knowledge.

"They're here," Giuseppe said. "I believe they're here."

Elia was confused, wondering why Giuseppe felt the need to dance around what he really wanted to say. "Who's here, Giuseppe? The enemy?"

"No. No, not the enemy. The men I saw in my dream. They're here."

"The men with the names you showed me?" asked Elia, trying to make sense of everything he was hearing.

"The very same," Giuseppe said.

"So what you're telling me is that two men, bearing the exact same likeness of the beings in your dream, just showed up on our doorstep?" asked Elia, unbelieving.

"Yesterday actually," said Giuseppe in a matter-of-fact tone. "Michael Dina and his men were escorting them from Fiumicino. They're the reason we had that standoff with that century yesterday."

Elia spoke a single, "Huh?" and then stood in silence.

Giuseppe exhaled heavily, ready to go into detail about the previous day, but was interrupted by a frantic Sword as he ran from the front of the square. "They're back!" was all he could get out, and it was all Giuseppe and Elia needed to hear.

The three men ran through the square like hell was on their heels. Giuseppe could hear men chanting and yelling with excitement and victory, and he knew it wasn't coming from his own men. As they drew closer, the sound of boots and rhythmic marching crescendoed into a terrifying cadence. Giuseppe and Elia feared for the worst, and the closer they got, the farther away they wished they could be.

The line of men standing between them and the terror beyond was significantly larger than from yesterday's encounter, but Giuseppe knew that Rome bolstered a legion of six thousand soldiers, so nothing they had could stand up to whatever Nero threw at them.

Once the men darted through the line, they were pleasantly surprised to see only about forty men standing before them. They were chanting a word he did not understand: "Anastauro."

"Elia …" Giuseppe said, trying to get his friend's attention. "Elia, what does that mean?"

Serra turned to look at Giuseppe, desperation in his wide eyes. "It's Greek," he said, but before he could finish, two large military trucks drove to the front of the forty-man square, their beds covered in heavy red blankets. "It means impale … but was usually used to describe a crucifixion …"

Giuseppe quickly cut his head toward the two green trucks before them. As he stared, the driver's side door of the right vehicle opened, and the centurion from yesterday emerged, smiling. He stood, gripping the door, and then, lifting his left hand into the air, immediately silenced the chanting. "What can be more painful than a bullet, Giuseppe?" asked the glowing soldier in reference to his threat from the previous day, smiling from ear to ear. When Giuseppe refused to answer, the centurion jumped down from his vehicle and walked toward him.

Before he reached the Crown of the Milvian Guard, the Swords behind Giuseppe quickly aimed their weapons at the man. "Oh, don't blow this out of proportion," he said, halting with his hands in the air. "I'm not here to hurt you … just them." He then snapped his fingers, and eight men, four on each vehicle, tugged the red coverings off the beds of both trucks.

Two men then pulled levers, beginning a series of metallic clanks that pounded in Giuseppe's head.

Two crosses, fixed to mechanical hinges, shot forward like catapults, loaded with instead of rock or stone, one man and one woman, hanging on nails in both wrists and two nails piercing their ankles on each side of the stipes. They screamed in anguish as their own weight bore down on their wounds, their breathing labored by their outstretched arms. Giuseppe could see dried blood crusted in dark red rivers flowing down their bodies. From behind the screaming victims, Giuseppe noticed more dried streams starting from their backs dripping down their ribs. They had been whipped, and hard, with a cat–o'-nine-tails, he thought, knowing Emperor Nero's love for Roman torture. To breathe, the man and woman needed to lift their bodies, pulling on their impaled arms and pushing up with their pierced ankles, causing horrible pain.

"Abele and Eula Fortuna," the centurion said, pointing at the two hanging sufferers. "They had been hiding the two men in your possession. Now they pay for their insubordination."

Giuseppe was speechless as he looked into the agonized faces of Daven's and Adam's saviors. This unbridled display of complete ruthlessness made him sick to his stomach. Out of his peripheral vision, Giuseppe could see Elia covering his eyes, unable to gaze into the face of violence and evil. Neither of them were able to do anything to ease the suffering of this benevolent couple, and it pained them to their soul.

"But if you would only just give us what we want," said the man, turning to face his victims, "then I will cease this public display of retribution and relinquish them into your custody."

"Either way, someone will die today," said Giuseppe, weighing his options.

The centurion turned once more to face Giuseppe. "Now why would I kill two perfectly good workhorses?" he said, feigning a look of shock.

"I know exactly what happened to those 'workhorses' your regime used to build Nero's wall," said Giuseppe, unconvinced.

"A harmful rumor," said the centurion, turning once more toward Abele and Eula, who were quickly losing their battle.

Giuseppe weighed his options. He knew that if he gave this man what he wanted, he would either kill Daven and Adam right before his eyes or take them away for some other sinister purpose. If he refused, then these poor souls would slowly and painfully drift into death. He looked once more into the faces of both Abele and Eula, watching them shake and groan with every movement they made. He knew that because of their age, their bodies would never be the same even if they were taken off their crosses at that exact moment. In fact, they would most certainly succumb to their wounds within days, if even that long. With this new thought and the acceptance of Abele and Eula's inevitable demise, Giuseppe turned away from the unbearable sight and walked toward his men.

Eula was in utter misery. The nerves in her wrists shot daggers through her arms with every moment she hung without the assistance of her legs. They would pop and send an electric pain through her hands, tingling her fingertips, painting a horrid grimace on her face. Her vision was blurred, and her eyes filled with warm tears that streamed down her cheeks. Her ankles were locked in place, unable to pivot on the spikes that had been driven through them. So much air was building up in the core of her body, as she couldn't exhale without pulling or pushing up on the nails imprisoning her wrists and ankles. It ached and stung, causing her heart to beat fast and hard in the distress it was experiencing. Her thoughts were loud, with a consistent bargaining to the divine, begging for a quick end.

She looked to her right, her eyes darting uncontrollably as she searched for her love. Abele had ceased his cries of pain what seemed like an eternity ago, and Eula searched, hoping that the man she adored had given up his soul and was at peace. Once she laid eyes on him, she saw his chest heaving quickly as his body gasped for oxygen. He hung his entire weight on his wrists, his legs clearly unable to lift anymore as they convulsed with an intense tremor. She longed to call out to him, to tell him she loved him with her entire being, but words were too much for her body.

She turned her eyes forward, focusing on Saint Peter's Basilica and on the statues adorning it. Christ the Redeemer was in perfect focus to her out of the blurred surroundings about it. She prayed to the image of Christ bearing his cross, begging and pleading for release. Eula thought of his own suffering, hoping that the one she prayed to would empathize and take her and her husband away. She saw the man the centurion had been speaking to walk away from them. He lifted something to his mouth and then lowered it once more. She turned to her husband as a loud pop echoed out and crackled as the sound dissipated. Abele's head and body instantly sagged with lifelessness, his chest still and the pain on his face gone. Eula then looked again to the statue of Jesus and noticed a bright flash of light come from beneath the green cross; then, the same pop and crackle, and after that, peace.

Giuseppe looked behind him at the two lifeless bodies hanging without pain or suffering on their crosses and saw the centurion's face scrunch up with intemperate anger and hate. Giuseppe wanted so badly to convey his thoughts in full to this man, but he refused to sink to the level of the Aurean officer. Instead, he weaved his way through the line of Swords, calling out to Elia to follow him. Once he reached the colonnade on his way to the Milvian Guard barracks, he looked again to the crosses, now on fire, and watched as the trucks and forty men pulled away and dispersed.

"I was wondering when I'd see you again," said Charles, sitting in a chair within a small hotel room, facing the window. He didn't turn to look at who had entered his domain, but he already knew who the visitor was, and he was quickly becoming agitated.

"Sathariel," said a man similar to Charles's height, same transparent skin, and deep, dark eyes. He wore a long black robe with loose sleeves, along with a wide red belt untied in the front. He had an ancient feel about him, and he exuded a personality so regal that none would hope to relate.

"Don't … call me that," said Charles with a sharp tongue.

"Our mother named you Sathariel. Why do you wish to separate yourself from that affectionate and maternal act?" asked the mystery man as he shut the door behind him.

"I was her last son. The final child born before her disappearance. That name only reminds me of her vanishing. It may as well have been her sentencing," said Charles, his thoughts reaching far back in time.

"We all desire to reunite with her," said the man as he sat down by Charles. "But you are taking a dangerous approach. One that could very well destroy our chances."

"It's been eight hundred years, Thamiel," said Charles wearily. "I'm tired of you taking your precious time."

Thamiel smirked at the mention of the number of years that had passed since their mother's disappearance. "You are young, Sathariel," he said, still smiling. "Young and stupid. You want what you want with immediate results. Tell me … if you plant an olive tree, will it break ground in a day? No … patience and care are required, so that when it blooms, it will be on the earth for thousands of years," he said while standing once more. "Our way is slow, yes, but our way will bear fruit. If you continue on this path, you will only hurt us, we the children of Lilith."

Charles's thin lips stretched across his face as he turned slowly toward his older brother. "Get out," he said, concentrating on each word, writing it across his face.

Thamiel stood from his chair and slowly glided to the door. "You will be the end of her and our race," he said without looking at Charles. "How fitting that you were her last child."

Charles sat and listened as the door opened and closed. In his mind, he was the only hope his mother had, and everything that he did was for her. He had even convinced a third of his brothers and sisters to join him in his more progressive strategy to find their mother. That kind of following aided his mind to truly believe that his crusade was the right course of action. He knew that the mystery of her place of being was guarded and hidden within the Vatican, and he was convinced that Giuseppe was the man who possessed that secret. Charles harbored an intense hatred of humanity and believed humans to be a blight on the earth. His kind, the lilim, were the true inheritors of the earth, or so he believed … like Jacob stealing Esau's blessing and inheritance. Charles would see his mother again, he would hear her speak his name, and he would once again be Sathariel.

Daven dreamt he was standing on the coast of his hometown, looking across the gray sea at the horizon. The clouds were large, painting their blue canvas with white mountains as they slowly smeared across the sky with the breeze. He closed his eyes and took in the sounds and smells of his home, feeling the smooth rocks of the coastline under his bare feet. It was peaceful and calm, and he desired nothing more than to sit and listen to God.

As he opened his eyes, he saw someone standing in his peripheral vision looking at him. He turned to see Adam, who had a look on his face that asked, "Where are we? How did I get here?" It took Daven by surprise and awoke him to lucidity. Before he could say anything, an intense hurricane wind blew in from the ocean. The salt burned their eyes, and it was impossible to keep their footing. Both men shielded their faces with their arms and hands and felt the land under their feet move as they were pushed farther from the shore. Daven looked down to see the water quickly covering the sand and rock he was standing on, and as he peered behind him, the houses and buildings of his home broke apart, beaten by the fierce waves invading his vanishing tranquility. Soon, Adam and he were standing in the middle of the deep dark ocean below them, and the wind had slowed to a breath.

The two stood, terrified, as the clouds slowly began to part, revealing a white, searing sun. They winced in pain as their eyes watered, irritated by the blinding light, but they were then quickly met with a powerfully booming voice.

"Do not fear us," said the bodiless words. "Rejoice."

Daven and Adam gazed into the sky, the light no longer painful to behold, and saw two beings with seven black wings each and robes that filled the entire firmament positioned above them. They fell quickly to the water below, putting them at the same height as Daven and Adam. The two friends were then moved forward at a great speed to meet the angelic beings. Both men fell with fear and trembling, their bodies unable to hold their weight.

"Do not fear us," the beings said again. "Rise."

Daven pushed himself to his hands and knees, trying hard to look up.

"We meet you here, in a safe place, to present you with a holy mission from the divine."

Daven then felt two hands lifting him to his feet. He looked into the eyes of the first winged man and saw white fire burning into his mind. When he spoke, glowing coals could be seen to fill his mouth, making every word cleansed and pure. Daven looked to his right at Adam and saw the same thing happening to him. "What do you want with us?" Daven asked once he regained his footing.

The angel looked at him and smiled. "You are worthy vessels," he said, stepping back. "Carry us and rid this world of the evil that has risen within it."

Daven and Adam looked at each other and nodded, then turned to their angelic counterparts. "Yes," they both exclaimed.

"Then it is done ... We are Senoy and Sansenoy, and now we all are one."

With this, Daven and Adam were enveloped by a torrent of fire, and then they awoke.

Adam opened his eyes calmly and sleepily. He looked over at Daven, who was still asleep, and sat up. He rubbed his eyes and felt a gritty substance on his knuckle that burned his eyelid. He felt it between his fingers, seeing that it was white and grainy, then placed it on his tongue. "Salt?" he said in confusion as Daven rose from his bed.

"Man, I just had the absolute craziest dream ever," Daven said, running his fingers through his hair.

"Yeah ..." said Adam, not entirely listening to Daven. "Yeah, I think I did too."

Daven looked over at Adam as the man continued tasting his finger. "What in the world are you doing?" he asked while rubbing his own eye.

"Salt," Adam said as he looked at Daven, lifting his index finger in the air.

Daven then felt the same gritty substance on his finger and tasted it as well. "What the ..." he said, looking perplexed. Both men then looked at each other with slight fear in their eyes when a soft knock was heard on their door.

"Daven? Adam? Are you awake?" asked a soft, feminine Italian voice.

"Yeah ... Just one sec," said Adam, standing up. He walked to the door and unlocked it. Having developed a habit of locking every door that contained him, he sheepishly looked past the corner to see a short, middle-aged woman with black hair and big black eyes.

"Hi, Adam, my name is Michela Tarallo. It's good to meet you," she said, smiling a motherly smile.

"How do you know my name?" asked Adam rather coldly.

Michela smiled, laughed, and answered while ignoring the manner of his retort. "Giuseppe said Adam had red hair, and unless you're Deirdre, you must be Adam."

Adam looked down and smiled. "Yeah, I guess that makes me Adam," he said, reaching out to shake Michela's hand.

"Is Daven awake?" asked Michela, tilting her head to look into the room. Daven peeked around Adam to see her.

"We need to bathe," he said, looking at Michela with desperation.

She laughed from her core, finding the two men's dry humor amusing, and motioned for them to follow her. She took them to the sublevel showers and provided them with towels, combs, shampoo, and soap.

Michela waited for about forty-five minutes before calling out, "You two still in there?"

Daven shot his wet face out from behind a wall. "Getting sixty-year-old insulation out of our hair. Sorry, just haven't bathed in days."

Michela shooed Daven away, crossed her legs, and sat back in her chair with a book. By the time the two had finished scrubbing the dirt and grime and horror off their bodies, Michela had nodded off.

"Isn't it some kind of bad luck to wake a sleeping Italian woman?" asked Daven quietly to Adam.

"Not unless you're in slapping distance," said Michela with her eyes still closed. "You two ladies finished getting ready?" she asked, closing the book resting on her knee.

"I like you," said Daven, grinning. "You remind me of a lady I know."

The three drifted into silence. Michela already knew that the Fortunas had been killed. She felt a deep sorrow for Daven and Adam and wanted nothing more than to see them smile. Michela's own sons had lost their lives during the Vatican Revolt, and even though she had told Giuseppe time and time again that she held no resentment toward him, Giuseppe did everything he could to make up for it. She knew that he had assigned her to Daven and Adam to help her remember her own sons through them.

"Let's get you some new clothes, shall we?" she said, reaching up to squeeze their shoulders.

"You're really short," said Daven, trying to lighten the dismal mood.

"And you're going to learn not to call me short," said Michela, jumping to smack him in the back of the head.

"I think we're going to get along very well," said Adam, jumping up the stairs.

The three made their way to the ground floor and over to the kitchen. Daven and Adam had only eaten one granola bar each that Michael gave to them on their trek across Rome, so they were eagerly waiting to put something in their aching stomachs. The cafeteria was empty, aside from the cooks in the kitchen, so the two men were treated with overzealous portions of whatever they wanted, and so they sat with a mountain of food and ate themselves into exhaustion.

As they were finishing up, Scott and Deirdre walked in, looking for Michela.

"So these are the guys Emperor Nero's throwing half of Rome at us for," said Scott jokingly.

"Is that an American accent I hear?" asked Adam excitedly. He was feeling out of place since their start at being refugees. Daven was Canadian, but he was also not a fan of "American narcissism," as he so eloquently put it, so Adam felt distance between even himself and Daven at times.

"No way!" said Scott as Adam jumped up to embrace the complete stranger in the middle of the cafeteria. The two began speaking about their homes, interests, and love of music, which happened to be the same.

Deirdre sat down by Daven, noticing again how nervous he became around her. "Why aren't you singing the 'Star-Spangled Banner' with those two?" she said, poking fun at the other men's patriotism.

"Oh …" laughed Daven, unable to look at Deirdre without blushing. "I'm not American. I'm from Canada."

"I see," she said, nodding her head as she drummed on the table. "I've always had a thing for lumberjacks," she said, smiling and winking.

"Oh, ha ha ha," laughed Daven facetiously. "And I've always been aroused by the IRA."

Deirdre belted out a loud laugh just before covering her mouth. Scott and Adam stopped talking, startled by Deirdre's outburst. "Sorry," she said, brushing her hair out of her face. "That was just inappropriately funny."

"Be careful there," said Scott to Daven. "You know what they say about redheads."

Daven smiled. He hadn't had much practice around women the last three years, so he felt safe to tread lightly and remain shy when it came to the one woman he had an attraction to. He had hoped to run into her today, and he felt a surge of happiness shoot through his body when he saw her walk into the room. All in all, Daven hadn't really spent much time looking at her, as he would only glance at her and then look away quickly so as not to be caught eyeballing. Daven loved the company of this more feminine redhead rather than the one he had spent the last three years with.

"Hey, have you been shown around yet?" Deirdre asked after a small awkward silence.

"Well, I think Michela was just about to show us the rest of the barracks," Daven said, looking at their den mother.

"No, I mean the city," Deirdre said, dismissing the barracks as "boring."

"I don't think Giuseppe wants them out of the barracks quite yet," said Michela, not entirely comfortable with the idea.

"Oh, come on," said Scott, noticing the chemistry between Deirdre and Daven, "What harm could it do? As long as they stay out of the square, I'm sure they'd be fine."

Michela threw her hands in the air. "Godspeed," she said, standing up to walk out of the cafeteria. "Bedtime at eight o'clock!" she yelled before the door closed behind her.

"So … where to?" asked Daven, standing up.

Deirdre stood from her seat and motioned for Daven to follow her. "How about the basilica?" she said as she walked toward the doors of the cafeteria.

Daven turned to look at Adam and smiled. Both men were overly excited to associate with people their own age, and it served to alleviate the stress of being wanted men. Once Daven and Deirdre entered the colonnade, Deirdre noticed Daven halting in his tracks, scared to step foot in such an open area as the ovato tondo. "They'll see me," he said shakily. "Can we stay in here?"

Deirdre nodded, feeling faintly guilty for not taking into account everything he had just gone through. "Yeah, of course," she said, resting her hand on his shoulder. "I've always enjoyed walking through here. The world doesn't seem so big."

"Thank you," said Daven, embarrassed for feeling so nervous. "I'm sorry. It will probably take some time to get used to walking out in the open so freely."

"No apologies," said Deirdre, smiling up at him. "I know you and Adam have been through so much." She quickly tried to think of something else to talk about to take Daven's mind off his fear. "So how does it feel to be trapped here with all of us?" she asked, clearly changing the subject.

Daven laughed, noticing the diversion, but he appreciated her thoughtfulness. "I've always dreamt of coming here," he said, looking up. "But I guess Adam and I are outcasts even here in a way. First it was being the two whitest people in Domus Aurea. Now it's being the two non-Catholics in a Catholic land."

"Oh really, eh?" poked Deirdre. "My mother would never approve," she said, testing the water for Daven's reaction.

"Don't worry," he said, noticing her veiled flirting. "I'm still as celibate as a nun, so maybe she would be comfortable knowing that."

"Maybe so," she said with a toothy grin. "I'll ask her next time I speak with her."

Daven knew it was impossible to contact anyone outside of the Aurean peninsula. "How long has it been?" he asked.

Deirdre looked up with a look of heavy thought on her face. "I'd have to say probably a little over three years," she said, not sounding overly depressed. "What about you?"

Daven looked at his feet as they slowly made their way around the square. "I haven't seen them for about four years," he said with sadness. "I went to school in the States, which is where I met Adam. I was going to fly back after our trip ... here, but obviously that never happened."

"I'm not doing a very good job at lightening the mood, am I?" she asked, sensing that both Daven and she were sinking into sadness. "But this should help," she said just before bolting out of the remaining stretch of the colonnade. Daven was caught off guard but instantly followed suit as she turned to the doors of the basilica and ran in. He stopped short and looked all around. He had dreamt since he was young about wandering the gigantic, four-hundred-year-old structure and was about to enter into a dream guided by, as he thought, an angel.

It was everything he thought it would be. The sheer magnitude of the interior was staggering, and with every step, he could feel the weight of the basilica pushing down on him. The floors were extremely ornate and a work of art in and of themselves. The walls and piers climbed like huge trees along the borders of a forest decorated with cherubim and floral motifs. Just down a way toward the enormous dome that sat like a crown on the structure, Daven could see crepuscular rays beaming into the building like he had seen in so many pictures before, but none could do justice to actually witnessing them. Below the dome was Saint Peter's Baldachin, its bronze structure lit with the sun's rays, and the four Solomonic columns spiraling up to the canopy. Still at the front of the nave, Daven looked right to see Michelangelo's Pieta, noticing how the young, beautiful face of Mary was devoid of sorrow and emotion altogether. He felt as if the basilica itself was void of humanity, with the expressionless statues positioned along the nave all the way to the transepts.

"It's a sight to behold, don't you think?" yelled Deirdre from the Papal Altar underneath the dome and baldachin. Daven walked slowly toward her, gazing at the ornately decorated vaulted ceilings above him. It was certainly more than he expected, but there was a sadness that hung like a fog within every corner and every opening. It felt like the building itself was utterly alone, a barren woman weeping, sorrowful of the lifelessness within her.

"It's a lot to take in," he said without looking back down. "So quiet."

Deirdre walked down to him, looking up just like he was. "You know," she said, looking at him, "there's more to this place than just the roof."

Daven looked down, still with a fascinated look on his face. "It's beautiful, all of it," he said, smiling. "Everything in here is just perfect."

"Aw, thanks!" said Deirdre, playfully twisting Daven's words. He smiled and looked down at his feet. It was true—he thought she was beautiful—and she knew it. Deirdre found it strange as well that she was able to freely express her emotions to this, by definition, stranger. She had been in love once, and that love still held a painful place in her heart. He was dead, but his face was still fresh in her mind—his smile, his eyes, even his bloodied and lifeless expression as he lay dead on the battlefield after the Revolt. Deirdre had all but moved on, but she felt as if she was disrespecting the memory of her lost love by so openly and freely expressing her attraction to Daven.

Instantly her countenance fell, and she lost the glow about her like a snuffed-out candle. "Do … do you think we could finish the tour later?" she asked with an empty look.

Daven noticed the immediate change in demeanor, thinking that he had done something to cause the change in mood.

"Sure," he said, standing back. "Do you mind if I stay in here for a bit?"

Deirdre nodded wordlessly and turned to walk away. Daven wanted to reach out to the woman but knew that it was best to allow her the time alone she needed. He then turned to the baldachin again and made his way to the stairway leading down to the grottoes. As he reached the bottom, looking out to the Tomb of Saint Peter, he felt as if he wasn't alone, like a dark secret was being kept within the halls of the dead before him. It was eerily ironic, given the feeling of emptiness above and the feeling of unsettling life where nothing should be living. This was not a place he wanted to explore alone, and so he quickly made his way back to the surface and then to the Milvian Guard's barracks.

CHAPTER 8

VENGEANCE IS MINE

September 18, 2035

"I'm sorry, Alban," said Innocent as passively and gently as possible. "I will not sanction your request. It is utter cruelty and destructive. We are supposed to be protectors of the innocent, not executioners!"

"These men are endangering the entire city just by being here!" argued Alban. "I myself witnessed both incidents of Domus Aurea's show of power! You call my wishes cruel, but I saw ultimate cruelty when those poor souls were crucified in front of my very eyes!"

"We live in a cruel world," said Camillo quietly, attempting to suppress Alban's passionate anger. "The adversary begets violence and horror, not these poor men we are supposed to be protecting. You say that those you saw crucified were unjustly murdered, and I agree, but what do you imagine would happen to these men if we just handed them over? The Fortunas were martyrs, and God has accepted their souls into his kingdom. We can't nullify that sacrifice by abandoning Daven and Adam."

Alban dropped into his chair, one that he had yet to sit in as he had been standing for his entire argument, and slouched. "Then if we do nothing, we may as well be burying the knife in our own chest," he said as he placed his hand over his eyes in an attempt to dramatically express his bottomless despair. "Taking our own lives. Is that not worse?"

Innocent sighed, tired, wanting to lay this argument to rest. "Alban, I am not handing over these men, and that is final," he said with irritation.

"In fact, I am about to go meet these men myself. I want you to accompany me. You will see the face of Christ in these two, and you will come to appreciate our decision to provide them asylum. Remember what our lord said: 'When I was hungry, you gave me food. When I was thirsty, you gave me drink. I was a stranger, and you welcomed me. I was naked, and you clothed me. I was sick, and you visited me. I was in prison, and you came to me.' We are simply of his flock, and we will carry out his will." Innocent then rose from behind his desk and beckoned to Alban and Camillo to follow him.

Alban was not particularly happy to be visiting the men that he deemed an attractant to death. The cardinal priest was not a sociable man, and meeting new people was something he had avoided for three years. He wasn't even keen on carrying on conversation with people he got along with, much less those he wasn't fond of.

"Please, Alban, if it's in your capacity as a holy man, don't embarrass me," said Camillo as he tried to speed up to Innocent, who was now surrounded by six Swiss Guard.

Alban felt a twinge of sharp pain toward Camillo's resentful remark. He knew he had an issue with allowing his anger emotions to boil over, but he also knew that even Saint Peter himself had a hot temper, even going so far as being venerated as the very first pope. Alban wasn't without fault, but he also wasn't a hopeless cause like so many around him believed.

The group of nine reached the entrance of the barracks, which was being guarded by two Swords. The Swords and Swiss Guard saluted one another, and after, the two guardsmen stepped aside and allowed the procession to continue inward. Making their way to the top of the barracks was agonizingly exasperating to Alban, given his unwillingness to take this trek in the first place. He knew they were making their way to Giuseppe's office, and he still harbored some anger toward the man.

Giuseppe's two office doors were wide open, and each man could see the Crown sitting behind his desk. Giuseppe saw the oncoming group and signaled for them to enter. The six Swiss Guard entered the office first, with Innocent, Camillo, and Alban following. Daven and Adam were standing on either side of the large fireplace and remained silent after the group stopped their movement. Giuseppe stood from his chair and situated himself between the two and the group of nine. "Your Holiness and Your Eminence, this is Daven Jones and Adam Gilmour, our new residents."

Pope Innocent hurriedly pushed past his protectors and shuffled his way to Daven and Adam. "Ah, the scourge of Domus Aurea!" he said with squinted eyes and a large cheeky smile. "It's an honor to finally meet you!"

Daven and Adam couldn't resist the urge to smile back at the unnaturally chipper white-robed man. "It's good to meet you too, sir," said Daven, borderline laughing.

"Your Holiness," coughed Alban, unable to overlook such, as he saw it, disrespect.

Innocent turned and scowled at Alban with a look that caught all those behind him off guard. The pope was always smiling, so such a polarizing change of face was shocking. "Ignore Alban," he said, turning back around. "He holds the concept of titles a little too high."

"I'm sorry," said Daven. "We're not aware of all the formal eloquences within this church."

"This church?" said a perturbed and increasingly angered Alban. "It is the church! The universal church, and you will show her respect!"

At this point, Daven and Adam stared at the man with a look of disdain. Pope Innocent had had enough and finally lost the bottomless well of patience he was known for having. "Alban Sommer, you *will* keep your mouth shut, or I will personally throw you out this closed window myself! Shut your mouth and have some self-control!"

"We're not going to get along with you," said Adam, breaking his silence. "This is apparent."

Alban was both embarrassed and furious. He had no intention to stay any longer, and so he turned with a red face and vacated the room.

Innocent turned to face the boys once more with an embarrassed look written on his entire being. "I have to apologize for that outburst," he said, unable to look the men in the eyes. "A man in my position should never lose his temper like that."

Adam looked at the short man. "Jesus flipped tables in the temple," he said, patting the pope's robed shoulder. "I'd say you are doing just fine."

Immediately Innocent's face lit up, and his cheerful bearing reemerged. "Wise words from a young soul. You will be well received here, I just know it. Perhaps sometime later we could dine together? I'd love to hear all about your escapades in Rome and your lives outside of this country."

Daven and Adam agreed with excitement and bade farewell to Innocent after greeting Camillo and the Swiss Guard protecting them. They were happy to see how human Innocent was and respected his intolerant stance on old formalities. Both Daven and Adam could tell the man wished to be seen as just a man and nothing more.

"Well, I'd say that went exceedingly well, all things considered," said Giuseppe, indirectly referring to Alban. "His Holiness is a kind man, and I know he'll do anything he can to make life here more comfortable for you."

"I've got to say that I wasn't expecting such a laid-back attitude from him," said Adam. "I expected more hand-kissing."

"Nobody wants their hand kissed," said Giuseppe, laughing. "Least of all Pope Innocent."

"Well, I'm going to head in," said Adam. "It's getting late, and I'm still feeling the effects from our trip."

Giuseppe said good night to the men and walked back behind his desk to take care of a few more daily tasks. Daven walked with Adam to their room but continued onward to the cafeteria to get a drink. The barracks were quiet and dim, save for the night watch, and Daven felt comforted knowing there were protective eyes everywhere. The silence served to amplify any sound he made, like the stair railing running through his hand and the muffled thud of his feet on the carpeted steps.

Once he reached the bottom floor, he took a look around at the sparsely furnished area, thinking the bland construct of the barracks paled in comparison to the structures around it. He made his way to the glass doors of the cafeteria and walked through to its half-lit interior. Ahead of him, he could see a figure sitting in the dark, back to the door. Daven flipped the switch and saw that it was Deirdre. The redheaded woman turned, squinting to see Daven standing by the door. She smiled at him and turned away. Daven lightly walked over, trying to silence the loud clopping of his shoes hitting the hard tile floor, and sat across from her.

"You thirsty?" he asked. "I am."

"No, I'm fine, thank you," she said without looking at him.

Daven stood up and grabbed a water. "Do you mind if I sit over here and finish this?" he asked from the end of the bench.

"You don't have to sit all the way over there, silly," she said, glancing over at him, trying to hide her troubled mind.

Daven smiled and slid down to face her. "I like water," he said, chugging it down. "You never appreciate it until you're running through an unfamiliar city with armed men tailing you in hot pursuit."

"I really can't imagine," she said with genuine concern in her voice.

"I'm sure you could," Daven said, taking another sip, "and I'm sure you were imagining what that was earlier today."

Deirdre crossed her arms on the table and rested her chin within the walls of her elbows. "I'm really sorry about that," she said, slowly tilting her head to hide her eyes. "I had a moment."

"Bipolar, eh?" he asked in a seemingly joking manner.

"Uh ... no," said Deirdre, slightly put-off. "Why would you ask that?"

"Oh, I didn't mean anything by it," said Daven without skipping a beat. "I am, and sometimes I'm very happy, and then I'm not in the blink of an eye."

Deirdre felt marginally bad for misinterpreting Daven's question. "I'm sorry ... I didn't mean that the way it came out."

"Don't apologize," said Daven, setting down his drink. "Adam and I aren't the only ones who have seen horrible things in this world."

Deirdre sat for a moment and saw the face of her love flash before her eyes again. It had been happening more since Daven's arrival, and she couldn't understand why. "You're right," she said. trying to keep her answers as vague as possible. "I was reminded of someone I lost a long time ago."

"It might help to speak openly about it," said Daven, standing up. "But I'm not one to force emotional revelations. My therapist always tried that. Never helped. But know that when you want to talk to someone, I'd love to be that person."

Deirdre left her head cradled in her arms, but she smiled a smile she hadn't felt in a long time. "Thank you, Daven," she said with a knot in her stomach and lump in her throat. She felt a rush of newfound happiness surge through her body, comforting her and filling her with excitement. Daven wasn't ignorant to tragedy, and she could sense a sorrow within him that had the potential to swallow him whole, but from her point of view, it only served to strengthen his resolve and fueled his will to overcome.

She listened as his footsteps slowly drifted out of earshot, and then she prayed for God to keep her from spiraling into the depths of her mind. She felt that Daven had something special within him that set him apart from anyone else around her, and she prayed that this strength could swallow her and give her the will to move forward and upward.

"So here we are … tempting fate once again," said Daven as he and Adam looked down the desolate tracks of the now almost defunct railway of the Vatican. The large archway opening the city walls to Rome was now fenced off with an openable gate for the occasion when the city actually received supplies.

"We've been tempting fate for years now," said Adam as he quickly walked to the gate to find a way out. "What's a little more temptation?"

"Well, this thing is definitely a hardware store job," said Daven, looking at the galvanized pipe fittings that made up the gate.

"Honestly, I don't think the Aureans want in," said Adam. "If they did, they would be."

Daven kept tugging on the bars of the gate, trying to find a way to get from one side to the other. "Well, we're not trying to get in," he said, looking underneath a small gap on the bottom of the gate. "Hey, help me pull from down here."

The two men gripped the bottom and pulled back with everything they had. Their efforts paid off as the gap gave way to enough space for them to scuffle underneath. The distance traveled wasn't much, but the sensation of being on the other side of the Vatican's walls was unsettling.

"All right. Let's stick close to the wall and keep hiding spots in sight," said Adam, feeling overtly nervous.

The men needed to move from the southern part of the city to the north, as the other gates were heavily guarded, and from there to the Fortuna's. It was a little less than a mile from their current location to their old residence, which was long enough to keep the two on edge for the entire trip. The night was warm, and the ambient sounds around them put forth the misleading feeling of peace and serenity. They moved in short spurts, taking in every bit of the outlying cityscape when they stopped to look for patrols. The two men made sure to wear darker clothing to blend in with the shadows. They weren't about to get arrested and possibly executed when Abele did everything he could to give them a fighting chance. But they felt a tug on their souls that caused an irresistible response that they couldn't deny, and so here they were in the heart of the lion's den, searching for their loved ones.

As they arrived on the opposite side of the street from their old household, Daven and Adam noticed how empty and desolate it looked. "I don't have a very good feeling about this," said Daven, looking up and down the road for any sign of life.

"I haven't had a good feeling about this since we walked out of the barracks," Adam said, marking his apprehension about leaving the Vatican. "But we can probably get in through the kitchen window. No lock on it, remember?"

The two looked up and down the road once more before sprinting across to the alley on the left side of the house. They noticed the garbage bins were still filled with trash from the last day they were there. Abele was meticulous about keeping up with his home, and this small inconsistency spoke volumes to them.

They arrived underneath a small window just above the kitchen sink and slowly opened it. Daven crawled in first and then reached down to help Adam climb up. It was eerily quiet inside, devoid of Eula and Abele's essence, and it caused a level of anxiety to build up within them. The creaking and groaning of the warped wooden planks beneath their feet were intensified by the tomb-like silence of the house, and the men winced with every step. The table and carpet covering their old hideaway were both still intact and seemed unmoved by anyone who may have been searching for them.

"Upstairs?" Daven whispered as they crossed into the front portion of the two-story house. Adam nodded silently, and the two moved swiftly to Abele and Eula's room. The door was closed, which was a good sign considering Abele's insistence on sleeping within a secure room. Daven gripped the doorknob and looked at Adam. The two silently mouthed a countdown and opened the door.

It was as they feared. The room was empty, and the bed was unmade.

They had hoped that Abele eluded his captors and left with Eula, but no clothes were missing, and Abele's hidden stash of money was still where he left it. "No ..." whispered Daven, fearing the worst. "This can't be happening."

Adam slumped down onto the disheveled bed and rested his face in his hands. "We've killed them," he said with complete despair. "This is all our fault, and there's nothing we can do about it."

Before Daven could try to comfort his ailing friend, he heard the front door open and close with a slam. "Closet ... now," he said as he skated across the floor to the small enclosure still filled with clothes. Adam followed suit and wedged himself into the coffin-tight space. They listened with fear as two sets of footsteps made their way up the stairs. They listened intently as a conversing pair of strangers came closer and closer to their hiding place.

"Someone was definitely here," they heard one man say. "We closed this door when we arrested the wife."

"What are you nervous about?" asked the other. "We've got guns."

Daven again held his breath as the two Aurean men placed themselves at the foot of the bed, just outside the closet door. "Remember that weird scream?" joked one of the soldiers. "It sounded like something out of an old monster movie."

The other man laughed. "Didn't she faint too?" he asked, going through drawers. "Look! There has to be at least a thousand euros here!"

"Come on, split it with me!" begged the other soldier. "It was my idea to come here in the first place."

The two argued back and forth for about five minutes, finally coming to an agreement. Daven and Adam could hear them splitting the money and moving the conversation along. "So were you there earlier today?"

"Of course I was there. I'm in your century, you idiot," said the man who found the hidden money. "Didn't last very long, did it?"

"No, it didn't. But I'm not complaining. Crucifixions can last for a pretty long time."

"Yeah, but it didn't work," answered his peer. "The whole point was to draw out those bastards, but I don't even think they saw it."

Daven's and Adam's blood pressure were building to a slow boil. They were almost positive these men were speaking of Abele and Eula's death, but they couldn't be sure. Fear was spiraling around them like a tornado, and it only depended on a name to confirm what they were aching to avoid.

"So what else do you think we can grab?" said the other soldier, changing the subject.

"I don't know. Anything, I guess. It's not like they're coming back anytime soon."

The two men laughed again heartlessly. "Yeah. I mean, if being nailed to a piece of wood didn't kill them, then that bullet to the chest would," said the soldier, chuckling as he walked to the closet, opening the door.

The soldier didn't have much time to process the next few seconds after looking inside. Daven landed a furious right hook onto the man's nose, breaking it and sending him falling straight back onto the floor below him. Adam pounced onto the second man, knocking his gun away and mercilessly beating him into unconsciousness. By the time he looked over to Daven, his friend had the soldier's neck gripped in his fingers, shaking him, tears pouring from his eyes.

"Daven ... Daven!" he said, trying to pull him away, but it was too late, and the soldier's bloodshot eyes looked up at him vacant of spirit. "Dammit, Daven," Adam said, but before he could chastise his out-of-control friend, the soldier behind him regained consciousness and frantically searched for his weapon.

Adam dove forward and wrapped his arms around the man's legs, trying to pull him away from his pistol. The soldier freed one of his legs and kicked Adam in the head, causing him to recoil in pain. Daven watched as the soldier rolled onto his right shoulder, aiming his weapon at Adam. It happened both in the blink of an eye and in slow motion, and before he knew it, Daven had jumped in front of the soldier's crosshair to pull Adam out of the line of fire. The weapon went off with a flash and a deafening crack, and Daven cried out as a sharp searing pain shot up his right leg.

Adam stood as Daven fell, and he jumped over to the armed soldier as the man attempted to gain his footing. Adam knocked the man back down, but the Aurean still held his pistol and swung its barrel around, pointing it into Adam's face. Adam grasped the gun and, with all his strength, turned the man's firearm toward himself, slipped his thumb around the trigger, and pushed. The second shot wasn't as loud, as Adam's ears were still ringing from the first, but the smell of burned gunpowder filled his nostrils.

The concussive blast reverberated through his skull, and a dizzying effect kept him on all fours. He looked over to Daven, who was rolling in agony, holding his ankle. Adam crawled over and pulled Daven's hands away so he could assess the damage. There was an immense amount of blood, but he saw that the bullet had gone clean through, possibly missing all the bones in his shin. He grabbed a shirt from Abele's dresser and wrapped it around Daven's leg.

"We have to go, now," said Adam, helping his friend to his feet. "And we have to be quick. I know it's going to be painful, but we don't have any other choice."

"I can do it," said Daven through short breaths. "I can do it ..."

Adam helped Daven to the door and then turned around. He grabbed a photo of Abele and Eula off their nightstand and tucked it under his arm. The two hobbled down the steep stairs and eyeballed the street through the front window. Adam couldn't see a soul outside and quickly opened the door, helping Daven down the front steps, shooting across the street to the opposing alleyway.

Daven was slowly slipping out of consciousness through sheer pain, blood loss, and exhaustion. Later he could barely recall the trip from the Fortunas to the iron gate cutting the railroad in two from Rome to the Vatican. Adam dragged his friend from one end to the other and limped with him from the station to the Milvian Guard barracks. He burst in and shouted to two Swords on watch to aid in getting Daven to the infirmary.

Daven awoke some time later to two voices shouting at one another. As his vision regained its focus, he could see Adam and Giuseppe in hot debate, arms flailing with anger.

"How could you keep this from us?" yelled Adam, obviously talking about the Fortunas' death.

"We didn't want you doing something rash and stupid," Giuseppe said with a slightly less intense voice. "But obviously that happened anyway."

Adam threw his hands in the air and twirled around to see Daven awake. Both Giuseppe and he went to opposite sides of the bed and began spitting out every bit of information they had on Daven's condition.

"So it looks like the bullet completely missed the tibia and fibula and went straight through the middle," Adam said with concern.

"You didn't lose too much blood contrary to how it seemed when you arrived," said Giuseppe, referring to Daven's blackout.

"I just don't do well when it comes to blood," Daven mumbled. "That or needles."

"Well, you were out for most of the needlework," said Giuseppe, trying to cheer Daven up. "So basically all you need to do is rest."

The three sat quietly for a moment, no one desiring to continue the argument that occurred just seconds prior to Daven's awakening, but Giuseppe needed to speak to the men about their rash decision.

"I can't say that I would have done anything different if I were in your position," he said, softening the blow, "but two Aurean soldiers are dead because of your actions, not to mention Daven's injuries. If anyone investigating those murders doesn't assume that it was your doing, then they're dense and idiotic."

"Maybe you're right," said Adam, cooling off. "But we should have been kept in the know. These people saved our lives and put their own in danger just by keeping us under their roof."

"Lucius Nero is an evil, twisted excuse for a man," said Giuseppe, trying to make Adam understand the terrible mistake he and Daven made. "If you had been caught, you would have suffered a fate much worse than the Fortunas. I did the only thing I could to ease their passing, but you two wouldn't have had the same option if you had been apprehended."

"Ease their passing?" said Adam, his anger boiling over once again. "Their passing wasn't eased, Giuseppe! They suffered! Who knows what might have happened before they arrived outside the square? Jesus was whipped and starved before he had to carry his own cross. What do you think probably happened to them?"

Giuseppe rubbed his forehead, feeling a headache coming on. He couldn't blame Adam for being so on fire about the Fortunas' death, but he wanted them to understand that the Fortunas' death was also a sacrifice. One that could have been voided due to the boys' thoughtless actions. "Adam, what happened to Abele and Eula was neither my nor your fault. They were murdered by a psychopathic tyrant. But if you and Daven had been caught, their deaths would have been even more meaningless than if you had lived. Which you did. Take that anger and sadness and turn it into something useful."

"What would be useful?" asked Adam.

Giuseppe thought about his dream and the boy's uncanny resemblance to the angelic beings within it. He was still unsure of what its meaning was, but he knew that if he asked them to fight with him, he could also keep them under his watch. "Tomorrow, once Daven is able to speak without drooling, I'll present you with a proposal, and if you accept it, you'll have the opportunity to fight your enemies with my full backing and approval."

He turned around and left the two men alone. Daven was still in a drug-induced stupor, and Giuseppe wanted to give him some time to recuperate. Adam waited for Giuseppe to begin ascending the stairs before turning around and asking Daven about something that had been picking away at his mind. "Are we going to keep ignoring what happened this morning?" he asked.

"Are we even sure about … it?" asked Daven, gesturing to an invisible object in front of him. "Yeah, I had a weird dream that was unusually clear and specific, but that doesn't mean you had the same one."

Adam was a notoriously skeptical man and wasn't one to latch on to coincidental occurrences without first researching every possible avenue of explanation. But the nature of his dream was so vivid and so different from anything he had ever experienced that it warranted deeper prodding and careful examination. "We dreamt the same thing, Daven," he said confidently, trying not to leave room for question in Daven's mind. "I woke up on a rocky shore facing a gray sea. After a few minutes, or hours, I couldn't tell, this gale-force wind blew the ocean in my face, burning my eyes with salt, the same salt you and I both woke up with in our beds," he said with surety. "Then the angels."

Daven couldn't forget the angels. Their image was burned onto his psyche like a brand on leather hide, and their words had been documented into his mind like a stylus etching information onto a record. If asked, he could relay the dream in its entirety in seamless perfection with the speed and accuracy of a computer accessing a file on a hard drive. He couldn't forget the angels … Not their names, their description, and especially not their haunting familiarity. Daven felt like he was undergoing an out-of-body experience when he faced the angel Sansenoy. He also couldn't shake the feeling that this angel was following him and watching him from some unseen vantage point, protecting him and preparing him for some as of yet unknown purpose.

"Do I need to go on?" asked Adam, hoping Daven would see the special nature of their ordeal without much convincing on his part.

"Yeah, you're right," said Daven, bowing to Adam's validity. He sat in silence for a moment, his mind wandering to a less grand aspect of the vision. "We were home," he said finally, in a seemingly deviatory change of subject. "On the shores of Nain ... My home, that is." Adam noticed a distant look in his friend's face, like the man saw something outside the white curtains of the infirmary that wasn't visible to his own eyes. "It was where I stood just before hopping on a plane to the States. I think I always knew I was in a dream when I saw it that night, but everything was so real. The smell, the wind, the cold rocks of the shore that always hurt my feet. I wanted to believe I was home so badly, but I couldn't shake the truth."

"Why do you think we were there? In your hometown?" Adam asked, feeling neglected, wishing he could have seen his own home instead.

"I'm not sure," Daven said, sensing his friend's jealousy. "But there is something I've been wondering. What was the name of your angel? Do you remember?"

"Senoy," said Adam.

Daven was then convinced that they had experienced a shared vision at this point. He decided that an interpretation would be the next step in discovering the true message within the cipher of information they had been presented with. "What does it all mean then?" he asked Adam. "What was the point of all this if we're left without a straightforward answer? It just seems so useless to choose an audience, present them with information, and then leave them without a way to understand."

"Maybe it wasn't a message," Adam said after a moment of thought. "Maybe all it was meant to do was make us aware of something. In fact, as far as I can remember, they actually asked us something. Asked us to carry them, and from what I can gather, we agreed."

Daven's head was beginning to burn with the amount of questions that were pouring through it. What had happened was real, and it confused his mind and stressed his body. All he wanted at that point was to leave the infirmary and walk outside. He knew the rest of his answers would present themselves when the time had come, and if their vision was any indication, he knew the answers would be just as otherworldly and epic as the initial thought-provoking presentation before it. "I honestly don't know," he said, feeling the effects of his painkillers more intensely than before. "And right now I don't think I can think about it anymore."

Adam had been so consumed by the attempted interpretation of their dream that he had completely ignored his friend's well-being. "You're right. You need to rest," he said, standing up. "I didn't say thank you tonight. You saved my life. I won't forget that."

"Well … I probably will," Daven said with his eyes closed and his head nodding from side to side. "You can thank me again tomorrow."

Adam laughed as he turned around to leave. Daven had successfully fallen asleep before he reached the doors to the infirmary, and Adam felt that fairly soon he would be drifting into a dreamless slumber as well. Tomorrow, they would hear Giuseppe's proposition and decide for themselves how effective their involvement would be. Adam was well aware of how their currently set path was leading to nowhere, but they needed to see someone pay for their suffering. They had essentially lost everything, and the anger they felt was fueled by the constantly negative turn of events that had been afforded to them. Adam wanted to stand atop Saint Peter's Basilica and fiddle as Nero's Rome burned to the ground. Nothing short of a horrible end to Nero's reign would satiate Daven's and Adam's bloodlust, and it scared him to feel such unrestrained hatred. But for the time being, all he wanted was rest and a chance to absorb every horrible event that had transpired up until that point—and a chance to mourn and a chance for vengeance once he rose the next day.

CHAPTER 9

A PATIENT
MAN'S VIRTUE

September 19, 2035

A single century of Aurean soldiers stood facing the Golden Palace. It was the same century led by the man who oversaw the crucifixion of the Fortunas. They stood silently and stoically as their ruler, Lucius Nero, emerged from his throne room within the restored Pantheon. The eighty men collectively stomped their right foot and threw their rifles up to rest on their left shoulders, barrels pointing to the sky. Other politicians and military leaders populated the Piazza della Rotonda. The obelisk and fountain in the center of the square were left within an empty twenty-foot radius, with Nero standing atop a ten-foot podium directly between the two center columns of the Pantheon.

The grand exterior of Nero's throne room was more in line with the ornate style of its original ancient Roman beginnings. The stone exterior had been whitewashed and stamped with marble statues inlayed along its facade. The pediment was adorned with a golden rendition of the coat of arms of Domus Aurea and the dome lined with plated bronze. The lamps within the square were primarily fueled by oil, keeping an antiquated atmosphere over the tyrant's massive complex.

From the western side of the Pantheon, a cavalcade of eight horses, four pulling and four pushing, slowly transported a giant hollow bronze bull, a Brazen Bull, in between the obelisk, fountain, and porch of the throne room. Directly behind the procession of horses, the decanus of each tent group within the century escorted the centurion who oversaw the Fortunas' execution to the location of the Brazen Bull. He was stripped down to nothing, ropes binding his hands and feet, with his head shaved.

Once the parade of horses and men halted their movement, the century executed an about-face, showing their backs to their shamed leader. "Unbridled anger and failure to lead are characteristics of an unbalanced and unworthy leader," said Nero, breaking the deathly silence that had hung itself over the square. "The military strength of Domus Aurea, in and of itself, is and should be enough to bring our enemies to their knees. However, I leave the power of leadership and the essence of my right to rule this blossoming empire in the capable hands of your superior officers. When these men fail in their appointed tasks, it is a blight upon this Domus Aurea and an imperfection upon my face!" His voice began to increase in volume and ferocity, and there was a fire in his eyes that shone to all around him. "This man before you was appointed the responsibility of apprehending two men, who murdered three of your own and possibly two more since yesterday, but he failed in his duty. Even after being given a second chance to stare down our enemy into submission, this man was unsuccessful. Now these murdering psychopaths are moving freely throughout our great city and are distributing their own brand of justice on your brothers–in–arms!" Nero then looked to the ten decani and signaled for them to carry out the execution.

The sentenced centurion did not go silently. He began screaming with complete terror and anguish in his voice, begging and pleading for his own life. "Mercy, please!" he cried. "Just one more chance to prove my loyalty!"

Nero descended his podium and marched toward the terrified man, who was convulsing to the point of being unable to stand anymore. His skin was white with fear, and sweat was pouring off him in rivers. Nero crouched down and grabbed the man's chin. "This is your chance to prove your loyalty," he said quietly. "Show your men what happens to failure. Your death will be imprinted on their minds forever, and they will do anything to avoid a similar fate. Now … do your duty."

Nero then sauntered toward the bull and opened a hatch on its side.

He moved away as the decani, who were forced to carry the immobile individual by this point, transported the now silent centurion to the bull and pushed him inside. Even as the hatch was closed and locked, the condemned man remained hushed and still within the belly of bronze.

Nero made his way back to the podium and ascended to its summit. With a small flick of the wrist, he signaled for the fires to be lit and then sat and waited for the end. It wasn't long before the bull began to vocalize with a low and intense growl. Inside was a carefully engineered pipe leading from the inner workings of the bull to its nose and mouth. Its purpose was to mask the screams of the slowly cooking man inside and to turn his cries of pain into sounds of an angry bovine. A sickly sweet smell began to fill the nostrils of all in attendance, and it caused many feelings of nausea and discomfort. Eventually the bull's growls became shorter and weaker and soon ceased completely. Nero commanded the century to turn again to face the Brazen Bull, while two decani made their way over to the brass encasement, extinguishing the fire underneath and opening the hatch. The curled and warped body of the man tumbled out, blackened and smoking, with much of his skin peeling and flaking off. As he hit the ground with a sickening thud, the man's boiled blood splattered across the square, slowly trickling into the cracks and crevices of the imperfect pavement.

"Cremate the remains and place the urn inside the Catacombs of the Conquerors," commanded Nero, standing from his seat. "In the end, he fulfilled his duty."

The catacombs were located on the outskirts of the city, like the burial sites of ancient Rome, and were constructed during the first year of Nero's rule. He was heavily involved with the design and architecture of his tomb, much like a pharaoh overseeing the construction of the pyramids. The massive product of the immense undertaking was reserved for Nero, the Lazio Legion, and martyrs of Domus Aurea; it was a vast marble complex that spanned an area of three square kilometers, overseen by a special guard called the Ferrymen.

The ten decani wrapped the body in a white sheet and tied the remains to the top of the bronze death trap. Nero quickly walked to the dead centurion and removed the bloodstained white sheet from his face. He reached down to a pouch tied to his sword, removed a single gold coin, and placed it within the lipless mouth of the shamed hero. "For your journey. May Charon allow you safe passage across Styx to your home in the Elysian Fields."

The procession continued onward, followed by the leaderless century, to the catacombs. Nero sank back into his palace, leaving his politicians and military leaders standing alone in the square to disperse on their own. After a small amount of time, the Piazza della Rotonda sat vacant of life, with only the red stain of death remaining to show that anyone had ever even been there.

Adam woke the following morning after venturing into Rome and was still in a small amount of shock after killing the Aurean soldier the previous night. He was becoming increasingly disturbed at Daven's uncanny ability to kill without hesitation, but he knew his friend and brother was a good man at his core. Adam never thought twice about Daven's intentions, but he also knew his friend had a teetering awareness. He thought his friend had a brilliant and bright way of thinking and had always considered this fact with how unbalanced he was; it was the price of a beautiful mind, and he was constantly amazed at Daven's intellect.

He rolled over and saw that it was already ten in the morning; he forced himself to sit up. Adam hadn't had time to mourn Abele and Eula. All his mind's eye could see was Eula's smile every night Daven and he returned home from work. He remembered how Abele draped his arm over the front seat of his vehicle whenever they went from home to work and vice versa. It was his way of shielding the boys from the eyes of Domus Aurea, and Adam felt unbearable guilt for not being there to shield him in return.

Adam opened one of the drawers in the dresser at the foot of his bed. Michela had gathered a number of things for him to wear and snuck them in during the night while he slept. He liked to think that Michela embodied the spirit of Eula and that he would find in this woman the same soul of motherly love that he saw in Eula every day. It made him smile and feel comforted by the idea that he would still see her in this new woman, and so he decided to celebrate Eula's life rather than mourn her demise.

After dressing, he made his way down to the infirmary to check on Daven. He knew the bullet wound was probably extremely painful, and the small hospital was limited on whatever painkillers they had in stock. He opened the door and saw Daven sitting up on the side of his bed surrounded by a number of nurses and Giuseppe. "What's going on?" he asked nervously, hoping the gathering was a positive one.

Giuseppe turned around and motioned for Adam to see what the fuss was all about. The nurses and he parted so Adam could look at Daven's leg, and what he saw added to an already long list of questions. "How is this even possible?" he asked anyone who could answer.

"Your guess is as good as mine," said Daven with just as much astonishment within him as Adam.

Adam looked closely at the scarring that had appeared where a large wound had once been. "It was there last night when we carried you in here. I watched the nurse wrap it up!"

"I couldn't feel any pain at all when I woke up," Daven said, rehashing the previous night's events. "The nurses came by this morning to check on the wound, but when we took the bandage off, nothing was there."

"Does anyone have any idea?" Adam asked again, trying to understand how something like this could happen.

The nurses and Giuseppe shrugged their shoulders. Several ideas had been bounced around, but the presented solutions were even more unbelievable than the miraculous nature of the healing itself.

"Are we all really trying to ignore the giant elephant in the room?" asked one of the women, finally building up the courage to speak her mind.

"And what elephant would that be?" asked Giuseppe with curiosity in his voice.

"We live in the religious center of the Catholic world, and yet we're sitting here afraid to say the word 'miracle,'" she said, walking to Daven's bedside. She grabbed the man's ankle with a strong hand. "Does that hurt? I know it doesn't because it's completely healed. Like nothing even happened. Not even a twisted ankle!"

The remaining nurses, and Giuseppe especially, felt the wrench of embarrassment. This young woman was absolutely right, and it gave Giuseppe a feeling of pride to see such faith come from someone with a mind so fresh. "I can't argue with you," he said, surrendering to her wisdom. "And I don't want to."

Both Daven and Adam looked at each other with an unspoken understanding. They had been experiencing odd occurrences since becoming residents of the Vatican, and their shared dream, or vision, was only the beginning of an ever-increasing list. The dots were presenting themselves, but it was up to the two men to connect them to unveil the full picture, and it was a big picture indeed.

Giuseppe had been presented with his own veiled picture days before these two men had arrived, but unbeknownst to him, Daven and Adam's portrait, and his own, were only separate pieces to something incredible. Eventually, the three would be witness to a divine painting of epic proportions, and their parts in the completion of that image would be immeasurable.

After a short moment of uncomfortable poking and prodding at Daven's no longer existing ankle wound, the nurses went their separate ways, taking care of the other patients in the small infirmary. Giuseppe grabbed two chairs for Adam and himself and set them by Daven's hospital bed. The two boys weren't exactly sure where Giuseppe was about to take the conversation, but he calmly sat down and motioned for Adam to join him. It was clear that Daven and Adam were uneasy about Giuseppe's uninterpretable exterior, especially after the previous night's catastrophe, but Giuseppe didn't mince words, and so he quickly began his dialogue. "I said last night that I would present you with a way to fight your enemies that I could fully support and one that would give you what you need to accomplish it." Giuseppe stopped for a moment to make sure the men were following and listening. "But it needs to move beyond anything personal if we're to continue. Vendettas are dangerous and will cloud your judgment, and if you are to accept my offer, you won't have room for them anyway."

The men hadn't given thought to their desire to avenge Abele and Eula. It seemed so natural to feel an unquenchable longing for justice, but it had never once occurred to them that their wishes would have to factor in those around them. Giuseppe needed to rein them in, but at the same time he knew the boys couldn't just stand aside and allow evil men to continue their rampages unchecked. "The offer I'm presenting you is this … Join the guard. Fight with me and make this city a better place."

Daven and Adam looked at each other with apprehension. "I don't know," said Daven. "I don't really see what good we could be doing by standing around on top of walls or guarding gates."

"But I have something quite a bit more extravagant in mind for you," Giuseppe said, moving on to a more specific description of his proposal. "There are four levels to the Milvian Guard. Uriel's Swords are our foot soldiers and the largest unit of all. They're commanded by Uriel's Mouths—Elia Serra, Raul Vezzi, and Margo Ruis. I command the entirety of the guard as Uriel's Crown, but I want you two for Uriel's Eyes, Scott and Deirdre's group."

"Well … that sounds interesting. But who is this Uriel that everyone seems to be a part of?" asked Adam, halfway jokingly and halfway curiously.

Giuseppe laughed, having underestimated how much he actually needed to explain. "Uriel, by tradition, is the angel who guards the Garden of Eden. There's a more specific reason as to why we chose him as our angelic comparison, but that's a story for another day. The Eyes that I'm asking you to join are our special operations unit and, here recently, are tasked with going out into Rome to gather information and take on distinct missions. So in essence, they are the special forces of the guard."

Daven's and Adam's shared interests were piqued much more at the idea of becoming specialists rather than ceremonial soldiers, and it showed on their faces in an obvious manner. Giuseppe smiled, seeing their eyes brighten, and it gave him a contented feeling knowing he had given them a purpose and something to fight for. "So does that mean we have a deal?" he asked, knowing the clear answer.

"I think we can jump on that," said Adam with a grin. "So where do we begin?"

Giuseppe explained who they would be reporting to in the following days and suggested they meet with Scott and Deirdre for a closer look into the daily tasks of the Eyes. "Deirdre and Scott are two original members in the Eyes, so getting some good one-on-one time with them would benefit you, I believe. Azael Vargas will be your superior officer and will be training you as well. You'll meet him early tomorrow at about o seven hundred hours, so rest up once you can."

"Is it untactful to assume that you somehow knew we'd agree to this?"

asked Daven, catching on to Giuseppe's ulterior motives. "Considering the prescheduled meeting with our sergeant made before our conscription?"

Giuseppe laughed, clapping his hands together. "I have this uncanny ability to pinpoint whether two young men such as yourselves would willingly agree to join a secret and special task force to fight an absolute monarchy run by a psychotic!"

"You're a great judge of character," said Daven with a beaming smile. "I'm rather excited to show these monsters they can't run unimpeded through Italy anymore."

Hearing someone refer to the peninsula as Italy gave Giuseppe a smile. It had been so long and even he had begun calling his home Domus Aurea, but it carried him forward to a place in time when everything could be better, and that was enough to revitalize the fight within him, one that had been waning slowly over the years. "And so you will," he said softly and confidently.

Giuseppe left the men in order to take care of the paperwork involved with conscripting two men in a militant branch reserved for Catholics, but times were different, and any amount of help was needed and welcomed. Daven jumped out of bed and arched his back, popping the ligaments between his vertebrae and releasing what felt like weeks of built-up strain. "I've got to find something a little less revealing to wear," he said, pulling the two ends of his gown together.

"What's there to see?" asked Adam with a dry execution. "All you've got is that 'Made in Canada' tattoo and a flat run all the way to your ankles."

"Glad to know someone noticed," said Daven as he rummaged through some drawers next to his bed. "Well, this isn't much better …"

Adam looked over to see Daven holding up a plain white T-shirt and thin white pants. "Well, then, your options are escaped psych ward patient or escaped psych ward patient with nothing to hide."

"I'm going with modest psycho," Daven said as he pulled the paper-thin pants up. He had difficulties tearing the gown off, given the unbreakable knot tied around his back. "These things …" he said, struggling to move the looped lace over his head. "I could dock the *Titanic* with this knot."

"You could also house a bird and her eggs in the nest you call hair," Adam retorted, noticing how disheveled Daven's mop was.

"Am I not?" Daven said, patting the top of his head with a confused look on his face. "I swear I had a family of blue jays living up there."

"Ah, so you were going full Radagast," Adam said, referencing a character from Daven's favorite legendarium.

Daven smiled as he remembered how content and happy he was whenever he read his favorite books. He was always able to fully immerse himself into any good story, allowing it to take hold of his spirit and transporting him somewhere that was better than the life he was leading. Now it felt like he had been cast into a horror story, and he was the next character to suffer at the hands of the monster creeping through its pages. After grabbing the clothing he had been wearing the night of his accident, he shot up the stairs to his room to find something a little less attention-grabbing to wear.

Adam walked outside to get some fresh air and to wait for Daven to change clothes.

"Hey, man," said Scott, startling Adam as he stood by the doors.

"You scared me," Adam said, holding his chest, feeling his increased heart rate. "What are you doing standing all creepily over there?"

Scott laughed as he pulled a cigarette and lighter out of his pocket. "I have to hide when I do naughty things," he said, lighting the small white bundle of tobacco leaves.

"You mind?" asked Adam, not having had a cigarette since they were chased into Fiumicino.

Scott pulled another one out and lit it for Adam. "You know these things are bad for you," he said sarcastically.

"Your last name must be 'Obvious.' Scott Obvious, captain of Uriel's Eyes," said Adam with a long and satisfying draw of his cigarette.

"Captain Obvious I am," Scott said, stomping out the ashes of his finished roll. "But not of Uriel's Eyes. That honor is reserved for Azael Vargas."

Adam smiled, knowing there was someone else who understood his sense of humor. "Yeah, we're meeting with Azael tomorrow—Daven and I, that is."

"Why's that?" asked Scott, lighting another cigarette.

"Giuseppe got Daven and me to join your group," he said, savoring the taste of the burning leaves, enjoying the smooth hot ash filling his lungs. "Said it would probably keep us from getting ourselves killed."

"Yeah, I heard about your tour through the city last night," said Scott, slightly impressed by the fearless gall of the two men. "You've got some balls, I'll give you that."

"Giuseppe doesn't share the same point of view as yourself," Adam said. "Which is why he conscripted us in the first place. To keep us from killing ourselves."

"Ah. If you want to kill yourself, you'll do it. Under Giuseppe's watch or not," Scott said, understanding the nature of the men's inspiration to fight. "I am sorry about your friends," he said, meaning well. "Life isn't fair. Never has been. I know you didn't see what happened to the Fortunas, but sometimes that's worse. Your mind creates these horrible images to fill in the missing spaces of your memory. I respect your desire to make these men pay for their inhumanity. I can also empathize with that desire. Just be successful at whatever you're planning. Don't negate their sacrifice, and rest assured knowing that your faces were the last things they saw. You and Daven. I know they loved you. I didn't know them, but I know they loved you. Dying for your friends. There's no greater love, right?"

Adam was surprised with Scott's display of brotherly advice and caring words. He couldn't speak, as he was trying to mask his shaky voice and watering eyes, but Scott wasn't a stranger to emotion, and he wasn't one to ignore it either. "You're going to have to learn that holding it in isn't going to help. It's going to come out one way or another. Either it'll be now when you're around friends or when you're trying to protect them. You choose when that is."

Adam couldn't hold back at that point. He hadn't been able to completely mourn for Abele and Eula, and so he fell to his knees and wept bitterly. His body shook uncontrollably, and his legs lost their ability to stand. His tears were hot, and his face tightened into a contorted look of complete sorrow. Adam could feel Scott's firm hand grip his shoulder, and as he looked beside him, he could see that the man had crouched down with him. He heard the door behind him open and knew it was Daven. His friend collapsed beside him and embraced him, joining his sorrow with his own tears. They were friends, but more than that, they were brothers. Brothers who were joined by a common loss and a desire to right wrongs.

They were finally allowing the fire burning within them to break the surface of their skin and show outwardly. Instead of hiding their loss and faking a strong exterior, the two crouched next to each other, heads leaned together, and allowed grief its day in the sun.

It wasn't a short affair. The two men weren't just mourning Abele and Eula. They mourned for Jean, a man who made a brief appearance in their lives to get them home and lost his life drawing the attention of the enemy away to buy Daven and Adam more time to escape. A sacrifice they felt they didn't deserve. They also mourned for Lorenzo, a man they knew they would never see again, but one who risked his life just by giving them a purpose. Strangely enough, they also mourned for the five men who had died by their hands. Five men who would still be breathing if not for Daven and Adam. Five men who might have changed their ways if given an opportunity but now lay breathless and still under the weeping eyes of those who loved them.

Daven finally wandered off by himself to find a place where he could think and be alone. He settled on a patch of grass by the Eagle Fountain, lying on his back to stare into the blue through hanging branches of the trees above. The clouds slowly panned across the sky, passing like time, unaware of the struggles of men and careless of their conflicts. Daven could swear he felt the earth rotating beneath him, taking him through night and day, around the sun, through the galaxy and the universe. No matter what he did, nothing could stop him from being wherever he ended up. Life played out as it would, with or without his approval. Even if he lay where he was and never moved, he would be where the universe took him whether he fought it or not.

It felt as if time was moving slower around him. Perhaps it was because he had time to take everything in, and that ability added to his perception of life, a way of stopping and smelling the roses. In that moment of time, life was beautiful. He wasn't sure if it was due to recent experiences that allowed him a clearer look into this realization, but he was where he was for a reason, and whatever that could have been, it didn't matter. He shut his eyes and inhaled deeply, letting the sounds and smells of that moment consume him.

The darkness behind his closed eyelids began to shape into the images of his imagination. He saw his mother's face, smiling and loving, full of pride and ideations that her son could do no wrong. Convinced that he was the most talented man she had ever laid eyes on, perfect and with unlimited potential. From the first moment she held him began a love that would never diminish, and whenever he visualized her face in his mind, he knew that all she saw was her baby, forever and always.

He remembered his father. The strongest man he had ever known and a superhero in whom no weakness could reside. But to his son he reserved a drawn veil, which when pulled away revealed an image of a diamond full of emotional facets, unhidden and fully expressed, teaching his boy that a man is not ashamed of showing love, joy, and sorrow and that a good father shows these unabashedly and liberally.

Daven loved his family beyond words. The day he left for school, he was embraced by proud parents but parents who found it difficult to let him go. He would never forget how it felt to be so loved, and that feeling was the last thing he had associated with them. He didn't know if he would experience those feelings again, but if he did, it would be the one contributing factor that saved his life in a world so cruel. The faces of his parents, and those of Eula and Abele, painted his mind and were always there to greet him when he needed them.

He opened his eyes again and was pleasantly surprised with the face of a beautiful woman staring down at him. "What are you thinking about?" asked Deirdre, her hair hanging down the sides of her head, blocking out the sun.

"Philosophy, the mysteries of the universe, what I'm going to eat later," responded Daven, short and to the point.

"You know, for as smart as you make yourself out to be, you sure do some stupid things," she said, moving to lie down beside him, trying to hide her obvious dismay.

"What was I supposed to do?" he asked her, vaguely seeking her approval. "These monsters killed two people I loved in a horrific public display of violence. They didn't deserve anything less."

Deirdre understood why Daven viewed his brand of justice the way he did, but she also knew how self-destructive it could be, and she cared too much to see him fall into the bottomless pit of never feeling completely satiated, leading a life of vigilantism until the day he died. "You're not the only person who's experienced loss, Daven," she said, tiptoeing around how she truly felt. "I had a situation arise not long ago to avenge someone I loved beyond words. But instead of letting my baser instincts take hold, I took a path that I have yet to regret."

"So are you saying that I fell to my baser instincts?" asked Daven, feeling slightly rebuked by Deirdre.

"What do you think happened?" she asked very carefully, feeling nervous about pushing Daven away.

He sat up and rested his arms on his knees. "I'm a stubborn man, Deirdre," he said, looking at the fountain in front of him. "But I can't argue with you. I killed a man with my bare hands. Plus I got shot. I'm clearly heading down a bad road."

Deirdre bolted up with a shocked look on her face. "You got shot?" she yelled with angered confusion. "Shouldn't you be in bed? Or in the hospital?"

"You would think so, right?" he said while rolling up his pant leg. "But there's something odd going on around here." He began explaining everything that had happened since last night, sparing no details in order to portray just how unbelievable his words actually were. Deirdre was pleasantly accepting of Daven's far-fetched point of view. She had no reason not to believe him given the number of witnesses involved and the reliability each of those individuals was known to possess.

"Healed or not, you could have been killed, Daven," she said, still upset by his brazen disregard for fate. "Where would Adam be if you had died?" she said with increased castigation. "He would be alone, with no one to relate to. We may be the good guys in this fight, but we are still strangers no matter how you spin it."

"I wasn't the only one to step into dangerous waters, Deirdre," Daven said as he stood up to walk away. "Adam was there with me, and he's just as guilty of diving in without testing the water as I am."

Deirdre jumped to her feet, walking after Daven. "But I'm talking to you right now," she said, pointing a sharp finger at him. "And Adam came out unscathed. Not you!"

"Because I saved his life!" Daven said, spinning around, wide eyed and tired of being reprimanded. "And why does it matter to you? You don't even know me!"

Deirdre was taken aback by his unfiltered words. "I care because you're a human being. One who wants to fight for a better world, and one who will go to any length to see that happen. And maybe I care because I see you as someone who could actually succeed in doing that."

"Deirdre ..." he said, realizing the hurtful nature of his words.

"No," she said, slowly walking away. "If your intentions are to burn up on some self-righteous crusade, then leave me out of it. I'm not losing someone else, and I'm not falling for another martyr."

Daven wasn't sure what she meant by her words, only that she viewed him as a suicidal fool bent on revenge. As much as he wanted to disagree with her, it was a painfully accurate description of his intentions. He saw no boundaries to his holy war, and it didn't leave room for any more loss. Unfortunately, it could potentially destroy the affections of those who wished to become closer to him. How many more lives would he directly or indirectly destroy on his mission to rid the world of evil, he asked himself. If it cost him the love of others, was it really worth it?

He watched as the redheaded woman walked farther and farther away. It was the first time he had seen the fiery personality associated with women of her ilk, but it was a logical reaction to men like him who stampeded through life, not caring who crossed his path. He wanted to reach out to her and apologize for his harmful words, but Daven was prideful and couldn't bear the path of passiveness. Instead, he fell slowly backward, landing softly on the thick grass below him. He closed his eyes again, waiting for the faces of those he loved to reappear, but instead of his parents', the Fortunas', or even Adam's, it was only Deirdre's, her smile calming his angered soul, and eyes he could lose himself in for hours.

CHAPTER 10

AN INVESTMENT

September 20, 2035

G iuseppe and Azael Vargas made their way to the shooting range in the Milvian Guard Barracks. Morreti had spoken to Azael about Daven and Adam's situation and made sure that the sergeant was willing and able to take on new recruits. "I'm willing to take on any recruits you have for me," Azael said with excitement. "In fact, I've heard much about them already. They seem to be adept at surviving in these dark times."

"They are indeed," Giuseppe said, feeling a small amount of pride for their discovery. "Their exploits are one for the books."

"Anyone who can take down multiple Aurean soldiers empty-handed either has an unnatural amount of luck on their side or Michael the Archangel himself as a guardian," Azael said, eager to meet the two boys.

Giuseppe was disappointed to hear that Daven and Adam's run-in with the Aureans was now seemingly common knowledge, but he wasn't at all surprised to see how much had slipped outside of the few men he had told. "That is true, but it wasn't at all due to a warrior's instinct."

"Maybe it was," said Azael without missing a beat. "Admit it. You wouldn't be showing them to me if you didn't already think so."

Giuseppe shook his head and grinned. "Perhaps not. I concede to your point of view," he said with a slight bow.

As they made their way down the long corridor leading to the armory, they were pleasantly surprised to see Daven and Adam already waiting for their day of training. Giuseppe introduced the three men and made his way back to his office.

Azael began the training with firearms, a Glock 17 9mm, the standard-issue weapon for the Vatican Gendarmerie. Neither Daven nor Adam were familiar with any kind of weapon, which added to their already strained nerves. Both men held the gun far from their bodies, pointing the barrel toward the ground, their index fingers wrapped beneath the trigger guard.

Once Azael spent some time showing the men how the weapon worked and how to properly maintain it, he led them to the firing range to familiarize them with gun safety and, finally, how to utilize the gun.

He positioned the men within their own ranges and placed their targets at a distance well suited to their beginner's skill level. The two men couldn't help but grin with reined-in excitement, and so they lifted their pistols and emptied their clips hurriedly and blindly.

Azael's vision was sorely lacking with his age, so he was unable to properly gauge the men's accuracy until he had their targets right in front of his eyes. "Go easy on us," Adam said as Azael inspected their shots. "I'm pretty sure I kept my eyes closed the whole time."

"Well …" Azael said with calm surprise, "this may be the absolute best example of beginner's luck I have ever seen." He flipped the large sheets of paper to show the men the product of their handiwork. Each man had a tightly packed bunch of holes directly within the center of each target. They were as much amazed as Azael but laughed it off as a ridiculous circumstance and one that could not be replicated.

Azael hooked another two targets up and moved them just a small distance farther than the previous two. "Okay, guys, try to keep your eyes open this time around," he said with a smile. The men emptied their clips once again and pulled the posters back to again assess their accuracy. This time around, Azael was less humored by what he saw and more amazed. The same instance had occurred, and he was confused, impressed, and speechless. "Your eyes were still closed," he said, still trying to understand what was going on.

"I can't help it," said Daven, both embarrassed and prideful. "I guess it's a nervous twitch."

"Me too," said Adam, agreeing with Daven. "I don't know why, but I can't help it either."

Azael sat for a moment rubbing his chin. "I think I might have a way to make things a little more difficult for you." He then brought the men to a reactive gun range, complete with randomized popup targets set on individual tracks.

"So how does this work?" asked Adam, unfamiliar with the setup.

"Don't shoot the good guys," Azael said vaguely. He flipped a switch beginning a countdown and stepped back to observe. From his point of view, it seemed as if he was watching two skilled shooters taking down every target with extreme accuracy and dexterity. It was unreal to him, and he was beginning to wonder if these men were everything they claimed to be.

From Daven's and Adam's point of view, it was a very different picture than what Azael could see, and a strange one at that. The two men were honest when they told him that their shut eyes were simply an unavoidable reaction, but it was a misleading honesty. Their eyes may have been closed, but their vision was still sharp and clear. They couldn't quite explain it to even themselves, but it was as if their physically veiled eyes opened a gateway to new sight, with heightened senses and reaction time. By every definition, Daven and Adam could see but through eyes not of their own. This was the third mystery added to their repertoire of strange occurrences, alongside their shared vision and Daven's expedient healing, but mysteries were tedious things, and answers would be less stressful.

"I think it's time for an upgrade," Azael said, taking the pistols away from them. He returned with two Heckler & Koch MP5 submachine guns and two Carbon 15 carbines. He wasn't gathering weapons to merely challenge the two but rather to observe and be entertained by how unnaturally efficient they both were. He wasn't let down, either, and was astonished by how these men could do what they were doing with their eyes closed. Eventually, Azael brought every weapon in the guard's armory to the men and called Giuseppe in to see for himself.

As the Crown of the Guard watched in awe, he likened the display to a well-choreographed dance, devoid of fault and error. This went on for a good half hour, but soon, Daven and Adam became winded and needed a break. "After what I just watched, I wouldn't think you two needed a breather," said Giuseppe.

"It didn't even look like you two had to try," Azael said with his arms crossed, laughing.

"I've been walking for years now, but after a while, even that gets tiring," Adam said, short of breath. "I'm going outside for a minute."

Daven sat back for a moment, hanging his pistol from his fingers, his mind wandering. He had always seen people using firearms through vicarious eyes, but he was learning to operate these properly in order to protect himself or take lives. He wasn't sure why it was nagging at him so much considering the lengths he had previously gone to to protect his friends or even himself before. In those moments, he didn't have time to think. He acted out of instinct and did what needed to be done to survive. Now, as he reflected on his past slayings, it ate away at his core. The looks on their faces haunted him, looks of fear and silent bargaining. At those moments in time, he only saw them as soulless enemies, nothing more. To him now, they were people and people with lives that were ended at his hand.

"Daven," said Giuseppe as he sat down across from him, noticing the man's forlorn look, "what's on your mind, son?"

Daven smiled, still looking at his weapon. "I've experienced things that any number of people would never see in their lifetime. Most of those instances I have processed and come to terms with. But killing … I can't wrap my mind around the gravity of taking someone's life. Not to mention how many I have murdered personally."

Giuseppe sat back and groaned from an aching back. "We are beings of free will, Daven. We make our mistakes, but there is always redemption. I won't lie and say that the horror of taking a life somehow recedes after a certain amount of time, but the memory soon quiets to a manageable level. It didn't take long for me to peg you as a spiritual individual. You just have to take advantage of the one thing that can redeem you, and time is the ultimate redeemer. That and God."

"Time may be the ultimate redeemer, but the mind is our greatest accuser. I am far from forgiveness at this point, Giuseppe," Daven said, still not looking up from his gun. "Not just from my God, but from those I have hurt, and gaining forgiveness from God's children is much more difficult."

"Who is it that needs to forgive you?" asked Giuseppe.

"A woman," Daven said as he finally lifted his eyes to look at Giuseppe.

Adam moved to the side of the barracks, out of sight from any wandering eyes. Scott had given him a small pack of cigarettes after their conversation the previous day. He pulled one out and lit it, then slid down the side of the building, hoping to calm his nerves. He shut his eyes, letting the smoke fill his lungs, relaxing him and soothing his mind.

"Maybe you're easier to talk to than your friend," said a familiar voice sneaking up on him.

"I need to tie a bell to you," said Adam, opening his eyes, startled out of his relaxation.

"Why are men so stubborn?" Deirdre asked, straight to the point, ignoring Adam's quip, still upset from her confrontation with Daven.

Adam sighed as he picked himself back up. He inhaled a long satisfying draw of his cigarette, prepping himself for a winless argument. "It's all we have since women are always right," he said with light sarcasm.

Deirdre wasn't a dim woman. She noticed Adam's playful jab, but she also realized that he wasn't the source of her anger. "You noticed that, eh?"

Adam wrapped his right arm around the woman's shoulders and hugged her like a brother would a sister. "You have to be patient with Daven," he said, well aware of her troubles with his friend. "We've only just found solace here. For three years, we lived in constant fear of bearing the brunt of Domus Aurea's wrath, and here recently, we did."

"It's not that I don't take that into consideration," she said. "But I don't understand the reckless response to that wrath."

Adam looked up, formulating a retort that would clearly explain their actions. "We didn't witness Abele and Eula's death, and we were left without closure. Scott helped me understand that point by saying it was worse not to see it happen. That our imaginations would violently fill in the blanks. He was right, and so when we heard those soldiers talking about their murders like they were remembering a good movie, they might as well have driven the nails in themselves. We acted rashly, I understand this, but I don't think it would have transpired any other way."

"I'm no stranger to loss either, Adam," Deirdre said, unconvinced. She had come to a realization that in order to properly convey her point of view, she would need to revisit a moment in her life she dreaded seeing again. "I watched someone I loved die in my arms. He bled to death while I sat there and did nothing but cry. I'm convinced my inability to act was the reason he died. Seeing that happen wasn't easier than not seeing it. It's there every time I close my eyes, Adam. It will never get better, no matter how much time passes."

Adam lowered his head. "I'm sorry; I didn't know."

"Don't apologize, Adam," she said, forcing a tearful smile. "I can't imagine what you two have gone through. The way the Fortunas' lives were so brutally ended and being on the run for so long. But nothing is harder than losing your reason for living. It's just how you approach your life afterward that matters."

"You're a wise woman," Adam said, yielding to her way of thinking. "It must be that red hair," he said with a wink.

"You think? I'd agree, but you're a redhead, and wisdom eludes you," she said.

"Such a comedian," Adam said, laughing while putting out his cigarette. "You know, Daven's lucky to have you in his life. Whether either of you see that yet or not."

"And what do you mean by that?" Deirdre asked, pretending to be ignorant toward his allusion.

"You're not fooling anyone, woman," Adam said, his back to her as he walked away. "Now if you'll excuse me, I have to go shoot things."

Deirdre watched as Adam walked around the corner and through the barracks doors. She hadn't really achieved what she imagined she would, like finding out how Daven's mind worked or how he truly felt about her, but it appeared that she had made her feelings fairly obvious. Adam seemed relatively sure about his assumptions, and Deirdre couldn't confirm or deny any of it given her undecided stance on the subject as it were. The thought of Adam's implication as being truth wasn't an unpleasant thought to her, but at the same time, she felt that rushing that thought into reality would be unpleasant and possibly dangerous.

Daven and Adam were still mysteries to her, walking into her world from the fog hanging heavily over Domus Aurea. These men weren't just war refugees, begging for asylum while cowering behind others. These men were hurricanes with angry and destructive power, focused on those who had wronged them, sparing no man who would stand against them, but there was much more behind the clouds of their storm. There was a still and dormant terror that waited, eyes closed and resting for the day when the clouds receded and the world would stand in support or cringe in fear.

Michael Dina and the members of his fire squad reached San Marino the same day after Daven and Adam's safe arrival in Vatican City. Lieutenant Colonel Dina's battalion of eight hundred men was spread out south of San Marino in Domus Aurea, mostly in Rome, and the second battalion of the same guard, led by Ciro Bucato, took the north. It was the only guard in the militia to be deployed outside of San Marino, while the Guard of the Rock and the Guard of the Council remained within the small country for defense purposes.

Michael had planned to bring the news of Ric's death to the man's family and return to Rome, but three days later, he sat behind a dumpster, bleeding from his shoulder and praying for a miracle. After reporting to Carlo Romano, the colonel and leading commander of the militia, Michael was made aware of a secret Aurean invasion that was moving into parishes of Sammarinese municipalities close to the border of Domus Aurea. The Le Marche Legion was slowly moving centuries into these parishes and building their numbers gradually. The government of San Marino was keeping the knowledge of the measured invasion quiet in order to move into a position of defense and to recall the Guard of the Phoenix back behind national borders.

It didn't work. Three days after arriving in his home country, Michael took a company of men to observe the municipality of Fiorentino after it was brought to their attention that an Aurean century had set up camp within Cerbaiola. Unfortunately, the century was well aware of Lieutenant Colonel Dina's arrival, and it was waiting.

Michael took a small group of men to wander the small parish incognito, blending in with the locals, looking for potential fortified structures, and gauging a potential reclamation of the small town. Unfortunately, the Sammarinese inhabitants of Cerbaiola had either been imprisoned or killed, making Michael's and his men's attempt at blending into the town's populace, impossible.

The century had placed their own men to walk the streets in plain clothes in order to divert the eyes of any militiamen who could be watching. The town had a small number of Sammarinese soldiers who kept watch, but the invading Aurean men were swift and intricate, cutting communication to the militia's higher-ups off completely and eventually killing every soldier there. The century watched and waited as Michael and his men wandered the streets, attempting to fool their enemies and acquire intelligence. Lieutenant Colonel Dina had reached a small building complex when he heard shots ring out just down the street. Before he had time to react, a bullet pierced his right shoulder, sending a burning pain through his collarbone and down his arm. He was quick and dodged several more shots before reaching a dumpster in between two buildings.

"Move in on all fronts!" he radioed to the remaining company, which was set up in the trees surrounding the town to the north. "All men on this frequency, move in on Cerbaiola!"

Michael could hear bullets pelting the walls of the large dumpster. The voices of his enemies grew louder and closer with every passing second. The pain in his shoulder was unbearable, and he was completely unable to move his right arm. His head was swimming and buzzing with a panic-inducing fight-or-flight instinct that he was incapable of responding to. Michael was sure that today would be the end of his life, so he decided that instead of cowering behind trash, he would instead throw himself into the skirmish and take out whom he could.

He collapsed to the ground and stuck his head around the corner of the green metal bin. He saw an Aurean soldier on top of a building adjacent to his position, one he assumed had been shooting at him but whose eyes were now diverted down the street to the south. Michael rolled onto his left side, grabbing his rifle. It was difficult for him the keep his crosshairs still because of his uncontrollable shaking, but he pulled the trigger and prayed.

The sound of gunpowder exploding in his ear caused his hearing to muffle and his eardrums to ring with a high-pitched scream. The back of his assailant's head burst open with a bloody haze, dropping him over the edge of the roof and down to the street below. Michael sank back, exhausted by the tiny amount of energy he exuded to give himself a few more minutes of life. Through his hazy vision, he saw a small group of Aurean soldiers retreating to the north, firing on an invisible enemy to the south. He wondered why their enemies were withdrawing on that particular route when his men were pressing into the town from the same direction.

"Lieutenant Colonel Dina!" crackled a voice over his radio. "Lieutenant Colonel Dina! Michael, come on, tell me you're there!"

Through blurry vision and a drifting mind, Michael grabbed his walkie-talkie and responded with slurred speech. "I'm here," he said as his consciousness faded, "in an alleyway off the main street." Michael's arm fell, and his radio dropped with a crack as he passed out from pain and blood loss. As his vision faded with black static, he could see the boots of an unknown number of men running to him and crouching down to take him to a field medic.

He woke after an unknown amount of time on a cot within a white tent. His shoulder had been hastily wrapped but well taken care of. It was obvious to him that the drip bag hooked into an IV was morphine, and he was extremely grateful for it. Michael was still foggy but interested in what had transpired since his blackout.

He stood up groggily, using his IV pole to lean on and to walk with, drawing back the entrance to his tent to look at a large camp. "Lieutenant Colonel Dina, you shouldn't be standing," said an unfamiliar field medic quickly walking toward his commanding officer. "Let's turn around and sit you back down."

"What happened?" asked Michael through half-closed eyes. "I just want to know what happened."

The medic sat Michael down on the stiff cot and began taking vitals. "I'm part of Captain Maroni's company. We got the word to head home from Rome two days ago."

"You're part of my battalion?" asked Michael, short of breath and barely conscious.

"I'd salute you sir, but my hands are a little busy right now," the medic said, changing out his morphine drip.

"So it was your company from the south?" asked Michael, seeing everything come together. "Where's the rest of the guard?"

"Colonel Romano split us into ten companies and sent us to every town close to the border. All those that were known to have Aurean soldiers stationed in them at least," the medic said, completing his tasks. "We had arrived earlier today and were just observing when we saw all hell break loose."

"Why weren't we informed that we were walking into an ambush?" asked Michael with quiet disgust. "Four of my men died because of that."

The medic could feel the tension rising in the tent. It wasn't his responsibility to command his company, but he still felt that it was his neck on the line. "We were commanded to remain radio silent within four miles of the border," he said, hoping to divert the blame from his captain. "Colonel Romano didn't want to alert the Aureans to our plans."

"Romano …" Michael said with disdain. Colonel Carlo Romano had been appointed as the commander of the San Marino Militia directly after his predecessor, Ermano Burrei, stepped down. Colonel Burrei devised a plan to infiltrate Rome in an attempt to rid Italy of Domus Aurea two years earlier, but when the militia marched on the capital, a mass murder of Sammarinese occurred instead, causing Burrei to step down and eventually take his own life. When the Captains Regent were choosing from the six lieutenant colonels of the different guards, Michael was made aware of Romano's likelihood to become the new colonel of the militia and was extremely vocal regarding his opposition.

Romano was an exceedingly reactive man, unable to formulate proper strategy that did not involve throwing soldiers into a burning fire. Regardless of Michael's efforts to bring these points to the attention of his superiors, Carlo, who was well aware of Dina's vocal disapproval, was promoted.

Colonel Romano's first act as the new commander was to send the Guard of the Phoenix, Michael's guard, throughout Domus Aurea, spread thin and barely able to defend themselves. Michael was certain that his obvious protests against Romano were what landed him into the situation he was in. He was also beginning to believe that the colonel was going to inhuman lengths to punish Michael for speaking his mind, especially after this most recent catastrophe.

"Find Captain Maroni and send him to me," Michael commanded the medic. "I feel some changes need to be made, and soon." He was finished with Carlo's thinly veiled attempts to rid himself of Michael's so-called insubordination. The colonel wasn't just putting Michael's life on the line, but that of every man under his command as well.

After a moment, Captain Maroni arrived, slinking into Michael's tent, nervous after being updated by the medic. He didn't speak but saluted and stood board straight in front of his commanding officer.

"At ease, Carmine," Michael said, rising from his bed. "There's no one to blame here."

Carmine looked at Michael and began speaking his mind. "Something needs to be done," said Carmine about Romano's homicidal tendencies. "Eventually he's going to succeed in getting what he wants, and we both know he won't stop there."

Michael made his way to the opening of the tent, motioning for Carmine to follow. "I guess I always thought that I could just fight him off alone, but four men died because of his belligerence. It started with me, but now it's gone too far."

"So what are we supposed to do?" asked Carmine. "I hate to say it, but a coup could mean even more lives lost."

"I know, but if nothing is done, then Romano could very well end up ruling San Marino with fear. Just like Nero does with Domus Aurea," Michael said, walking outside. "the Captains Regent are too scared to handle any kind of militant decision-making, and since the militia is the only thing standing between us and Nero, Romano has in a way been tenured."

"That seems to be true," Carmine said, sighing, "but even if it weren't, the fact remains that he is depended upon. By the very leaders of our nation. And—"

"The fact that he commands the entire militia?" asked Michael rhetorically, cutting Carmine short. "Can we be sure that he actually owns the loyalty of everyone below him?"

"Speaking for myself, there's no doubt in my mind that the man is psychotic," said Carmine with utmost certainty. "I just can't think of a way that it would work without someone becoming a martyr."

"Carmine, we are an army of martyrs," Michael said, pushing the opening to the morgue tent aside. "Some of us become them early on so the rest of us can keep moving forward."

Captain Maroni bowed his head to the four covered bodies. It sickened him to his core to know their deaths could have been easily avoided and even more so to know that a man who claimed to properly lead these men was responsible. "Tell me what to do," he said without looking away from his dead brothers-in-arms. "As far as I'm concerned, you are the only commander these men and this militia needs."

"I just want someone who will do right by their men," Michael said, still with an unbroken gaze focused on the dead men. "Someone who will constantly fear the consequences of their actions."

"I still believe that man should be you," said Carmine. "But this is a multistep process, and we've yet to begin."

Michael let the cloth partition close again and turned to look at the camp full of soldiers. "We start with one man," he said, speaking to Carmine while watching the movement around him. "Take your company and find Lieutenant Colonel Bucato. Don't speak to anyone about our conversation until you find him. I'll send you with a letter. Once he is informed, bring him here. If we can gain his support, then we'll have a regiment of support.

Carmine saluted his commander and began yelling out orders. Michael felt as if he had just been thrown bleeding into shark-infested waters, but he knew if he didn't act, he would be torn to shreds, attracting more carnivorous men to those who took the plunge with him.

"What's going on?" asked Salvador as he and Joseph walked toward their leader and friend. "Are we moving out?"

"Not us," Michael said, quickly walking to the medical tent. "We need to stay out of sight for the time being. Gather the company. We're going to execute one hell of a disappearing act."

CHAPTER 11

HIDING IN PLAIN SIGHT

September 23, 2035

Six men lay naked and unconscious inside an empty hotel room. The shades had been drawn, and the lights were off. Slowly each man woke, unaware of their location but calm and unafraid. Their minds were foggy, and each move they made sent their hearts beating through their chests. They were unable to speak to each other, but the desire to converse wasn't within them. Through their peripheral vision, they could see something moving, but the objects would disappear when looked at directly. The sounds of light breathing entered their ears, shaky with desire, yearning for warmth.

"The want for power is a convincing motivator," said a disembodied voice coming at them from all directions, "able to push a man over barriers he may never otherwise overcome. Not because of some physical inability, but because of the deplorable deeds he may have originally found too shocking to act out."

A dim white glow entered from above the six men's heads. It shone down from above their prostrate bodies, gradually intensifying as if the source of this light were approaching from afar down a long dark road. "Humanity is a disgusting breed, one that I would rather see purged by fire off the face of the earth, but you also shine brightly, if only quickly, and that burning power within you is something I envy."

The men remained docile and fearless while the voice continued speaking. Suddenly, six faces peeked in at them from the direction of the white light. Its source was the eyes of six women with sharp features, bleached-white hair, and translucent skin. They were female lilim, and the male voice speaking to the men was Charles. "Our kind is dying. Dwindling away with the absence of our mother. Breeding with one another in a disgusting and incestuous act, deluding our bloodline and destroying our legacy."

"S-succubus," stuttered one of the men, becoming more aware of his surroundings.

"Ah. An accurate, if not overly superstitious, title," Charles said, moving out of the darkness and standing at the foot of the six men. "Your life, if harnessed properly, can and will create a power that will burn away the imperfections of the earth. As appalling as joining our likenesses is to me, I must look past my own opinion and look forward to my people's survival. I will control an army so terrifying that I will be able to choke the location of my mother's whereabouts from my enemy's last breath with ease. All because power is a convincing motivator."

The six lilim moved around to straddle the six men. Their naked bodies seemed to glow with an eerie white color, blue veins flowing like rivers over their perfect forms. They were long beings, taller than any normal man, with their straight white hair flowing down past their knees. "We thirst," each lilim said in unison. "Satiate our barren bodies and breathe new life within us." Slowly they crouched down over the men, breathing in their souls' light and wringing them out like a wet sponge. In the end, the succubi rose up from the remaining husks of the six men, the lilim's cores glowing bright and swelling with unnatural life.

"Burn them," Charles said to three lilim who had just walked into the hotel room. "It won't take much. Their bodies will burn like dry leaves at this point."

The lilim grabbed the remains of the six men, each lilim hoisting one under each arm. The bodies were stiff and mummified, weighing hardly anything and easily lifted by the lilim's unnatural strength. "What will they be?" one of the lilim asked Charles.

Charles sat for a moment, thinking about one of the men associating the lilim with a succubus. "In mythology, an incubus breeding with a human woman begot a cambion. Half human, half demon." He then looked at the six lilim, all of which were swelling with gestation at a rapid rate. "These life-bearers aren't myths, but we can adopt the name. It's fitting."

"Cambions," the lilim said. "Wasn't Merlin said to be one?"

"These monsters we're creating will not be named," Charles said sternly. "Lilith named us out of love. These things will only be used to wreak havoc. Nothing less. No names."

The three lilim bowed with respect and continued carrying out the dry human remains. Charles looked at the six lilim and then at their stomachs. "I don't know your names," he said to the lilim in front of him. "I need to know. I need to be able to separate you from these things you carry. You're still children of our mother. No matter what festers inside you."

One of the six stepped forward, cradling her round womb. "This is Yishai, Llyn, Lautium, Cĕolsige, and Hilera," she said, going down the line behind her, "and I am Tŭnash. The eldest of those before you. You refer to yourself as Charles, but that is not your name. What did our mother name you? I know it. But do you remember?"

"Not until I see her again," he said to Tŭnash, distance in his eyes. "Not until I hear her call me by my name will I utter it."

"Then we are the succubi until then as well," she said, moving back into the line of her sisters. "Our army is growing. Find us more."

October 15, 2035

Daven stood below the baldachin after almost a month of training for the Eyes. He was alone, as he normally was, but this time was different. He peered down into the grottoes searching for his courage. The grottoes terrified him still, and he couldn't figure out why that fear still remained. It wasn't because of their synonymous nature with death, and it wasn't the feelings of absolute loneliness that crept up his neck whenever he was near it that scared him. In fact, the grottoes weren't the issue at all. It was what lay below them that gave Daven feelings of panic and anxiety. Something dwelt within the halls of the necropolis, not living, not dead, something heavy with menace. Today, though, Daven was determined to find the source of his fear and to confront it.

Adam and he had learned a lot about themselves over the course of their training regimen. Strange things that didn't make natural sense, but things that had been witnessed and were continually seen even though they defied reality. Their talents were not acquired in the normal sense. They seemed to have always been with the men, unseen and lurking, waiting to be brushed off and scrubbed clean. These abilities had instilled in Daven a sense of elevated bravery, and he was testing that newfound courage by overcoming what he thought to be an irrational fear.

He made his way down to the grottoes and then to the necropolis below them. He had studied the ancient Roman tombs and knew their names and to whom they belonged. Daven felt that being familiar with his surroundings might make it easier on him when he made the jaunt into the ancient underground below the basilica.

Daven felt a strong pull to a certain mausoleum near the bottom of Saint Peter's Tomb, one that took control of his body and mind, calming him to his surroundings. It was as if his fear and the source of the attraction to his destination were fighting one another, and the attraction was winning. He stopped in front of the mausoleum named Lucifer, painted with an image named Light Bearer within it, its namesake, tilting his head slowly to look in. "It's about time you grew some balls," said an eerily familiar voice from within.

Daven walked in, slowly, looking for the man whose voice he'd heard. Suddenly, to his right, the culprit sat looking at him as if Daven had stumbled into his home. However, the presence of the man himself wasn't the issue; it was the mirrorlike resemblance of himself, like looking into his own eyes, that shocked him.

"I was wondering if you'd ever show up," Daven's doppelganger said, smiling.

Daven stuck his hand out, hoping to feel glass on his fingertips, but there was none, and the only thing he felt was the skin of the man in front of him. "Who are you?" he asked.

"Are you really all that surprised?" asked the man. "You've seen stranger things before me. That was the point. To make seeing me now a little bit easier to understand."

"Strange things are always strange," Daven said, still ill at ease. "But I guess this isn't anything new."

The man smiled, still sitting. "I'll make it a little easier for you then. I'm Sansenoy. Pleasure to meet you on this plane of existence."

Daven rubbed his face and grinned in disbelief. "Is this some kind of joke?"

"If I were joking," Sansenoy said, ignoring Daven's disbelief, "I'd be laughing. I laugh at my own jokes."

Daven rubbed the temples of his skull. "How am I supposed to believe that you're Sansenoy?" he asked.

"Do you have a twin, Daven? Or do you have a tendency to ask yourself questions while staring into a mirror?" asked Sansenoy, increasingly irritated. "Here I am trying to make it easy on you to understand what's going on, but you're a little dense, if I do say so myself. I could always go the normal angel route and come up with something horrifying. Would that help?"

Daven settled down and finally began coming to terms with the obvious supernatural event going on before him. "I never expected angels to be so short-fused," he said after both individuals relaxed.

"You call this short-fused?" Sansenoy laughed. "Have you read Genesis? Sodom and Gomorrah?"

"Don't tell me that was you too," Daven said, feeling comfortable now to have a down-to-earth conversation with his angelic counterpart.

Sansenoy looked away with humbled diversion. "Yeah, it was," the angel said quietly. "And I was only doing what I was told, so temperament wasn't a factor. But it's a good example of what we're capable of."

"No kidding," Daven said, beginning to feel the proper level of amazement for what was going on. "So why come to me now? Why contact us in a dream, only to come to me physically now?"

"The dream got your attention," Sansenoy said. "But now is a time for conversation." He then stood up and walked to the center of the small space and looked around him. "There is something here, in this place, that should be protected and has been protected for over a century."

"Are you going to tell me where it's at?" asked Daven, waiting to be included in the age-old secret.

"No," said Sansenoy without hesitation. "You only need to watch this place and guard it. Eventually you will learn, but you have enough to handle at the moment."

"So what do I do now?" asked Daven, looking around the stone room.

"Let the current take you," Sansenoy said from an invisible location. Daven looked around trying to find the angel, but he had vanished without a trace. Daven again sensed the overwhelming feeling of doom with the absence of his guardian angel, as he had affectionately named him. Daven felt eyes crawling over his skin, unknown entities standing behind him, disappearing whenever he would turn to confront them. He skidded with haste out of the city of the dead and back to the floors of the basilica. Once he reached the open stairwell, he could hear someone quickly walking from above and then peeking over the railing down at him.

"Either you completely forgot about me, or you're the stubbornest person I've ever met," said Deirdre as Daven made his way up.

"There's no forgetting you," Daven said, smiling. "But stubbornness isn't a trait reserved only for men."

"Oh, I know," Deirdre said as she opened the small gate at the top of the grotto stairs. "I just wanted you to say it before me."

Daven walked through the opening and stood in front of the woman. "I'm sorry, Deirdre," he said without breaking his gaze. "You were right to be angry. Adam and I acted rashly and hastily. All we wanted was to make sure Abele and Eula were okay, but when we heard what we heard, I didn't even think twice."

"Daven ..." she said, trying to speak her mind, having come to him to apologize as well.

"Not done," he interrupted. "I promise you I'll never be so careless again. But I am not done punishing the heartless, and even though I won't use my new position in the Eyes to go on a murderous rampage, I'm not holding back either."

"I wouldn't imagine I could tell you how to live your life, Daven," she said, sounding marginally disappointed. "But what could possibly keep you reined in?"

Daven looked into Deirdre's face. "You, maybe?" he said after a moment of delay.

"I need to tell you, before anything else, how … terrified I am," she began, about to break down one barrier standing in her way to happiness, but she was cut off before she could delve into the painful recesses of her mind.

"Hey!" yelled Adam from the nave. He looked like a tiny insect superimposed on the giant structure behind him. Deirdre gave a long and irritated sigh, as her rehearsed speech to Daven had been interrupted. "Sorry, guys, but Giuseppe wants us in his office. We might be going out into the city soon."

Daven and Deirdre looked at each other, briefly protesting the command in their heads. The two hadn't spoken much in the last month, given Daven's strict training schedule and both individuals' obstinacy after their argument. Yet the two had been in each other's thoughts and dreams since the beginning, their feelings for one another growing with each day. Both were hesitant and scared to allow each other a closer relationship. In their minds, the more they loved someone, the more likely they were to lose that person.

Daven, Deirdre, and Adam were the last three to arrive to Giuseppe's office. Azael, Scott, and Marco, along with the remaining two members of the Eyes, Sergio Monti and Liana Belluzzi, both of whom had been in Rome for the past two weeks watching the hotel for signs of interest, were already there.

"Now that everyone is here, Liana, Sergio, you have the floor," said Giuseppe, sitting back in his chair as the man and woman in front faced the Eyes.

"For the past two weeks, Sergio and I have been keeping an eye on the Hotel San Pietro on the corner of Via Anastasio II and Via Pietro De Cristofaro."

"Pun!" yelled Marco.

"W-what?" said Liana, caught off guard.

"You said keeping an eye …" said Sergio, leaning in to explain.

Liana stared at Marco for a short but awkward amount of time and then continued. "Anyway, while we were watching, a man whom we have identified as Felice Savoca made frequent and routine trips to the hotel.

Each time, we were able to listen in to him conversing with an unidentified man who never appeared to leave the premises."

"I have transcribed for you here the main points outlined during each conversation," said Sergio, handing individual binders to the members around him. "There's a similarity linking everything we heard during our stint, and it's not good. It turns out that this Savoca fellow is a mediator for Mister Nero, and it looks like Nero is in league with whoever has made his home in the hotel."

"Do we know what they're planning?" asked Scott, skimming through the transcript.

"Seems like an alliance of some sort, but who the other half is, I'm not sure," said Liana. "They were careful when they spoke, almost as if they knew we were listening. We still don't know who Savoca has been meeting with."

"So why are we getting involved?" asked Deirdre. "Nero can form alliances left and right if he wants, but we're protected, in a sense."

Sergio sat back on Giuseppe's desk, nervous about what he was going to say. "We're getting involved because the word *Vatican* came up a total of over two hundred times in their conversations. Not in a good way."

Everyone's hearts in the room dropped. They began reading the instances Sergio had mentioned and were fearful of what was said. "Well, this is a change of luck," said Marco.

"Or misfortune," said Scott, tossing the transcript behind his back. "So what do we do? What can we do? I knew our watchful peace wasn't going to last, but this looks to be unstoppable."

Giuseppe stood up and walked around to the front of his desk, standing between Sergio and Liana. "We don't lose hope. Believe it or not, we have more to us than our enemy would like to believe. More to us than they would ever expect."

Azael moved to the center of the room. "I am sending a team of five operatives into the city tonight. Myself included. We will infiltrate the hotel, apprehend the two men involved, and acquire what knowledge we can."

"Why tonight? Why so quickly?" asked Deirdre with unease, nervous to jump into action with so little information under their belts.

"Felice and the unknown man agreed to meet tonight. Even going so far as to mention that this would be the last time they would meet for a considerable length of time," said Azael.

"This smells, looks, and feels like a trap," said Marco, closing his binder and adjusting his shoulders.

"That's exactly what it is," said Giuseppe, not hiding the truth. "But I have faith in your abilities. If I didn't, I would never consider this option."

"So who will be going?" asked Marco, eager to hear the roster.

Azael stood straight and placed his arms behind his back. "I will be leading the mission tonight. Under me will be Scott Farrell, Liana Belluzzi, Adam Gilmour, and Daven Jones. The rest of you will remain here to help in the interrogation of whomever we bring back to Vatican grounds."

No one in the room reacted to Azael's roll call. All were rigid, standing in stunned silence. Daven and Adam had only just completed their training, and yet Azael felt comfortable enough to allow these two greenhorns the opportunity to watch his back. "Dismissed," said Azael, seemingly unwilling to explain his choices.

Deirdre was furious with Azael. She wasn't about to let the decision go unattested, but she waited for her fellow Eyes to dismiss themselves before cutting into her superior officer. "You cannot be serious!" she yelled once the last soldier left the room. "Daven and Adam? Are you moronic? They don't have the experience! Are you punishing me for something? What did I do? Why am I not standing behind you? Why are you doing this to me?"

Azael was not angry with the woman and had known his decision would cause strife between himself and Deirdre. "It was not an easy decision," he said, lightly grabbing her wrists and holding her still. "But it was one that I could not avoid. Daven and Adam are unnaturally gifted in their abilities, and I need people on this mission whom I have seen in action."

"But why not me?" she kept asking over and over again, tearing up out of feelings of betrayal.

"It would have been you," Azael said softly, trying to calm her down. "But I've been informed of the feelings you have for Daven, and I couldn't risk that distraction on the field."

"There's nothing there!" she said sternly. "Daven is just another boy added to the long list of people I tolerate in this city." She turned around and stormed out but was quickly hindered by Daven, standing before her with a look of hurt and melancholy in his eyes. Then she watched him turn and walk away without a word spoken. She turned around once again and looked at Azael. "I'm sorry," she said with an expressionless face. "I can't be here right now."

"Deirdre," Azael called out as she turned and quickly walked to her quarters, silent and disparaging.

That night, the members of Uriel's Eyes met in the Apostolic Palace, along with Pope Innocent and all the high-ranking cardinals within the city. The five Eyes who were entering the city knelt in front of Innocent and the long line of robed cardinal priests, waiting for the pope's blessing.

"Does this feel weird to you?" whispered Daven to Adam.

"Just shut up and do it," Adam harshly whispered back.

"Almighty and eternal God," Innocent began praying, "those who take refuge in you will be glad and forever will shout for joy. Protect these soldiers as they discharge their duties. Protect them with the shield of your strength and keep them safe from all evil and harm. May the power of your love enable them to return home in safety, that with all who love them, they may ever praise you for your loving care. We ask this through Christ our Lord."

"Amen," said everyone in unison, except for Daven and Adam, who fumbled the rhythm.

"Wow," said Adam quietly to Daven. "We're not Catholic, but we are Christian. We know how to end a prayer."

"Yeah, I don't know what happened there."

The men and one woman rose from their kneeling stance and shook Innocent's hand.

Alban stood in the background, looking especially irritated at the informal farewell.

"Your Eminence," said two voices from his side.

He looked over to see Daven and Adam standing side by side, smiling at him. "Good to see you finally learned some manners," he said, unimpressed.

"You're right," laughed Daven. "Now we're just waiting on you," he said with an exasperated grin.

Alban grimaced in disgust. He wouldn't tolerate insolence, especially being a man of his stature. "One day your blatant disrespect will find you out. As far as I'm concerned, you two have no place here," he said, facing the two men. "You do not know the meaning of veneration, and because of this, you will never belong."

Adam displayed a meager smirk and crossed his arms. "You see that man over there?" he said, tilting his head in the direction of Pope Innocent. "Since the first day I met him, he earned my respect and Daven's as well. Not because he demanded it, but because he is a respectable man. He's kind, compassionate, friendly, and down to earth. I can approach him and not feel like a burden. And you know what? He's the pope. No, we're not Catholic, but that doesn't matter. I feel compelled to respect him because he is a good man."

"You, on the other hand," said Daven, taking over, "couldn't gain the respect of a brainless pile of dog crap. We came over here to try being civil with you, even going as far as bending to your demands for titular reverence, but instead of noticing that, you continue being miserable and unbearably immature." Daven turned around and walked away, unwilling to give Alban any more of his time.

"He's right, you know," Adam said, watching his friend walk away. "He may have said it in an untactful manner, but he's right. I hope one day you can get past your hatred and learn to relax."

Alban's familiar red face was beginning to show itself once more. The rising searing fire of his angered words welled up in his core, ready to explode. However, before he was able to speak, Camillo moved in front of him. "Enough, Alban," he said quietly but forcefully. "I heard everything, and I am tired of your embarrassing actions." Alban attempted to defend himself but was immediately cut off by an index finger in his face. "You did not become who you were for respect. Because if that was the case, you would be failing miserably. Do you want the respect you feel you are owed?"

"Yes. Yes, I do," Alban said calmly and quietly.

"Then follow me," Camillo said, looking around with a shady countenance.

The Eyes all made their way to the armory room of the barracks. The five soldiers moving into the city later that night began arming themselves and changing into their uniforms. The dress was typical of urban warfare, black and lined with pockets. Their knees and elbows were strapped with protective pads, and they wore open-fingertipped gloves. Each soldier was fitted with a netted black hood, unrestrictive of their peripheral vision, with a white mask, devoid of expression, fitted with glass lenses, programmed with tactical vision. Its primary purpose was to appear inhuman, emotionless, and unnerving.

A tactical vest was draped over their clothing, fitted for submachine and pistol magazines. The soldiers were carrying Heckler & Koch MP5 submachine guns and Beretta M12 pistols into battle with them, compact and easy to maneuver around corners. Once everyone was outfitted, Giuseppe stood against the blue lockers, the reconnaissance team to his left and the investigative team to his right. "Tonight is straightforward. Carefully move in, extract, and move out. Hostility must be avoided at all costs. Once our captives are safely back in the Vatican, our investigative team will acquire whatever information they can. The safety of our home is at stake, so these men should never be made aware of their whereabouts or who we are. Are we all on the same page?" After a resounding "Yes, sir," Giuseppe dismissed those in attendance and left Azael to finish up.

"We move out in ten," he said, short and to the point.

Deirdre sat in a distant corner. She was feeling especially horrible after her outburst earlier that day and couldn't bring herself to speak to either Azael or Daven, even though she feared for the men and wanted to wish them well. Deirdre hoped to catch their eye in a passing glance, but Azael was too engrossed with preparations, and Daven was making it a point to avoid her.

"Deirdre," said Liana, walking to her female colleague, sensing her distress, "I hope you're not upset with my being chosen over you," she said, fearing derision from her. "It didn't have anything to do with our skill level. Just luck of the draw, I think."

Deirdre pulled herself out of her sulking state of mind. "Of course not, Liana," she said with a genuine smile. "I just have a lot on my mind is all."

Liana smiled at the woman and knelt down in front of her. "You have too much strength in you to let whatever has a hold on you win," she said, placing a hand on her shoulder. "No matter how terrible that hold may be."

"Tenacious self-pity," Deirdre said, clasping her hands together. "But you're right. I just need time to let the dust settle."

"Sometimes we don't have that luxury. But you know yourself better than I," said Liana, rising up.

"You're an intuitive woman," Deirdre said without looking up.

"'Intuitive woman' is redundant," Liana said, walking away. "You should know that."

Deirdre smiled again and watched as her friend caught up with her team. She saw Adam looking her way, smiling out of obvious pity but also from a caring standpoint. Daven was adjusting his vest. She hoped to catch a glance, but he pulled the white mask over his face, never once looking at her. She decided to be patient, bowing to her own intuition and humbling herself instead of ripping the mask off Daven's face and begging him to forgive her. She would instead wait, taming her own anger and obduracy. Praying that Daven could do the same.

The team arrived at their destination shortly after preparing themselves in the barracks. They had made their way to the back of the hotel searching for the stairwell. Liana and Sergio had pinpointed the exact floor and room, so the team climbed to the roof of the building and quietly opened the access door, dropping into the main stairwell.

The hotel itself was empty of traveling occupants, but each member of the team felt a strange and uneasy presence that permeated throughout the entire building. "It feels like the Shining in here," whispered Scott, failing in an attempt to make the situation lighter. Azael whipped around and stared heavily at him. Even through the emotionless facade that his commander wore, Scott could sense the silent "shut up" that was aimed at him.

Azael and Liana led the team down the crisscrossing corridor of concrete steps until they reached their floor. There was a thin window, lined with a checkered inner frame set at the corner of the door. Liana peered down one end of the hall through the same window as Azael looked down the opposite way across from her. There was no sign of life. No pacing security, no men standing outside of doors, no one.

"This is most definitely a trap," whispered Liana to Azael. The commander didn't respond, only indicating through signals to open the door and move in.

They bolted down the hallway in single file, weapons out front, gliding without sound across the carpeted floor. Once they reached their destination, Adam, Daven, and Scott lined themselves opposite the door hinges, waiting to move in. Liana and Azael gripped the handles of a weighted battering ram, set to break into the room. It happened fast, faster than Daven and Adam expected. After Liana and Azael broke through, Scott led the two other men into a small room, populated by only Felice Savoca and, unknown to them at the time, Charles Monroe.

It was almost instant. Charles jumped from his seat and shot his hand out, palm toward the invading soldiers. Scott, Liana, and Azael instantly collapsed, but much to Charles's surprise, Daven and Adam remained standing. He attempted once again to take Daven and Adam out, with a look of complete confusion and surprise laid out across his face, but instead of seeing the two men's eyes roll into the backs of their heads as they fell backward, he was presented with a far more terrifying image.

As Felice cowered in the corner, Charles watched as a blinding white light emanated from behind the eclipsing silhouettes of the two men. Their eyes lit up in an explosion of flame as their jaws dropped to a gaping maw, revealing another blinding spike of light, pouring out like a jet engine's exhaust. Seven wings twitched and shook as they unfurled outward into a black feathered circle, the tips of each wing lit with a candlelight flame. "Sathariel," bellowed one voice from Daven's and Adam's mouths, "you have forced our hand. Forced your fate upon yourself. But we have hope that redemption can be found in you."

"Why are you here? Why have you returned?" screamed Charles from on his knees, arms extended outward, trying to block the light and the hurricane wind that came with it from his eyes.

"A question asked out of contrived ignorance," said the voice, low and trembling. "We will only say this once. Stop your rampage, convince your siblings to cease their search, and we will allow you to live. If you disobey us, we will retaliate. As you once so eloquently stated in threatening messages of your own, you have been warned."

The light vanished instantly, leaving three laid-out Eyes lying still, with Felice hiding in the corner, arms over his head. Charles looked at Daven and Adam, who were standing before him, still and stoic. "Leave," the voice said, now sounding distant. "You know what to do." Charles darted out of the hotel room and into the hallway. He looked down to the end to see three lilim staring at him.

"What did you see, Sathariel?" asked Thamiel, the other two lilim remaining silent.

"You know what I saw." Charles scowled, walking quickly in their direction. "And unless you want to die, I would suggest we all leave. Now." Charles pushed by them, hurrying to get far away from the hotel.

Thamiel watched as he left, standing still and unwavering. Instead of following along, he turned to look back and saw Daven and Adam standing and staring, their white masks glowing ever so slightly.

"Thamiel," said the same low, thundering voice, "obey."

Inside, Thamiel was terrified, having not seen these angels in hundreds of years, but on his surface, he remained stern, even amused. He nodded to the two and slowly made his way after Sathariel, fearful of this reemergence of a power that had been absent for so long.

Scott's, Liana's, and Azael's ability to move leapt back into them with a fury, sending them jumping up like an electric shock had just run through their bodies. All three removed their masks and stared at Daven and Adam with unbelief.

After a moment of lost words, Scott spoke up. "Can you please explain to us what just happened?" he asked, unable to process the event.

The two slid their masks up, shocked in and of themselves. "You saw that?"

"Saw, felt, almost pissed myself," said Scott, being the only talkative one of the three.

"I had been waiting to see where all this dream stuff went," said Adam to Daven. "Apparently there's some validity to it after all."

"Validity to what?" asked Liana. "Catching your eyes on fire?"

"We're just curious, boys," said Azael, trying to keep a level head. "It's not every day that you see someone transform into the embodiment of 'holy hell.'"

"I think before we do any explaining, we need to take our package home and unwrap it," said Daven, referring to Felice, who was still shaking in the fetal position inside the room.

"You two are something else," Azael said with a smile, sliding his mask back down and walking to apprehend Felice. "More than I believe any of us know."

CHAPTER 12

SEVENTY TIMES SEVEN

October 16, 2035

T he lilim had been constructing underground tunnel systems and
habitats for thousands of years. Especially under cities and capitals
within powerful nations or empires. The tunnels served a strategic purpose,
allowing the lilim to control the growth and decline of human civilizations.
The lilim had secretly been contributing to the undermining of evil men
through subtle hints to opposing forces or intervening directly. Until now.

The city under Rome was the central hub of lilim activity since the
rise of Domus Aurea, housing the eldest of the children of Lilith and the
militant lilim responsible for changing the course of war. At the onset
of Italy's dissolution, Lilith's eldest met with the world's most powerful
and influential leaders, threatening them into inactivity. Great Britain,
however, attempted to invade and stop Nero's path of destruction. The
lilim were true to their word and burned London, causing British forces
to retreat before even setting foot inside the peninsula, keeping Aurean
forces safe and allowing them to grow.

The core of Lilith's Roma, as her children were apt to calling Rome,
ran underneath the Tiber River, with small tunnels branching off to areas
below the streets and structures of the world above. The inner workings

of the underground city were unimpressive, composed mainly of stone support columns and large wooden crossbeams, but the lilim hung large, colorful banners, some braided into rope figures, interwoven and decorated with metallic lamps burning with an otherworldly fire. Behind the largest banners covering the walls, softly glowing white lights, seemingly held by nothing, lit the surroundings, saturating the colors with a glowing hue, creating tunnels of soft enclosures.

It had been a long time since Charles wandered through the main halls of the deeply hidden, underground containment. He remembered how much he took for granted the beauty of this place, wandering aimlessly, ignorant of the artwork around him. It was still difficult to appreciate the city given the purpose of his visit.

"Do you know why the three have returned?" asked Thamiel rhetorically.

"I only saw two," said Charles, quietly being difficult.

"One would be enough to eviscerate you into a cold pile of dust," said Thamiel, carefully dancing around anger. "We have been searching for our mother for hundreds of years … carefully, slowly, and quietly. Because of this, the angels have left us alone. Until you decided to take the search into your own hands, destroying and tossing whatever gets in your way aside like a child looking for a toy."

Charles and Thamiel continued walking in silence until they reached a compartment with tall, soaring ceilings. Inside were seven lilim, Lilith's eldest, standing in the shape of an arrowhead. Thamiel walked to the tip, leaving Charles in the middle between the two lines of lilim.

"I thought about your question," said Charles, leaving no time for the others to speak.

"What question was that?" asked Thamiel.

"About why our nuisances have returned." Charles began walking back and forth, drawing shapes in the air with his hands. "You see, the three were never meant to wipe us from creation. As unbelievable as it may seem, we are still part of God's handiwork; therefore, it could be said that when our mother was still active, the angels were part of nothing more than population control, veiled behind the divine command to punish her. So when she vanished, the angels ceased in their task."

"Get to your point quick, Sathariel," said Thamiel, growing exasperated.

Charles scowled at the mention of his name. "And I thought I was the impatient one," he said, forcing a smile. "They're back because I got too close. They're back because I have risen as a real threat to their holy mission. They're back because they know I will succeed."

"They are back because you are a fool," said an ancient-looking lilim to his left.

"Chaigidel," said Charles, faking his joy, "you were always the toughest older sister, weren't you?"

"I was tough because I always thought you had the potential to lead our family," Chaigidel said without moving. "But I was wrong. You are psychotic and suicidal, and if you were to lead, you would lead us into oblivion."

"It won't matter what you think," said Charles, still smiling. "When I'm there to welcome our mother home, our brothers and sisters will rally to me like sheep to a shepherd."

Chaigidel attempted to raise her voice in defiance once again, but Thamiel lifted his hand to silence her. "You have an opportunity to rejoin the fold, Sathariel," he said, his voice slightly elevated. "If not, you will die. Here and now."

Charles wasn't expecting such a harsh ultimatum. You're a fool, Charles, he said in his mind. The young lilim honestly expected to refuse their demands and leave to fight them another day. The children of Lilith had strict laws against fratricide, but it was obvious that times were different, and they were desperate. "Th-the laws," he stuttered quietly.

"The laws? The laws?" Thamiel laughed. "You are not fit to limit our decisions with something you clearly have no regard for. The laws were made to keep our family strong and united, and we were until your belligerent antics ripped a quarter of our numbers away from us."

"Didn't know it was that much," said Charles, pleasantly surprised.

"What is your decision?" Thamiel asked, obviously tired of the banter.

Charles sat, his mind racing with contemplation. If he agreed, he feared he would never see his mother again. However, if he disagreed, he would most certainly be killed. He opened his mouth to bargain once more, but before he could speak, a gleaming metal point thrust itself through Thamiel's chest. The elders quickly spun to the sound of their brother's shocked gasp, watching him collapse, blood spurting from his chest. Charles saw one of his own, standing still, with a bloody dagger in his hand. The young lilim mouthed the word *run* as the seven elder lilim pounced on him, ripping him limb from limb.

Charles felt like he was running through water, fear gripping his heart like a vise. He knew he was no match for the seven most powerful lilim on earth, as he was still young and still developing his strength. Although his stamina in a battle was considerably better than older lilim, great power came with age. He could hear his follower screaming in agony as he raced through the corridors. You coward, he kept repeating to himself over and over again in his head, turn around … face them, but he knew he couldn't. Both out of fear and of duty. If he turned back, the young lilim would have died for nothing.

He rounded the corner of the exit beneath the ruins of the Colosseum, within the confines of the hypogeum, waiting for the feel of the nighttime air on his skin. Charles hadn't thought about what he would do once he was free of the long stone halls, populated by thousands of angry lilim after his blood, but as he burst out and saw the starry sky above, he felt safe.

"You are certainly a man of repute," said Tŭnash, standing with a thin black robe loosely draped over her shoulders.

"We need to move," he said, passing by the succubus.

"Should we leave the city?" she asked without moving.

"No. Find me a place where we can lay low for a while. I won't deny that I fear my siblings greatly, but I won't run with my tail between my legs."

"So be it," said Tŭnash, slowly following after Charles. She curled the corner of her mouth with a sly smile, reveling in the thoughts of the futures of her and her leader.

"Just say something! Say anything!" screamed Felice, handcuffed to a chair.

"They've been sitting there for forty-five minutes, Giuseppe," said Deirdre. The two sat in an interrogation room within the Gendarmerie Barracks, watching in secret from behind a two-way mirror. Sergio and

Marco sat across from the fearful mediator, wearing the same white masks as their militant counterparts, draped in formless black cloaks.

"It's working," said Giuseppe, staring through the glass.

"Tell us," said Sergio, breaking a long and anxiety-ridden silence for Felice. The interrogation masks were fitted with a voice modulator, changing the wearer's voice into a terrorizing growl.

"Tell you what?" he yelled, hopping up and down in his seat.

"Why were you meeting with the lilim?" said Marco.

Felice looked back and forth with confusion. "I've been meeting with him for months! What do you want to know?"

Sergio ticked his head to stare directly at Felice. "What does Nero want with the lilim?" he said with precise enunciation.

"He doesn't want anything to do with the lilim," Felice said as if the interrogators were supposed to already know. "The lilim sought out Nero!"

"Nero and the lilim already have an alliance," said Sergio. "What underhanded deals would he be making? He has the power he desired."

Felice laughed borderline maniacally at this notion. "Are you serious? Nero is completely unsatisfied! He wants an empire! Not a plantation!"

"This was bound to happen," said Deirdre. "The lilim helped Nero as far as they wished. Now he's getting cabin fever and making deals with that rogue lilim."

"Charles," Giuseppe said, still locked in an unfocused stare. "His name is Charles Monroe."

Deirdre slowly turned to look at Giuseppe. "And how would you know this?" she asked with unsettled nerves. Giuseppe ignored the question and continued to watch.

"What does the lilim want?" Marco asked.

"I don't know what the lilim wants exactly, but he is promising Nero the empire he's desired if he'll destroy the Vatican," Felice said, growing more tired by the second.

Both Sergio and Marco looked to the mirror. Giuseppe flipped a switch, revealing Deirdre and himself, and then nodded to complete the interrogation. The two men rose from their seats and placed a black hood over Felice's head. "P-please don't kill me," sobbed Felice. "I'm begging you. Spare me …"

"Speak a word of our meeting to anyone, and your life will be forfeit," said Sergio as he and Marco walked Felice out. "We will be watching."

Once the three men exited the small room, four gendarmes took the man away.

"Forfeit?" laughed Marco, removing his mask.

"Demons are articulate beings!" Sergio laughed, defending his word choice. "Would he have been as scared if I said we'd kill him dead?"

"You really think he's going to believe we'll be watching him?" asked Deirdre. "I mean, if we're watching him, why would we need to capture him to ask questions?"

"I never expected my interrogation skills would be so ridiculed!" Sergio said.

"We got everything we needed," Giuseppe said with satisfaction. "You did well."

"What will happen to the man?" asked Marco.

"He'll be taken to San Marino," Giuseppe said, watching as Felice disappeared behind a corner. "I spoke to the Captains Regent earlier about taking in a political prisoner."

"I can't believe they agreed," said Deirdre with surprise. "They're not scared of retaliation?"

"We're hoping for a reform on Felice's part," said Giuseppe. "The Sammarinese have promised to treat him with dignity and mercy. Perhaps he'll answer to kindness and reciprocate in turn."

"A long shot," said Deirdre but not out of skeptical apprehension, "but at least he'll be watched."

"Won't Nero be looking for him?" asked Sergio, nervous about the possibility.

"Nero wouldn't even send a bloody three-legged schnauzer out if his mother was captured by Somalian pirates," said Marco.

"Fortunately for us, Marco's right," said Giuseppe as he watched Azael walk down the hall toward them. "But we still need to be cautious."

Azael quickly walked up to the group, still in his gear, aside from his weapons and mask. His face showed signs of obvious exhaustion, his shoulders slumped and lethargic. "Go well?" he asked, sighing hard.

"Very," said Giuseppe, quickly avoiding the details. "Ready for a debriefing?"

"You bet, but it's going to be hard to believe," said Azael, still breathing heavily.

Giuseppe and Azael met in the Crown's office after seeing the infiltration team. He noticed how uneasily silent they all were, but he attributed it to their contact with the lilim and left it at that. Giuseppe sat behind his desk while Azael slumped in his chair across from him. As tired and obviously shaken as Azael was, he flew through his debriefing like it was nothing, being as detailed and thorough as he possibly could. Giuseppe listened intently, doubtless and totally believing. He felt only excitement as Azael described Daven's and Adam's transformation and the fear in Charles's eyes when he saw what he saw.

"So that's it," said Azael, placing everything he knew in front of Giuseppe. "Take it how you will."

Giuseppe leaned back and let out a loud weighty laugh. Azael turned red under the impression that Giuseppe didn't believe him. Before he could defend himself, Giuseppe chirped happily, "It's one thing to have faith in an ideal, but it's another to see it come to fruition."

"You obviously know something I don't," said Azael in confusion.

"You saw it for yourself, so it doesn't bother me to tell you now, but I admit I had ulterior motives for insisting Daven and Adam go with you," Giuseppe said, still smiling. He began from the onset of his strange experiences, like his dream, proceeding to Daven's and Adam's unnatural forte for weapons combat and stealth. Giuseppe was always on the precipice of complete belief, but it took three of his most trusted friends to see it for themselves to push him over.

"Where are they?" asked Giuseppe, rising from his chair, eager to see the two boys.

"Asleep and dreaming," said Michela, walking through the doorway, clothes and towels tucked under her arm. "I heard what you said. And if it's true, then it's an amazing truth. But your angels are slobs."

"Good to see their humanity is still intact," said Azael, walking to Michela to help lighten her load. "Wouldn't want them becoming too celestial, would we?"

Giuseppe said his good nights to the two laundry-laden individuals and then shut himself in. He prepared himself for a deep and revitalizing sleep as he crawled into his bed. The moon outside his window was full and bright, its glow holding the darkness at bay. He remembered the morning after the initial dream that started it all, how he witnessed an oncoming storm, and his feelings of hopelessness that came with it. Tonight, he looked at the same sky, but instead of despair, he only felt hope, pure and simple.

"You should have seen it," said Liana, beaming, sitting cross-legged on her bed. "It was the most amazing thing!"

"Are you sure it wasn't just the lilim's hold on you? A side effect?" asked Deirdre, overly unbelieving.

Liana rolled back, laughing. "You're trying to rationally explain a supernatural event with another supernatural event?"

Deirdre rolled her eyes at herself, pointlessly angry at her dull wits. "When you're right, you're right," she said, quickly trying to move the conversation along, "but what's with all the fawning?"

Liana rocked forward, eyes squinted at the accusation. "What do you mean?" She scowled.

"Well, you have puppy-dog eyes and sparkly stars coming out of your ears," Deirdre said dryly.

"You should see what's coming out of my butt," Liana said, tossing a pillow at Deirdre as her target shrieked with laughter.

The affair didn't last long after Scott burst through their door, agitated and disheveled. "Shut it!" he yelled. "I may have to live beside you two squealing eight-year-old slumber partiers, but at least let me sleep after one in the morning!"

Both Deirdre and Liana pulled their pillows to their chests with feigned looks of shock and irritability on their faces. "We could have been having a sexy pillow fight! At least knock!" yelled Liana as Deirdre laughed.

Scott pivoted to walk out. "I could only be so lucky," he said with saggy eyes and a frowning expression.

As he shut the two women in and jumped in bed, Deirdre turned to Liana. "So what does this all mean?"

"This means that someone has seen our struggle and taken pity on us," said Liana.

For a moment, the two sat in silence. It was a calming thought, reassuring and mentally absolving. They could rest easy that night, confident that a blanket of protection had draped itself over them.

"Daven is pretty cute, though," said Liana, grinning, breaking the serious tone.

Deirdre pounced in defense, retaliating with an outstretched index finger, bony and sharp. "You're treading on thin ice, you gowl!" she said with her lips pursed.

Liana recoiled with a laugh. "I knew it!" she yelled with satisfaction. Scott banged twice on the wall from his room, silencing the loud voices. "I knew it," she whispered.

"I'm not having this conversation with you," Deirdre said, lying down with a slam. "I already feel like Scott was right. We are little girls."

"Oh, don't pout, Deirdre," Liana said. "I've known for a while now."

"You have?" Deirdre asked, feeling slightly ashamed.

"Yeah," Liana said, leaning forward, resting her chin in her hands. "You two avoid each other like the plague, but only because both of you are too stubborn to admit being wrong. When you pass each other, I can see that harnessed aching in your eyes. You want to look, but you don't, even though it takes every ounce of energy not to. All that, and the fact that you didn't deny my assertion in the first place."

Deirdre hadn't been aware of how obvious the whole ordeal was, but Liana was intelligent and a woman. It probably hadn't taken her long to figure it out. "I'm just scared," she finally admitted. "Even though I feel like I've left my past where it died, it continues to rise up and pull me back in. Every time I see Daven smile at me, the fluttering in my stomach gives way to a bottomless drop, sucking me down. Then all I can see is Morgan, choking on his own blood as I cradled his head in my useless hands." Deirdre began to cry withheld tears, attempting to hold back the sorrow associated with the painful memory. "I loved him. I still love him, but I feel something for Daven I haven't felt for years. My soul wants happiness, but my mind lashes out at the thought of loving someone again, fearing that it might be taken away from me again."

Liana walked over to Deirdre, pulling her in close. "You and Morgan had something unique and rare. Everyone knew it, and even though it grossed us all out, we knew it was real." Deirdre quietly laughed through her tears, wiping her face with the back of her hand. "We are meant for one love in our lifetime, but just because we are meant for something doesn't mean that it's untouchable and unsusceptible to tragedy. But we are still meant to love someone, even after life changes its course drastically and we're left as alone as we've ever been, so when that new love presents itself, take it, because you are meant to have it."

"When did you turn into such a philosopher?" joked Deirdre, trying to pull herself back to a lighter mood.

"Not a philosopher. I only passed enough classes to be a motivational speaker," Liana said, rocking her friend back and forth.

"Partied too much?"

"Partied too much."

Liana pecked her friend on the forehead and walked off to her bed. It made her feel good and useful to aid someone as close as a sister to her, and it was what she loved to do, having a talent for it.

Deirdre lay back for a few minutes, but her mind's throttle was still wide open, keeping her far from sleep. Liana had quickly passed out after her romp around their room, and she was a notorious snorer, so Deirdre decided a walk in the late-night air would be good for her.

The world was still and quiet, except for the almost inaudible hum of the dim streetlights around her. It was a warm and humid night, calming and cozy but empty and lonely at the same time. She made her way between the Swiss Guard Barracks and the Tower of Nicolas V on her way to the colonnade. Walking the curved breezeway was something she did on sleepless nights, the repetition of columns reminiscent of counting sheep.

Once she completed her first round leading up to the vestibule of the basilica, she stopped, her right shoulder facing the front of the entrance doors. She didn't know why she stopped, but she felt compelled to go in and wander.

She always thought the inside looked significantly larger without anyone in it, but tonight, it was enormous. The arches that bridged over her loomed like the rings of Saturn, stretching from horizon to horizon, millions of miles away. The heavy marble floors pulled at her with a force much stronger than earth's gravity, making her limbs heavy and cumbersome. As she moved through the basilica, she felt like an ant inching along the surface of the moon, never reaching her destination and never belonging.

As breathtaking as the view was, it wasn't anything she hadn't seen before. She always gave the building the proper scan of the eyes as it deserved, but she hadn't wandered it aimlessly in a long time. There was one aspect of the basilica she hadn't properly taken in for her entire stay within the Vatican, and it lay beneath.

She opened the small gate below the baldachin carefully and quietly, like she was trying not to wake some unseen person sleeping in the church. Slowly she descended down and farther down to the necropolis, feeling an uneasy sensation creeping up her spine, sensing ancient eyes watching her and waiting. It was dark in the tunnel, but there was enough light for her eyes to see shapes and shadows. Her ears perked up as she neared the halfway point, hearing what sounded like someone having a conversation with themselves, whispering so she couldn't recognize the voice. Every fiber in her being was screaming for her to turn around, but Deirdre was a curious woman.

The closer she got, Deirdre saw that there were two men, one with his back to her and the other standing in front of him. She still couldn't make out what was being said, but before she could get any closer, the man facing her looked over the other man's shoulder, staring at her with bright eyes, startling the woman into stillness. She blinked as the other man turned to face her, but in that split second, the second man had disappeared.

"Deirdre?" asked the man still covered by darkness.

She recognized his voice. "Daven?" she asked, feeling the nervousness slip away. "What are you doing down here? Who were you talking to?"

"Myself," he said, unmoving, still veiled by shadow. "What are you doing?"

"Couldn't sleep," she said, moving closer to him. "Went for a walk and found myself down here."

Daven didn't say anything. He wasn't keen on being hurt by anyone, and he felt an unavoidable need to even the score before forgiving. It was worsened by his feelings of betrayal after her harsh words earlier that night, and so he was unwilling to do much talking.

"I-I heard about what happened tonight," she said, trying to keep Daven's interest in their flimsy conversation.

"Dammit," Daven muttered under his breath. He didn't want to let up, but the thought of continuing his own brand of punishment felt cruel and unusual. "Yeah," he said louder. "There have been a lot of weird things happening to Adam and me, but this took the cake."

Deirdre smiled at Daven's lengthy answer. "Yeah ... I wish I could have seen it," she said, inching closer.

"I don't know what this all means," he said, lowering his head while sticking his hands in his pockets, "but Giuseppe promised to talk to us tomorrow, so ..."

The two stood in silence for a moment, staring at the ground, both unwilling to concede to the other.

"Well, I'm going back to bed," Daven said, walking past Deirdre. He stopped and looked behind him. "You coming?"

Deirdre smiled without making eye contact and then caught up to him. They walked side by side, both mulling topics of conversation around in their heads. As they rose from underneath the floor of the basilica, Deirdre reached out to grab Daven's hand, stopping him on the top step of the stairwell. "I'm sorry," she said with a shaky, quiet voice. "I know it probably isn't enough to convince you that I'm telling the truth, but I really am sorry. More than I can express."

Daven turned his body to face her completely. "Why did you say it?" he asked calmly but sternly.

"I don't have a reason," she said, rolling her eyes. "I can give you all sorts of excuses, like I was angry or that I felt betrayed or cast aside," she said, waving her hands. "But it doesn't excuse what I said ... But I can tell you that it wasn't true."

Daven walked down to her step, moving in close. "So I'm not just a man on your list of people you tolerate?"

"I'm pretty sure I used the word *boy*," she said, smiling. "But no. I was angry, but not because I was stuck back here, waiting for all of you."

"That's what it seemed like," Daven said, unconvinced.

"I was scared. Scared for all of you, but mostly, scared for you," she said, looking up at him.

Daven couldn't help but smile. "I don't think there's anything to worry about anymore when it comes to me," he said as any anger he had for Deirdre left him.

Deirdre's countenance changed from a smile to a scowl. "Don't you even start thinking like that," she said, catching Daven off guard. "You can't think like that anymore. Even with everything you've learned about yourself, your life is always much too important to gamble with."

"You're right," he said, bowing to the woman's lecture.

"Good," she said, nodding her head like a chastising mother. "Daven, at some point, we need to talk about some things."

Daven smiled and squeezed her shoulder, leading her forward as he followed close behind. They walked slowly out of the basilica into the breaking day. The dark of the night and light of the new day were visibly separated in the sky, with a small number of stars still hanging from the darkness. Deirdre looked up and took the sight as a sign, reflecting her life pushing the sadness away, replacing it with new love and happiness.

CHAPTER 13

SPORADIC

October 16, 2035

"Be lion-mettled, proud, and take no care who chafes, who frets, or where conspirers are. Macbeth shall never vanquish'd be until great Birnam Wood to high Dunsinane Hill shall come against him," said one of three men standing watch on the eastern slopes of Monte Titano in San Marino, by the Guaita Fortress.

"Enough of your Shakespearian dribble," said another man, irritated by his fellow soldier's ambiguous remark.

These Sammarinese militiamen gazed over a moonlit forest sloping down onto the flatlands of the small country. The wooded area wasn't especially large, but it was big enough to hold a sense of otherworldly wonder within its branches. This seemed to be increasingly apparent over the course of the past two weeks, and a relatively young legend had begun to circulate through the ranks of the militia.

"I suggest you develop some class, Roland," said Mirko, slightly disgusted by his friend's lack of culture. "We could all learn something from Macbeth's blind ambition. So blind that he neglected to properly interpret a prophetic vision, and because of it, he lost more than he could have imagined."

"Why don't you just come out and say what is on your mind, sans the pretentiousness," said Roland, rubbing the bridge of his nose.

Mirko sighed heavily. "A living forest spelled the downfall of a tragic hero in Macbeth. Now here we are faced with our very own version, treating lightly what could potentially be a serious problem."

"Oh, come on now," said Roland, his voice elevated in volume. "You can't really believe that forest is haunted."

"Guys," said the third soldier, Benito, "what in heaven's name is that?"

The three gazed down on the treetops as a pale white woman dressed in glowing blue garb stood among the branches, her body floating high above the forest. They were speechless and noticed that she was staring directly at them with unblinking eyes. All three felt a pang of fear and surprise as they looked without turning away from the ghastly image.

"Well, I'm not entirely sure how to explain this one," said Roland, his eyes wide with unbelief.

"That's the problem with you rationalists," said Mirko with a passive-aggressive jab at the term *rationalists*. "You feel like you have to explain everything with grounded science, even if the explanation you come up with is more unbelievable than the otherworldly event you're attempting to dismiss."

Roland wasn't listening. His mind surged with thoughts attempting to properly diagnose the situation. Everything he tried to apply as a solution to this problem fell flat and made no sense. He was like a child stubbornly trying to shove a square peg into a circular hole.

Suddenly a loud whisper permeated his skull, causing dizziness and blinding pain. He could shape the voice by opening and closing his mouth, like wind passing through the pipes of an organ.

"Come to me," the voice said. It echoed and reverberated around him, but he quickly noticed that the others weren't responding to the voice as he was. He clapped his hands over his ears, but it wasn't as effective as he hoped.

"Roland, are you okay?" asked Benito, placing his hands on the shoulders of his ailing friend.

Roland couldn't hear him, and he could barely feel the grip of Benito's hands around him.

"Oh, stop it," said Mirko, thinking Roland's reaction was in jest. "You've made your point."

"I don't think he's kidding around, Mirko," said Benito. "He's shaking like a leaf in a hurricane."

Mirko looked down on his friend, placing his head between the floating apparition and Roland's head. Suddenly, he too was gripped by pain and fear as the same voice shot through his skull like a bullet. He fell over onto the ground but was immediately relieved of the specter's hold on him. He looked up, seeing that Roland was still stumbling around in shocking agony, and then he thought of a way to stop the madness.

"Sorry about this," Mirko said as he kicked his friend hard in the ankle, sending Roland tumbling down in front of him. His idea seemed to work as Roland's expression changed from pure pain to alleviation. Benito had fallen to the ground as well, hoping to avoid, successfully, the sharp agony of the specter's voice.

"Is it still there?" asked Mirko loudly to Benito. His ears were still muffled and ringing from the piercing audio, but the pain was gone.

Benito sat up precariously, widening his eyes and ever so slightly peeking over the stone side of the stairwell. His head darted back and forth, but after a few seconds, his face emulated Roland's own when he noticed the absence of their ghost woman. He shook his head, and Mirko relaxed his muscles, lying flat on the ground next to Roland.

"I have to get down there," Mirko said after a moment of silence. "I have to find out what that was."

Roland rolled over onto his elbow. "You're a fool if you think you'll get me down there with you."

"I'm going alone," said Mirko as he stood up, his legs wobbling, trying to find their strength.

"You'll hear no argument from me," said Benito, unashamed of his fearful apprehension.

Mirko stood still for a moment while he regained his composure and strength. The night didn't seem so calm anymore even with the absence of the forest's banshee. Mirko was jumpy to say the least, and his hearing was coming back with a vengeance. As he moved deeper into the woods, every snapping twig, every crumbling leaf, sent his heart sailing, pumping adrenaline throughout his body. Even the sounds of his own footsteps seemed to be foreign in nature, not of his own making. The moonlight became weaker with the thickening of the foliage around him. He peeled the Velcro covering of his flashlight pouch back and removed the small, handheld lamp, clicking the rubber button on the bottom. A bright bluish-white LED light pierced the wall of night in front of him with a concentrated beam only feet in diameter. He twisted the head of the light, widening the ray into a dim circle. As he lifted it up to guide him, he swore he could see two figures dart to the side of the beam, as if to avoid it.

"Hello?" he asked feebly, his body trying to keep quiet while his mind wished to inquire. Mirko realized he was fixated on one area of the woods instead of searching from side to side. He attributed it to irrational fear and fought with his body to respond to his commands. "Who's out there? I just want to see you, talk to you."

Still no response. In fact, Mirko realized that the sounds of the forest around him had all but stopped. No crunch of dead plants, no whisper of wind through branches, no chirping of insects, and no sound of his own breathing. It felt like someone had wrapped a thick scarf around his head, blocking out every sound of the world around him. Suddenly he felt a presence behind him, and it shot fear straight through his veins, freezing his limbs and sucking the will to run out of him.

Finally, after fighting with himself for what seemed like hours, Mirko slowly turned his whole body to confront the presence behind him. It happened fast, so fast that he didn't have time to be scared. Two black figures stood mere inches from his face and immediately placed a black hood over his head. His body was unable to handle the sheer terror of what was happening to it and finally shut down to escape the horror unfolding around him.

It didn't feel the same to Adam. A looming sense of dread and terror crept through his mind, something he hadn't felt in a long time. Adam's dreams of late were full of life and purpose, fueling his waking mind with ambition and happiness. This was different.

The dream placed him on a field of dead grass, with a gradually sloping horizon on a gray sky. One cross stood twenty feet ahead of him, black with soot and cold, absent of life. There was no wind and no noise, but his mind replaced the silence with thoughts of unease. He found himself walking slowly toward the cross, but it was not something he was able to stop. The closer he got, the more the setting before him began to come alive.

Small tendrils of smoke began flowing into the wood, as if its dry fibers were inhaling it with oxygen-deprived lungs. The small lines of gray and black began growing into torrential billows, filling the black with the fuel of a nightmare. As Adam neared, he could see small particles of ash pouring out of the wood, like tiny insects flying together to form shapes and patterns. As the ash condensed, Adam saw the anatomy of a woman begin to mold into being. The skeletal structure moved and writhed in pain as fibers of muscle ran along the black bones of the slowly shaping body. Organs filled empty pockets within the framework, her lungs expanding and deflating quickly and shallowly. Adam stared in fear as white eyes appeared in the woman's smoldering ocular cavities, their brown irises darting back and forth. Red veins ran like rivers along the white orbs as their healthy color quickly began to peel away in pink flakes. Suddenly, as charred black skin covered the horror beneath it, the woman shrieked in pain and agony, being silent only to inhale deeply to release another banshee wail.

"Why?" she begged, tears turning to steam as they ran down her blackened skin. "It hurts, Adam; the fire burns!"

"I'm sorry, Eula. I'm so sorry," he said as he fell to his knees, fists pounding the ground, bleeding and bruised.

"Don't listen," said a voice from far off, but it was soon dampened, and Eula's cries became overbearing once more.

"You slept while we burned!" Flames poured from her mouth like fire from a dragon's mouth.

"We didn't know," Adam said, unable to look up from his bleeding knuckles. "We couldn't know."

"You knew," said Eula, her voice growing more and more accusatory. "You knew we couldn't hide you for long, but you hid under our watch anyway, and we paid for your cowardice."

"Daddy, don't listen," said the childlike voice again, floating on the wind like a feather.

Adam lifted his head, looking for the source of the words. He cupped his hands over his ears, trying in vain to drown Eula out. "Who's there?" he cried out.

"There is no one here," said what remained of Eula, her voice lowering in pitch to a vibrating growl. By now, the blackened husk of her body and head seemed to be fueled by a white flame that torched the surrounding area. "You are alone with me in this place, your punishment."

"Daddy, wake up."

Adam, through his searing eyes, saw a little girl peering at him from behind the charred wood of the base of the cross. Her blonde locks waved and floated with the intense rising heat generated from the fire. "Sarah?" he asked as his nightmare came to an end.

Adam sat up slowly in his bed, inhaling audibly with a gasp.

"Sorry I'm late," said a voice as Adam struggled to open his eyes. "The enemy has seen fit to make your nights miserable, I imagine."

Adam's vision began to focus in the dimly lit environment, the only light to be seen coming from the hallway outside his room. He saw the silhouettes of a man and a little girl standing next to one another. "Am I still asleep?" he asked the strangers in the room.

"You're in between dream and reality," said the man. "Like hearing a voice in a dream as the room around you fades into existence."

"Speaking of fading into existence, is there any particular reason I can barely see right now?"

"That's all you, buddy," said the man.

"Is that you, Daven? It's got to be. You sound like an asshole, and Daven is capable of being quite the asshole," said Adam as he vigorously rubbed his eyes.

"Language around the little lady," said the man.

Adam once again opened his eyes to a focused, albeit dark, room around him. It wasn't the man that he noticed first, but the same girl from his dream that grabbed his attention. She had soft, bright blonde hair that reached past her shoulders. Her eyes were an eerily organic green, with wide staring pupils, and the moment Adam peered into them, he knew who she was. His daughter, standing in his room, peeking from behind the strange individual at the foot of his bed.

"How is this …" asked Adam in shocked confusion.

"Your life will be filled with inexplicable occurrences from here on out," said the man. "I figured this may be the best way to introduce myself to you personally. My name is Senoy, and I am a part of you now. Part of you in a way that has yet to be fully revealed but has been sparsely hinted to you for quite some time."

Adam was barely listening. All his attention had been drawn to his daughter, Sarah. "Baby, is that you?" he asked as hot tears welled up in his eyes.

"Where did you go, Daddy?" she asked sheepishly. "Mommy cries a lot. We miss you."

Adam covered his mouth, trying to hide the overwhelming flood of emotion, but the quivering surge flowing through his body was uncontrollable. "Oh, baby, Daddy would do absolutely anything to come home. But Daddy just ... just can't do that right now."

"But we miss you so much," she said, becoming increasingly upset by the idea of being left alone again.

Senoy crouched down to the little girl's height. "Your daddy is going to be a hero, Sarah," he said, running his fingers through her soft hair. "He's going to make the world a much better place. He's going to make you and your mommy very proud. In fact, I'm fairly sure that he's going to save the world, and after he does, your mommy and you will remember him as the man who defeated very, very bad people, so that you and your mommy can live a life free of danger."

Sarah turned to look at her father. He had reined in his tears enough to appear strong and stoic in order to relieve her fear, but his red, puffy eyes revealed the truth. "I'm going to see you again, baby. I promise you that. You tell your mommy that I love her so much and that I dream about you two every night."

Adam finally embraced the little girl as she drifted off to sleep. To him, it was the single happiest moment of his life after the terrible events he had recently endured.

"She will remember this," Senoy said as Sarah began to fade away in Adam's arms. "You need this moment of happiness to prepare you for the road ahead."

"What must I do?" asked Adam as he watched Sarah fade completely. "This is happening so fast. I'm scared, and I'm not afraid to admit it. I feel like I'm up against the unknown. An unknown that because of its obscurity makes it that much more terrifying."

"You will know all in time. First, you must know who we are to you and Daven. Sansenoy has spoken to him already, and now that I have met with you, the next step can begin. Giuseppe will explain his mission for you, and once you know that, Sansenoy and I will speak to you in full. Do not fear. We are with you in this realm, and we are also a part of you. Do not fear, child of God. You have been seen as worthy."

At this last word, Adam drifted into a dreamless, restful sleep.

He'd been here before. He'd been everywhere before, but the beauty of this world had never lost its appeal. He had watched mountains crumble and rivers trickle into streams. He had seen wind carve beautiful sculptures out of rock and sand and witnessed the rise of human civilization. A purpose was all he desired, but a millennium had passed since he had walked with a goal in mind. The sound of his voice had become a memory, along with the sounds of companionship.

His skin was thick and calloused with extreme age, numbing it to cold and heat. A deep, resonating pain was all he felt anymore, and no amount of time could dull its searing torture. His hair had grown well past the length of his body and was used to robe himself in braids and knots. Twigs and leaves decorated the filthy dreads, creating a moving habitat for all sorts of insects, but the sight of the man was not displeasing and was awe inspiring given his ancient appearance and otherworldly quality. His eyes were his most unnerving feature, sunken in dark, bony, wrinkled pits. A shadow cast itself over them, leaving only a small prick of reflective light to peer through, hiding any sense of emotion toward any onlooker.

He stood at the point of a fjord on Seiland Island in northern Norway, the wind blowing through his hair and thundering in his ears. Suddenly a voice permeated the raucous noise with a piercing whisper.

"Go east. Help him."

The man stood without answering, inhaling heavily through his nostrils. The smell of the sea was warm in an otherwise cold environment. It reminded him of his home and the salt of the ocean there. It also reminded him of the smell of his brother's blood.

CHAPTER 14

QUESTIONS AND ANSWERS

October 17, 2035

"Followers are too scared to exhibit signs of curiosity," said Michael to Mirko as the latter sipped on a cup of tea.

"Seems to me you might be attracting some unwarranted attention through your unorthodox tactics," said Mirko, referring to earlier the previous night.

"It got your attention," said Michael. "Is it safe to assume you may have some reservations toward your current leadership?"

"You mean Carlo?" asked Mirko. "The man's neurotic if we're being blunt."

Salvador began laughing. Michael turned with a smile to his friend. "Yes. We are being blunt," he said as he turned back, "but his behavior has become psychopathic."

"More than usual?" asked Mirko.

Michael began pacing within the large tented area. "His actions nearly cost me my life. His actions cost me four of my men. I can no longer function in a society where my enemies and my supposed allies wish me dead."

"The man has never been secretive about his feelings toward you," said Mirko. "I think he alluded to you several times in a speech he made about failure."

"I think I was there for that one," said Salvador. "Someone heard me questioning whether or not he was just stupid or if he was cleverly underselling his own intelligence to throw us all off. Woke up the next day in Michael's battalion. Best joke I ever made."

"Is that what's happening to me right now?" asked Mirko. "Am I waking up in Michael's battalion?"

"You're waking up to a choice," said Michael. "Your dissatisfaction with Carlo's control has been noted. Now the decision lies before you. Help us take our home back. Help us put the leadership of San Marino back into the hands of those more suited for the task."

"Am I to assume you're the one who wishes to take that place?" asked Mirko, somewhat put-off.

"Not in the least," said Michael. "My hands were made for a different set of responsibilities. But I'd rather see the office liquidated before keeping Carlo in it."

"I think we can all agree to that," said Mirko. "So how does this work? Pledge of allegiance? Paperwork? Blood ritual?"

"Your word will suffice," said Salvador, growing tired of Mirko's dry witticisms.

"Then you have it," said Mirko with a nod. "So, I'm guessing you've begun some kind of clandestine conscription?" he asked as he set the empty teacup on his cot. "How successful has that been?"

"It's been decent," said Salvador, arms crossed as he leaned against a tent pole. "But good things do not come quickly."

"No," said Mirko, "no, they do not. I guess my real question is, are you being met with positive results?"

"Yes," said Michael with a smirk. He reached forward to pull away the cloth partition, revealing a camp full of faces familiar to Mirko. "I guess you can say we are."

There were close to fifty men rolling up tents and packing away equipment. Some turned to smile at Mirko, who was wide eyed and surprised at the number of friends he saw. "How did you manage this?" he asked Michael without breaking his gaze.

"A directional loudspeaker and her," said Michael, nodding his head in the direction of a woman clad in a white robe. The same specter Mirko had seen earlier. "We pinpointed a particular message toward these men and women and yourself through the speakers. Laura here worked as a sort of magnet attracting your sense of curiosity, luring you here to us. Unfortunately, you were the first to leave your group alone. The rest were too frightened to venture here without those who kept watch with them. Which is why we need to move fast. There's no doubt that your friends up there have already reported your disappearance and may be close to searching for you. Could be they already are."

"How do you know my word is gospel? How do you know I don't want to be found and am just giving you what you want to live until that happens?" asked Mirko.

"Like I said earlier," said Michael, "followers are too scared to exhibit signs of curiosity. We've been watching you for a while now and have seen the dissatisfaction in your eyes. Those who are loyal to Carlo will run to him in moments of fear or change. You, on the other hand, and those around you, saw the first opportunity to escape your cage and took it. We preyed on your inquisitiveness, and now you have no desire to leave. Do you?"

"No, I don't," said Mirko with conviction. "Where do we go from here?"

"I'm not saying he's a replacement, but you have to admit his vocals are fairly spot-on," said Scott as he and Adam walked the gardens.

"I cannot confirm or deny your opinion," said Adam, exhaling gray smoke from a cigarette.

"I don't think you understand what that actually means," said Scott in passing. "But Layne's own mother even said DuVall sounded like him."

"Bah. I'm done with this conversation," said Adam, waving his hands in defiance. "At this point I'd listen to Macy Gray if it was new."

"You must really hate your ears," said Scott as he turned to the sound of footsteps behind them. "Five bucks says he's here for you."

"You have money?" said Adam as he turned to face the man quickly walking toward them.

"Oh, hey, Vergil," said Scott, recognizing the Sword as he approached. "Why the brisk pace?"

"Still burning through that last coffee," Vergil said, stopping and smiling at the two men. "I'm actually here for Mister Gilmour."

"You can pay me later," Scott said to Adam with a smile. "Do you mind if I escort Adam myself?" Scott asked Vergil. "I'm assuming Giuseppe wants to speak with him?"

"You'd be correct, and that's fine by me," Vergil said as he jogged onward. "This stuff is shooting straight through me. I need to find a bush."

Vergil quickened his pace and rounded a corner, vanishing from view. Adam and Scott spun around to head back toward the barracks. It was still early morning, with a clear blue sky. The wind was cool and light, just enough to blow Adam's long hair past his ears. The two walked in silence beside one another, eyes straight forward, taking in the sunlit trees and buildings around them. It was almost enough to draw their attention away from the events of the past few months, but no matter how beautiful the surroundings, Adam, and especially Scott, knew the current events of their lives were about to be brought back into view.

"Do you ever still think about escaping?" asked Scott. "You know, going home and forgetting about everything you've seen here?"

"Should I not?" asked Adam, indirectly answering Scott's question. "It's my purpose in life. I couldn't think of anything more I could ask for."

Scott smiled thinly, glancing quickly at Adam and then looking back without speaking.

"What?" asked Adam, confused.

"You realize at this point, there's no going back," Scott said with gloom. "You may be able to go home, see your wife and daughter. Maybe even succeed in forgetting, for a little while that is, everything that has happened, but you've been marked. We may not know very much about it yet, but your life is about to take an even more drastic turn."

"I never asked for any of this," Adam said with elevated emotion. "My decision to come to Italy was to broaden my horizons. Learn more to seize any opportunity that arose before me. Apply those lessons to any career I chose for myself, so that my family could live in comfort. It wasn't a selfish decision. My family was first and foremost in my mind. They still are. The fact that I've been trapped here for so long confuses me. Why am I being 'marked'? I don't want any more responsibility. I don't need to be part of some convoluted scheme to make things right again for anyone but my family. I don't know what happened the other night, but I'll tell you right now and whoever else is listening," he said, glancing to the sky, "count me out."

"Unfortunately," Scott said, "I don't think you, or myself, have any choice in the matter. You're about to learn something that may change everything you think you know about this life. I believe your tune will change when you realize your family, and everyone's families, may just rely on you and Daven alone."

Adam didn't speak. He just looked down and continued walking. Scott wasn't one to mince words, but he knew none of what Adam was about to learn would be easy to process. He began to think of ways to ease his friend's ailing mind.

"You may be right, though," said Adam rather lightheartedly.

"I may be right about what?" asked Scott.

"DuVall is a dead ringer for Staley now that I think about it."

Scott laughed and nodded in agreement.

"Fear. My life is ruled by it. The day I took what was mine, I learned the only way to retain what I acquired was to rule with it. I don't deny the accusations that so readily float off the lips of my people. Denial is the fear of acceptance. I revel in their hatred and distaste. It fuels my resolve to show the world that plebeian opinion need not regulate the powerful. I do not consent to the will of the governed. They can't seem to agree on anything anyway."

"That annoyance transcends humanity," said Charles from the darkness of a far corner. "Mankind, lilimkind, it makes no difference."

Nero slowly turned to face Charles with a scowl on his face. He sat in a dark wooden chair with deep red cushioning, but instead of rising, he sank and turned to peer out his window once more. It was noon, and the sun was high in the sky. Its warm rays permeated the inside confines of his bedroom, illuminating the gold trim and marble floors, enhancing their natural vibrance. Nero's bed sat within the middle of the room atop a stepped dais, a canopy drawn closed around it. Charles stepped out from the only shadowed corner of the room, far from the door and any window, leaving the wonder of how he entered the room in the first place.

"It seems our mutual distaste for our brethren is the reason for our union," said Charles as he stopped next to Nero.

"I've been reconsidering our alliance," said Nero, still staring out his window. "You've promised much but delivered little."

"You must forgive me," said Charles with a passive-aggressive smile. "I forget your years, along with your patience, are much shorter than my own."

"Patience I have," said Nero. "Results I do not."

"Have you forgotten our deal?" asked Charles. "Bring the Vatican to its knees, and your empire will flourish. The Catholics still retain their secrets."

"And have you forgotten your promise?" asked Nero without skipping a beat. "Remove your kind from posing a threat, and the rest will fall into place."

Charles stood silent. The emperor in the making had a valid point, but both were overly stubborn and would not concede to the other. The two felt action by the other was required before moving onward with their end of the bargain.

"My eldest brother, Thamiel, is dead," Charles said. "The eyes of my siblings are upon me. If there was ever a time to proceed with whatever plan you may have, it's now."

"So that is the reason for this bold meeting," said Nero with epiphany. "I would never see you, especially in broad daylight, otherwise."

"This latest occurrence should alleviate some of our past restrictions," said Charles with insincere excitement.

Nero was not convinced. He knew that with the death of Thamiel, the lilim's anger would be at an all-time high. Initiating a plan that went against his formal agreement with Charles's siblings would recoil with deadly consequence. It would take more than an indirect death to cause Nero to act on Charles's behalf.

"For an ancient being, you're quite the fool," said Nero. "Grasping at straws like you are, I would think you were out of options. You did not intend for Thamiel to die. I can still smell the shock on you. While the absence of the Eldest does allow for some room to plot, it by no means gives us the right to act."

The pain hit Nero like a train moving at full speed. His throat closed so fast that his lungs burned with the shock. His eyes clouded with tears, and his brain instantly surged with an intense panic. He gripped the mahogany armrests, twisting and writhing with fear.

"Fear? This is fear," said Charles as his silhouette blocked out the sun. "You say you rule with it, but from my point of view, you can barely control it."

The lilim moved in close, face-to-face with the man in a cold sweat. His fingers dug into Nero's face, anger pushing from behind each digit. The man began kicking and shuffling his feet, trying in vain to acquire some stability, but the more he struggled, the more his mind began to slip.

"Never test me again," said Charles as he released Nero. "You are mine to use. You will do as I say, and when you have completed your task, I will reward you. Not one moment sooner."

Nero lurched forward, retching hard past the point of vomiting. Spit, bile, and tears streamed from his mouth, nose, and eyes as he collapsed to the ground. By the time he looked up, Charles was gone, leaving Nero to wallow in his shame and anger as he threw the ornate chair across the room, smashing it into splinters on the marble floor below.

A soldier ran into the room after hearing the crash. He moved toward his leader, grasping his shoulders in an attempt to lift him to his feet. "Sir! Are you okay? I heard the noi—."

Nero slammed his fist into the soldier's mouth before he could finish, breaking several teeth in the process. Once the bleeding man fell to the ground, Nero began kicking him in the stomach with unhinged fury.

"No one! Ever again!" He screamed with every strike. "I will not be made a fool of in my own home! Never again!"

Adamo Gozi, the legate of the Lazio Legion and one of the men with Nero during his visit to Lorenzo's bakery, heard the commotion and ran in to hold back his infuriated leader. "Rein it in, you idiot!" he screamed as he threw Nero off the near dead soldier. "At this rate, you'll kill us all before long! Then what?"

Nero quickly pulled his sidearm from its holster and pointed it straight at Adamo's face. He didn't recognize the man at first, and without thinking, he pulled the hammer back, milliseconds away from squeezing the trigger. Adamo did not move, trusting Nero would recognize his best friend and ally before any harm could be done. Time for Adamo moved cringingly slowly. The opening of the barrel was the only thing in focus, and the sound of his own breath was the only thing audible. Finally, sense slowly seeped into Nero's brain, and the screeching of his hot blood surging through his ears and head dissipated, his vision clearing to recognition of the man in front of him.

"I was going to kill you, you fool," Nero said, his stubbornness unwilling to compromise with his sense of self-error.

"I'd have shot you first," Adamo said as two other soldiers rushed to their beaten brother's side.

Nero scoffed internally at the idea with a smile. "You've always liked pushing your limits," he said as he tossed the firearm haphazardly to the side.

"I learned from the best," Adamo said, still put off by Nero's attack on the battered soldier. "Perhaps you might adopt a sense of self-control to add to that fury of yours."

"What do you want?" Nero asked, noticing Adamo's strained humor.

"The citywide holding cells at our security checkpoints have been completed," Adamo said, moving straight to the point.

"The tunnels?"

"Finished as well," Adamo said. "We can safely move prisoners from the checkpoints to Mamertine Prison without utilizing city streets."

"Good," Nero said, and rarely, "What of the workers?"

"We gave them a choice after they finished construction," said Adamo. "Conscript or populate the prison."

"I imagine our strength in numbers has risen?" asked Nero, very sure of himself.

Adamo's reaction skipped a beat. "All were imprisoned," he said very carefully.

Nero did not move. For a moment, Adamo sincerely thought Nero was legitimately depressed by the answer, but the thought was short-lived. "How many exactly?" Nero asked calmly.

"A number over three hundred," Adamo said. "But it is possible to reconsider."

"No," Nero said, still unmoving. "I want them dead. Make it public. Make an example of them all."

Adamo hung his head slightly. "Is that wise?" he asked with a sigh. "There has to be another way."

Nero turned his head to look over his shoulder. "Wise?" he asked. "I'm not sure if it is wise to ask such a question. You may be my closest friend, Adamo, but I am still your leader and superior. All that grants you, however, is my hesitation to pull a trigger on a gun pointed at your head!" His voice crescendoed to a concussive head and reverberated through the room.

"Dead then," Adamo said through his teeth with a curled lip. "Dead just like the rest." He turned and walked away with his hands grasped behind his back, but before reaching the door, he turned once more. "Do you want to be present for the execution? Wait, of course you will. You thrive off horror."

Nero did not react or respond. Instead, he watched as Adamo closed the doors behind him, finally being left alone once again, gathering the pieces of his broken chair and piling them in the center of his room.

"How do I explain any of this?" Giuseppe asked Elia. "There's so much to tell. So much that is fundamentally unbelievable. I do not envy Daven or Adam. To be at the center of this storm and be so uninformed."

"I truly believe everything they have experienced thus far has somewhat blazed a trail of understanding," Elia said, wiping dust off the fireplace mantel in Giuseppe's office. "I do believe, however, that being open to anything they find hard to swallow should be an element in this as well and something we should be willing to do."

"I find most of it hard to swallow myself," Giuseppe said, squeaking back and forth in his wooden office chair. "And I have answers. I may need your assistance when words fail me."

Elia nodded his head as Adam and Scott entered the room. The four exchanged hellos and took their respective seats as Scott made his way out. The room was quiet aside from the creaking of the loosely hung ceiling fan above them, but it was not an awkward silence. The three (other than Adam) knew to keep conversation to a minimum, but the thick, anxious air around them caused a certain aching in their bones.

"Adam, I want you to know that whatever you learn here today, just remember you are not alone," Giuseppe said, trying to easily coax the revelations along.

Adam was about to respond when Daven finally arrived, disheveled and looking exhausted. "What happened to you?" Adam asked as Daven sank into the remaining empty chair.

"Late night," was all Daven could muster.

Giuseppe leaned forward in his chair, placing his elbows on his desk with his fingers interlocked in front. He did not make eye contact, mulling an introduction to what he wanted to say around in his head. He knew whatever he said, it would be almost impossible to digest right off, but knowledge is power, and Daven and Adam would need all the power they could get.

"There is more to this life than meets the eye," he began. "I think you two are well aware of this fact, and I think you are beginning to see just how far that extends. You've survived for three years in this city because a madman with a sick dream saw fit for you to suffer. You've lost so much and endured more than I could ever imagine, but there is even more to your suffering than is readily visible. Nero is not the source of your misery. Nero is a puppet, a marionette to a puppeteer with a darker purpose behind the strings it pulls. There is a blackness that controls Nero, so well in fact that Nero himself believes he is independently making the world his own. But he is being used as a powerless figurehead to pave the road to a singular purpose."

"You're telling us that someone else is making Nero horrible?" asked Adam. "I feel like you're trying to excuse Nero of the atrocities he's committed."

"Far from it, Adam," Elia said. "Nero needs to be stopped. That much is certain, but one of the ways to end his reign is cutting the head off the serpent itself."

"Yes," said Giuseppe, thankful for Elia's clearer explanation. "And that is why you're here today. You two are the blade to be used to cut the fangs from the real danger."

"I'm still not clear on what this real danger is," said Daven, slowly waking. "I mean, I imagine it has something to do with our night on the town, but I'm no closer to understanding what that actually was."

Giuseppe gave a moment's pause and decided to nix the slow introduction in favor of diving headlong into the truth. "Mankind is not alone on this earth. We believe we are the stewards of the world around us, but there are others. Others that have sat on the sidelines since the beginning but have recently begun springing into motion, and we are directly in the midst of it all. Not just as humanity, but more focused—as the Vatican itself."

"The lilim," said Elia, attempting to translate Giuseppe's roundabout dialogue, "the Children of Lilith to be exact."

"Was that man from the hotel a lilim?" asked Adam, trying to accept the far-fetched notion that there were other intelligent beings on the earth besides humans.

"Yes," said Giuseppe, "yes, he was. A male lilim bent on violently acquiring information from the Vatican that has been kept secret for over a century, but first, the lilim themselves and who they are."

Elia took the reins. "According to ancient Jewish folklore, God created man and woman at the same time. Adam and Lilith," he said, hoping the two boys would accept this notion without question. "Lilith was unwilling to submit to Adam as a wife, and so she fled on wings to the shores of the Red Sea, where she would lie with demons, giving birth to the lilim."

Daven snickered. "Wow. You do realize you led that fact with the word *folklore*, right? Are we supposed to accept this as the truth without some kind of tangible evidence?"

"Well, yes," said Elia. "But you have evidence. You have met a lilim in person, and you have already fought with him in the form of something you can't explain. Do not just dismiss that occurrence flippantly. It is pivotal to everything we are telling you at this moment."

"He's got a point," said Adam. "That did happen."

Elia continued. "Lilith and her children have, for millennia, been a blight to humanity, spreading disease and pestilence to keep our numbers down. Every major plague that has decimated the living was introduced by the lilim."

"But Lilith vanished," Giuseppe said, taking over. "Her children searched for her for hundreds of years but could not find her. It wasn't until the year 1912 that the secret of her place of rest found its way to the Vatican. The lilim quickly learned of this and have been after it since the beginning of Nero's Reclamation."

"The lilim are actually the masterminds behind Nero's rise to power," said Elia. "They gave Nero everything he needed to take Italy for himself, successfully trapping us within the Vatican so they could search without fear of us moving the secret."

"The Milvian Guard was created to fight both the Aurean powers and the lilim," said Giuseppe, "but the lilim are our top priority."

Adam and Daven sat dumbstruck, attempting to assimilate everything they had just been told. In a matter of five minutes, their world had been turned upside down, but it was not the end of the stream of information being fed to them, and they knew this. "So where do we come in?" asked Adam.

"Lilith and the lilim had their own plagues of a sort to contend with," said Elia. "Three angels God had originally sent to retrieve her: Senoy, Sansenoy, and Semangelof. When she refused, they swore to kill a number of her children every day she neglected to return to Adam. We believe these angels are more than just names when it comes to you two."

"No, no, no," said Daven. "There is no way what you're thinking is possible in any way."

"And why is that?" asked Giuseppe.

"Because!" Daven said, feeling a headache welling up behind his eyes. "It's just ridiculous. The world doesn't work that way."

"After everything you've seen. Everything that has happened to you. The effect the lilim had on your teammates. The transformation you underwent at the hotel. The unnatural speed with which you were healed of your gunshot wound. You still can't accept what we're telling you?" asked Elia with some irritation.

"I can," said Adam. "I can accept it."

Daven looked at Adam with confusion. "Adam," he said, "there is no way what they're thinking can be possible. There's no way we've been possessed by angels. Saying it out loud makes it sound even more nonsensical."

Adam was tired of Daven's disbelief. "Is it so easy for you to forget things?" he asked. "Do you remember the dream we had? Do you remember what you were telling me about the grottoes? According to you, you've actually had extended conversation with someone who called themselves Sansenoy! Someone who would vanish in front of you like they were never there in the first place! What is it going to take to make you believe?"

"I do," Daven said finally. "I do believe. I just don't want to." He sank in his chair. To believe would mean accepting the future that lay ahead of them. He didn't want the responsibility of battling some ancient evil. All he wanted was happiness, and he was close to achieving that with Deirdre. Something he hadn't felt in a long time.

"I understand how this may feel," said Giuseppe. "It is not easy to hear, and I know how scared you must be. There is nothing wrong with being fearful. It keeps your wits about you, but you must realize, we cannot do this without you. You were chosen for a reason. What that reason may be, I'm unsure, but you are not alone. Whatever road you choose from this point, we will be with you. All of us."

Daven and Adam nodded in unison. They were certain at that moment what it was they had to do, as difficult as it was to accept. Shouldering the responsibility of fighting an immensely powerful enemy was a daunting task to undertake. Not only would they need the skills to take on Nero's Domus Aurea, but they would need the knowledge and blessing of the angels they had apparently begun housing within their own souls.

"How do we know?" asked Daven. "How do we know this is exactly what our purpose is?"

Giuseppe opened his mouth in an attempt to answer Daven's question, but his attention was directed to Elia, on whose face was written both shock and awe. His eyes were wide, staring in the direction of Daven and Adam. Giuseppe turned to face the two boys, who had the same look of wonder in their own eyes as well.

It was a familiar portrait to him. The two men from his dream stood behind their respective vessels, every detail the same as it was in that wide, cold void he once found himself in. The same names that had ornamented the foreheads of the angels now had been placed on Daven's and Adam's. It was undeniable proof for all the men in the room of the intent behind the angelic visitors. The boys were no longer scared or apprehensive. Those negative emotions were replaced by wonder and empowerment—and excitement most of all.

"Do not fear. Take heed," said a voice that did not come from either being. "These men have been divinely chosen for the task set before them. This war is one that must be fought by the children of Eve, the children of God."

A backlit fog, one that was familiar to Giuseppe, began to seep into the room. It throbbed with every word that was spoken, and he finally realized it was the source of the disembodied voice.

"Keep vigilant," it continued. "Do not sway or become dismayed. You are worthy. You are the hope of man. You will be victorious."

Suddenly, all was quiet. The room was left empty of anything otherworldly, leaving Giuseppe, Elia, Adam, and Daven alone and silent. There were no questions left within them. No trepidations or disbelief. The importance of their mission was etched into Daven's and Adam's brain and soul. They knew they were backed by not only their friends and allies, but by something entirely celestial.

"What do we do now?" asked Daven.

Giuseppe looked at the two men and smiled.

CHAPTER 15

A Letter from
a Mother

To my one true love,

I dreamt of you ever since I was a child. My young days were filled with caring for a plastic doll, changing its diaper, giving it its soother, changing its clothes and feeding it. I've kept that doll ever since; it sits on the bookshelf in the den. You've always asked why I held on to it for so long, and I admit to some level of embarrassment as to the reason. I guess to me that doll embodied my desire to be a mother and to care for someone bigger than myself. It's what you have to do as a parent. Realize that you are no longer the number one person in your life and that everything you do from that point onward is about raising this precious being to be someone extraordinary. I believe I succeeded when it comes to you.

When your father and I found out that I was pregnant, I nearly fainted. Your father actually did. I can't say I was surprised, given that my mind and body were prepping for that day for as far back as I can remember. The nine months that it took to make you were the longest of my entire life. Not because of the weight gain, agonizing pain, nausea, sleepless nights (I could go on), but because I couldn't wait to see your face. The day you came into this world, wailing and kicking, with a full head of thick dark hair, I wept with happiness. You were the most beautiful thing I had ever seen, surpassing every mountain, forest, ocean, river, lake, construct, and work of art I had laid eyes on. Your father came in as you cried, your tiny little face red, and called out your name. You stopped instantly and looked at him. I know they say that babies can't see anything tangible when they are first born, but I swear in those moments that you saw him and you recognized his voice. He began crying, as you may have guessed, considering he has always been a crybaby, and we both sat, looking at you move, for hours. You didn't fall asleep for a full day, it seemed. Your energy infected us all, and it still does to this day.

As a toddler, you were such a source of happiness, to yourself and to everyone around you. Your intellect was something to behold. The way you articulated your words and how your answers stemmed from logic and not imagination. Your talents bloomed so early, and we became those annoying parents who thought their child was the reincarnated Mozart. The only difference being that you actually were. Or at least I believed it to be so. Your musical ear, your way with words and artistic prowess, fascinated and amazed me, and I'm so proud of you for utilizing those talents.

Your young adult days brought with them pain. We never knew. You never knew. The struggles you dealt with were more than just a burden. They were a curse. The imbalance in your mind pushed your limits, making your life a nightmare to live every day. The brilliance of your high moments was so bright and colorful. Your charismatic personality infected everyone around you, but your curse shocked those who didn't understand. A mother is supposed to be strong for her children, but I fell apart as I watched you weep bitterly in a crumbled heap on your floor that one night. Carrying you out of your apartment to take you home with me was the scariest thing I've ever encountered. Your depression left you immobile, and your weeping left you drained. Mental illness runs in our family. We always knew this, but seeing you suffer the way you did left me speechless. I felt at fault that I allowed this sickness to pass through me to you. But with that pain came dazzling talent. You could do anything you wanted. I remember coming home one day to the sound of that old dusty piano playing "Moonlight Sonata" and asking how long it took you to learn it. You said half an hour. I was so proud. You could play any instrument you put your hands on. You could draw anything that came to mind. You could broadcast an image into anyone's head with detailed precision just through the written word.

I knew you were meant for great things. I knew you would reach millions with your abilities, and I knew you would travel the world so that number would reach billions. I never knew that the day you left would potentially be the last day I would ever see your face. I see your beautiful smile and piercing eyes in my dreams every night, but all I want is to hear you call me Mommy once again. I can't begin to tell you how crushed I was to see your light fade on a television screen. Especially when no answers could be given as to what had transpired. I still don't know what happened to this day, three years later, and I can't keep going any longer with these questions pouring through my mind, wondering if you are still out there or if you've been buried and forgotten on foreign soil. So today, I write this as a form of closure, to mentally and spiritually allow you the rest you so greatly deserve. My world is over with the closing of these words, and I will seal this letter with my love and soul. I'll place it in the arms of that doll on the bookshelf and keep the memory of you alive through everything your life was and could have been. I love you so much, Daven. I love you more with each passing day. I will see you again in the bright eternal, and I will stare into your beautiful eyes once again with pride in my heart and tears on my face.

I can't bear to close this letter.

CHAPTER 16

DECISIONS

October 18, 2035

His boots clicked quickly and angrily down a hall in the Aurean Ministry of Defense. Benito Gozi had been summoned by his older brother and legate, Adamo, to discuss an unnerving change of plan put forth by Nero. He was a younger man, in his midtwenties, with a fiery personality that had landed him as the primus palus, or senior centurion, in the Lazio Legion's first cohort. Although his abrasiveness was widely noted, his leadership skills were fabled.

A command had just come down from Nero ordering Adamo and Benito to plan an attack on the Vatican. Benito was aware of the implications this entailed, knowing of the lilim and their restrictions. He did not enjoy the idea of being involved in whatever insane idea Nero had in mind, and he hoped his brother would back any attempt to stop the matter before it got worse.

"What is he trying to pull?" Benito asked as he slammed Adamo's office door behind him.

"Not now, Benito," Adamo said as he placed a book back on its shelf.

"Yes, now!" Benito yelled, pounding his fist down on Adamo's desk. "We can't dignify this with any kind of serious thought. You know what will happen!"

Adamo turned slowly with slit eyes, disarming Benito with a single look. He walked to the corner of his office in front of his desk. "Sit," he said as he forcefully slid a chair toward Benito.

"I don't understand," said Benito, quieter and less offensive. "For years one of our top limitations was to refrain from even looking at the Vatican. Now he wants us to actively begin planning an invasion? Has he forgotten? This is a game to the lilim, and if Nero breaks the rules, the game is over. And so are we."

"There are more players in this than you are aware of, Benito," said Adamo calmly. "We associate ourselves with those who are winning. With those who can get us what we want. Just like any race, runners can fall behind and lead. Right now, the runner we bet on is losing. However, we've been given an opportunity to change our wagers."

"You don't truly believe that, do you?" asked Benito, skeptical. "You're just repeating what he's told you. Isn't this true?"

Adamo paused. "I'm not paid for voicing my personal convictions. Neither are you."

"Personal convictions aside, I have no want or need to march into Saint Peter's Square knowing it could mean taking my last step," Benito said. "What has changed? There's no way you agreed to this without some kind of resistance. You've always been the only one who could stand up to him."

"Obviously what I think is inconsequential," Adamo said, confirming his reservations. "We've made it this far. I think we are obligated to follow Nero further."

"You still haven't answered my question," said Benito. "What has changed? What are we marching into hell for?"

Adamo finally sat down at his desk. He rubbed his eyes with the palms of his hands and sighed. His job was to lead, not question, but he was teetering on the edge of opposing action. The lilim were clear about interfering with their hidden task. They had made their intentions clear: leave the Vatican unmolested so their kind could look for the answers to their standing question, and Nero would receive the empire he so richly desired. Adamo knew Nero would never go against such a powerful ally when his every wish was at stake unless a better offer was presented.

"I trust him, Benito," said Adamo with sincerity. "He may be unhinged at times, but he is a good leader. If you trust me, trust him as well."

Benito stood and walked toward a window facing the Via Venti

Settembre as a century of one hundred men marched by. These men put their lives on the line to protect Domus Aurea and her leader. It did not sit well with him knowing these soldiers might die by his hand. Although the command came from Nero, it was his and his brother's voice that would have them marching forward.

"If we do this, we do this right," said Benito. "I don't like going against the lilim's wishes, but I despise watching my men die even more. So although I disagree with this move completely, I will put forth my all. For my men's sake. What is our time frame?"

"We act slowly," Adamo said. "I have no date set as of yet. I want this to go over without resistance, so we tread lightly; there's no sense in rushing in. The problem does not lie with Vatican forces; this much is certain. What happens after we lay waste? This is what I fear."

"So we plan for retaliation?" asked Benito. "We plan for the recoil?"

"Yes," Adamo said. "We become proactive. Not reactive."

Benito rested his forehead on the giant window framed by flowing red curtains. "It just doesn't seem right. It isn't sitting well with me," he said as the century marched out of view. "We sit here in this room and plot their demise like it's nothing. They're just chess pieces to us. Disposable and easily manipulated. If we commanded them to start a fire and then march into it, they would without hesitation. Is this what we are to Nero? Pawns on a checkered board? He doles out commands flippantly, and we follow them blindly. So far, the lilim have had him reined in. What happens when he finds out he can function without them?"

"He can't," Adamo responded. "He can't function without them."

Benito finally understood. "You want him to fail," he said with realization. "You want the lilim to intervene."

"I don't want him to fail," Adamo said. "I want him to refocus. He is dealing with a dangerous lilim that has promised him everything he has ever wanted in half the time. If this lilim can pull off what he is promising, then so be it, but we need to plan for the worst. I'm hoping that if or when this invasion turns south, Nero will correct his course."

Benito continued looking out the window. The clouds had parted, and the sun began to shine in his eyes, causing him to squint but not turn away. There were some days he wished he was ignorant of the lilim's existence, but a man in his position needed to be aware of his surroundings.

He trusted Adamo more than anyone. Family was family, and blood was the ultimate word of trust. Nero was a force to be reckoned with, but he was only one man and an unbalanced one at that. He was capable of great feats, but it was due time for a mistake to be made, and Benito felt this would be one.

"What's on your mind, brother?" asked Adamo.

Benito turned around and sat back down at Adamo's desk. For a moment, he fidgeted with a paperweight, picking it up and letting it fall with a short click. "What if we tell the lilim what Nero is planning?" he asked Adamo without making eye contact.

Adamo sat back in his chair, interlocking his fingers across his chest. "I wouldn't even know where to start or where to find them."

Benito was happy his brother hadn't shot the idea down without thinking it over. "Maybe we don't need to find them. Maybe they have already heard us."

Adamo was about to answer when one of the soldiers guarding his door walked in. He stood in the center of the room, his weapon resting across his torso, with a look of emptiness in his eyes. Neither Adamo nor Benito spoke; instead, they both looked at the man, waiting for something to happen.

"We hear all," the soldier said with an unfamiliar voice. "Nothing escapes our gaze, and nothing deafens our ears. We understand your position. We will speak again."

Suddenly the soldier's mind was released. A look of shock moved across his face, fearful that he had interrupted an important meeting, sensing the tension in the room.

"I'm sorry, sir!" he chanted as he saluted. "I did not mean to disturb your meeting."

"All is well," Adamo said with a slight smile. "You are dismissed. Return to your post."

Benito turned to Adamo. "I've never actually experienced something like that before," he said, looking at his arm as he rolled up his sleeve. "I've got chills."

"There's no getting used to it," Adamo said, remembering some past event. "But this does change things. For now, we continue with our plans."

"I agree," said Benito. "Keep me informed. I'll be around."

Benito rose from his chair, dipped his head to his superior, and left, shutting the large wooden door behind him.

Deirdre opened her eyes and groaned. She had slept well past twelve in the afternoon, feeling groggy and weak as she placed her feet on the ground. Liana had already woken up, having made her bed and left without waking Deirdre.

"Why did she let me sleep so long?" Deirdre mumbled to herself as she rubbed her eyes and yawned. She slipped on a pair of jeans and a white cardigan, then sat down in front of a mirror to brush her hair. It was a jumbled red mess, thick and wavy. The brush ran roughly through the curls, tearing pieces out and clumping itself on the bristles.

"What I wouldn't give for some decent hair products," she said, looking at the brush.

After a few minutes, she heard a light knock on her door. Setting the brush down on the chest of drawers, she stood up, wrapping the open cardigan around her body. Deirdre gripped the knob and slowly opened the door. Daven stood there with his hands in his pockets looking especially exhausted, but he smiled a weak smile and diverted his gaze downward at his feet.

"Hey there," Deirdre said with a grin, reaching out to grab his wrists. "Sorry if I look terrible. I just woke up."

"I don't think you've ever looked terrible a day in your life," Daven said, still quiet and reserved. "You want to take a walk?"

Deirdre smiled. "Yeah, let me put my boots on. Want to walk the wall?"

Daven nodded and watched as she slipped the brown boots on; they reached to just below her knees. It was the first time he had looked at her through affectionate eyes knowing the same was being reciprocated. She was beautiful. Everything about her seemed perfect to him. Her eyes, her smile, the way she walked, the way she looked at him. He felt lucky; even after everything he had endured, she made it all go away.

"Shall we?" she asked as she hopped up from the bed.

"Let's go."

The two made their way west to the fountain of the Belvedere Courtyard, walking across the warm asphalt of the parking lot that surrounded it. The buildings loomed in over them from all four sides, their windows reflecting the empty world. After a few minutes, the couple passed into the Old Gardens. The foliage was thick, shading them from the afternoon sun. The smell of decaying vegetation filled their noses, wet and dirty, feeding the old forest that grew around them. The sunrays bled through the branches and leaves above their heads, warming the surroundings and adding to the sense of calm Daven and Deirdre were feeling.

The two had walked, speaking little, all the way to the farthest wall. The stone protector climbed forty feet into the air, angling inward at the top. Daven had wondered, even though the walls were thick and sturdy, how they could keep such a force like the Aureans at bay. It seemed nothing could keep them from destroying the life they had built there, but knowing what he knew now, it wasn't much of a mystery anymore.

"I've walked these walls so many times," Deirdre said, running her fingers along the stone as they walked, "but it never gets old. It makes the world feel bigger."

"I still feel caged," said Daven, walking with his eyes staring at the path below him. "The world felt small before, but when all this happened, it got smaller. Then when we arrived here, it got even smaller."

"Well, if you look at it that way," said Deirdre. "But sometimes the world only needs to be big enough for two people."

Deirdre reached out her hand and grasped Daven's. The man's heart leapt through his throat, beating hard and fast, pulsing adrenaline through his body. He had wanted to reach out to her for a long time, but he was slow when it came to Deirdre. He wanted things to be perfect, not rushing and not pushing, leaving a forceful persona behind. He couldn't help but smile, something Deirdre awkwardly pointed out.

"You're so cute," she said, grinning from ear to ear. "Like a grade-schooler. Have you ever held a woman's hand?"

Daven looked at her, his smile zipping into a grin. "Yes. A long time ago, but I'll never forget."

Deirdre noticed the sinking in Daven's voice. "Sorry," she said. "Did I touch a nerve?"

"No, it's okay," he said. "Just memories at this point. Nothing we need to worry about now."

Deirdre disagreed. "It is something to worry about. Maybe not worry, but something that needs to be talked about."

"Some people just have a way of living on in your mind no matter what you do," Daven said. "They take a piece of your soul and hide it away, forgetting about it forever. No matter how the end arrives."

Deirdre nodded her head in agreement, dropping Daven's hand in the process. "I was married once," she said, shocking Daven and halting his movement. "He died during the Vatican Revolt. It feels so long ago, but it really wasn't. Some nights, I can still smell his blood on my hands and the feelings of uselessness creeping back over me, just as I felt that day he died. I've tried associating my life with him with something other than death, but I can't. No matter how hard I try. I won't lie. I still love him. I think I always will. Just like you said, they take that piece and hide it. Morgan took it the day he bled out in my arms." Deirdre turned back to look at Daven with tears in her eyes. "But a piece is only a piece. I still have more to give. I haven't taken what we have lightly, and I didn't jump into this to forget what once was. You came into my life like a comet hitting the earth, something I couldn't ignore. You've become a frustrating and blinding light that I've come to adore more than anything else. I can't hide it anymore, no matter how much you drive me insane with your stubborn personality."

She looked at Daven and blushed. "Oh, my God," she said as she covered her face. "That just came pouring out. I'm so sorry."

Daven walked to Deirdre and embraced her. "Thank you," he said. "Thank you for showing me everything. I never knew about your husband. I'm so sorry. I've never experienced a loss like that, and I can't imagine how that's affected you. You're a brave woman. Braver than I'll ever be, but I hope I can change, having experienced life with you."

Deirdre rested her head on Daven's chest, listening to his heart race. "What about you?" she asked him. "Have you ever been in love?"

Daven stood quietly, his thoughts racing. "Once," he finally said. "We were characters in an old story of forbidden love. The more we fell for one another, the more the world wished to tear us apart. I was young and headstrong, causing more harm than good, but I truly thought I was fighting for something worthwhile. The problem was that I was going about it all wrong, and I ended up hurting someone I am—or was—madly in love with." Daven stepped back and crossed his arms. "I look back now and realize that her family was only doing what they thought was best for their daughter, but at the time, I was certain of their so-called cruel intentions."

"Sounds to me like something Shakespeare may have written," said Deirdre with a sly grin.

"Something like that," said Daven, forcing a smile, "but I'm convinced Romeo and Juliet had it easy compared to myself and … her."

"Her?"

Daven continued avoiding eye contact. "I live with the scars; no need to be reminded of the pain by dredging up an old name."

"So if I remember correctly," Deirdre said, moving the conversation along, "Romeo and Juliet met with a painful and tragic death. How is that easier?"

"They died together," Daven said as the faint smile faded from his face. "Better, in my opinion, than loving someone from afar, knowing you'll never feel your heart leap at their smile, never lose yourself in their eyes or hear their voice say, 'I love you,' ever again."

Deirdre felt for Daven as she stood in silent regret, wishing she hadn't forced him to relive a painful memory. "I'm sorry. We don't have to talk about it if you don't want."

"No, it's fine," he said, forcing another weak smile through an empty countenance. "I enjoy seeing her face, even if it's only through the eyes of recollection."

"So, what happened?" she asked apprehensively.

"We flew too close to the sun," Daven said, leaning forward. "Our embrace was loosened by familial intervention, and we lost our wings. We reached out so far to touch once more that our bones themselves stretched and cracked under our intense will to be together again. The moments we were together toward the end were filled with sorrow and tears. We were left not knowing if that instance would be the last we saw each other, but you learn to appreciate those times so much more when there is the threat of separation. I remember the last time I saw her face. It replays in my mind like a residual haunting, constantly reminding me of something that has died and drifted into oblivion. I loved her more than I can express or even imagine. I loved her so much that I couldn't begin to fathom the depths of its potential, and it scared me to the point that I couldn't commit to the plunge, not knowing if it would drown me or revitalize me from a life of cynicism."

"Why did you let her go?" Deirdre asked, noting Daven's clearly expressed longing for the unnamed woman.

"I was weak," Daven said with a tired voice. "I fought for years to gain the respect of her family, but the internal battle I fought with myself weakened my resolve. I knew then that I couldn't win her parents' adoration, but instead of bowing out and allowing for an easier life for her, I caused a rift between her and her loved ones with my spiteful actions. We began to fight constantly, and one night, I spoke our end. I dream of seeing her again some nights. In my dreams, she's far off, and it doesn't seem like she notices me, but then she turns and we lock eyes. She smiles that smile, and her eyes—those eyes make my knees buckle and my heart soar. We walk toward each other and embrace. I weep and tell her that I never stopped loving her and never stopped wanting her back. She tells me the same. Sometimes, in the back of my mind, I know it's only a dream, and I prep myself for awakening to a world without her. But other times I believe it is complete reality. Which makes waking so painful. I will never heal from her, but I hope that she realizes that I don't want to, and I hope my Ashbee knows that I will never forget the sound of her voice and the way it kills me inside."

Deirdre's heart sank. How could she stand up to such a woman? How could she replace that emptiness in Daven's heart?

"But that voice, that dream is real now," Daven said. "I've found a smile that eclipses anything I've seen before. I've stared into eyes that outshine the gaze in my memories. You've burned away the sadness and longing I've felt for so long. You're everything I've ever wanted."

Deirdre's heart rose to the middle of her throat, pushing happiness through her body. She stared at Daven, taking in everything he was, seeing him as someone to bring love back into her life.

"Oh, what the hell," she said as she jumped, wrapping her arms around the back of his neck, pulling herself up to Daven's face and pressing their lips together with ardent force.

"I won't apologize for that," Deirdre said, still hanging from Daven's neck, "and I plan on doing it again very soon."

Daven laughed, picking Deirdre up in his arms, repeating the process Deirdre started. "I won't apologize for that either," he said. "Because I also plan on doing it again very soon."

Deirdre pulled herself close, listening as their heartbeats intertwined in rhythm. "I love you, Daven," she said with closed eyes.

"I love you, Deirdre," he answered, the sound of his voice vibrating in his chest, allowing Deirdre to both listen to and feel the words she had always wanted to hear once more.

Chaigidel stood facing a large stone wall within the many corridors of the tunnels under Rome. These halls had housed many lilim for millennia, allowing them both strategic placement within a once powerful empire's capital city and safety. The wall in front of her was burrowed into, creating inlaid shelves filled with ornate bowls. She stared intensely at a new vessel that had been placed in the middle of hundreds of old, tarnished ones similar in make. The ashes of Thamiel had been placed within it, surrounded by those of the brothers and sisters gone on long before. Thamiel had been the first lilim to die in hundreds of years and the first to be killed through fratricide.

"You will never find rest," she muttered to herself. "Like Hagar and Ishmael, the lilim are cast from God's sight. All we ever had was each other."

"Disobedience begets punishment. Your wandering in death is of your own doing," said a whispered voice from behind her.

She knew the voice, and there was no way she could ever forget. It was over one thousand years ago, on the shores of present-day Moraine Lake in the Valley of the Ten Peaks. Chaigidel was a young lilim lying on the shores of the emerald lake under the stars of twilight. There were three hundred other lilim lying on the waterside that night with her, peaceful and alone. Lilith spread her progeny around the world in an attempt to keep them safe. The native human population kept their distance, naming the area the Place of Starry Eyes, as the lilim's eyes reflected moonlight like a cat's. She remembered the crack that echoed off the mountains like an explosion of thunder and lightning as a blinding pinprick of light appeared above them. Four hands pushed through the opening, pulling the hole apart in four different directions, revealing a heavenly realm behind the night sky. Three beings emerged, silhouettes of white fire, each clutching sharp pillars of lightning. They were massive, standing taller than the mountains around them, with black shadowy wings growing from behind their celestial bodies. With their wings, the angelic beings walled one hundred lilim within, Chaigidel being spared by inches. She remembered watching as the swords of light came down, burning the hundred into ash, and then ash into nothingness.

"It has been decreed," the three spoke in unison. "By the eternal creator, it is so."

Chaigidel fell to her knees as the three stepped back into the opening, and then watched as the four hands pulled it closed, leaving silence and stars in its wake.

"It's been a long, long time," she said, returning from thought to reality, still staring at Thamiel's grave. "Are you here for your hundred?"

Chaigidel turned around to see two men dressed in radiant white robes staring at her through hot, burning eyes.

"Our promise requires Lilith to refuse an offer made long ago," the man on the left said. "Lilith is incapable of decision. You live because she is hidden."

The lilim turned back to face the wall of ashes, silent in thought. She knew what the angels were offering, but arriving at a decision was difficult to achieve. "Our kind would eventually die," she said after some deliberation. "All newborn lilim come from Lilith. We are all siblings of one another, and therefore we do not lie with each other. It deludes our bloodline."

"You will die if you continue this crusade," the angels said. "We have chosen warriors to carry our essence within them. They will continue our work where we cannot. Our mission was to punish Lilith. Our vessels' mission is to punish you."

Chaigidel did not answer in defense. She was tired and drained from her time of mourning. Her family would continue their search, no matter what threat befell them, but her eyes grew heavy with the thought. "Tell me," she asked the angels, turning back around. "Where is the third?"

"He is coming," they said in unison, and as Chaigidel blinked, the angels were gone.

A lilim turned a dark corner, walking to Chaigidel and tilting his head to touch his right shoulder, signifying the rank of the eldest sister in front of him. "I heard speaking," he said. "Are you alone?"

"I am," she said, still with an unbroken gaze. "I was talking to your older brother."

The lilim nodded and began to walk away. "Where do we go from here?" he asked her, stopping short of the corner.

"We make the Catholics bleed," she said. "And once the skin is broken, we will swim in their veins and infect their minds. There, we will find our answers."

The lilim tilted his head once more and smiled. "My sister, it will be done."

"Yes. Yes, it will."

CHAPTER 17

UNHINGED

January 16, 2036

S everal months had passed without incident for the occupants of Vatican City. The burden of repetition spread once again through the minds of those protecting the city, boring them into semi-insanity. Milvian Swords decorated the tops of the city's walls, attempting to present a more intimidating face to the Aureans than was actually there. Scott and Adam sat atop a section of the north wall, with their legs hanging off the side facing the city. Both sucked down on a cigarette that hung loosely on their lips, letting the ash fall onto the streets below.

"I could never get Daven to do this," Adam said as his gaze became unfocused on the landscape in front of him.

"What? Smoking?" asked Scott, turning his head toward Adam. He blew smoke out of the corner of his mouth, trying not to rudely puff it in Adam's face.

Adam laughed. "Yeah," he said. "That, too, but he hates heights. He acts like a worried mother whenever I do stuff like this. He thinks if he looks away, I'm going to fall or something."

"Sounds like a little something my mom would do," Scott said. "But I outlived her, so I guess I should have been the one doing the watching."

Adam was slightly put off by how nonchalantly Scott spoke about his dead mother. "What the hell, man?" he asked with a hiccup laugh.

"Leukemia," Scott said. "But she never showed an ounce of fear. Even after losing almost a hundred pounds in a month. She pretty much gave death the finger as her last word. I respect her memory by remembering how strong she was. I guess my dark humor is a symptom of that."

Adam silently agreed and lifted his cigarette back to his mouth.

"What about you?" asked Scott. "You have parents?"

Adam laughed. "No, I was a Cabbage Patch Kid," he said. "I had the beady, soulless eyes and everything."

"You're a jackass. You know what I mean," Scott said with an irritated smirk.

"As far as I know, I still have parents," Adam said, part jokingly, part depressingly. "My mother is also my rock. My sister died when I was eighteen. We knew it was going to happen, but that just killed us slowly. She had slipped into a coma after years of blood thinners caused bleeding in her brain. My mom crumbled the day she died, but even then, I have never seen more strength in anyone else since that day. I know it still cuts her to the bone when the anniversary of her death arrives, but she puts on a happy face and celebrates her life rather than mourning her passing. But now her last remaining child may as well be dead. I wish I could just reach out and let her know I'm fine. That I'm still breathing and doing everything I can to get home."

"Mothers have that instinct," Scott said. "They worry all the time, but they know when their child is fine."

"I hope you're right," Adam said as he flicked the cigarette butt out into Domus Aurea. "I really do."

The sky opened up after Adam stopped talking. The rain was relatively warm compared to the cold in the air, but it still made Adam shudder.

"Come on, man," said Scott. "Let's get out of the rain."

It was cold. Very cold, and dark. He walked slowly across the landscape, his boots heavily laden, keeping him firmly planted on the earth. The ground was flat and wet, making his already laborious footwear that much harder to move. He could sense the animals of the surroundings staring at him, curious, knowing he didn't belong in their home. The elements moved quickly past his ears, creating a deafening noise, making it hard to keep his eyes open. Although it was a difficult journey, it wasn't anything he hadn't experienced before.

This place used to frighten him, the otherworldly creatures of the perpetual night a horror to behold, but he had been here several times in the distant past. The monsters of this world stared at him. Much like inhabitants of a small village nervously observing a stranger passing through their town unannounced. Now, the only fearful element of his place of being was the eyes of the giants that moved like smoke around him, effortless and perfect.

He had a purpose now. Something he hadn't been blessed with for some time. The voice had asked him to help, and help is what he would do, with no questioning in his quiet mind. He knew that this holy mission would give his life new meaning, and for the first time in millennia, a smile graced his lips.

It was cold. Very cold, but it was always cold at the bottom of the sea.

"What is it, Alban?" Camillo asked as he flipped through the pages of a book while sitting at his desk.

Alban slumped into a chair across the room. He was clearly distressed, but it did nothing but irritate Camillo.

"You're intruding on my quiet time, Alban. Tell me what you want."

Alban sighed. "I-I don't know if I can commit to … whatever it is you have planned for me," he said without making eye contact. "I feel a twinge of unease with the situation."

Camillo eyed Alban through the top of his glasses, set his book down, and removed the frames from his face.

"You agreed without hesitation when we last spoke," Camillo said with a soft voice. "Am I to understand that you do not wish to acquire the respect and power you have always desired?"

"I am a man who does not think before he speaks on some occasions," Alban said with a forced smile. "I'm afraid I agreed in the midst of overwhelming excitement."

"Finally," Camillo said. "Something you and I both agree on. Your unbridled and boisterous personality. Not your decision."

Camillo rose from his chair and walked toward the cardinal. "I am not critical of your apprehension, Alban. It is a quality rarely found in yourself. I am, however, confused as to where this change of heart is stemming from."

"Fear," Alban said, looking up for the first time since he entered the room. "I'm afraid of the repercussions."

"Ah," Camillo said. "However, the powerful have no reason to fear. Their subordinates take on that responsibility. They claim accountability for consequences. I think, however, this may be a matter of trust."

"Trust?" Alban asked.

"You don't trust me," Camillo said. "You don't trust I can keep my word."

"But it's not in you I need to place my trust, is it?" Alban said with a curled lip.

Camillo smiled back. "How astute." The man leaned against his desk and crossed his arms. "Then trust that I know what I'm doing."

Alban's thoughts were chaotic of late. According to his peers, it had had a positive effect on his demeanor, shutting away his fiery persona in favor of a quiet, anxious thinker. Although he had become tolerable to the people around him, his body was plagued with health issues, most notably a festering ulcer in his stomach. His normal offensive self was a pressure release, using his rank as a sort of castle tower to shout down from, but he was no longer the top of his world.

"Perhaps I am just untrusting of the men behind the curtain," Alban said. "I am a third party in all this. Much responsibility lies with me, but I am blind in the scheme of things."

"This will be something you must overcome mentally, Alban," Camillo said with some compassion. "View your partially veiled eyes as a blessing in disguise. Too much knowledge is enough to drive a man insane."

"Just tell me I'm not being used for some higher sinister purpose," Alban asked with a sweat-covered brow.

Camillo sighed. "We are all puppets of a sort, but the realization of this fact is the first step to working toward a level of control. However, you have been promised power. Does it matter in what form it comes?"

"I suppose not," Alban said as he rose from his seat. "I believe I shall commit to the plunge, Your Eminence. Thank you for your time."

Camillo watched as Alban approached the open door. "Alban," he said as the cardinal turned to look at him. "Do not second-guess your choice. They abhor indecision."

Alban's countenance fell slightly, but he quickly forced it into a contorted smile. "I will not give them a reason to second-guess me."

"Good," Camillo said with a smug expression. "Not even once. They watch always and from all vantage points. You are never alone. Just as God is omnipresent and omniscient, so are our allies."

"To the future of Christ's bride, the church," Alban said with a bow.

"To the future of the church," Camillo responded.

As Alban left, Camillo lightly shut the door and returned to his desk. He placed his glasses on the tip of his nose and picked up his book once again. He was reading *The Death of Caesar*, smiling as his eyes slowly glided over the words describing Julius Caesar's assassination.

"I've seen rocks jump higher than that!" yelled Azael as he walked back and forth in front of the line of Eyes doing lunge jumps.

"I'd love to see that," said Deirdre, panting and red-faced.

Azael halted his march and kicked a rock up into his hand like a soccer player juggling a ball. "You see? Now with gusto!"

"I really hate cardio," Marco said with labored breathing.

"I hate that rock," Sergio said with the same heavy voice. "It really can jump higher than us."

"Please don't make me laugh," said Liana. "I don't have enough wind for it."

"Are you okay, Deirdre?" Sergio asked. "You're not your normal paper-white self."

Deirdre cut her eyes at Sergio. Her skin was flushed and glistening from the hour-long exercise regimen. "I'm very Irish, ye bollix. We're either pale with freckles or red with freckles. The latter could result in an arse whooping."

"I'd enjoy that," said Sergio with a grin.

Suddenly a rock soared from Azael's direction, smacking Sergio in the shoulder.

"Enough, you jackass!" Azael said as he continued his pacing. "Since I lost count listening to you dribble on, let's start back at one! Shall we?"

After what seemed like an inordinate amount of time, Azael blew his whistle and ordered the soldiers to stop.

"All right, guys, hit the showers," he said as Giuseppe walked into the gym.

The two began speaking in a low murmur as the Eyes began to wind down.

"You wanted to see me Azael?" Giuseppe asked as he watched the soldiers stretch.

"Yes, sir, but I could have met you. I didn't mean for you to come down here," said Azael.

"I was enjoying the weather," Giuseppe said as he removed his jacket.

"Last I checked, it was eight degrees outside," Azael said with a laugh. "But no one ever accused you of being too smart."

"That they have not," Giuseppe said. "So what do you have on your mind?"

Azael looked over his shoulder at his men. "They're restless, you know? It's been two months since our last foray. What were the fruits of our labor? Was it all for nothing?"

Giuseppe couldn't blame Azael for the question. He had been thinking the same thing for some time now. He knew steps needed to be taken to move forward, but it was a precarious path to follow. One wrong move could mean the end of them all, but indecision and stagnation could spell the same fate.

"I've done a lot of meditating and praying on the subject," Giuseppe said, still watching the Eyes. "I do feel that a careful approach is pivotal to our success, but I can't argue with your assertion. They deserve to see results." Giuseppe crossed his arms and exhaled through his nose. "We need to meet with them," he said finally.

"Meet with who?" Azael asked, hoping *them* wasn't who he thought they were, knowing Giuseppe wasn't talking about his men.

"The lilim you encountered was not of the main fold of lilim,"

Giuseppe said quickly. "We know that. I feel at this point, alerting his brethren may be beneficial for us."

"The enemy of my enemy," said Azael. "I'm not so sure, Giuseppe. Is it wise?"

Giuseppe nodded his head in the direction of Daven and Adam. "It is now," he said, still with his arms crossed.

Azael had forgotten about the Guard's new secret weapons. Although what he and the others had witnessed that night in the hotel was a sight to behold, it was the only example available demonstrating what Daven and Adam could do. It was time to put their abilities to the test.

"I wouldn't know where to start," Azael said, stubbornly clinging to his trepidation. "For one, how would we contact them? I'm assuming we would be keeping this knowledge within the Guard, but how do we handle this getting out? People will not be happy."

"The weight of responsibility lies with me, Azael," Giuseppe said. "You may feign ignorance if this were to become an issue, but I believe this is the right path to follow. We can't fight a third opponent. It's not feasible. Domus Aurea is one foe enough, but the lilim make it two too many. Having a rogue third could potentially raze us to the ground. I'm almost positive the lilim are worried this lilim will foil their plans by being too brazen. One wrong move, and the secret is destroyed."

"You're serious about this, aren't you?" Azael said.

"Very."

"So be it," Azael said as he beckoned to Daven and Adam.

The two men stood before their superiors, sweaty and panting. It was strange to look at these young boys as heroes or saviors. Just months before, they were scared and spiritually exhausted individuals having just fended off the entirety of the Lazio Legion. They had experienced loss and pain, fear and doubt, but now they stood tall in the face of death and hatred. Now they were vessels of insurmountable power.

"Boys, you have seen and done things that no one among you could possibly begin to explain," Giuseppe said before the two men could speak. "And I know we haven't made mention of it since it happened, but I believe it's time to test your abilities. It will mean you becoming our frontline defense against the lilim. I believe you are immune to anything they can throw against you. We've seen this in action. We know it to be true, but now is the time for us to send you into the field."

Daven and Adam were silent, but Azael and Giuseppe saw no hint of fear in their eyes.

"We need emissaries," Giuseppe continued. "We need to speak with the lilim, and you two are the only ones who can do this safely."

"Okay," Adam said with confidence. "What do we need to do?"

Giuseppe smiled. "Azael and I will get with you once a plan is in place. For now, prepare yourselves mentally. You may be the only humans in the world able to stand on equal footing with the lilim, but they are still creatures of a supernatural origin. Your own minds may be your greatest enemy when facing these beings."

"We trust you, Giuseppe," Daven said. "You've done so much for us, we'd be crazy not to trust you now."

"We will win this, boys," Giuseppe said with excitement. "Once the lilim fall, Domus Aurea will fall as well."

Daven and Adam waved farewell to Azael and Giuseppe as they made their way to the showers. The water was hot, but the cold outside made it that much more enjoyable. The two made sure to consciously enjoy the simple amenities every time they utilized them, especially after the short time they spent wandering the streets of Rome without said comforts.

"Will you two girls hurry up in there?" Deirdre yelled from around the corner. "He's my boyfriend, Adam! Keep your grubby hands off him!"

"I'm the one you should be scared for!" Adam yelled back. "Every time I drop the soap, I have a heart attack!"

Daven came around the corner after drying off, wrapped in a towel.

"Why do you do this to me?" Deirdre said, grabbing his hips. "We live in the most Catholic place on earth! I shouldn't even be looking at you right now!"

"My clothes are in my locker, you perv," Daven said. "You're insatiable, you know that?"

Deirdre growled and laughed as Daven walked down the row of lockers. She was happy. The happiest she had been since Daven's arrival to her corner of the world, and now, he was her world.

Scott came into the room as Daven and Adam were tying their shoes.

He was wearing a thick aviator jacket and was rubbing his hands together quickly.

"Hey, Adam," he said as he warmed his hands with his breath. "You have any cigarettes?"

Adam patted the pockets of his jeans and jacket. "No, man, I think I'm out," he said much to Scott's dismay. "Where have you been getting them anyway?"

"Ah, there's a store in Rome that gives them to me for nothing," Scott said casually. "I guess I'm going to have to head out soon."

Deirdre, Adam, and Daven looked at Scott with shock. "What the hell are you talking about?" Deirdre said. "You've been sneaking out into Rome? Are you insane?"

"I've been doing it for years, chickadee," Scott said with a furrowed brow. "Never had a single issue. In fact, I guarantee you I can take all three of you with me, and we'll all be fine."

"Oh no!" Deirdre said with disdain. "None of us are that crazy."

"Didn't you two do the same thing?" Scott asked Daven and Adam. "In fact, rumor has it that you got shot, Daven. I even heard that you killed an Aurean soldier in the process. So I think it's safe to say that neither of you can cast judgment."

"Hey, I didn't say anything!" Daven said in his defense. "In fact, I'll go with you!"

"The hell you will!" Deirdre said as she punched Daven in the shoulder.

"Yeah, I'm down for it," Adam said, stepping away from Deirdre's swinging range.

"Are you insane?" Deirdre asked Adam. "You'll be caught! And you know Nero has it out for you! If you get arrested, he's going to make an example of you. He won't just kill you; he'll torture you, and publicly."

"Deirdre, he's going to be fine," Scott said. "They won't get caught, I promise."

"They aren't going to get caught because they aren't going," she said. "Daven is staying here with me. I wish Adam would stay, too, but I can't tell him what to do."

"Babe," Daven said with a low voice, "I can't let Adam go without me. We've been through everything together. If something were to happen and I wasn't there to stop it, I'll never be able to live with myself."

Deirdre was not happy with Daven's plan. "Please don't," she pleaded. "I'm not going to lose you. I can't lose you. I can't go through that again."

Deirdre began to weep in Daven's arms. Flashbacks pulsed through her mind, imagining her late husband's blood seeping into the ground around them.

"Okay," Daven said softly. "Okay; I won't go."

Deirdre turned her face toward Adam. "Please don't go," she said with foggy eyes. "Scott, you too. Not for something so superficial."

"I'll be fine," Scott said. "I've literally done this hundreds of times."

"We'll be safe," Adam told Deirdre. "We'll be back before you know it."

Deirdre still wasn't sure, but there was nothing she could do to stop the two from doing what they wanted.

"Just be careful," she said with care in her voice. "Don't make me regret not tying you to a chair."

After a half hour, Daven and Deirdre walked through the doors of the barracks, leaving as Scott and Adam approached the Santa Ana Gate. They paid off the guard and disappeared into the night. Daven was quiet and Deirdre knew why, but she instead tried to cheer him up and not acknowledge his disposition.

"Are you hungry?" she asked, feeling slightly guilty and embarrassed about how she treated Daven.

"No, I'm fine," Daven said, kissing her on the cheek and smiling with closed lips. "Look, I know you feel guilty for keeping me here, but I'm glad you talked me out of it actually."

"You are?" she asked with elation.

"Yeah," he said. "I'm tired. Plus, I wouldn't have been able to go, knowing how it made you feel. It's fine. Really, it is."

Deirdre smiled, a load lifting off her shoulders, but even then, she still felt like she had nailed Daven to the floor.

"I'm going to go lie down," he said as he leaned in to hug her. "I'll come find you in a little bit."

The two gave each other a peck on the lips and parted ways. Deirdre watched him slowly ascend the stairs and then as he walked out of view. She still felt a measure of guilt, but she knew she couldn't lose him now. Not after how far she had fallen for him.

"Deirdre!" Liana yelled from the café. "Come here! I feel like I haven't been able to talk to you in forever."

Deirdre turned to see her friend sitting alone at a table. She knew she had been neglecting her other social relations, and so she felt obligated to sit and talk. The woman hoped it would take her mind off the events of the night, but she felt better knowing the love of her life was just seconds away.

"Where is this place?" Adam asked Scott as they quickly skipped through backstreets. "I really don't like being out here."

"Shut up," Scott hissed. "The more talking we do, the more likely we are to get caught."

Adam hushed himself in a hurry. He had no desire to be put through another stretch on the Roman streets, which made him think twice about his decision to be out there now with Scott. His nerves were on end, and the cold wasn't helping. Every picture Adam had seen of Rome looked warm and inviting, not freezing, but hot days bring tourists, not the other way around.

Adam could see his breath in the air and could hear the quivering from his body through it as well. Their boots scraped the loose concrete as they walked, echoing on the sides of the buildings. Every sound they made sent their hearts racing. It seemed like all of Domus Aurea could hear them scurrying around corners and across streets.

"Wait," Scott whispered. "Don't move. I think someone's following us."

Both men plastered themselves against the wall and held their breath. They listened as the same scraping footsteps made their way to their street. Adam's heart was buzzing in his chest as he watched a single silhouette slowly creep up to their position.

"I can see you," the shadow whispered. "I didn't think I was actually going to find you."

"Dammit, Daven." Scott choked. "What the hell are you doing out here?"

"Didn't like the idea of you guys being out here without me," Daven said as he crouched down.

"You weren't kidding about the mothering," Scott grumbled to Adam. "Well, just keep up and be quiet then. We're almost there."

The three made two steps before Scott stopped them again. "How did you convince Deirdre to let you come out here?" Scott asked as he slowly turned to face Daven.

Daven stood stoically and without an emotion on his face. "I killed her."

Scott paused for a short second. "I believe it," he said as he turned back to continue onward.

It was a short affair. The three entered the store like it was anywhere but Domus Aurea, purchased their items, and left. They even took a moment for Adam and Scott to light cigarettes in the cover of shadow.

"Is it strange to anyone else how quiet it is out here?" Daven asked as he stuck his head into the lit area under a streetlamp. "Guys, we probably need to get moving."

"What is it?" Adam asked, sensing the distress in Daven's voice.

Daven motioned toward the center of the street about fifty yards out. A man stood motionless in the shadows between the lights along the sidewalks. From what the three could see, it was clear that the man was not a soldier, but feelings of unease still washed over them—Scott most of all.

"Scott, are you okay?" Adam asked as his friend covered his eyes with his hands.

Daven lurched forward as Scott collapsed on the ground in a convulsing, sweating heap. Adam jumped in fright as the man moved down the street in mere seconds. Neither man had time to react before the figure was standing directly in front of them. As Daven jumped to his feet, he could see that the figure standing before them was indeed a lilim, but he was shaking.

"Please hear me," the lilim said as he flinched at some unforeseen oncoming attack. "I am not here to fight. Just to talk."

Daven and Adam felt a warm sensation come over them, as if their souls had left their bodies and were watching from a far-off distance.

"You are safe," Daven said as if his voice was not his own. "Speak quickly."

The lilim let out a relieved sigh. "We are aware of your troubles with Sathariel," he said as he straightened his back. "He has become a thorn in the flesh of our own aspirations, but fratricide is not permitted within our society."

"So you know of our plans," Adam said with the same distant voice.

"Your wish to have us handle the situation is, at best, far-fetched," the lilim said with more confidence the more the conversation moved forward.

"Then our exchange is finished," Daven said with Sansenoy's voice. "Leave us."

The look of impassiveness began to fade from Daven's and Adam's eyes.

"Wait!" the lilim yelled with panic in his voice. "There is a way we can work together."

The look of emptiness glazed over the two men's eyes once again. "Speak," they both said in unison.

The lilim let out another sigh of relief. "If you would remove the threat that is my brother Sathariel for the lilim," he said, "then we will cease our search for Lilith and any further conflicts with the Vatican until our mutual enemy is removed."

An unnerving curl at the corner of Daven's and Adam's mouths gave an element of life to their otherwise emotionless exterior. The lilim began to nervously chuckle with inhibited joy. The slight twitch of the men's facial muscles gave enough to signal an agreement, and so the lilim was confident he was successful in his mission.

"I am grateful to you," the lilim said with a bow. "For your aid and your willingness to listen."

The lilim was about to turn to disappear into the night, but before he could complete his turn, a second lilim dropped down from a rooftop onto his brother.

"You have become passive and weak!" he yelled as he rung the neck of his brother below him. "You sleep with the enemy when you should be looking for our mother!"

Daven walked slowly toward the two lilim below him. The attacker was so focused on acting out in anger toward his brother that he didn't notice as Daven reached out with his hand. A blinding white flash and a loud crack rang out in the street as Daven pressed his index finger on the head of the new lilim. It was like a deadly static charge had been defused, sending the lilim flying a full block down the street.

Adam checked to see if the first lilim was still alive, but the lilim's eyes were vacant of life. Daven rushed toward the second lilim with unnatural speed. The surroundings blew outward from where he stopped, knocking over streetlamps and shattering windows with a concussive blast.

The lilim began to laugh maniacally as he crawled backward away from Daven. "You hide in this weak husk of a man because you're scared to face us openly," the lilim said with blood streaming from his ears. "What are you hoping to accomplish with the farce?"

The air around Daven began to glow white and then ignited into wings of flame. "Our mission is to punish Lilith," a voice that was clearly Sansenoy's bellowed. "These men are here to punish you. The lilim and humans are cousins on this earth. You will be defeated by those you hate and see as inferior to yourselves. This is a mission not only to stop you but to humble you as well."

The lilim scrunched his face into a scowl as he spat at Daven, only to have it evaporate into nothing. Daven reached down and wrapped his fingers around the forehead of the injured lilim crumpled in a heap on the ground.

"This is a message to you, Sathariel," Daven said with glowing eyes. "Stop. Now. And you will be spared from death. Continue onward, and you will be destroyed along with the rest of your defectors."

The lilim then began to smoke from the inside out as his eyes caught fire. Within seconds, he was reduced to ash.

Daven and Adam were then released from the angels' hold, leaving them in the cold air and silence.

"I'm never going to get used to that," Adam said as he moved to Scott's side.

Daven began to walk back toward the store as Adam dragged Scott to the alleyway. Once Scott was safe, Adam moved into the light and then called out to Daven with fear in his eyes.

"Daven!" he screamed. "Get down!"

Daven fell to the ground as a hot, searing pain shot through his shoulder. The last thing he saw before he blacked out was the sight of two men pushing Adam to his knees as they hit him over the top of the head with a club.

CHAPTER 18

THE FAN

January 17, 2036

M arlon had been standing watch outside the Palazzo Pubblico in San Marino since the beginning of the day. Early on during his shift, the Captains Regent, Giafranco Bollini and Domenico Gozi, and the Colonel of the San Marino Militia, Carlo Romano, had arrived to discuss future tactics in the war against Domus Aurea.

It was not going well.

The Captains Regent had become increasingly more vocal in the previous months than their passive past selves, this being overtly clear at the present moment. Originally the Captains Regent held office for six-month terms, but during this time of war, the more battle-worn members of the government were chosen to act as the heads of state for an indefinite amount of time. However, even with their experience, Carlo was the seasoned war veteran who spoke the last word in anything involving strategy, but considering his recent track record, Domenico and Giafranco felt the need to become more involved.

"When an entire guard goes missing, then we know something is wrong!" Marlon heard Domenico yell. "Yet, you have done absolutely nothing to rectify this!"

"We don't have the manpower!" Carlo yelled back. "I can't send out more men when they're needed here! Our country needs to be defended!

I don't know why I am having to argue the merits of a properly fortified border!"

Marlon groaned. The cacophony had been escalating for a full hour now, and it was beginning to wear on his nerves, causing irritability to creep in.

"Carlo, you have to understand where we're coming from," Giafranco said, trying to calm the storm in the room. "Word spreads quickly in our small country, and it speaks of unrest. Your men are unhappy."

"Are you insinuating that they are running away because they are depressed?" Carlo said in a snide manner. "Maybe you are too far removed to understand the quality of soldiers fighting for you. They are not children."

"Not everyone is a miserable and calloused husk of a man!" Domenico hissed back. "Some people are capable of emotion and feel despair when faced with insurmountable obstacles presented to them by a superior!"

Marlon's mind dulled the voices of the screaming men to a muffled whisper. This wasn't the first time the three leaders had butted heads, and he knew it wouldn't be the last. It was no secret that unrest was spreading through the hearts of the Sammarinese like a sickness, and everyone knew who was at fault. Carlo came into power after his predecessor, Ermano Burrei, stepped down in 2033. Burrei headed a march on Rome in June of that same year that ended in a bloodbath. The people of San Marino were vehemently opposed to the militia's operation, but Burrei felt a desire to be the mastermind behind the fall of Domus Aurea and continued anyway.

Burrei was forcefully detained by the Sammarinese government after multiple death threats were received on his behalf. He was then given the opportunity to apologize on a public broadcast from the Public Palace and at the same time was able to step down as Carlo was being sworn in. Burrei's body was found two days later in his home, dead from an apparent suicide.

Now San Marino felt they would be lucky to have Burrei back. Carlo was a temperamental and belligerent man who was unable to think his decisions through to their long-term consequences. His defensive capabilities were to be reckoned with, but they were overshadowed by his inability to commiserate, a quality he felt he did not need. He was a dangerous man, one that needed to be put down for good.

Marlon had successfully blocked out the racket of voices bellowing from behind him. The sounds of wind and silence were all he could hear, and finally his mind was put at ease. The Piazza della Liberta was empty aside from a lone white statue at its center, the Statua della Liberta. She was beautiful to Marlon, a white marble warrior with an outstretched right hand and a flag clutched in her left. The woman wore a crown adorned with three towers, representing the fortified city of San Marino. Marlon prayed freedom would once again be enjoyed by all in his country, and within minutes, his prayers were answered.

His blurry vision focused on the opposite side of the square as a large group of soldiers and civilians marched up a narrow street from the south. He didn't feel threatened, nor should he have, as he watched the group of soldiers line up in front of the statue. Marlon saw Michael Dina emerge from the back of the company, a pistol in hand. Michael smiled at Marlon as he lifted the pistol, pointing it at the sky and firing. The crack was deafening, breaking the solitude of the early morning and sending a flock of birds scattering into the sky.

Marlon was forcefully pushed aside as Carlo and the Captains Regent ran into the square.

"What is the meaning of this?" Carlo yelled with a thundering voice. His eyes widened with confusion and fear once he recognized Michael.

"Surprised to see me?" Michael yelled back from the statue. "I've been waiting for this day."

"Lieutenant Colonel Dina," Giafranco said with surprised delight, "it is good to see you considering you are supposedly a dead man." Giafranco slowly turned to look at Carlo.

"It was my intention to remain dead for a time," Michael said with a return smile. "But I admit, it is good to be back among the living. I'm sure the Captains Regent need no explanation as to why I am here."

"We were wondering when you would show," Domenico said. "Keeping him here was a chore. As much as I love to argue with this grumpy old man, my voice was beginning to suffer."

Michael holstered his weapon and moved forward with haste. In his learned opinion, Carlo was a blight. He had put the men under him in grave danger in order to punish one man, Michael himself. He wasn't about to let Carlo off easy.

"You won't get away with this," Carlo said, glaring at Domenico and Giafranco. "I have friends with power you couldn't possibly imagine."

As Carlo turned to face Michael, a quick fist backed by fury landed on his jaw; his vision flashed white, and an intense pain cracked through his teeth. Carlo was unable to remain standing and fell to the ground, spitting blood.

"That was still less than you deserve," Michael said, shaking the pain from his hand. "You got four men killed and not the one you meant to."

Carlo spit a bloody tooth from his mouth. "You're psychotic," he said, lifting himself off the ground. "Do what you will. I'm not defeated yet, and I know you won't kill me."

Michael grabbed his pistol and pulled the hammer back in milliseconds, aiming it at Carlo. The Captains Regent lurched forward, standing between the injured colonel and the angered lieutenant colonel. Michael crouched down, looking around Giafranco's right leg at the injured military leader.

"Trust me," he said to the two men standing between him and Carlo.

Domenico quickly moved aside, being as he didn't care what happened to Carlo, be it imprisonment or death. Giafranco was less willing to step away, but he trusted Michael and bowed out.

Michael immediately pressed the pistol barrel to Carlo's head.

"Do you know what's happening right now?" Michael asked quietly of Carlo. There was no answer, from the colonel or anyone else in the plaza. "This is called restraint."

Michael slowly uncocked the weapon and lowered it. "Something you didn't show me or my men. Something you probably can't show. You saw me as a threat, and instead of going through proper channels like a perfectly sane man, you instead concocted an elaborate scheme to have me killed. Only instead, you killed four of my men. It's over, Carlo. You're dismissed."

Michael signaled to five men who detained Carlo and escorted him to Montale Tower, which was once again being used as a prison. The disgraced military man was silent, confident he still had the upper hand, regardless of his position within the San Marino Militia. He was a man of strategy and cunning, and Michael Dina was not the first person to stand in his way.

The civilians who accompanied Michael to the square began cheering as Carlo was carted away. Domenico edged closer to Michael and took him aside.

"You realize what this means," he said as the two looked out onto San Marino's landscape.

"I suppose I can't deny it," Michael said. "I began this mission to overthrow a monster, but I knew where it would lead."

"Neither Giafranco nor myself would have agreed to this if we didn't think you had the capability to lead these men," Domenico said, still looking out. "Have you given it any thought?"

"Every night," said Michael. "As they say, if you want something done right …"

"Do it yourself," Domenico, said finishing Michael's sentence. "So do we have an understanding?"

Michael stuck out his hand and shook Domenico's. There was no fanfare, no parade, no celebration of any kind. It was at that moment that Michael Dina became the leader of the San Marino Militia. Now he could lead his men properly, without fear of molestation and with compassion. He didn't view his home as a place of fear or danger any longer. His eyes didn't dart from building to building or alleyway to alleyway looking for a place to hide. He saw the beauty in his country and breathed a sigh of relief.

Adam gripped the bars of his cell and looked through them into the low-light room. Daven kept falling in and out of consciousness, never able to remember anything that had occurred beforehand, and was now passed out in the corner. Their prison was one of many security stations spread all throughout Rome, each one housing six small underground holding cells. Every station was accessible to the others by an interconnecting tunnel system extending for miles under Rome.

Adam looked left toward a stairway that led up to the station. The doorway was windowless and locked tight, with a dim yellow bulb casting a hazy glow down to his cell. To his right, another door, unlit and cold, led to the underground tunnels. Adam was aware of another prisoner in the low-lit jail, but no words were exchanged, and the man hadn't moved since Daven and himself were locked in.

"Where are we?" Daven groaned as he stirred from his unconscious state.

"Look at your arm," Adam said, still staring through the cold iron bars. He had scribbled the answers to every question Daven had asked after waking into amnesia onto his forearm. This had happened four times in the past hour.

"Oh," Daven moaned after about half a minute. "Well, this is bad. This is really bad."

Adam didn't answer. He spent three years trying to avoid this exact situation, and now it had become a reality. He was terrified, and it exhausted him.

"Since I don't have the answer written down on my arm," Daven said, "I'll just ask. Where's Scott?"

"I dragged him back into the store," Adam said, resting his wrists on the horizontal bar. "The owner took him behind the counter. As far as I know, he's safe."

Daven sighed. "Well, at least there's that."

The two sat in the quiet darkness for a time, their thoughts being the only conversation to be had. Daven knew by now that Deirdre was aware of his absence and had probably told Giuseppe. If he got out of this alive, he knew he'd be dead once he returned home. Adam felt especially guilty for Scott's predicament, knowing he was the sole reason for his lack of cigarettes, being that he had smoked half of them in a few days' time.

Daven began to search the cell, albeit unsuccessfully, for any weakness, finding only concrete above, below, and around, with cold bars to keep them in. He began slapping the walls, hoping to feel some semblance of anything hollow, but they were solid all the way through.

"Will you please keep it down?" a voice from the other inhabited cell griped.

Daven and Adam pressed their faces through the bars as much as they could. "How long have you been in here?" they asked. "Is there any way out?"

"Do you really think I would still be here if I knew of a way out?" the voice fired back.

There was something familiar about the man in the darkness that Daven could not place. The voice was a recognizable one, but it was not that of Scott or anyone else from Vatican City. He began to wonder if it was just his mind forcing a false memory to satiate his inquisitive thoughts, but soon, he would have his answer.

The door from atop the stairs opened, flooding the jail with bright light. "How long have we been down here?" Daven asked.

"Since the last time you asked?" Adam said. "About an hour, but we've apparently been here through the night."

Daven felt a rush of panic. He knew now, for certain, that Adam's and his absence had been noted, and Deirdre was either worried sick, fuming angry, or most likely, both.

An Aurean soldier descended the stairs with a clipboard in hand and stopped just before the two men's cell. His eyes never left the clipboard as he began to call out names.

"Cell two, Daven Jones and Adam Gilmour," he said. "Are you there or not?" His voice escalated, but still his eyes remained fixed on the paper in front of him.

"Maybe if you'd look up, you'd get your answer," Adam said, waving an obscene hand gesture.

The soldier, without moving anything but his eyes, looked up. "For someone who is most likely going to die a horrible death, you are incessantly troublesome."

"Incessantly?" Daven softly asked Adam. "What did you do?"

"I smashed his friend's balls in with my heel when they handcuffed me on the ground," Adam said without breaking his intense gaze. Daven snickered.

The soldier scribbled something down on his board and moved forward. "Cell five, Lorenzo Mita?" he said, much to Daven's and Adam's shocked surprise.

The two slowly panned their eyes toward the other cell and saw their old friend and former employer. He was disheveled and despondent, not seeming to care that Daven and Adam were there with him. "Where am I to go?" he grumbled as he fell over drunkenly onto the floor.

"You should be happy, Lorenzo," the soldier said loudly. "You'll die alongside the men who got you here in the first place. Take solace in the probability that you'll see them fall over dead before you're killed. In fact, I might put in a good word to the executioner. Maybe he'll shoot you last."

"Why don't you just shoot me now?" Lorenzo said as he rolled over onto his side, facing away from the rest.

The soldier shook his head and turned to walk out. "A pathetic display of humanity," he said as he ran the board along the metal bars. "Say goodbye to the sunlight!" He then slammed the door, leaving the men's eyes to once again adjust to the dim yellow light.

No one spoke. If what the soldier had said was true, Daven and Adam were directly responsible for Lorenzo's dilemma, and if so, there was nothing that could be said. The silence was palpable, and with each passing second, Daven and Adam felt more and more pressed to say something.

"What happened?" Adam asked with as much care as he could muster.

"You," Lorenzo said, then returned to a hushed state.

"Lorenzo, we're so sorry," Daven said, emulating Adam's careful tone of voice.

"Why?" Lorenzo asked. "You don't even know what happened."

It was quiet again. The two were unsure of how to move forward with the conversation.

"How about I fill you in?" Lorenzo said as he shifted to sit up. "After you got Abele and Eula crucified in a humiliatingly violent manner, the Aureans searched their house some more and found evidence of my involvement. Bear in mind that these people aren't satisfied with just arresting and killing you. No. They find it necessary to make your life miserable before doing so." Daven and Adam saw Lorenzo's shadow stand up against the bars of his cage. "So they locked my family in their house and set it on fire. While making me watch. While making me listen." His voice began to quiver. "I'll never be able to get the picture of my mother's burning silhouette out of my head. Her screams still fill my ears. They showed me her body after everything had been reduced to a smoldering pile of ruin. It was smoking from the inside out, and even though her face was unrecognizable, I could still see the features of her contorted, pain-filled expression. They kicked me to my knees and forced my face inches away from hers. They blamed me, insulted me, cursed me; but all I heard was her voice speaking their words. My only comfort is the fact that I wasn't shown the rest of my family."

Nothing could be said. Any words that were spoken now would just be an affront to Lorenzo. It would only sound like an excuse, so Daven and Adam kept quiet. All that could be heard were the sounds of Lorenzo sobbing, slurring what Daven and Adam could only guess were the names of the dead.

"It is our fault," Daven whispered to Adam. "We should have accepted death. We should have died with some dignity instead of cowering on Abele and Eula's front doorstep. Our lives for theirs. We've been responsible for too many dead."

Adam turned and gripped Daven's shoulders hard. "Don't do this to me now," he hissed. "Don't fall in. I need you to be here with me now. Not in your head." Adam turned in Lorenzo's direction. "You may blame us, and you may hate us, Lorenzo, but I promise you're getting out of here alive. Even if it's just to kick our asses, I'll make sure you live until that time comes."

"And how exactly are you going to do that?" Lorenzo said, slowly enunciating every word.

Adam opened his mouth, but before he could answer, a loud metallic clank and the sound of metal scraping on metal came from the door leading to the tunnels. A bright florescent light flooded the room, and three men walked through.

"Stay here," the first man said to the third. "Shut the door and wait for us to return. Find a corner to hide in."

The door closed again, and the darkness returned before the prisoners' eyes could adjust to the light.

"Daven? Adam?" an unfamiliar voice asked. "Don't be afraid. Stay where you are and don't say a word. We're getting you out of here."

The second man was already making his way up the stairs to the security station. He opened the door, allowing the sunlight to shine back into the dark. Adam was able to glimpse the faces of one of the men and recognized him, but he couldn't place from where.

"Well, I didn't receive any orders," the station's officer said loudly from the sunlit security box, answering to some indiscernible comment the second man had uttered. "These guys are the most wanted men in Rome. I'm not going to let them go without seeing something official."

"Call it in, then," the man at the stairs' summit said, handing the officer a radio.

The security officer took it with apprehension and walked out of Adam's view. The second man looked down at the first, Adam also recognizing him, and gave a look of anxious hope.

"What's going on here?" Adam whispered to the first man.

"Don't talk," he said and began walking toward the stairs.

The three men spoke softly at the top of the stairs as the officer handed the radio back to the second man. He smiled, and the two exchanged a bit of laughter.

"They expect us to follow protocol, but then they work outside of it at every turn," the officer said. "Follow me. I'll get the door."

The three made their way down the stairs and to Daven and Adam's cell. "Up against the wall with your hands behind your backs!" the officer commanded. "Palms toward us with your thumbs interlocked! If you move, I will not hesitate to beat you to death!"

Daven looked at Adam, silently asking if they should comply. Adam moved toward the wall and did as he was asked, resting his forehead on the concrete. His arms were forcefully gripped, and he sensed the cold metal of the handcuffs as they were tightly fastened around his wrists. The barrel of a pistol was pressed hard against the back of his neck as he was pulled from the wall and pushed toward the open cell. The officer was standing between them and the door at the top of the stairs as they were forced down the corridor toward the tunnel door.

"You move, and you die," the man holding the gun to Adam's neck bellowed.

The officer moved between Daven and Adam, unlocking the metal door for the other men. As they passed through, Adam listened as the door slammed shut, echoing down the long tunnel ahead of them. The barrel of the gun was lowered from his neck, and he was moved down another passageway to his left.

"Can I come out?" a voice from behind a pillar asked.

"Yeah, we're good," said one of the men from behind Adam.

Adam watched as Scott peeked around the corner.

"Holy mother of God." Daven sighed. "I thought we were dead."

Scott pulled the two men in and embraced them. "Guys, I'm so sorry," he said with fervor. "I should never have let you come out here with me. I swear to you, I'll make it up to you somehow."

"Would you mind taking a beating from an angry Irishwoman for me?" Daven asked in jest. "You'll probably die."

"Maybe my luck will extend to you too," Scott said as he turned to the two unnamed men. "Adam, I don't know if you remember our humorous exchange with those two Aurean soldiers earlier, but here they are. Paolo and Pietro. They were called by that store owner to come help me when you went missing. Apparently they've helped thousands hide when everything went down."

Daven turned to grip the hand of his savior. "I don't know how we can ever repay you. You're heroes, plain and simple."

Adam, knowing of his rescuer's benevolent intent, frantically ran toward the door of the jail. "We have to get Lorenzo," he said with panic. "We can't leave him here, Daven. I won't be responsible for his death. I won't be. Not another one. Too many have died because of us."

Pietro and Paolo detained Adam. "It's too late," Paolo said. "We can't go back in there. Once we have you safely back in Vatican City, maybe we can save him, too, but the likelihood is slim. If we had known …"

Adam tore away from the soldiers. "I'm not going anywhere without him," he said, trying to open the door.

Pietro put Adam in a restraining hold. "Look, you're going to get us all killed if you keep going on like this," he growled in Adam's ear. "Then you'll be responsible for even more deaths. Do you want that? Do you?"

Adam relaxed, and Pietro released him, causing him to collapse to his knees. Adam began slamming his fists into the stone floor. "Not again. Not another," he cried.

"I know this is difficult," Paolo said, crouching down beside Adam. "But we need to get moving. It won't take long before someone gets wise to our little stunt here and comes looking for you."

"How did you pull this off?" Daven asked, helping Adam to his feet.

"Fake ID's and a short-range radio," Pietro said. "Your friend here gave the 'order' to release you."

"I think I did pretty well, given I only had a few minutes to memorize my lines," Scott said. "But Paolo is right. We need to move."

The five moved down the white concrete passageway, with Paolo and

Pietro guiding in front. The tunnels were lit rather well, but this did not serve to comfort the men of the group. It was easy to hide in the dark, but with the light, they risked being caught by anyone who was in sight.

"Where are we going?" Daven asked, breaking the silence.

"There is an access hatch that leads up to Borgo Pio near your home," Pietro said. "From there you can travel unhindered. Once you are home, you will stay there unless ordered to leave by your superiors. This could have gone in a disastrous direction had our friend not called on us."

"You're not wrong," said Scott, still hushed. "Let's just get home."

The group traveled onward for another ten minutes, and then the lights in the tunnel shut off. No one said a word as Paolo and Pietro began desperately searching for an electrical box. Daven, Adam, and Scott heard the soft slap of the Aurean soldier's hands hitting the cement walls. Suddenly Adam's eyes adjusted to the darkness with unnatural speed and quality, just as a sixth person was approaching the group.

"Daven," Adam said with a whisper.

"I see her" Daven answered with the same low volume of voice.

"I think I've got it," Paolo said as he flipped a switch. The corridor lit up with bright sparks and a flash of light, knocking both Paolo and Pietro to the ground in a smoking heap, filling the passageway in black once again.

"Blue dots everywhere," Scott groaned, rubbing his eyes. "What happened?"

No one answered as a burning light began to swell from behind him. It had an orange hue, giving off heat like a wildly burning fire. He turned to see Daven and Adam in a state much like that of the night at the hotel.

"Well, I know what this means," Scott said, turning to face in front of him.

The sixth individual was a lone lilim, the light of Daven's and Adam's burning auras casting waves of shadow and light on the lilim's leery countenance.

"Get behind us, Scott," a voice said within Scott's mind.

He slowly stepped back, all the while casting an unbroken gaze at the lilim's unflinching stare.

"Speak your allegiance," Daven said with Sansenoy's voice.

"I do not fear you," the female lilim said with disgust. "You slew my brother in cold blood and left his ashes to blow away with the wind. His soul will never find rest on the water side of the starry night because of you."

"Your brother attacked and killed another of your kind," Daven said. "Fratricide is heavily punishable within your laws. How do you defend his actions?"

"Do not quote law at me when you have no understanding of what it means," the lilim spit. "I am here to enact vengeance on behalf of my brother and leader, Charles Monroe," she said.

"But he did not send you," Adam said with Senoy's voice. "You are here of your own accord and alone."

"You will learn of the power that is the lilim's," she said with fire in her eyes. "I may be alone, but I am fully capable of punishing you."

The lilim stretched out her left arm, her palm flat and fingers fanned out. Daven and Adam stared back, waiting for something to happen, and then they heard the click of a gun's hammer being pulled back from behind them.

"Guys," Scott said with pure fear coursing through his body.

Daven and Adam looked behind them, seeing Scott pressing his pistol against his right temple.

"Release him," Adam said with the commanding voice of Senoy, his own angered speech interlacing it from beneath.

"What will you do?" the lilim asked. "If you kill me, he dies. My hold will be ripped away, causing his muscles to clench, pulling the trigger. Then it will be on your head. This does not end happily. If you let me leave, he still dies. You have weaknesses, even now in this form, and I will exploit this one."

The essence of Sansenoy and Senoy left Daven and Adam at their command, leaving two dimly lit orbs floating above their heads.

"Please don't," Daven said with a shaky voice. "You want to see weakness in us? Here it is. Our human frailty and fear. You want us on our knees? I'll lie on my stomach at your feet; just please don't hurt him."

Adam stared at Scott, his mind whirling with potential solutions to their dilemma, unable to keep his thoughts in order. Time began to slip away, the look of Scott's horror-filled face burning itself into Adam's memories. He knew that if this was the last moment he spent with his new friend, this image would be the thing he saw every time he closed his eyes. This would be the recurring nightmare he was plagued with for the rest of his life.

The lilim began walking away while Daven stared with hatred, unable to move, fearing the repercussions. He shook with anger, both at the lilim and at himself. Daven felt like a coward, frozen with inactivity and inability. If he chased after, Scott died; if he stood still, Scott died. The most he could do would be to stay with his friend in his potential last moments.

"I'm so sorry, Scott," Adam said, with tears rolling down his face.

"This is not how I saw today going," Scott said in a final attempt to lighten the dismal mood.

Daven watched as the lilim rounded a corner, disappearing from view. He looked back at Scott, brimming with sorrow and disgust. At himself and Charles.

"Why can't we fix this?" Daven said, speaking indirectly to the ghostly, silent lights shimmering above their heads in the tunnel. "We're supposed to be able to stop things like this. Why aren't you helping us? We were supposed to be able to protect people from the lilim! Say something!"

The lights shone dimly, suspiciously silent and inopportunely absent of advice. Daven crouched on the ground and covered his ears. He was helpless and hopeless, waiting for the inevitable to occur as hot tears welled up in his eyes, distorting his vision while they dripped without pattern on the ground.

The gunshot caused him to jump.

CHAPTER 19

FAULT

January 17, 2036

"I feel I must reiterate, I do not feel this move is a wise one," Adamo said as Nero paced the interior of the Pantheon.

"I didn't call you here to listen to you dribble on like this," Nero said, continuing his hastened steps, not looking in Adamo's direction.

"But you did call me here for my advice, did you not?" Adamo said calmly.

"Advice," Nero said. "Not lecture."

"Good advice needs a stern voice at times," Adamo said with a veiled smile.

Nero halted his movement and peered upward through the oculus. To go against those who had placed him in his position of power, especially those as powerful as the lilim, seemed to be an unwise move indeed, but Nero needed to see his empire flourish. The lilim were long-lived and patient, but he was not, and if it meant taking an alternate and straighter route to his ultimate goal, he would do what it took to get there. Even if it meant following someone with a more dangerous but direct path in mind.

"I feel as if you are not fully invested in this anymore," Nero said as he watched the clouds pass by. "Your sense of initiative has dwindled, it seems, over the course of our mission."

This accusation angered Adamo. "I would see this through to the end.

The bitter end if need be, but I will not sit by and watch your impatience put that mission at risk."

Nero looked over his shoulder at Adamo, who was standing at the bottom of the dais to the throne. "Perhaps I am mistaken then. It's clear this is important to you, especially when you defend that dedication with fiery words spewed at the one man in Domus Aurea that could see you burn for insubordination. I will not, however, turn aside from my current path. It's not as if it will be hard to defeat the Catholics. For pity's sake, Adamo, they rely on a fantasy to protect them! A big man in the sky who shields them from the boogeyman under their feet. A red devil wreathed in fire, poking at them with a pitchfork from below. It's a blight, religion, as cliché as that may sound, but I'm only echoing the thoughts of men before me who wished to open the minds of humanity. It's an idiot's illusion, the mind's primal instinct to explain away the sad reality of life. We all die."

"That we do," Adamo said. "But you're as religious as the next man, Lucius."

Nero was not amused. "How so?"

Adamo slowly stepped up the dais to the empty throne, placing his hand on the armrest. "The idea of God came from the desire to explain the world around us. Bad things happened because we were disobedient, good things because we listened. This God created us, and so, since we were created in his image, we, in turn, created him. Or so you would like to think."

"What are you going on about?" Nero asked, irritated.

"After these explanations satiated our thirst for knowledge, we turned it into religious law. Complete with rules, saints, prophets, and so on. Scientific thought, while more direct and factual, is still in its infancy. Soon, it will be its own religion, complete with rules, saints, prophets—You see where I'm going with this. We already idolize celebrated minds like Einstein, Sagan, Newton. Their word is law. Their ideas have universal implications that cannot be broken. For all intents and purposes, you are a disciple of these prophets. You're even ready to carry out a crusade in the name of reason and the rational. Your religious conviction."

Nero laughed, his voice bellowing through the circular interior, bouncing off the walls like a rubber ball. "Very good, Adamo, very good. I suppose I'm a priest then, am I? So be it. I'll prey on the ignorance of my laymen. Send them out, control their little minds for my own benefit. Let them spill their blood so I can take the Holy Land unmarred. I've already begun. Have I not?"

"Am I nothing more than a layman to you?" Adamo asked.

"No," Nero said. "You're my disciple. Would you die for me, Adamo? Would you cut the ear from the soldier's head who came to take me away?"

"You're a troubled soul," Adamo said with a snicker. "But I do value your friendship, believe it or not."

"And I yours," Nero said as he turned to look at his primus pilus. "And friends do not lead each other astray. Wouldn't you agree?"

Adamo sighed. "My apprehension is not indicative of mistrust, I assure you. Lucius, your mind is bright and buoyant, and your reach is far. I only serve as an anchor to your mind as it traverses the waves of your intellect."

Nero tapped the tip of his own nose. "You've got a little brown …" he said as his voice trailed off into an airy laugh.

"Shove it." Adamo smiled. "You're intent on following through with this, aren't you?"

"Trust me, my friend. I've seen it," Nero said as he tapped his temple. "In here. It plays out like an opera. The voices of our men as they storm the square sing like a choir of tenors. The sounds of the stone churches as they collapse concuss like percussion. It's beautiful."

"And the sound of the lilim wreaking havoc as vengeance? Is that the fat lady singing?" asked Adamo passive-aggressively.

"Fine," Nero said. "I concede the possibility that this is madness. But all revolutions arrive from a bit of insanity."

Adamo's thoughts ran wild at the idea. There was no stopping Lucius Nero from playing out what burned in his mind. Adamo finally realized it wasn't that Nero didn't fear the repercussions of playing against the lilim; it was that he trusted his primus pilus to protect him from such occurrences. This alone kept Nero on his path without fear of consequences.

"They know. I'm sure you're aware of this," Adamo said with fear in his voice.

Nero grinned. "They're listening to us right now as a matter of fact."

Nero quickly glanced upward to the oculus. Adamo followed his leader's gaze, catching a fleeting glance of a shadow as it moved down past the opening's horizon, disappearing from view. This greatly unnerved him, knowing with certainty that the lilim were keenly aware of his, as they would see it, lapse in judgment.

"We don't have a lot of time," Nero said with an almost nervous quiver in his voice. "Are you with me, or are you not?"

"There are things you have not told me," Adamo said. "I need to be let in."

"All you had to do was ask," Nero said. "Walk with me."

The four men sat around Scott's body, a bloody handkerchief covering his face. Pietro had tried to clean up the blood, but his attempt only seemed to smear it, making it look worse than if he had just left it. Paolo had taken most of the shock from the overloaded electrical box and was laid out on the cold ground. Daven stared blankly at Scott's still hand, his face streaked with dried tears. Adam was unable to look at the body. Instead, he gazed intently at Scott's sidearm, which had skidded across the ground after being dropped.

"What if Senoy and Sansenoy are the angels of death?" Adam grumbled to Daven. "We've been the cause of so many lives lost, both directly and indirectly. Would it be so hard to believe?"

Daven didn't answer.

"We've lost our ability to choose," Adam said as he inched his hand closer to the pistol. "Agreeing to this union was the last choice we ever made. Our lives have been part of a rigorous set of bullet points on a list, the angels checking off each completed step as we carry out their will. I won't let them use me to ruin more lives. This is my choice. They can't take this from me."

Adam snatched the pistol from the ground and held it under his jaw, pulling the trigger to a muffled click, and then nothing. He opened his eyes and found he was floating in a sea of black, dotted with tiny white pinpricks that glowed dimly around him.

"Well, that wasn't so bad," he thought, assuming he was dead.

He held his hand out, cupping one of the white flecks of glowing dust in his palm. His eyes focused on it as he came to the realization of what he was holding.

"Makes everything seem so trivial now, doesn't it?" a voice said from an unseen vantage point. "When you can hold a star in your hand. Look closer."

Adam pulled the star up to his nose, focusing as hard as he could on an almost invisible blue dot moving slowly inside the radiant light of the small sun.

"I know what you're thinking," the voice said. "Why should anything outside the realm of humanity care at all about such an insignificant speck of nothing? About the lives that thrive on it, the wars fought on it, the minds thinking and creating on it. Yes, these elements mean everything to you, but in your eyes, this blue ball is your entire world."

"You're terrible at this cheering-up thing," Adam said, his eyes still fixated on the Earth and Sun. "If that is what you're trying to do."

"When a mother finds out she is pregnant," the voice continued, "the first thing she does is look down. Down at the life growing inside her. She doesn't think about how tiny that new life is. Barely large enough to even matter, some would have you think. But to her, this new life is her whole world. Her whole existence. That, Adam, is how we see you."

"Then why does the world fall around me?" Adam said, still staring intently at his hand.

"Bad things happen because you live in a cursed world," the voice continued. "The cold hard truth is: you did this to yourself. But we do intervene."

"Who are you? God or something?"

A man of Middle Eastern descent stepped out of the darkness. His hair was black, curly, and short, his face covered with shadowed scruff.

"No, but we do trade recipes on occasion," the man said as he stopped just in front of Adam. "We've met before, you and me. I'm Senoy."

Adam looked away with a measure of disgust. "After all this time and after everything I've been through, you've stayed coldly silent. Forgive me if I seem put off."

"Would you like me to hold your hand?" Senoy said. "Give you a shoulder to cry on?"

"That would be a start," Adam said begrudgingly. "You've thrown

Daven and me into the fray without so much as a word of instruction. We've seen everyone we care about fall one by one by the hand of hatred because they stood between us and fate."

Senoy's face remained stoic and unreadable. He was a being of an almost eternal quality and had been placed in every situation imaginable. This was nothing new to him, but he was not one to take blame so flippantly.

"Not all things are part of a divine strategy. Bad things happen, as I have said, but these incidents are not always dead ends and can be redeemable. Scott's death is not random, however. As much as it may seem like his light has diminished for no reason at all, that flame has simply been moved to a place unseen by you. Do not believe for one moment that his purpose is finished. Scott will be much more involved in your mission than you realize."

"If you have taught me anything," Adam said, almost as if he didn't hear anything Senoy had been saying, "it's that things can always be worse. Here I thought being separated from family and other loved ones was the worst thing that could happen to me. I never knew how wrong I could be, but if history also has taught me anything, it's that mankind has the ability to overcome anything in the face of adversity. I, however, also believe that the spiritual realm is working in tandem with me. I trust God; therefore, I must trust you."

"This gladdens me," Senoy said with a smile. "So we will forget the attempt you just made to forfeit your life and start again. After you."

Senoy stepped aside and pointed his hand toward a warm light ahead of Adam. The next thing the man knew, he was staring at Scott's gun once again but with a different plan in mind.

Daven was oblivious to the voices within the concrete corridor. The gunshot had deafened his ears, quieting any word of comfort Pietro or Paolo could give. *Daven,* a breathy voice hissed from beneath the covering over Scott's face. *There's a plan, Daven,* the voice whispered. *A plan for everything … Not your fault … Keep going …* The clearly distraught man looked lazily across the long hall, the faces of the men around him gazing caringly at him, silently moving their lips in sympathy. *Get up … Get up … Get up …*

"Get up, Daven," Pietro said, reaching his hand out to assist Daven to his feet. "This is not your fault. You know God has a plan for everything. There is a plan. You have to keep going. We all have to keep going, or we'll die here. Get up."

Daven craned his head back, staring at Pietro's hand through dry tears. His hand lifted of what seemed to be its own accord and gripped the hand of aid above him.

"There we go," Pietro said. "On your feet. Paolo, Adam, let's move Scott. We need to get him home."

Paolo moved to grab Scott's body beneath his shoulders, but a hand stiffly halted his movement. Daven moved without eye contact to place himself above Scott's head, grabbing him gently by the arms. Scott's body was relaxed and still warm, as if he was sleeping peacefully beneath the covering over his face. For one split second, Daven thought he might wake his slumbering friend, but he felt the twinge of reality pierce him as he lifted Scott's deadweight.

The concrete corridor stretched on for an eternity as Daven and Adam carried Scott to a locked manhole under Borgo Pio just outside Vatican City walls. Paolo pulled out a giant metal ring with an inordinate number of keys looped along its circumference and proceeded to climb the metal ladder to unlock the circular cover.

"Give me a moment to see if the coast is clear," Paolo said, grunting as he flipped the cover over onto the street above.

Daven and Adam laid Scott's body down, Daven cradling his friend's head in his lap, both hands covering the entrance and exit wounds in the dead man's skull.

"There's no more blood," Daven mumbled. "It's gone."

"I need you here with me now, Daven," Adam said, trying to break the veil of fog clouding his friend's thoughts. "We can't fall apart now. Not with so much riding on us keeping to the path."

"I'm scared, though," Daven said, his eyes still fixated on Scott.

"I am, too," Adam said.

"No," Daven said, finally looking up, "I'm scared of the day things like this won't affect us anymore. I'm scared of what will happen to make moments like these seem tame in comparison. What will make us numb to death?"

Adam had no words. It was a legitimate question that deserved an answer, but he had none to give.

"Eight bells, and all's well," Paolo said quietly, poking his head down into the tunnel from the street. "But we need to be quick."

Pietro climbed to the top to join his friend on the street. Daven and Adam lifted Scott's body to the men above, allowing them to pull him upward. Adam was the first through the manhole, the cool night air causing feelings of vulnerability and shame. Daven was the last up, quickly scooting off to the side for Paolo to close and lock the entrance to the tunnels below.

"The Porta Sant'Anna is just over there," Pietro said, pointing in the direction of the walls of Vatican City. "Hopefully your guardsmen will recognize you and allow you through. Otherwise we'll have to find a place for you for the night. Can't have you on the street."

"They'll recognize us," Daven said. "But I don't want them to."

Paolo and Pietro checked the intersecting street to see once again if the area was empty. The two guardsmen at the gate stood at attention, clutching their weapons close, unaware of the four men in the shadows. Pietro signaled to Daven and Adam to move forward with Scott, Paolo and himself following behind with their weapons drawn. The guards twitched toward the direction of the men with the barrels of their rifles pointed forward.

"Daven? Adam?" One of the guards at the gate said with a hushed voice. "What in the world happened?"

Adam shuffled past the guard without an answer, looking past Daven's head as Pietro shook the hand of the inquiring soldier, whispering inaudibly to him about the events of that night. The second guard lowered his head in sorrow, signaling Adam that the knowledge of Scott's death was about to spread like wildfire through the city.

Daven didn't remember moving through the doors of the barracks or laying Scott's body on a stretcher. He did remember, and would never forget, the look of Liana's face when she barreled through the infirmary doors. Word had reached Giuseppe, who had been talking to Liana when he heard the news, and so both individuals arrived at the same time. Liana grabbed Daven's face so hard, he fully expected her to rip it off.

"You idiots!" she screamed, with red, puffy eyes streaming with tears. "You killed him! Over cigarettes! Over stupid cigarettes."

Adam attempted to restrain her but was instead slapped to the ground as she spun around in red-hot fury. She then seemed to forget about everyone in the room and wept bitterly on Scott's chest.

"They loved each other," Giuseppe said, calm and still but clearly distraught and, even worse, disappointed. "They kept it quiet, but it was like something from the pages of some old love story. I never expected it to turn into this tragic romance."

Daven and Adam remained quiet.

"I want to say that everything will be fine and that this isn't anyone's fault," Giuseppe said with foggy eyes. "But the truth of the matter is that Scott is dead, and all three of you are to blame." Giuseppe walked past Daven and Adam, then stopped and sighed. "'For if you forgive others their trespasses, your heavenly father will then forgive you,'" he quoted from scripture. "But I cannot forgive this. Not yet. You will be escorted to your room, and you will stay there until I decide how you will be reprimanded. Don't attempt your disappearing act you have become so adept at performing. I will have guards on your door and men on the wall watching your window. This childlike behavior is unbecoming of you. Especially with the responsibilities you have been entrusted with."

Giuseppe waved them away as two Swords flanked them and began walking them to their quarters. As they reached the top of the stairs, Deirdre was emerging from her room, clearly having awakened from a deep sleep.

"Daven," she said with a furrowed brow, "what's going on? What happened?"

"I'm so sorry," he said, unable to look her in the eye. "Please forgive me."

"Baby, what happened?" she asked, her voice beginning to quiver with worry. "Have you seen Liana? She's not in bed. Please, you're scaring me!"

Deirdre watched as the two Swords stood at attention after shutting Daven and Adam off in the room. Her mind was burning with anxiety, panic, and questions. She knew the guards would not be able to answer anything she asked, but she still looked at them with inquiring eyes.

"The infirmary," one said, sensing her distress; then he returned to his stoic, rigid stance.

Deirdre ran with everything her tired body could muster.

CHAPTER 20

WHERE IS YOUR VICTORY?

January 18, 2036

Rudolf Anrig's legs were burning. He had received the call while visiting Saint John's Tower, located at the westernmost tip of the city. *The pope's life has been threatened* were the only words he heard before running headlong to the Apostolic Palace. He was not the only one moving with haste toward the pope's residence, but he was the fastest.

"You two with me!" Rudolf yelled to two Swiss Guards as he slammed through a line of gendarmes in front of the Apostolic Palace. "The rest of you get with your superiors. I want this entire structure locked down!"

Rudolf scurried to the top floor of the palace to the papal apartments, making his way to a small chapel near the pope's office and quarters. Adriano was there, doling out orders quietly on his radio as Innocent sat next to him. The old man didn't seem particularly worried at all, but Rudolf knew better, as Innocent was renowned for hiding his emotions extremely well.

"Do we have a name?" Rudolf asked Adriano.

"Anthony Dawkins," Adriano answered. "He's a gendarme. Relatively quiet individual. Keeps to himself. I have never had any issue with him in the past, but you know what they say about the quiet ones."

"In what form did this threat arrive?" Rudolf inquired.

"You wouldn't believe me if I told you," Adriano said as he walked in the direction of the pope's personal quarters.

"Try me," Rudolf responded as he followed close behind. "These days, I wouldn't scoff at any strange notions. I'm constantly being proved wrong."

The men walked into the pontiff's room together; Adriano walked toward a window and pulled back the heavy curtains. "His Holiness found a brick lying on the floor this morning with the words *mors tua, vita mea* carved into it with, I'm guessing, a human fingernail. There was blood in the marks, but we were able to ascertain that Dawkins was the culprit by fingerprints he left on the object."

"Your death, my life," Rudolf said, translating the Latin through a foggy mind. "I guess that's fairly straightforward, but there is a lot I don't understand."

"Like how a man could throw with enough force an object nearly sixty feet through glass made to stop bullets?" Adriano said as he picked up a shard of glass from the floor.

"After finding the body of a grown man wrapped around the tip of the obelisk in the square, a brick through bulletproof glass seems mundane," Rudolf said. "What perplexes me is why he would go through all this trouble. Why bring so much attention to himself?"

"Maybe he grew tired of going unnoticed. Maybe he's a closet narcissist," Adriano said.

Rudolf had already moved on to another set of conversational points in his own mind. He knew the most difficult task that lay ahead of him would be keeping Innocent still long enough to find Anthony. "I'm assuming you've begun a search?" he asked.

"I have. I assumed you would handle security. Would I be correct in my supposition?" Adriano asked.

"I was going to grab a nap," Rudolf said in jest, "but I suppose I can babysit. You know you got off easy, right?"

Adriano laughed. "His Holiness is a bit of a restless soul in times of stress, but I can't imagine I'd be any different."

"Maybe it's time we got back," Rudolf said. "Just to be sure he hasn't rearranged the chapel."

The two men hadn't spent much time in Innocent's private bedroom, but the situation in the chapel had changed drastically since their short time away. A gendarme had just arrived from a short search of the city and was desperately looking for Adriano.

"Sir!" he yelled from the southern entrance of the chapel. "We've located Dawkins. He's holed himself up in the Church of Saint Stephen."

Adriano immediately began taking action. "Has contact been made with him? Have any demands been made?"

"Nothing as of yet, sir," the gendarme responded. "We've secured the area but are awaiting your orders. If you'll accompany me."

Adriano moved toward the gendarme. "Rudolf, the building's yours. I'll radio in with updates."

"Should we contact Giuseppe?" Rudolf asked as Adriano moved away.

"Why?" Adriano asked. "Is something strange going on that needs his input?"

"I suppose not," Rudolf said sheepishly. "But he does command the largest militant force in Vatican City. Wouldn't it be downright idiotic *not* to contact him?"

"Their concentration is on city defense," Adriano said with faux deflection. "But maybe he has some men to spare. The Eyes maybe?"

"Sir, we need to move," the gendarme said with unease.

"You're right," Adriano agreed. "Contact him if you wish, Rudolf. I'll go make sure we don't need him."

Adriano walked out of view, following hastily behind the gendarme. Rudolf turned to walk back to the chapel, which had two Swiss Guards guarding the entrance and eight more within the confines of the room. Innocent was sitting still in the center of the room, which came as a surprise to Rudolf, even to the point of anxious worry.

"Are you okay?" Rudolf asked Innocent as he sat down beside the emotionless pope.

Innocent forced a smile. "That's the first time today someone has asked. It's been *Your Holiness, don't leave this room* and *Your Holiness, please step away from the window.* They treat me like a child trying to poke a toaster with a fork."

Rudolf was amused. "It's protocol. They are only doing as they are commanded."

"I understand this," Innocent responded. "I've always fought to be treated as an equal among my peers. During the Angelus Address, I would stand in the square with my brethren. I never wanted to stand above them like a king, untouchable and far removed. Now, when my life has been threatened, the world stops, and everyone with a gun in the city has rallied around me."

"You are the Bishop of Rome," Rudolf said, "the leader of Roman Catholicism. Surely you knew the ramifications before you agreed to all this."

"As I indicated," Innocent said, "my intentions were to lower the papacy to ground level. Be a person and not *holy*. No man is holy. None but Christ."

"Still," Rudolf said, "you must concede to the fact that many around you still view you as their Holy Father. If you wish to be a grounded leader, respect their points of view."

Innocent laughed. "Wise words from a Swiss. I will do as you say and concede. But I will only do so in my office."

Rudolf was uneasy. "I'm not sure that's wise."

Innocent stood up and shuffled toward the exit. "If I'm the Holy Father," he said, turning his head toward Rudolf, "then I have to have some seniority in making my own decisions."

Rudolf stood up and hurried after him. "At least let me and some of my men stand watch over you. After all, my job is to protect you, and I can't do that from the hallway."

"But they can," Innocent said. "I'll allow you to sit in a chair by the window. Otherwise, your men can keep watch outside my office. I need to get some work done, and I can't do that with people standing around me watching."

"It's folly to argue, isn't it?" Rudolf asked.

Innocent grinned and walked to his office, Rudolf following suit. The pontiff scurried behind his desk and sat. Rudolf watched as the man placed a small set of glasses on his nose, opened a large book, and began to read. The leader of the Swiss Guard silently grabbed a chair and sat down by the window, looking out on the square in the quiet and warmth of the sun shining through the glass.

Every rooftop in the vicinity had a sharpshooter's barrel fixated on the Church of Saint Stephen. Adriano stood against the giant rear wall of the basilica facing the church as a column of flashing lights from gendarmerie cars circled Dawkins's position. No contact had yet been made with the would-be assassin, but his whereabouts were without uncertainty in the building before Adriano. The inspector general had lost his escort in the shuffle of gendarmes surrounding the barricade, but he knew the man had taken a position of watch.

"As far as we know, he's located somewhere in the transept," said a gendarme as he briefed Adriano. "We've heard nothing in the way of demands or anything really. He's been silent as a grave."

"Do we have any visual confirmation?" Adriano asked, staring blankly at the front of the church. "Or are we just going on hearsay?"

"It's our best guess," the gendarme said. "We've only been able to get close enough to check the nave. All we know is he's not visible in that area."

Adriano began walking toward the barricade but didn't stop there. As he pushed his way through the wall of gendarmes, the officer who briefed him ran after him.

"Sir!" he yelled. "Where are you going?"

"We know absolutely nothing," Adriano yelled back. "We don't have time to wait around and theorize."

Adriano walked to the front door and opened it. The interior was silent, almost eerie and deathlike, so quiet that Adriano expected to hear Dawkins breathing from the transept. There was, however, no sound to be heard.

"Anthony Dawkins!" he yelled into the church, his voice echoing loudly off the walls. "This is Inspector General Adriano Gabrieli. If you're here, let it be known!"

Nothing.

"I am armed!" Adriano said as he moved inward. "If I so much as think you are going to fire your weapon, I will not hesitate to rain hell itself down upon you!"

Still nothing. Adriano signaled to the men behind him to move into the church. As they spread out into the nave, Adriano inched forward slowly and kept his eyes focused on anything that might move. Finally, a man came into view, sitting on a pew at the front by the altar. He was hunched forward as if he was praying, but there was no movement. Adriano still took caution but began to move more quickly.

"Anthony?" he asked with a borderline whisper. "Anthony. Speak up."

Adriano moved to the edge of the pew and pointed his gun at Anthony. The aspiring assassin did not move or breathe.

"I need every available unit to the palace immediately!" Adriano yelled as he ran to the entrance of the church. "Let's go, people! Move now!"

The gendarme who had been following Adriano since the briefing walked over to Anthony to see what had spooked the inspector general. Dawkins was slumped over, blood dripping from his lips into a dark red pool at his feet, completely white and most definitely dead.

"I can say with certainty that this is the quietest it has ever been around here," Innocent said, scribbling randomly on a sheet of paper on his desk. "I thought silence would be conducive to concentration, but it only serves to intensify my wandering thoughts. Maybe some music would drown out the demons, wouldn't you agree, Rudolf?"

Innocent looked up in the direction where Rudolf had been sitting, but an empty chair was the only thing in view. Innocent quietly stood up and glided around his desk. He thought he was in a dream, one of loneliness and silence, but he felt eyes on him, coming in from all directions. The man felt an overwhelming urge to run, but his legs were heavy, and the way out seemed so far away. Finally Innocent decided to sit at his desk, against his better judgment, and wait for what was coming.

From the entrance to his office, Camillo strolled in with a man the pope did not recognize trailing behind. Innocent sat confused as Camillo and his mysterious guest approached him. An overwhelming sense of fear consumed him, but the old man kept his composure, almost as if he had come to terms with what was about to unfold. Although he was not a man easily intimidated by mere mortals, a sense of uneasiness and strange aura surrounded the unknown individual standing before him, and Camillo's suspicious presence did not ease the situation.

"Your Holiness," said Camillo, smiling and with a condescending tone.

"Camillo, my friend, how can I assist you and your guest?" said Innocent, holding back the fear in his voice.

Camillo approached Innocent and situated himself in front of his leader and friend. "I'm afraid we have a situation that only you can remedy. Bear in mind that this will affirm the safety and survival of the church here on earth. It will not be in vain, I swear to you this."

Innocent stared emptily into the eyes of his trusted advisor and saw nothing but evil intent. At that point, the pope, though the most powerful man within the Vatican, was powerless.

"What do you mean, Camillo? I'm afraid I don't understand," said the increasingly frightened man, unable to hold back the quiver in his voice.

"A common response for your kind," said Camillo's companion. Much to Innocent's surprise, the man had made his way behind the pope's chair in a matter of a split second. Innocent's heart jumped, and suddenly his reality slowed. His vision became tunneled and his auditory reception blurred and muffled. He was rendered completely helpless and was a puppet in the hands of, as Innocent had finally realized, the lilim. In the buzzing of his skull, Innocent could make out the voice of the being behind him.

"Mankind is terrified by what they don't understand. Therefore, they fight, murder one another, formulate their own views of reality rather than accept truth as it is, and divide their lands rather than live in harmony. You cannot be allowed to continue as you are. Nature and God must purge you, but instead, humans cling to hope, believing a change is imminent." The lilim placed his hands on Innocent's temples and leaned down to whisper in his ear. "Even my brothers and sisters believe this to be true. You see, they wish to find our precious mother and leave humanity to destroy our world, but I know better. Mother Lilith would be so disappointed to see her garden overrun by weeds and vermin, and I wish to cleanse this paradise and reinstate its majesty before her awakening." The lilim stood straight up and closed his eyes. "And this begins with you."

Innocent was completely incapacitated at this point. The lilim's hands felt like two massive vise grips wrapped around his entire body, keeping him from moving, breathing, or even thinking on his own. The door to his office began drifting farther away from his sight, and the sounds entering his ears seemed to originate from a far-off distance. What had been just a steady buzzing in his head turned into an earthquake-like tremor that blurred his vision and drowned out the voice of the lilim.

"Who are you?" Innocent yelled, unable to hear his own voice.

"My name is Charles," the lilim revealed.

The voice penetrated everything Innocent was experiencing, silencing the shaking in his skull. A light began to seep in from his peripheral vision, comforting him and removing the fear from the horror he was feeling.

"Come," a voice commanded that was not his own nor Charles's nor Camillo's. "It has been long enough."

Camillo watched as Charles released Innocent's head, blood pouring from the pope's eyes, ears, nose, and mouth. His forehead hit the wooden desk with a knock as his shoulder rested on the corner of the desk, keeping his body from falling onto the floor.

"Begin your conclave," Charles said as he walked past Camillo.

"You will keep your word?" Camillo asked.

"Free my movements within your city," Charles responded. "Once I have what I want, I can wield and award power liberally. Nero will have his empire, and you will have your church. The emperor has already agreed to your terms. Your church will be the official religion of the Aurean Empire. I will have my mother, Domus Aurea will spread globally, and your faith will flourish."

"I will summon the College," Camillo said.

When Camillo turned around, Charles was gone. He glanced over at Innocent's body with sorrow in his heart. The man had a deep respect for his leader but knew in the coming times that Innocent would not be strong enough to keep the church from collapsing from within. The image of Innocent was too much to bear.

"I'm sorry, my brother," he said. "You will live forever in God's kingdom. Forgive me."

Camillo walked out of Innocent's office, stepping over the unconscious bodies of Rudolf and the Swiss Guards who had been standing watch. The sound of Adriano and several gendarmes could be heard rising from the stairwell, and so Camillo lay himself down among the scattered watchmen, waiting for the sounds of grief to fill the halls.

CHAPTER 21

THEY WEPT

January 18, 2036

The Church of Saint Anne had a line of mourners entering and exiting its doors. Members of the Swords of Uriel passed Scott's modest wooden coffin as it sat below the altar. The Eyes, apart from Daven and Adam, flanked Scott's body as Giuseppe and the Mouths of Uriel stood behind the container. Liana was crouched by the coffin, crying bitterly over Scott's head.

"Give them time," Raul said to Giuseppe. "Daven and Adam have accepted much if not all the blame regarding Scott—"

"Rightfully so," Margo said, interrupting Raul with disdain.

"But," Raul continued, glaring at Margo, "I know they'll come around. Those three were so close."

"I was overly cold to them," Giuseppe said. "They had just watched their friend die."

"They needed a measure of reprimand," Elia chimed in. "But we all know how Scott could be. He left the confines of the city on more than one occasion. I'm sure Daven and Adam were not the reason for the trip."

"I'm not sure if you people realize this," Margo said, his voice elevated above the whisper the others had been conversing in, "but we are standing over the body of our dead comrade. Dead. Murdered under the streets of Rome because those two idiots decided to get themselves thrown in prison. He should have left them there to rot for all I care."

"Margo," Elia started to say.

Giuseppe placed his hand on Elia's shoulder and turned toward Margo. "If you feel so inclined, walk out of this funeral right now and speak your words to those two."

"I think I just might," Margo spat back.

"Then don't be surprised when they break your jaw," Giuseppe yelled.

Giuseppe pushed past the line of Swords and stormed out of the church. Elia and Raul looked with disgust at Margo.

"Rein it in, you piece of—" Raul hissed.

"Let him be bitter," Elia said, cutting Raul off. "He'll hold it in his soul for a lifetime. Learn to forgive, Margo. Learn to channel your anger. Direct it at the evil that rules this world. Not at your allies."

"Those dimwitted children are not my allies," Margo growled. "And I'm going to do what none of you have the balls to do yourselves."

Margo took the same path Giuseppe had stomped out on and tore off in the direction of the barracks. Elia crouched down beside Liana and placed his hand on her shoulder.

"The pain is long-lasting," he said empathetically. "There is no silver lining to be seen right now, but I promise, it will show. I won't tell you to find solace in the fact that Scott lives on, because that realm of lasting life is too far away to be held or seen, but I will tell you to keep that thought in mind when sorrow allows for it. Do not hold in the pain. Do not hold in the anger. Just control it."

Liana slowly turned her head to look at Elia. She could see the pain of life carved in the lines of his face, the cloth over his eye a testament to his struggle. But she could also see his conquering spirit, the stoicism that held him up through years of trial and the inability to back down under immense pressure.

"What if I can't control it?" Liana asked with a raspy voice, her throat damaged from hours of weeping and yelling.

"Prayer, patience, and the gun range," Elia said with a grin.

This forced a smile, which pained Liana on the inside. She had no desire to show any form of happiness. The anger in her needed a release, and that anger kept forgiveness at bay.

"Don't harbor resentment," Elia said, referring to her feelings toward Daven and Adam. "You've lost more than anyone could stand to bear, but so have they. This was not their doing. You and I know full well who is behind this tragedy. The enemy is with the lilim. Not with your friends."

"I know," Liana said with slight disappointment. "There was no one else to blame at the time. I overreacted, but I would have burned from the inside out if I hadn't let the anger release."

"They need to hear it from you," Elia said.

Liana looked down at Scott. His face was remarkably lifelike, the color in his cheeks still red, but the light was gone. She cradled his face in her hands, with a look of serenity and contentment in her eyes.

"I'll go to them," she said quietly, "but I can't leave him now. Not yet."

Elia squeezed her shoulder and stood up. From the entrance to the church, Elia watched as Adriano burst through the line of Swords, coming to a stop to search for someone of authority. His eyes met Elia's, signifying that something horrible had just occurred.

"Where is Giuseppe?" Adriano yelled from the entrance.

Elia ran to Adriano. "He left in the direction of the barracks. I think to Daven and Adam."

"We need your soldiers along the wall as soon as possible," Adriano said in a hushed voice. "All of them."

"What's the rush?" Elia said, confused. "They deserve a chance to bid their friend a farewell."

"They'll get their chance," Adriano said. "But this is urgent."

"What's going on?" Elia asked.

"His Holiness is dead," Adriano said, choking back tears. "I found him in his office just minutes ago. I don't know what's going on. All the Swiss Guards protecting him, along with Rudolf and Camillo, were unconscious. Just lying on the floor. Camillo is gathering the College as we speak. My men will patrol the interior of the city while the Swiss Guard keeps watch at the Sistine Chapel. Your men will present themselves on the walls and the square."

"I'll tell Margo and Raul immediately," Elia said with shock. "I'll let Giuseppe know myself."

"That makes my job easier," Adriano said. "The time for mourning will come later. For now, we need to act."

Adriano pivoted on his heel and exited the church. Elia stood for a moment, processing the information that was laid on him. His body and mind ached for rest and a chance to grieve, but his duty came first. He knew when he looked over his shoulder that Raul and Margo would be staring, a look of inquiry in their eyes, but the words had not come to him yet, and he feared being the bearer of terrible news.

"We should be there," Daven said to Adam.

"It wouldn't do any good," Adam said. "Besides, Giuseppe said we could have a private viewing once everyone else has seen the body."

"Scott," Daven said sharply. "He's still Scott."

"You know what I mean," Adam said, aggravated. "What I'm saying is it would cause more harm than anything else. We're still the bad guys at this point."

"You'd think forgiveness would be overflowing in a place like this."

"What would you do?" Adam said. "Liana loved Scott. We were the first in line to be blamed."

"You see where that got us, right?" Daven said. "Word of mouth spreads. Right or wrong."

"It's a moot point," Adam said. becoming increasingly agitated. "Just be patient. You've never been one to take things slow."

The two had been confined to their room since returning from Rome, with nary a soul to visit or speak to them. They had not slept since the previous night and had successfully fought the urge to sneak away during the twilight. Daven alone had taken the brunt of the blame to heart and had an aching desire to speak to Dierdre above all else. The pain of wondering kept him awake and kept him worrying. He knew his thoughts should be focused on Scott, but all he could think about was how Dierdre had reacted to the news. Did she hate him, have no desire to be around him, had moved on in the short time since he had seen her? These questions were his immediate existence.

"I can't just sit here anymore," Daven said as he stood up. "It wasn't our fault, Adam. Why are we letting them think it was?"

"Because it's what they need!" Adam yelled. "The ability to cast blame is therapeutic."

"Then why not blame who is at fault?" Daven asked.

"Because the lilim aren't here!" Adam yelled again. "And we are. They can see us. We are an object they can fixate on."

"We've proven what we're capable of," Daven said. "Why do they treat us like children?"

Adam didn't have an answer. He had wondered the very same thing but had since let it sleep at the back of his mind. They ventured into Rome out of protective instinct, not as a childish endeavor.

"Open the door!" a voice yelled at the door, three loud pounds shaking the walls of their room.

"I'm not doing this anymore," Daven said, anger rising in his countenance.

Margo opened the door and came stomping in, lunging at Daven viciously. Adam jumped at the men, violently attempting to defuse what was about to transpire. Daven took a hard and sharp strike to his left cheek, Margo screaming at him with every swing.

"You two have been nothing but trouble since you arrived!" Margo screamed. "You let Scott die, you've brought the entire Lazio Legion down on us, and you are probably responsible for the lilim killing our men and displaying their corpses all over the city! You've even managed to get yourself shot in the process!"

Daven was through. The anger in Margo's eyes fueled Daven's rage and lit the explosive force that propelled him forward. He didn't speak, landing with a weighted thud onto Margo's chest, punching so savagely that the anger on Margo's faced turned wide eyed and repentant.

"Daven!" Adam screamed, trying to pull Daven off Margo before he killed the man. "Daven, stop!"

"No!" Daven bellowed. "I'm not rolling over like an old dog anymore! Scott's death was not our fault!"

Finally, the sight of Margo's unconscious head bouncing off Daven's fists defused his wrath. He slowly raised his body off Margo, shaking the pain and rigidity out of his hands. Margo began to come to just as Giuseppe entered the room.

"You got off easy," Giuseppe said to Margo as he helped the man off the floor. "I said they'd break your jaw; looks like you're walking away with just a damaged ego."

"He attacked me," Margo said, blundering through his words.

"You broke into our room and went straight for Daven's throat," Adam said accusingly.

Giuseppe looked at Margo, then Daven and Adam. "I'm readier to believe the latter," he said with a disappointed look directed at Margo. "You did say not fifteen minutes ago that this is what you would do."

Margo slumped over onto Adam's bed, clutching the sides of his head, silent like a child in time-out.

"Get to the infirmary, Margo," Giuseppe said. "Nod if you can hear me."

Margo stood and nodded, then walked out of the room in a daze. Giuseppe waited for Margo to shuffle out of earshot and then turned to Daven and Adam.

"My words last night came without thought," Giuseppe said, avoiding eye contact with the boys. "I cast blame before speaking to you first, and for that I am sorry. I can't take back what I said, but I can tell you with certainty that I don't blame you. I know how Scott could be. He was— is—a fire to be reckoned with but out of control at times. I don't need to know the details, but I know you did everything you could for him. Let that be of some consolation."

Daven and Adam remained quiet. In their hearts, a weight had been lifted. They respected Giuseppe beyond measure and had come to see him as a father figure, especially after the demise of Abele. Having him disappointed in them laid a guilt on their shoulders they could not contend with. They had lost friends and family in their journey, but losing the affection and admiration of the living would be the end of them.

Giuseppe prepared to speak more words of encouragement but was cut short.

"Crown Morreti!" Elia yelled through labored breathing from the stairwell. "He's dead. His Holiness is dead. We have to go now. Camillo has called an enclave."

Giuseppe didn't have time to think or question the details of the assassination. "Did you see Margo on the way up?" Giuseppe asked, nearing Elia.

"I did; he seemed a little worse for wear," Elia said half inquisitively.

"No time for that," Giuseppe said, strategizing with every step he took. "Are your companies on the move?"

"They are," Elia said, still breathing heavily. "Margo ran out the door as soon as I told him."

"Then we are on our way," Giuseppe said. "To either another day of life in Domus Aurea, or the collapse of everything we've ever known."

"Do you think that could happen?" Elia said with worry.

Giuseppe was on the verge of mental collapse. He had held it together for too long and had finally felt defeat creeping into his mind. "Dammit!" he yelled, crashing the palm of his hand down on the banister. Elia stopped short as Giuseppe slumped his shoulders and halted. "It's the beginning of a new hell. One I do not think I will live through. The sun is becoming dim the further I sink. There is this endless ocean of black that used to seem so far away but has since swallowed the shore and myself. I can hear the voices of the dead below me, their arms outstretched clawing through the dark abyss, waiting to feel my body in their grasp. They are the dead that I failed, Elia. They are all there at the bottom of the dark, with something else. Something big. Something that speaks softly, almost inaudibly; I can't make out the words, but I can feel their intent."

"What is their intent?" Elia asked as Giuseppe trailed off.

"To choke me with my failures," Giuseppe said with a tired voice. "You see, I failed the dead, but they are not symbolic of my costly frustrations. The infinite dark ocean I'm falling through is. The unseen source of the voice means to see me swallow it all. That is my hell. To consume all that is dark and unmentionable. Everything I've destroyed."

"You're forgetting something," Elia said, gripping the shoulder of his friend and superior. "The sun."

"What about it?" Giuseppe said, looking over his shoulder.

"The sun seems small plastered up in our blue sky. The ocean you are sinking in, almost eternal. But the sun, in reality, is giant, burning bright and fierce, giving life to our small planet, with its even smaller ocean. The sun, Giuseppe, is symbolic of your successes. It burns, even as you sink."

"If the one-eyed man is trying to cheer me up," Giuseppe said with a smile, "then I guess I should cheer up."

"What's the saying?" Elia said, walking ahead of Giuseppe. "'It is always darkest just before the day dawneth'?"

"I'll take it to heart," Giuseppe said, feeling more optimistic. "Now go. I want this city to be the safest place in all of Domus Aurea in minutes."

Elia dipped his forehead and exited into the bright afternoon sun.

Azael was in the middle of instructing the Eyes on how to aid the gendarmerie on patrolling the city and investigating Innocent's murder, but Dierdre's mind was a thousand miles away. She felt betrayed, despairing, and sorrowful. After watching Liana crumble to pieces when the news of Scott's demise reached her, Dierdre felt a large measure of guilt knowing the man she loved was still among the living. Especially when Daven had been present and had survived the encounter with the lilim.

Dierdre imagined the eyes of her peers staring through her, her mind creating a false narrative where they blamed her for being unable to stop the foray in the first place. She knew Scott and Adam were leaving the city that night, but her primary focus was not letting Daven leave with them. The woman felt like she should have and could have done more to prevent Scott's death from happening.

"Dierdre," Liana said, her voice penetrating the deep black smoke that had encompassed her mind. "Dierdre, are you ready?"

Dierdre looked up as the rest of the Eyes and Azael were leaving the room, breaking off into their assigned teams to begin the tasks appointed to them. "Yeah, sorry," she said. "I have a lot running through my mind. What are we doing again?"

Liana looked at her friend through concerned eyes. "We're assisting the gendarmerie with their investigation. Giuseppe thinks the lilim may have had something to do with this, and since the officers don't really know what to look for in that regard, we're to treat the assassination like it was deliberately carried out by a lilim."

"Okay," Dierdre said. "I guess we're on borrowed time at this point. Let's get going."

Dierdre began walking to the door, trying to push the anxious thoughts from the back of her mind.

"Talk to me," Liana said, stopping Dierdre from exiting the room. "You've been on the other side of the world mentally all day."

"If that were true," Dierdre said, with almost slurred speech, "I'd be much happier. Far from here. Far from Domus Aurea."

"You need to come back to reality," Liana said, firmly but with care. "The past isn't going anywhere. We both can address it when the present has been addressed."

"There's a lot that needs addressing," Dierdre said. "Sometimes so much that its weight keeps you from moving forward."

"My weight is lying in a coffin, alone, still, and cold," Liana said. "I'll help you with your burden if you help me with mine."

"Compared to yours," Dierdre said, "mine may as well be a feather pillow. Forgive me, Liana. I don't deserve to be so dejected."

"Loss is loss," Liana said. "Pain is pain, and sadness is sadness. Everyone feels those qualities in their own way. Don't disregard them because someone else's despair seems to be worthier of the emotions."

"Even so, I think you have a point," Dierdre said. "I can compartmentalize with the best of us. Let's go. We have more pressing matters than my instability."

Liana and Dierdre made their way from the barracks to the papal apartments, where Innocent's body still resided. It was quiet outside— no mourners, no bells, no news. The walls around the city bore a line of Swords, guarding the city from any onlookers gazing in from Rome. Small patrols of gendarmes could be seen, popping in and out of view from between buildings. The rest of the Eyes remained unseen, as they were intended to be, but Dierdre knew it was not the soldiers of the Lazio Legion that they were looking to protect the city from, but those who moved about concealed as well.

The Swiss Guard was front and center all around the palace, guarding from every vantage point, protecting from those who would seek to disrupt the process of procuring answers. Their faces seemed chiseled from stone, but their eyes were darkened by sorrow.

"I don't know what to make of this," a gendarme said as he escorted Dierdre and Liana to the scene of Innocent's death. "There are no signs of a struggle, no outward signs of trauma, and no one who was on this floor when it happened remembers seeing anyone coming in or out. The only thing that can be confirmed is the fact that everyone remembers waking up on the floor having lost, at the most, ten minutes of consciousness. That and the blood. It's as if the inside of his skull turned to liquid and seeped out of his eyes, nose, mouth, and ears."

It was obvious to the two women at that point what had transpired. Their job now was to divert suspicion to something less supernatural in order to keep a level of calm blanketed around the city. As much as could be left after such a horrendous tragedy.

"Had anyone left the building before the murder took place?" Liana asked as she entered Innocent's office.

"Witnesses say Inspector General Gabrieli left the building with one gendarme within an hour of His Holiness's murder," the investigator said. "After which, Commander Anrig stated Innocent and he entered the office where His Holiness sat at his desk, and Anrig situated himself by the window in that chair. He then stated that he lost sense and awoke on the floor outside the office."

"I don't suppose the commander is still in the confines, is he?" Dierdre asked, staring at the congealed blood under Innocent's head.

"No, ma'am," said the investigator. "He is personally standing guard at the Sistine Chapel, where the College is attending the conclave."

"Already?" Liana asked. "His Holiness hasn't even seen a proper burial! Six days before burial, nine for mourning, fifteen until the conclave. Innocent is lying in a pool of his own blood, and Camillo is already looking to replace him."

Dierdre understood Liana's point of view, but times were different, and Pope Innocent himself was not a man of tradition. "I don't think Camillo is doing it out of contempt or the desire to replace Innocent out of derision toward his legacy. We, and to a larger extent the church, need a leader. We can't wait for ceremony."

Liana knew what Dierdre said was true, but she believed a time of healing was pivotal to the process, especially when trying to make the right decision, but there was no time for argument.

"Adriano was the one who discovered the body, correct?" Liana asked, disregarding the issue of the conclave.

"Correct," the gendarme said.

"Did he notice anyone among the unconscious who was not present when he left the first time?"

This question triggered a visual sign of distress on the officer's face. "There was one," he said delicately. "Cardinal Lombardi."

Liana looked quickly at Dierdre.

"I'll get to the Sistine Chapel now," Dierdre said, bolting toward the stairwell. "But don't expect miracles! You know they're not going to let me in!"

"What's going on?" the gendarme asked, clearly shaken.

Liana didn't answer. Instead, she walked over to Innocent's body, his head pale and cold, with dark dried blood covering his face. "What did they do to you?" she asked through tears. "They think they've won. Those children of that devil. They've taken you. They've taken Scott. They won't take the world. Not with us standing in the way." Liana lifted her head and wiped her face. "We're done here. Call Doriano and let him know he can move the body. No autopsy, as usual. We can keep to tradition for that at least."

"Are you sure?" the officer asked. "Do we have a cause of death?"

"We have more than that," Liana said. "We have answers. We have a purpose."

CHAPTER 22

THE BEGINNING
OF THE END

January 18, 2036

"Scott, Innocent, Abele, Eula. How many more are we going to let die at the hands of evil because of our inaction?" Daven said.

"What could we possibly do?" Adam asked earnestly.

Daven thought about it. Their skills hadn't been tested fully, but he knew what the two of them were gifted with. In the end, Daven's and Adam's abilities were above human capability. Senoy and Sansenoy gave them their essence, powers of a supernatural quality, but as to the limits or lack thereof, neither of them was aware of what they may be.

"Why don't we find out?" Daven asked, a look of recklessness in his eyes. "We've spent so much time being angry at the angels for bringing this on us that we've overlooked the fact that we are extraordinary."

"This positivity coming from you is unnatural." Adam laughed. "But I wouldn't even know how to begin. It's not like we've been presented with an exorbitant amount of leads."

"Ask and you will receive, seek and you will find, right?" Daven said. "Maybe it's that easy. Maybe it's always been that easy."

"So, we just ask?" Adam said with disbelief.

Daven looked around the room, his eyes searching for something that was not immediately visible, but something he knew was there and had always been there. "Sansenoy? I could really use some advice if you're skulking around here somewhere."

It was quiet for a moment, just enough time for Daven to feel foolish, but like appearing from some unseen vantage point, Senoy, Sansenoy, and some unknown third angelic being stood in the center of the room as if they had always been there.

"It's about time you two pulled your heads out of your butts," Sansenoy said.

The three appeared in similar fashion: unfocused shadowy bodies, black eyes, and white wings draped over their bodies like cloaks. The third being's face was evasive to the focus of Daven's and Adam's eyes, unable to be seen.

"You left us with almost nothing in the way of instruction," Adam said, annoyed. "You've sent us out on autopilot, but what happens when some unforeseen hurdle gets thrown in our path? We need to know how to avoid or overcome it."

"Use your imagination," Senoy said.

"We need real teaching," Daven said. "Not some stupid PBS rainbow imagination load. Tell us what to do. Tell us how to do it."

"Hold out your hand," Sansenoy said to Daven. "And think of fire."

Daven held out his hand and thought of a candle flame. In the center of his palm, a small pinpoint of light appeared, white-hot, then lessened in its magnitude to a flickering candlelight, simple, yet amazing in its existence.

"Bigger," Sansenoy said. "With control."

The candle flame grew in intensity, engulfing his hand entirely but not burning him. Adam held out his own hand and shut his eyes. In his mind, he imagined his daughter as he had seen her the night Senoy appeared to him, thinking of her blue eyes and blonde hair, her smile and laugh. Before him the little girl appeared, her hand placed within his.

"What are the limits?" Adam asked, tears welling up in his eyes.

"You can't click your heels and wish your way home like Dorothy," Senoy said. "But you can see it whenever you like. Just don't expect it to be lasting."

The little girl began to distort to those surrounding Adam. Daven began to realize that her image formed based on how Adam saw her, and he was seeing her through tears.

"She is who you are fighting for," Senoy said. "The war you are fighting is bigger than this city, bigger than Domus Aurea. This fight covers the earth and all who inhabit it. You wanted counsel? A lesson? Think of what you need, and it will be so."

"When it comes to your enemies," Sansenoy added, "the scarier the better."

Daven grinned. The room around them melted away like an artist covering his work in black paint. Nothing remained but Daven, Adam, and the angels. Daven screamed black fire, his body vanishing in the flame's shadow, his face white as a specter delivering some terror-filled message in the night. He shut his mouth, and the flames burned within his body, glowing blue inside him and outlining his form. Six wings outlined in a gray hue began spinning behind him like the blades of a windmill, slow at first, then fast, blowing the darkness away, the horror rising off him like smoke revealing the room, himself, and reality once again.

"Now that's using your imagination," Sansenoy said. "Got the hang of it now?"

"Well, I'm not as imaginative as he is," Adam chirped. "But, yeah, I'm sure we've got it now."

"Good," both angels said. "Now that that's out of the way …"

The third angel's face immediately came into focus, shocking both Daven and Adam in an instant.

"Can this be?" Adam asked. "Was this the plan all along?"

"Maybe not the plan," Senoy answered. "But you know the saying: God can work all things for good."

The third angel came out of the shadow he had been standing in behind his brothers, smiled, and introduced himself. "I am Semangelof," he said with a smile. "But you can call me Scott."

Daven and Adam slowly inched forward, shock still plainly written on their faces as they gripped Scott's shoulders and pulled him in to embrace him.

"Death is the great divider," Sansenoy said. "Driving a rift between the living and the eternal. Its pain is sharp and lasting, but it is not forever. You are so constrained by time. It limits your vision, creating the illusion of permanent separation, but to all who believe, there is hope. This is what keeps your soul at peace when your mind yearns for reunion. A reunion that will come. Everlasting life and light."

"What about Innocent?" Daven asked. "Is he with you?"

"Innocent is in paradise," Sansenoy answered. "He is at peace and happy."

Adam stepped away from Scott, looking the being before him up and down, trying to process everything, then glaring his eyes at Senoy and Sansenoy. "Who killed Innocent?" he asked sternly. "Who took him from us?"

Senoy looked back, unfazed by Adam's severity. "The one you call Charles Monroe," he said. "He has his hands in every facet of the world you have become accustomed to for so long. His command brought the lilim that murdered Scott. He himself killed Innocent and the men whose bodies he left strewn across Vatican City. His ultimate goal is to find his mother Lilith, and he will control Domus Aurea and the Catholic Church to get what he wants, regardless of his siblings' apprehension."

"You must find him," Sansenoy continued. "You must remove him from Domus Aurea. He is close to achieving success, and if he does, the war is lost."

"And that's where I come in," Scott said. "I may not have been the most astute individual in life, but death has granted me some insight. You need direction? I'll direct."

"When do we begin?" Adam asked. "And where do we go?"

"There's a building north of the city on the corner of Viale Giulio Cesare and Via Ezio," Scott began. "He waits there for the way to be opened into the Vatican."

"Is Innocent's death the beginning of his plan?" Daven asked.

"Innocent's death was but a gear in a ticking clock, counting down the minutes until the pawns are in place. Charles hand winding the machine into life," Sansenoy said. "But the second hand clicks closer to midnight with every word spoken here. It is time to move."

Daven and Adam cleared their minds of every worry and every trepidation. They both knew this would be the start of a journey unstoppable, leaving no time for goodbyes or explanations. They prepared themselves mentally and spiritually, then walked out of the barracks and into Rome under the new moon of the night.

"You know the laws, Dierdre," Rudolf said. "No one is allowed in until the conclave is finished. Under no circumstances. I can't explain it any clearer than that."

"This conclave may have been forced, Rudolf!" Dierdre said with an elevated voice. "I know it seems crazy, but I can't willingly let this happen."

"Then I'll make it easy for you," Rudolf said. "It's not up to you. Your will cannot be done. Accept that this is happening and take your investigation elsewhere. When the conclave is finished, then you can ask all the questions you'd like."

Dierdre's frustration was being stoked to an unmitigated heat. "It may be too late by then, Rudolf."

Before Rudolf could express his thoughts in another way more suitable for the argument, the doors of the chapel opened, revealing Camillo and a throng of cardinals behind him.

"Considering our present dilemma, we must obviously forgo tradition for a more practical formality," Camillo said with a blank look. Dierdre expected the dean to acknowledge her grievance, but before she could speak, Camillo continued forward with his thought.

"But I could at least indulge in the proclamation," Camillo said.

The cardinals parted ways for two men, one being the Cardinal Protodeacon. "I announce to you a great joy!" the Protodeacon bellowed. "We have a pope! The Most Eminent and Most Reverend Lord, Lord Alban, Cardinal of the Holy Roman Church Sommer, who takes to himself the name Gregory XVII."

Alban, now known as Gregory, moved to the forefront of the cardinals and began to impart the Urbi et Orbi blessing, with an almost fake smile on his face. As Gregory stammered on, Dierdre gazed dumbfounded at what she considered a gross miscarriage of power. Innocent hadn't been dead for more than twelve hours, and already he had been replaced—and by someone not fit to bless anyone. The words he said were drowned out by the boiling blood in her ears. Nothing but the *amen* response made it through to her understanding. As everyone around her listened with acceptance in their hearts, Dierdre refused to sit and watch the farce unfold.

"You did this," she whispered in Camillo's direction. "You let this happen. You've been planning this all along."

Camillo eyed her from where he stood, an almost unnoticeable smile on his face, one that was not related to the celebration at hand. Dierdre turned away and marched out toward the entrance, the voices of the men echoing in the distance until the sounds of her footsteps drowned them out.

It was a sight to behold. The first cohort of the Lazio Legion stood before Adamo and his brother Benito under their banner among ceremonial torches. Tonight was the night in which Nero's plan came to fruition, and the Vatican became part of the Aurean Empire. Up until now, Adamo had been pessimistic at best, but seeing such ferocity under careful control was inspiring. Even under the quiet of the night, battle cries and chants drummed in Adamo's mind. He now knew that this was the right step to furthering the empire. Charles had held up his end of the bargain, and now Nero reciprocated by reducing Vatican City's defenses to nothing.

"Tonight begins the spread of Domus Aurea!" Benito yelled into the cohort's carefully placed square of soldiers, the men responding with a resounding cadence of cheers. "The germ of obstinacy that has plagued the heart of this great nation will be eradicated! The sickness that has held our Golden Lady back from embracing the rest of this planet's children into her bosom will finally die, and our Aurean light will shine upon the planet. A light rivaled only by the sun itself!"

"Bosom?" Adamo laughed over the shouts of the soldiers.

"Shut up," Benito answered. "It's effective wording."

Benito held up his hand to silence the men. "Let tonight's eminent victory fuel the fire that will drive this machine past our current borders! Let it spread like a raging blaze across the earth with such power that humanity will flock to it for warmth in this cold world! You men will go down in the annals of history as the first of many great warriors who will follow in your footsteps! They will speak of you as if you were gods, and they will clamor to reach the pinnacle of greatness that you will build here starting tonight! Every new beginning comes from another beginning's end! Ignis Aureo!" Which meant, For the Golden Fire. The cohort repeated this motto over and over, giving Adamo chills.

Benito signaled a command for an about-face, the perfect stomp of boots thudding in perfect unison. The resulting dead silence left even the slightest whisper audible throughout the entire rotunda in front of the Pantheon.

"Move," Benito said, his voice like a lit match in a pitch-black room, seen and heard by all.

The cohort began moving in the direction of Vatican City, marching in perfect form and harmony.

"The remaining cohorts will surround the city," Adamo said to his brother. "Yours will move into Saint Peter's Square at my command. You will avoid bloodshed at all costs unless fired upon. From the point of entry, we will wait for word from Nero."

"They started the revolts of 2032," Benito said with hope. "I pray they try again."

"Your bloodlust will be the end of you," Adamo said. "You are a great leader. Don't fall to lunacy."

"Lunacy is the spark for advancement," Benito said. "But I will submit to your advice."

Adamo looked at his sibling with worry in his eyes. "You are my brother, and I love you. But sometimes I see the strongheadedness of Nero in your soul. Avoid that life. Avoid the turmoil that comes with it. I can't be the voice of reason for both of you and still reserve a level of sanity for myself."

"Maybe so," Benito said. "But perhaps I can embody the best of both worlds. I am capable of balancing my own mind."

Adamo smiled. "I forget you are not the little boy I fondly remember from all those years ago. You have grown to be the man our father would have always wanted you to be."

"Ah, don't get all sentimental on me now, brother." Benito laughed.

"Especially when we should be shedding our emotions in favor of a strong spirit."

Adamo watched Benito jump down from the platform they had been standing on. He was frightened for his younger sibling, aware of the edge the man was teetering on, swaying back and forth between a level head and unhinged cruelty. He gazed off into the distance, unmoving, waiting for the cohort to move out of view, Benito having ridden on horseback to the front of the line. He knew Nero would have wanted an update on the campaign's proceedings by now, and so he turned away from the empty rotunda and walked into the Pantheon, the click of his boots echoing off the domed roof as he made his way to his emperor's throne.

CHAPTER 23

FIRE FROM WITHIN

January 18, 2036

"Why do you trouble your mind with such thinking?" Tŭnash asked Charles. "Death is not a luxury we lilim possess."

Charles was sitting slouched in a chair on the upper floor of a building he had acquired for himself. A place to retreat to when his mind became heavy with thought. "Luxury?" he asked. "In death we do not rest. Conscious just enough to know we are doomed in it. Blackness forever. What did we do to deserve such a fate except for being born to a mother sought after by the demons of this world? I am angered by her costly decision, but I am grateful for her unwillingness to submit. I acquired this characteristic."

"You would see her return to Adam?" Tŭnash asked, surprised and appalled. "You would guilt her into such foolishness? And you claim to be grateful for her unwillingness to submit."

Charles was not at all taken aback by Tŭnash's recoil. He had kept this desire a secret for so long he had almost forgotten it completely himself. It was a selfish want, one that caused him great distress, but her return would mean the end of the angel's onslaught. "I'm not in the mood for a lecture," he said. "It is my own burden to bear. In the end, it will be her decision, but I will try as I might to convince her of the merits of her return."

"I would see us all burn before she returned to a life of submission and misery," Tŭnash said.

275

"You would see your family burn?" Charles yelled, kicking the seat back. "I fight for my mother. Everything I do now, I do for her! But I will not live a life of constant worry because of a choice *she* made."

"You had me fooled," Tŭnash said with disgust. "I truly believed you were doing this because you loved our mother. Now I see you are doing it for your own benefit."

Charles slammed his hand into Tŭnash's throat so hard her body left the ground. He gripped her neck and squeezed. The other succubi stood quickly, ready to defend their sister. "Never question my devotion," he said, articulating every word with rage. "Never again. I love my mother. I have done more than the entirety of lilimkind to see her returned to us. But as much as I quarrel with my brothers and sisters, I will not watch them be diminished to a pile of ash."

Tŭnash eyed her sisters, giving a silent command to back down. Charles lowered the succubus quietly, the anger lessened in his heart. He was prepared to divert the confrontation when the entire building shook, like it had fallen from a great height.

"The legion?" Tŭnash asked.

Charles shook his head. "The time is not right. There is nothing in their arsenal that could be felt here from the square."

The lights flickered, and then all went dark. From below, Charles and the succubi could hear their followers scream in horror as the sickly-sweet smell of burning flesh and hair rose to their floor.

"What is it?" Tŭnash asked calmly but with undertones of terror in her voice.

Charles looked at the wide space in front of them where the stairwell was—black smoke, thick like ink droplets bleeding into a pool of water rising up from the hell unfolding below them. "They're here."

There was no time for fanfare, ordeal, or ritual. Innocent's body was dressed in modest apparel, lying in state beneath the dome of the basilica. Alban, now Pope Gregory, stood silent over the body as fewer than a hundred onlookers stood by. Giuseppe was the lone member of the Milvian

Guard in attendance, along with Adriano and Rudolf. The Commander of the Swiss Guard was especially distraught, seeing as it was his sworn duty to protect his Holy Father from all danger. He was inconsolable and stood alone at the head of Innocent's resting place.

It was dark, with an encircling of tall candelabras lighting the funeral. Innocent's body had not been prepared aside from being cleaned and dressed by Doriano. His remains lay inside a hastily built wooden coffin, his final resting place a recycled stone sarcophagus sitting within the Chapel of Saint Veronica under the basilica in the grottoes.

"He was a light," Camillo started to say, "in this darkness that has been brought upon us. That light has now left us, but where that fire once burned bright, new breath can rekindle new flame from the ashes."

Giuseppe kept quiet. Dierdre and Liana had relayed their suspicions about Camillo hours before the funeral, and he was inclined to believe them. Rudolf affirmed the fact that Camillo had not been present before the blackout, but a Swiss Guard reported seeing Camillo enter the palace with an unrecognized man—tall, pale, with an otherworldly quality about him. Giuseppe's temper had been thin of late, and it had become almost transparent since Camillo had arrived.

"Whose breath rekindled the flame?" Adriano said quietly. "The same one who snuffed it out?"

Adriano glared intensely at Camillo. Giuseppe had not made Adriano aware of his suspicions, but it was clearly obvious that he had not needed to. Gregory had not moved since his arrival, staring intently at Innocent's body with a look of regret on his face, but he sensed the growing tension around him and spoke up.

"I could never hope to replace this man. I fear my light will not hold back the shadows as his could. I can't do it alone. I need your blessing."

Giuseppe did not recognize the man before him. Before he was Gregory, he was Alban Sommer. Power-hungry, short-tempered, overzealous. Perhaps with the elevation to his new stature and the adoption of a new name, Gregory was shown what it meant to acquire the power he so longed for, and it wasn't what he expected.

"You have it," Rudolf said, breaking his silence. "I will protect you if you'll have me."

Gregory smiled and nodded. The rest of those in attendance, including

Giuseppe, agreed and gave their blessing as well. Something none of them thought they would ever do.

The procession made its way down into the grottoes of the basilica, where Innocent's body was laid to rest within the stone sarcophagus. As the top of the container was set atop the encasement, Elia burst into the quiet chapel, a look of fear in his eyes.

"Giuseppe," he said, sadness and despair in his voice, "Curre," which was an operation known only to Giuseppe and his lieutenants, the word Latin for *run*.

"How bad?" Giuseppe asked.

"The entire Lazio Legion has the city surrounded," Elia said. "Their first cohort has pushed our men out of the square."

Giuseppe began instructing the higher-ups on the hierarchy to find shelter and prepare to evacuate the city. Camillo, Gregory, Rudolf, and the few cardinals in the group made their way farther into the grottoes, to a location unknown to even Giuseppe himself.

"You know what I have to do," Giuseppe said to Elia.

"Get it and keep it safe," Elia responded, referring to the document holding the secret of Lilith's location. "What are your orders?"

Before Giuseppe could answer, the flames on the candelabras surrounding Innocent's grave intensified, like a focused wind had blown through the room. The fire swirled into a twister of heat and light as the form of a man appeared within it. At first, the figure was too bright to look at, but as the fire returned to the candles, the form of the being became visible.

The man was robed in white light, but his features were human and recognizable.

"Do not fight the forces at your doorstep," the man said. "Remove your men and move toward San Marino. The city is lost. Lost to the armies of Domus Aurea and to the snakes that have made their home here."

"Who are you?" Elia said, his vision restored.

"My name is Semangelof," the angel said, "but I bring with me my vessel."

The robe of light diminished, leaving just a man standing before Giuseppe and Elia.

"Scott?" Giuseppe said with joy. "Can it really be you?"

"You can't fight them and win," Scott said, moving in close to the two men. "This has been planned for a long time now. Camillo, Nero, and Charles. You were never meant to win against them, Giuseppe. We were never meant to make it out of this alive."

"I knew it," Elia said with anger. "Camillo had Innocent killed, Giuseppe. He put Gregory in power because he knows he can control him. With Camillo and Nero working together, this can't end well."

"Camillo wishes to see his church become the state religion of Domus Aurea," Scott said. "Billions of faithful working in tandem with whom Nero bends to his will. Nothing will stop him. But your task is not with them. Bring the lilim to their knees, and everything will fall into place. You will fight Domus Aurea—this cannot be avoided—but your concentration must be on keeping Lilith hidden."

"This begins with getting the secret out of the city," Elia said. "Go, Giuseppe. I'll gather our men and move them toward San Marino."

"They'll kill us all," Giuseppe said. "How can we just move into Domus Aurea without blood being shed?"

"Their eyes are fixed on Vatican City," Scott said. "But it won't be for long. You have to move now, or else all of you will die. Now go."

Scott's image moved back into the robe of light as it dispersed back into the candle flames.

"Get the word out," Giuseppe said. "I will meet you in San Marino in two days. Do not wait for me. I promise to see you there."

Giuseppe and Elia embraced, no more words being spoken between the two. As Elia ran headlong to find Margo and Raul, Giuseppe moved farther down into the ancient Roman necropolis where Daven liked to roam. Even with winter still lingering in the air aboveground, the narrow passages down below were warm and humid. The lighting was dim, and the air was unnerving. An artificially generated high electrical field was present in the tunnels, working as a slight deterrent to any who would search the halls of the necropolis. The fear the air brought with it would keep trespassers still long enough for guardsmen to arrive.

Giuseppe pushed the fear to the back of his mind and moved down to mausoleum "U," the Lucifer Tomb. There he entered, staring toward the back wall at the red depiction of the Light Bearer, contrasting with the bland concrete color surrounding it. It was here that he placed his hand, running his fingers along the painted Lucifer on horseback. With a strained push, the portrait receded into the wall, then sliding to the left, disappearing from view, revealed a small chest situated behind bulletproof glass.

Giuseppe placed his hand on a large sensor, after which the glass door clicked, opening outwardly, leaving the chest accessible. Reaching in, Giuseppe placed his hands on the container just as the foundations of everything around him shook. The shock wave hit the man hard enough to knock him to his knees, the sounds akin to the earth itself ripping in half—cracking, quaking, and clapping of stone, plaster, and marble crumbling above him and beside him. The lighting, though low to begin with, shut off, leaving Giuseppe in total darkness with the secret of Lilith's location, the one document the lilim would go to any length to acquire, clutched in his arms.

Daven and Adam stood in the middle of a blackened smoke-filled room. Just moments before, a gathering of lilim, all followers of Charles, celebrated the successful assassination of Innocent and the ongoing annexation of Vatican City. The arrival of the two men ceased all merriment. Although the lilim were unaware of who these men were, they sensed the danger, elevating their fear.

That was all Daven and Adam needed. *This won't hurt,* Daven said. *The fire burns quickly.* The lilim jumped into action, leaping with hive-like proficiency at the two men. The front line of lilim evaporated with a flash of light and smoke, causing the remainder to recoil in fear. Fear that fueled what Daven and Adam were capable of doing.

The men's faces then drained of color, leaving white skin, black eyes, a gaunt appearance, and a wide-open mouth, a mouth that revealed a furnace of heated metal. As they leaned over, the glowing-hot liquid poured out, forming into a blade of fire. The men cut the air in the direction of the remaining lilim, burning and melting the flesh off their bones. The angelic forms of Daven and Adam knelt and slammed the blades of their swords into the ground in front of them. A ripple of molten liquid spread out from the point of impact, leaving nothing but ash and bone in its wake. Pulling the swords from the ground created one last quake of energy that left nothing but ash and smoke in the now silent room.

"We just vaporized about twenty of those guys," Daven said amid laughter.

"Yeah, we did," Adam said, "but remember, it hinges on their fear of us. Don't forget what happened with Scott. That was just one lilim. She wasn't falling for anything we were dishing out, and it got Scott killed."

"I won't lie. When I saw Scott put that gun to his head, I lost all concentration," Daven said. "So in other words, we just need to be careful."

Adam moved forward through the room. The walls were black with soot, and the remains of brittle bones crunched under his feet. Out of the corner of his eye, Adam noticed movement. "Daven," he said, "we've got a live one."

A lone lilim sat slumped in a corner, an arm missing and half of his leg blackened and dead. His breathing was labored, and his face showed fear and pain plainly. "You see us as evil," he said through grunts and sighs, "but from where I sit, you are the evil ones."

Daven and Adam crouched down in front of the lilim, the injured lilim cowering and twitching.

"All we want is our legacy," the lilim said. "Without our mother, we die out. Extinction is something all forms of life seek to avoid. Why is it that our mission has received divine intervention?"

"Your mother has promised to cause pain and agony to the children of Eve," Sansenoy said through Daven. "She has been the cause of much turmoil throughout human history. Pestilence, drought, famine, even the fall of many empires. Her sins are tenfold."

"Why do her sins require the eradication of her children?" the lilim asked, coughing blood up between words.

"They wouldn't," Senoy said through Adam, "if you would leave her to rest."

"You have the ability to reproduce through your own kind," Sansenoy said. "Take this path, and you live."

The lilim laughed painfully. "This deludes our bloodline. Our power would diminish."

"And this is why we fight," Sansenoy said. "Your ultimate desire is power, under the guise of love for Lilith. Your lies are visible and your intentions transparent."

Adam gripped the remaining arm of the lilim and squeezed. From within, the bones of the lilim ignited, burning him from the inside out.

"Charles is still here," Daven said, looking toward a set of stairs in the center of the back wall of the room. "Why don't we end this right here and now?"

"After you," Adam said as he released the ashes of the lilim. "But remember, fear is our power. In them, not us."

The two men walked toward the stairs as a dark fog began materializing around them, moving up the stairwell ahead of them.

CHAPTER 24

OUT OF THE PAN

January 18, 2036

Benito and Adamo scaled the rubble of the collapsed dome of Saint Peter's Basilica. Centurions moved through the city, taking prisoners and executing those who resisted. Adamo was not happy with the events of that evening, but the end result was what mattered.

"This was supposed to have gone down without violence," Adamo said from atop the stone and plaster. "Then again, maybe that's what I was meant to believe. Do we not want an alliance with the new church? Why wait for our contacts within the Vatican to replace the seat of power when this was the plan all along?"

"Nero has no desire to ally with the church," Benito said. "But our strange friend you have been so quiet about seems to require it. You know how Nero can be. Bring down the enemy and salt the earth. We stand upon that briny pillar."

"Then what will stop him from desecrating our own graves?" Adamo said. "If he'll stop at nothing, then what happens when he bulldozes over those who stand in his way?"

"Don't stand in his way then," Benito said, hopping down from the pile of rubble as Camillo was being escorted to the two men.

"What is this mockery?" Camillo yelled as he stood toe to toe with Benito. "The deal was to leave the city unmarred!"

Benito slapped the cardinal to the ground. "From where I stand and from where you kneel, you have no room to make such demands."

"I do when I'm the only one keeping their word," Camillo said, spitting blood from his mouth. "But you have taught me a valuable lesson tonight, so for that I thank you."

Benito grabbed Camillo's chin with force. "What do you know of keeping words? Did you not vow to serve your Holy Father? Protect and keep? His death is on your hands. We acted just as you have. You and I are the same."

"Stand down, Benito," said Adamo. "I sympathize with the holy man. Trust cannot be kept alive when we feed it lies." Adamo reached out his hand and lifted Camillo to his feet. "Sometimes our higher-ups subvert our own authority. This was not my intent, personally. But my desires are irrelevant in the scheme of Nero's own interests."

"Your ruler has nothing to fear from me," Camillo said, rubbing his jaw. "But our mutual benefactor may see this as a gross miscalculation."

"I'm inclined to believe you, holy man," Adamo said, glancing at Benito. "You gave the order, brother. Who gave it to you?"

"You already know, do you not?" Benito said, standing behind Camillo and Adamo. "Nero ordered me to bring down the dome. He saw it as a symbol of defiance."

"What will happen when the lilim see *this* act of defiance?" Camillo asked. "Nero is a man. The lilim are much more."

"The lilim need me more than they realize," said Nero as he marched up to the group of men, surrounded by his Praetorian Guard. "If they are as powerful as you say, then a crumbled ruin of rock will by no means stand in their way."

"Perhaps you are correct," Adamo said. "But where does that leave us with the church?"

Nero stared from beneath his brow at Camillo. The would-be emperor was not fond of religious thought, but he understood its place and draw in the world. "They have nothing I need, but their place will not be threatened. This city is mine now, but you may continue your traditions and rituals as you see fit. Let this night be a lesson in power. Let the world see that I am a fair ruler. Your ways will flourish under my hand as long as you obey. Where are their remaining forces, Adamo?"

"Aside from a few stragglers," Adamo said, "the city's militant forces retreated to the north. Per your command, we did not pursue."

"Excellent," Nero said with a smile. "They will most likely make their way to San Marino. Let them gather their forces in one area. A tightly placed target is easier to snuff out."

"What are your orders, my liege?" Benito asked.

Nero breathed deeply and stared into the moonlit sky. "Make this world my own."

"If we do not leave, we will all perish at their hands," Tŭnash said. "Your misguided stubbornness will be the end of everything you have worked for."

Charles heard Tŭnash's plea, but it was lost in the ripples of his worried mind. Even without seeing the destruction below him, he knew every one of his followers on that floor had perished to the angels. He was afraid, but more than that, he was angry. He stared intently at the top of the stairwell, waiting as time ticked by excruciatingly slow for the heads of the angels to appear. Charles caught a glimpse of the eyes of Daven and Adam, but for only a second. A rush of gray smoke flowed toward Charles and his succubus followers, enveloping the two men, but was stopped by an invisible wall, the lilim able to watch as it billowed and swirled against the unseen partition.

The gray mist began to slow its churning, leaving a still screen of murky smoke. Charles looked to the windows as an avenue of escape, but instead of buildings, only blackness with faint silhouettes of writhing beings in pain could be seen. There was nowhere to go. He looked back at the wall, but two pairs of eyes had appeared, red and round, with bright Hebrew names shining above them. A third pair of eyes appeared between the other two, another Hebrew name on top. Quickly and alarmingly, three hands pressed themselves against the unseen wall with a deep thump.

The middle being stepped out from the smoke, a man in the image of Scott, clothed in white with a cloth covering his eyes, although the red eyes were still visible through the fabric. He outstretched his hands toward the other beings as two swords began to materialize in either palm, the pommels pointing at Daven's and Adam's angelic likenesses.

The hands of Senoy and Sansenoy shot out from the cloud of gray, gripping the swords in a flash. Faster than Charles's mind could process, Senoy and Sansenoy shifted from the smokescreen to being behind him and Tŭnash. The blades of the swords pressed firmly on their necks as Semangelof extended his black wings around the room, leaving no exit.

"We are capable," Semangelof said. "Your followers have been reduced to dust."

"I gathered that," Charles said brazenly. "The smell of seared flesh gave it away."

"Your fear shines through your feigned courage," Semangelof said. "But your life does not end tonight."

Charles was confused. The entrance Daven and Adam made screamed death, but he would not argue with the angels. "Then why are you here?" he asked.

"Your voice gathers the masses to you," Semangelof said, still and unmoving. "Your endeavors speak even louder. Go to your siblings. If they see you willing to end your crusade, then perhaps their eyes will be opened to the fruitlessness of their own quest. Convince them to stop their search. Your kind will live and prosper."

Charles fell silent in thought, angered beyond measure. "Prosper? How will we prosper? Without our mother, our strength fades. Our search gives us purpose, but without the end result, we will either die out or live on through familial relations, a vile act in and of itself and an act that will delude the power within us. My answer to you is no. I will let my voice gather the masses to me, and I will let my endeavor fuel their resolve."

The fear in Charles began to subside. The blades of Senoy's and Sansenoy's swords moved away from Charles's and Tŭnash's necks, giving them just enough time to fly with speed toward Semangelof's wings. The lack of fear in the lilim caused the wings to curl inward like the paper of a scroll, revealing the window glass behind them. Charles and all the succubi leapt through the windows to the streets below, vanishing into the night.

"Well, at least he's gone," Daven said, the visage of Sansenoy retreating into the shadows.

"It's what was expected," Scott said, still in his white robes. "I didn't think he'd drop his mission, but he will leave the city. Without him, Domus Aurea's strength will lessen, though not enough to halt their advances."

"Well, then, if we're done here," Adam said, turning toward Daven, "we should probably get back to the barracks before anyone realizes we're gone. I don't want to get grounded again."

The two men walked toward the stairwell, but Scott stood silently with a look of remorse on his face. "I'm sorry, but returning to the city will not be possible."

Daven and Adam looked at Scott's tall image with confusion.

"What do you mean we can't go back?" Adam asked. "We don't have anywhere else we can go."

"Vatican City has fallen," Scott said, rather emotionlessly. "Camillo Lombardi planned the assassination of Pope Innocent and replaced him with Alban Sommer. Now Domus Aurea and the Vatican work together, Alban now known as Pope Gregory acting as a puppet to both Nero and Camillo."

The color in Daven's face faded. "W-what about Giuseppe?" he asked with a shaky voice. "What about the guard? What about the Eyes? What about Dierdre?"

"They have fled the city," Scott said. "San Marino is their destination, but it is not yours."

Daven raced past Scott as Adam yelled after him, "Daven! You're running toward a war zone!"

Adam ran after his friend but couldn't keep up. Daven had a fire behind him that propelled him through the streets toward Vatican City. He had an uncontrollable feeling that everything he loved and longed for had perished under the hand of Domus Aurea. If he lost Dierdre, no power in heaven or hell could save Domus Aurea or the lilim from his wrath.

The men rounded a corner and found themselves staring at a section of the northern wall dividing Rome from their home. Daven could see smoke rising from behind the stone separator that sent his mind and heart racing. He could see the faces of everyone he cared for and protected lying dead and cold under debris, covered in blood. It was enough to convince him to scale the wall and destroy everything in his path.

"They survive," Scott said, appearing from nothing. "There is nothing for you here. If you linger, the lilim will spread along with the Aureans, and everyone you know and love will die. Leave and save them. Stay and be the reason they are destroyed."

Everything in Daven told him to run after Dierdre and the rest of those who had fled the city, but Scott was right, and though he hated to admit it, Daven knew he was right.

"Where do we go?" Daven asked. "We have nothing."

"You have everything," Scott said. "You will leave the peninsula and reunite with your families. Until you are reminded of what is at risk, you will not fight with everything you have."

"Then I'm assuming you are leading the way?" Adam asked. "Because I'm lost here."

Scott extended his hand, motioning the way forward. Without a word of rebelliousness, Daven and Adam walked away from the city, never having witnessed the carnage on the other side of the walls, but they didn't need it to fuel their resolve. They knew what was at stake.

He waited until there was nothing but silence. It was dark outside, so he knew the cover of night would aid in his escape. He cradled a thick, acrylic frame with Robert Falcon Scott's journal entry encased within it. The collapse of the dome made it difficult to escape the necropolis, but Giuseppe was able to reach ground level through the excavations office. The Aurean presence in the city was obvious, with several patrol groups making their way through the small country, but Giuseppe was sure he could avoid any confrontations.

He stayed close to the walls of the sacristy, making his way toward the railway. Before he was home free, a patrol passed by the station.

"Be quick about it," one of the eight soldiers said to another. "You call yourself a man. My grandmother has a stronger bladder than yours."

"I've been holding it since Benito's speech," he said, inching closer to Giuseppe's position. "Just keep going; I'll catch up.

The soldier positioned himself just in front of Giuseppe, his back to him as he relieved his aching body. An uncontrollable anger came over

Giuseppe, watching as the man urinated on the wall of his beloved city. What happened next was out of his control, as if his body had taken over where his mind would not venture. His hands grabbed the Aurean, bringing him to his knees as Giuseppe struck him to the ground. The soldier choked pathetically as Giuseppe stomped his booted foot on his throat.

"This by far does not make up for what you have done here tonight," Giuseppe said with a hissed whisper, "but I will enjoy watching the life flutter from your eyes. I will remember every movement of your face—the fear, the shock, the frantic desire to live. But I will also remember how I felt being the one who took that life from you, just as you have taken my life from me."

Giuseppe dropped his knee hard onto the man's neck, feeling the stiff collapse of his trachea between the soft muscle of his throat. The soldier's eyes bulged, tears streaming down his bloodred cheeks. Soon, the life left his face, and Giuseppe lifted his weight from the dead man below him. The emotion caught him by surprise, shocking and disgusting him to the horror he had just unleashed upon the dead Aurean, but he didn't have time to reflect.

After slipping through the railway exit and out into Rome, Giuseppe made his long journey northward toward San Marino. He had no fear in his heart, as sorrow had left no room for anything else to reside. It had been several hours since the rest of the survivors of the attack had moved on, but he was one man and knew he could catch up. He refused to look back, thinking back to Lot's escape from the destruction of Sodom and Gomorrah, but bringing with him the fire of vengeance.